REGRET NOT A MOMENT

REGRET NOT A MOMENT

A NOVEL BY

NICOLE McGEHEE

LITTLE, BROWN AND COMPANY
BOSTON TORONTO LONDON

FIRST EDITION

The characters and events in this book are fictitious.
Any similarity to real persons, living or dead, is coincidental
and not intended by the author.

Library of Congress Cataloging-in-Publication Data

McGehee, Nicole.
Regret not a moment : a novel / by Nicole McGehee. — 1st ed.
p. cm.
ISBN 0-316-55853-2
I. Title.
PS3563.C36373R4 1993
813'.54—dc20 92-41732

10 9 8 7 6 5 4 3 2 1

RRD-VA

Published simultaneously in Canada by
Little, Brown & Company (Canada) Limited

PRINTED IN THE UNITED STATES OF AMERICA

To my mother, whose dreams for me have no limit,
and my husband, who helps make the dreams come true

CONTENTS

BOOK ONE

FAUQUIER COUNTY, VIRGINIA

1930

CHAPTER 1

DEVON hopped off the lathered black stallion and handed the reins to a groom, then scurried up the flagstone path from the stables to the main house. As she approached the Georgian brick mansion, she cast sheepish glances up at the balcony outside her bedroom window, certain that her maid, Alice, would be standing there, ready to scold her for her tardiness. Devon was sweaty, dirty, and smelled like a horse. Worse, she and Alice had only one hour to prepare her for the dinner party at the Magraths'.

A hectic fifty-five minutes later, Devon was ready.

"Not bad, if I do say so myself," said Alice, the proud expression on her matronly features belying her matter-of-fact tone. But then, her mistress always looked beautiful. If she had not, Alice would have been disappointed in herself.

Devon studied her reflection in the mirror and gave Alice, who was putting the finishing touches on her upswept hair, a smiling nod of approval. Dark and shining as the sea at midnight, Devon's hair was artfully interwoven with pearls. It created a striking contrast to her vivid, blue-green eyes. Her skin — flawless, roses-and-cream satin inherited from her mother — provided the perfect background for the rich sapphire velvet gown she wore.

"Not bad . . . for an old maid," Devon said mischievously, giving Alice a conspiratorial look in the mirror. "I would bet . . . let's see . . . a box of those chocolates you're so fond of that my parents are downstairs right now discussing my spinsterhood again."

"I don't believe in gambling, miss, as well you know," Alice primly admonished. "And it wouldn't hurt you to listen to your parents' advice." But she could not prevent a smile from appearing at the corners of her mouth. She loved the elder Richmonds, but she knew that Devon's marital status was a matter of choice. Devon was independent. Happy with her life. Still, Alice sometimes shared the Richmonds' disquiet as Devon turned down one proposal after another. And this year, there had not been as many. Of course, there were few bachelors left among Devon's friends in Virginia. And the Richmonds did *insist* on living most of the year at Evergreen instead of their town house in New York.

"Well, *I* believe in gambling. It's one of life's great pleasures," declared Devon.

Alice sniffed disapprovingly. "Well, you needn't poke fun at your parents' concerns, miss. One day you'll wake up to find all the young men who were pining after you have married, just like Mr. Hartwick."

"Then I'll have to content myself with my horses and my greenhouse," said Devon cheerfully, ignoring the remark about her former beau. She had not been in love with Brent and she was not sorry he had married her neighbor Helena Magrath. Devon was not the sort of woman who kept men dangling when she was not interested in them. She was too straightforward for that.

"Anyhow, I know Mother and Father are hoping that tonight I'll pass muster with the gentleman from New York . . . what *is* his name . . ."

"Mr. Alexander, miss. And you could do worse. They say he's very handsome and that he comes from one of the finest old New York families. I haven't heard one word against him. And you know the tongue on that Annie Sparks," she added significantly, referring to Helena Magrath's lady's maid.

"Well, if he doesn't have even one flaw, then he must be perfectly awful! I'm determined to dislike him," Devon said, only half joking. "Dinner parties become really tiresome when one has the impression that all the guests are holding their breath to see if the old maid will finally reel in a fish."

"Don't be vulgar, Miss Devon!" said Alice sharply. "I hope you don't say things like that in public."

Devon gave a merry peal of laughter and reached back over her shoulder to grab her maid's hand affectionately. "Of course I do! That's why I'm an old maid!"

"Ha! That may not be the joke you think! Lord knows, there's nothing wrong with your looks or your brains. It's only that tongue of yours." Alice meant to scold Devon, but she could not keep a note of affection out of her voice. She had loved Devon the minute she had laid eyes on her, almost twenty-five years before. How could she help but be proud of her charge when she was so lovely, in spirit and in body?

"Well," Devon said, her laughter bubbling over as she spoke, "perhaps this visitor from New York won't mind so much. Yankee girls are so much more outspoken."

"They say he's very charming, so I'm sure he won't appreciate poor manners," said Alice with mock severity.

"He sounds like a paragon. I shall hate him. I know it," said Devon firmly.

Devon had guessed correctly the topic of her parents' discussion as they waited for her in the library downstairs.

As Devon approached her twenty-fifth birthday, her parents were beginning to worry that she would never marry. Although the 1920s had changed the world, it was still true that once a young woman had passed the age of twenty-three, it was taken for granted that spinsterhood was a distinct possibility. At age twenty-five, it seemed a foregone conclusion.

"Maybe she is *too* sharp-tongued," Laurel said, looking up from the fine embroidery that was rarely out of her hands.

At the sound of Laurel's voice, her husband, ensconced in a leather wing chair in front of the fireplace, looked across the top of his newspaper. His wife sat in the matching chair opposite him, the light reflecting off her fine blond hair. As a young woman she had been remarkably pretty. At age fifty-three, her prettiness had given way to elegant grace. But to her husband, the lines around her eyes and mouth, the luminescent white strands in her hair, served as mementos of their many happy years together.

"Who's that, dear?" he asked.

"Devon. Maybe she speaks her mind too openly. Maybe her remarks are sometimes too . . . pointed. Do you suppose that is why she hasn't married?"

Chase lowered his paper thoughtfully. At least once a week he and Laurel discussed the possible reasons for Devon's unmarried state. Although Devon seemed happy as she was, the Richmonds both wanted to see her married. They did not like the patronizing comments their friends made about Devon's spinsterhood. They did not like to see the less attractive, less intelligent daughters of their friends pluck off eligible young bachelors one by one while Devon remained obstinately single. But most of all, they believed that Devon's future happiness depended upon her being married. Without marriage, her place in society would be that of an onlooker. And they wanted their daughter to experience the happiness of connubial love.

"I shouldn't think so, Laurel," said Chase after carefully mulling over her comment. "After all, I remember when she and the young Hartwick chap used to laugh the evenings away. Why, he was a great admirer of her wit."

"Well, there's a good example, Chase!" said Laurel excitedly, sitting forward in her chair. "Brent Hartwick liked that at first, but do you suppose he grew tired of it? Do you suppose she showed too much . . ." Laurel's sentence tapered off. She did not like to use the word *intelligence*. It was 1930, after all, why should a young woman have to hide her intelligence?

"Nonsense, Laurel, you and I have always been progressive. We taught Devon to ride and hunt as well as any man. We taught her to be honest and speak her mind. She even went to college! And I hope we have provided an example of marital fulfillment. If she's not married, it's by choice. After all, her sister is married."

"You can't think she wants to stay an old maid, like the Chapman girl. Why, no one invites that poor girl anywhere, except as a chaperone!"

"Of course she doesn't want that! But Devon claims she hasn't found a man who suits her," Chase said, with a helpless shrug.

A man who suits her, Laurel thought. It had seemed so easy for her and Chase to find each other. They had grown up as neighbors, made mud pies together as toddlers, taken piano lessons together as adolescents. They had always been inseparable. She gazed at her husband now. She supposed he could be called portly, despite his still-broad shoulders and strong arms. His balding head had once sported thick, dark curls; the hair that remained was now mostly gray. But to Laurel he was the most attractive man in the world. Why was it so difficult, then, for her own daughter to find the same contentment?

CHAPTER 2

BRIGHT light spilled festively from the long windows of the Magrath mansion. The sight made Devon's heart beat a little faster as the tires of her parents' Cadillac crunched on the circular drive. Parties always filled her with anticipation, and the Magraths' parties were among the most sparkling.

Built to resemble a French château, the lavish three-story Magrath home was a departure from the Georgian-style and antebellum structures that sprinkled the Virginia countryside. The architecture, a romantic fantasy of Helena Magrath's Francophile grandfather, was complemented by a houseful of valuable antiques gathered over the course of seventy years.

As Devon entered the richly gilded Louis XIV–style salon, an arm through one of each parent's, she searched the room for their hostess. All the faces she saw were familiar and she smiled at those closest to her. Then a circle of young people parted, and in their midst Devon saw a stranger.

Her scan of the room stopped at once and her gaze fixed on him. He was one of those rare people who, for no clearly definable reason, immediately draw the eye. He didn't blend into the crowd, he stood above it. His charisma was due to something beyond good looks; something beyond self-confidence. It was a combination of eloquent gesture, carriage, expression — a magnetism that absorbed the attention. Though John Alexander was completely unaware of Devon, she found her eyes locked on his profile.

He looked no older than many of her friends, but he moved with utter self-assurance. He was no taller than the other men in the room, but his manner of carrying himself made him appear more powerful. He had the look of an athlete, with wide shoulders tapering down to a narrow waist. He gave the impression that he was extremely capable — no . . . indomitable. His face was all male angularity, with a strong, almost stubborn jaw. His nose was slightly larger than average and had a small hook in it, which gave his face a keen, somewhat hard look. To Devon, the men standing beside him looked callow in comparison.

The Richmonds' hostess, Rosalind Magrath, spotted her guests and moved toward them. As she greeted the new arrivals, she looked over her shoulder to see what was so enthralling Devon. The young woman looked positively hypnotized. When Rosalind saw the direction of Devon's gaze, she smiled to herself. Giving Laurel Richmond a knowing look, Mrs. Magrath led the family across the vast room to meet the guest from New York.

Alexander turned as Devon and her parents approached. And he faltered in midsentence. Devon was looking directly at him in a way that made them seem alone in the room, and she was one of the most stunning women he had ever seen. He was captured by her, incapable of looking away. It wasn't just her remarkable looks — she had about her an attitude of daring that fascinated him. And she moved with the kind of graceful self-confidence usually found only in women at least ten years older. His eyes gripped hers as she drew nearer.

Devon was transfixed. She was unaware of moving through the crowd; unaware even of breathing. Unaware of anything but his eyes. And now she stood before him, staring up into those extraordinary eyes. Rimmed with long, dark lashes, they were so deep blue as to be almost navy. They were an arrestingly beautiful touch in a face that was otherwise ruggedly masculine.

"Ah, our guest of honor," Mrs. Magrath said smoothly, pretending not to notice the strange little island of silence amid the room's conversational hum. "Mr. Alexander, I would like to present you to our neighbors, Mr. and Mrs. Richmond from Evergreen — and this is their daughter Devon. As I mentioned, she is to be your dinner partner this evening."

The space between John and Devon hummed with electricity. "Then I am a very lucky man," he said in a warm, deep voice.

Devon almost never blushed. But now her mother was surprised to see that her cheeks were distinctly rose colored as she stared up at the stranger.

"How do you do, Mr. Alexander," murmured Devon. She didn't dare extend her hand to him. His touch would singe her, she was certain of it. The sheer physical impact of him left her almost breathless. She felt . . . naked.

And Alexander felt the heat in her. It was the kind of seductive heat that more practiced women tried to exude deliberately, but this young woman did it naturally. Yet he knew she was innocent. And this combination he found excruciatingly arousing. His eyes refused to release hers. He was thinking what it would be like to make love to her. To take her and —

"Devon Richmond! Are you avoiding me again?" A laughing voice broke the spell. The elder Richmonds drifted away as Devon turned her head to greet Brent Hartwick, her former beau. Hartwick had recently married the Magraths' daughter, thus Rosalind Magrath's generosity in partnering Devon with the handsome guest of honor. Hartwick was one of the few people the Richmonds knew who had taken a large loss in the crash of 1929. Most of the other wealthy residents of Fauquier County and bordering Loudon County believed real estate was the best investment and had scorned the stock-buying craze.

Hartwick was the exception. Born and raised in Upperville, Virginia, he had gone to live in New York, taking a job with an investment banking firm. As a gentleman of the 1920s, he had regarded his job as a pastime, nothing more. Until he became afflicted with stock-buying fever — and lost a fortune. Many believed that had been the reason he had stopped waiting for Devon Richmond to agree to marry him and had instead settled for the wealthy Helena Magrath.

Helena Magrath Hartwick quickly came to her husband's side when she noticed him talking to Devon. She was conscious of the gossip that surrounded her husband and Devon, and was particularly jealous of the other young woman.

"Devon, dear, how lovely you look!" exclaimed Helena.

Devon was irritated at Helena's habit ever since her marriage of condescendingly addressing unmarried women as "dear," as though she, Helena, were much older.

"Helena . . . dear," replied Devon, allowing a few seconds to elapse between the two words.

Helena turned to Alexander. "Devon is the most eligible young lady in the county. I promise she'll keep you amused. Why, you're lucky we didn't invite one of our younger ladies to be your dinner partner. None of them would be even half as good a conversationalist as Devon."

"And yet, a quick wit doesn't necessarily come with age, does it, Helena?" asked Devon pointedly, to the chuckles of John Alexander and Brent Hartwick.

Helena, glaring at her husband, pulled him away, throwing over her shoulder, "Please enjoy your evening," in a tone that implied she meant the opposite.

Devon turned to Alexander. "Was that wicked?" she asked,

wincing comically as though she expected to be reprimanded. She was more herself again — the interruption had given her time to regain her poise.

"Yes. And well deserved," replied Alexander with a snicker. "The moment I saw you, I knew you were a woman to be reckoned with."

"Well, I . . ." Devon looked up to find his blue eyes boring in to her, wiping all rational thought from her mind. Try to remember what you were going to say, she commanded herself. "I . . . I don't like being patronized, and I'm afraid Helena does that sometimes."

"I'm surprised she dares," John said with a droll look. Devon did not seem the type of woman who would meekly accept such behavior.

Devon simply smiled, annoyed that she couldn't think of a witty rejoinder. She could again feel the turbulence rising in her body. She had to avoid looking into his eyes. If she could avoid that, she could remain composed. He must think I'm a tongue-tied ninny, Devon thought to herself.

But to John, who did not know her, Devon seemed composed. She would not meet his eyes, so that brief glimpse into her thoughts that had so aroused him was gone. And he was sorry for that. He had the sudden urge to speak to her of the unmistakable electricity between them, but he suppressed it, falling back on small talk instead.

"Tell me, Miss Richmond, do you like New York?" He was uttering conventional phrases, but his rich voice sent goose bumps through her, as though he were blowing on the back of her neck.

"Yes . . . yes, in a way." What *had* he asked her? Oh, yes. New York. "We have a place there actually." The home to which she so casually referred was a stylish five-story town house, purchased after the recent sale of the family's Italianate villa on Fifth Avenue. Chase Richmond, like many who enjoyed old wealth, did not enjoy squandering it. He recognized that the era of Fifth Avenue mansions that occupied entire city blocks was coming to a close. The fact was, the Depression had caused many of the wealthy to scale down the wildly lavish socializing that had characterized the previous decade.

"Do you visit New York often?" John wondered why he had never met her before.

"Not too often," Devon said. As she spoke, she began to feel more in control. "I like to visit, but there are too many people. Besides, this is my real home."

"You don't feel isolated here, living miles away from your nearest neighbor?" John asked.

"Not a bit. I rather like it. As you can see, we are a close-knit society."

John found himself wanting to know more about what she thought, about what she did each day. He wanted to know everything about her. "Don't you get bored in the country?"

Devon was growing intrigued with the conversation itself now. She was amused at the man's assumptions about life in Virginia. "Mr. Alexander, I've never been bored a day in my life," she said firmly. "The occupation of my mind does not depend on others."

"No, I can believe that you do very well on your own." He wondered if he dared ask the question that sprung to mind. Would she be insulted? It would be interesting to see her reaction. "Would it be impertinent of me to ask why someone as beautiful as you has not married?"

Devon, now completely unself-conscious, turned to face Alexander squarely. "Probably." Her mouth turned up at the corners in a sly smile. "I suppose the Magraths have treated you to quite some amount of speculation on that subject?"

Alexander could not tell whether she was offended. As he was trying to decide, Devon burst out laughing. "Don't feel uncomfortable. Everyone we know speculates on that. The fact of the matter is, I've never fallen in love with anyone. A very simple answer. Why everyone tries to complicate it is beyond me. I'm simply not going to give up my independence for someone I don't truly love. And no matter how wonderful the rewards of marriage, one does give up a measure of independence, doesn't one? Is that why you, Mr. Alexander, have never married?"

Now it was Alexander's turn to laugh. He was thirty-two years old, and it was not uncommon for men his age to be unmarried. He was forward-thinking enough to know that it was unjust that Devon was questioned because she was unmarried while he could remain a perfectly respectable, even desirable, bachelor. Yet he was enough a man of his times to find her unconventional for even raising the point.

Turning serious, Alexander considered Devon's question. He had loved women, even been *in* love. When he was nineteen he had wanted to marry a young Frenchwoman he had met while visiting Italy. Of course his family had been adamantly opposed to his marrying a Roman Catholic, as hers had been opposed to her marrying an Episcopalian, and somehow the two young people had not had the will to fight their families' disapproval.

John's second love had been a young married woman of his own set. She had told him that her husband was cruel to her. Captivated as much by his role as savior as he was by the lady herself, he had willingly begun a passionate affair with her. He had begged Janine to leave her husband so that he, John, could marry her. He smiled to think of his naïveté at age twenty-three. Of course she had refused. Only when her attention began to wander to another young man of his circle did he realize how stupid he had been.

Since then, he was rarely without at least one mistress, but he never again had the desire to marry. John enjoyed being free to travel, to explore new interests, to go out when he felt like it. He did not want to answer to anyone. Furthermore, as more of his friends married, he noticed that their wives, no matter how exciting before marriage, all seemed to turn themselves into replicas of one another. They occupied themselves in the same ways and had the same thoughts and standards.

"I'm pleased to see that you're taking my question seriously, but you needn't take it *too* seriously," said Devon, breaking into his thoughts.

John laughed. "I'm sorry. I was trying to come up with an honest answer. Suffice it to say that judging from my friends, people turn dull when they marry."

For a moment Devon forgot her attraction to John. The generalization annoyed her. "I do *not* intend to turn dull!" she said decisively. Dull! She thought about her parents. They were content, but not dull. She thought about her sister, married to a diplomat and living in Paris. That wasn't dull.

"So you *do* intend to marry?" John asked, sensing her annoyance and anxious to move the conversation along.

"If I fall in love. And I'm certain I will." Devon felt suddenly shy as she said the words. Her conversation with this stranger had taken a surprisingly intimate turn!

"And what will you do to prevent your marriage from becoming dull?" He asked the question with real curiosity, all mockery gone from his voice.

Devon thought the question presumptuous, and was about to say so, but something in the seriousness of Alexander's tone, the studious curiosity in his penetrating eyes, stopped her rebuke. Instead, she carefully mulled over her response, allowing the silence between them to lengthen.

Finally, she said in a thoughtful tone, "You see, Mr. Alexander, you and I disagree on a fundamental point. You say that the institution of marriage turns people dull. I disagree. I believe dull people give the institution a bad name. Maybe they attribute their dullness, their lack of adventure, to the inhibiting influence of their spouse. People do what they want to do, Mr. Alexander. When interesting people marry, and they retain their independent interests even after they are married, I see no reason why their marriages should not be equally interesting."

"Well spoken, Miss Richmond," said Alexander, an admiring look on his face. "It is a point of view well worth considering."

The Magraths' butler entered the room at that moment to announce dinner. John turned to Devon. She knew he would take her arm, as custom required, but she was not prepared for the wave of desire that swept over her at the contact. For in that second, John Alexander gave her a taste of the secret, exquisite possibilities from which she had been so carefully sheltered — a sudden understanding of what it meant to share a man's bed.

Devon raised her eyes to his and this time he refused to release them. She could read his message of seduction as easily as if he had spoken it aloud. Her body tingled, as though anticipating his touch. For one dizzy moment, she thought he was going to kiss her.

Her face was upturned, inviting. He had only to bend down and . . . He wanted to rip through the conventions that prevented him from doing what he felt. And his eyes signaled this clearly. He didn't kiss her, though. He did much, much more than that in his imagination. And Devon knew it.

CHAPTER 3

DEVON was not surprised when she returned from her ride the next afternoon to find John Alexander having tea with her parents. Opening the heavy double doors that led to the library, Devon found the three cozily sitting in front of a crackling fire. John lounged on a burgundy leather love seat that faced the fireplace, while the Richmonds, as usual, occupied the matching wing chairs that flanked the little sofa.

The butler had told Devon that Alexander was visiting, but, once again, she was utterly unprepared for the physical impact of his presence.

"Mr. Alexander, what a pleasant surprise," said Devon. To her own ears, her voice sounded unforgivably shaky. She couldn't let him affect her this way!

"I see you've been riding, Miss Richmond. I'm sorry I didn't arrive sooner. I don't get a chance to ride frequently enough in New York."

John had been afraid that in the clear light of day Devon wouldn't live up to his memory of her, but she actually surpassed it. He smiled at her. A smile that absorbed her utterly. His teeth flashed white against his tan features and a lethally charming dimple showed on one side of his mouth.

"You like to ride?" asked Devon, a little breathlessly. "Perhaps you'd like to see our stables after you've finished your tea."

"I'd like that very much," said Alexander warmly.

"If you'll excuse me, then, I'll just freshen up. I'll be back in a few minutes."

Laurel and Chase exchanged a significant look. They were pleased to see the effect John Alexander had on their daughter. For once, she seemed flustered with emotion, a condition perhaps more attractive to suitors than her usual no-nonsense self-assurance, they thought.

"Alexander, what brings you to our part of Virginia?" asked Chase. He knew the answer already, for it had been the subject of discussion among the men of his circle.

"Mr. Magrath owns some real estate in New York I've been considering taking off his hands," replied John casually. Unlike many of the gentlemen of his day, John chose to work. He bought tenements in New York, renovated them, and resold them at low cost, but profit nonetheless, to former tenants. The hardworking immigrants who became John's buyers were given their first chance at living decently in the United States, and John made money from the sheer volume of buyers.

"A rather tough time for investors nowadays," said Chase.

"A time of opportunity, provided one was wise enough to avoid the stock-buying craze."

"Amen. Land is always the best investment."

Devon reappeared in the doorway. She had used the time alone to calm herself, and she felt more in control now. Still, the pounding of her heart was unnaturally fast. "Shall we have a look at the stables?" She was anxious to escape the confines of the house, the scrutiny of her parents. She wondered self-consciously if they could see the effect Alexander had on her.

"By all means," replied John. He rose and crossed the room-sized Persian rug to reach Devon.

When the two had left, Laurel picked up her embroidery, while Chase simply stared into the fire. They did not speak for a long time. Finally, Chase looked up to find Laurel looking at him, a satisfied smile on her face.

"How long do you expect to be in Virginia, Mr. Alexander?" asked Devon. Visitors to the vast estates of the South often stayed for weeks, even months at a time. Devon hoped that would be the case with John.

"Until my business here is concluded," he replied cryptically.

Devon did not feel that she knew John well enough to pry further, so she asked nothing more about his business. John noticed this and admired her discretion.

"You say you like to ride. Do you like to hunt?" asked Devon, gesturing to the rolling meadows around them. Indeed, the graceful brick manor house surrounded by century-old boxwoods was only a small portion of Evergreen. The Richmonds' land stretched to every horizon.

"Very much. Do you enjoy horseracing? That's more our sport in New York."

"I don't really know a great deal about it, but it seems a very exciting sport." In the brisk afternoon air, the atmosphere between them was less charged. They could relax somewhat, get to know each other.

The stables were some distance from the house and it was a cool day, so Devon walked down the flagstone path at a speed that had John hurrying to keep up. Even so, John absorbed with interest the details of the meticulously maintained grounds. The path's boxwood border was carefully trimmed so that not a leaf was out of place. In front of the hedge, flanking the little path, was a perennial flower bed, artfully designed so that something was almost always in bloom no matter what the season. John paused a moment and turned back toward the house, appreciating the casual richness of the ivy growing over the back portico and up the chimney, of the Palladian windows that graced the facade of the structure. Everything about the Richmond home bespoke quiet elegance, order, and care. There was nothing ostentatious about Evergreen — it had a comfortable, cozy quality despite its size — but every detail was of the highest quality. And there was a serenity to the place that John found a marked contrast to New York.

"What do you do here for excitement, Miss Richmond?" asked Alexander.

Devon reflected for a moment. "I'm not sure how to answer. Excitement isn't necessarily what we seek here. We travel for that," Devon added with a smile.

"You seem a very intelligent young woman. What do you do to occupy your time?"

"Well, for a while I was away at school, so I've enjoyed becoming reacquainted with our place."

John looked around him appreciatively. Freshly painted white fences in perfect repair stretched over rolling green hills. A small pond in a valley about half a mile away mirrored graceful weeping willows and the deep blue sky. Several horses, their coats gleaming in the sun, grazed in another field filled with yellow flowers.

Following his gaze, Devon remarked, "Those always bloom here in autumn. They make my sister sneeze terribly."

"Does your sister live nearby?"

"No, she lives in Paris now. Her husband is a diplomat."

"And what do you do when you are here?"

"Mostly I ride. I also train my own horses." Devon paused thoughtfully before continuing, "After our conversation at the Magraths', I can't help feeling that you seem unusually worried about the possibility that I may be vegetating here, Mr. Alexander. Is there a reason for that?"

Actually, Alexander expected someone as intriguing as Devon to be occupied with intriguing pastimes. That she did nothing that he classified as exceptional was a slight disappointment to him. "No . . . no. You just don't seem like the sort of person who would be content with life in the country."

Devon stopped, turned to face John, and looked keenly at him. Under her scrutiny, he felt embarrassed by his judgmental attitude. "I suppose I know very little about it," he admitted, looking down sheepishly.

His embarrassment amused Devon, who said coolly but gently, "Then we'll have to familiarize you with the charms of country life. That way, you can make educated judgments about its attributes relative to city living."

"You make me feel quite provincial," said John in an exaggeratedly apologetic tone, looking at her from under his brows. "Can you forgive my narrow-mindedness?"

Devon could not suppress a smile. "If you'll pardon me for making a generality," she said, not unkindly, "I find that many New Yorkers share your outlook. They can't believe that there is intellectual stimulation outside Manhattan, except, of course, in France or England. As you've pointed out, it is a somewhat provincial point of view." Devon concluded her words as they arrived at the stable, a massive white wooden structure with room for at least forty horses. Like the rest of the farm, it was spotless. "In fact, I'll show you a perfect example right now of how stimulating country life can be," she added, her smile growing larger.

Devon led John to a spacious stall. At first, John could not see within, then he spotted the most magnificent horse he had ever seen. The creature was entirely black, a shining, ebony vision.

"This is my baby," said Devon, caressing the horse's nose as it nuzzled her fondly.

"What a superb creature!" said John, in awe. "A Thoroughbred?"

Devon nodded. "A stallion. Sirocco is his name. Perhaps you'd like to come over tomorrow for a ride? We can even have a picnic if the weather is nice. You can take Sirocco," she said, giving him a sidelong glance. "I think you'll agree then that life in the country can be exciting after all."

"I'm not sure I should take you up on that offer, but I can't resist," said John, smiling. He was actually an excellent rider, and had even played polo in college.

Devon showed him several more horses before leading him to a large greenhouse beyond the stables. Stepping inside, John was overwhelmed by the rich perfumes that filled the air. Exotic flowers grew from hanging pots, as well as from flat trays and large planters on the floor. John observed species he had never before seen, even in the most exclusive florists in New York.

"What are all these?" he asked in wonder.

"Orchids mostly. Some gardenias that I bring inside for the winter. I love their scent. I grow jasmine too, for the same reason."

"You mean all this is yours?"

"It is. I experiment with plant breeding. Some of these species are found only in one place in the world." Devon walked over to a planter suspended from the ceiling. Over its side tumbled a mass of large red flowers, about four inches in diameter, that had petals like swallows' wings. Devon plucked one and handed it to John. On closer observation, he saw that each flower's innermost petals were a delicate waxy white with pink around the edges. "For example, this orchid grows only on the Caribbean island of Tobago. Nowhere else. Can you imagine that?" Devon asked dreamily.

"It's beautiful," said John. "How did you find it?"

"I went and got it," said Devon in a matter-of-fact tone. John looked at her in surprise. But without further elaboration, Devon turned and led him back to the house.

CHAPTER 4

LORETTA Morgan stretched dreamily, then settled back against the blue satin cushions of the chaise longue in a provocative pose. "This way?" she asked the man standing in front of her.

"No. Move a little forward, Loretta. Let's see more of you," he answered curtly.

Obligingly, the young woman leaned forward, further emphasizing her deeply exposed cleavage. "Better?"

"Perfect . . . okay . . . now!" Loretta gave a languid smile and looked up at the man seductively. As soon as she heard the camera click, the look of allure disappeared from her face and she stood up. Paying no mind to the photographer, she stood impatiently as her maid removed one sequined gown from her voluptuous body and replaced it with another. The photographer, busy with his camera, didn't even notice. To him, one famous actress was very much like another. They were all difficult. They were all prima donnas.

As if to confirm this, Loretta, now fully clothed, preened before the mirrors that covered three walls of her dressing area.

"Okay, Loretta, let's see a little leg."

Loretta went through the paces professionally and mechanically. Her mind was elsewhere. She was thinking of John Alexander. It had been three days since she had last been with him and she missed him, truly missed him.

She wondered at her chances of marrying John. At times, she had felt that he might propose. Then, suddenly, he would grow distant. Once she had mentioned the possibility to him, but he had treated it as a joke, saying, "Why ruin a perfectly good love affair, Loretta?"

That was easy for a man to say. But Loretta's public was beginning to wonder why their twenty-eight-year-old idol (thirty-four if the truth were known) had never married. Marrying a man like John Alexander, handsome and from a venerable old New York family, would enhance her career. And it would give her something no career, no matter how successful, could give her. Respectability.

She did not know why this last was so important to her. She had certainly not been brought up with it. Maybe that's why I want it so much, she mused.

CHAPTER 5

THE morning sun that streamed through Devon's open window warmed her body as she lay in bed. Not fully conscious yet, she was nonetheless aware of a delicious sense of anticipation. Shaking off her sleep, she tried to remember the reason for her happiness. Ah, yes, John Alexander. She sighed to herself. John Alexander was coming to the house today to go riding with her. The thought of seeing him filled her with a forbidden sort of excitement.

Devon had been brought up carefully. It was expected that her husband would be the first man with whom she shared a bed. But she was not cold. She had had the same sexual longings and schoolgirl crushes as her friends. And she had tingled pleasantly at the kisses of her beaux. But she had never met a man who could sustain that feeling. Now, she was excited at the prospect that John Alexander might possibly be a man she could love.

Singing merrily to herself, she threw off the cheerful white linen and lace comforter and hurried to the carved cherry armoire that housed her riding clothes. She selected pale gray breeches, a blue cotton shirt that enhanced the aqua of her eyes, and a mauve and gray Harris tweed jacket. After washing her face, she tied her hair into a ponytail with a lavender ribbon, finished dressing, and went downstairs to breakfast.

"Good morning, darling," said her mother, "you look lovely."

"Thank you. Mr. Alexander is coming over to go riding." Devon noted the look her parents exchanged and smiled to herself. She went to the Hepplewhite sideboard laden with blueberry muffins, eggs, and Smithfield ham. Devon helped herself to a generous portion of each, then joined her parents at the gleaming, banquet-sized mahogany table. The Richmonds had frequent guests, so the table was always open to its full length, but when they were alone the family sat together at one end. Despite the grandeur of the room, the family's emotional closeness gave their surroundings a warm glow.

Teasingly, Devon asked, "You both seem bursting to comment on my visitor. May I ask why?"

"It's not that at all, Devon, we just . . . we just —" Her father groped for words, but he found it embarrassing to discuss courtship with his daughter.

"We think Mr. Alexander is very pleasant, dear," interrupted Laurel smoothly. "And Mr. Magrath speaks very highly of him. Weren't you saying that we should invite him for dinner, Chase?"

"I don't remem—" Chase began, before catching Laurel's eye. "Why yes, now that you mention it. Yes, yes, of course. Only yesterday, Devon, I was saying —"

Devon was unable to stifle her laughter any longer. "Mother, Dad, you don't have to pretend. I would love for Mr. Alexander to be invited to dinner. I hope to have the chance to know him better and, yes, I think he's very handsome. Does that tell you everything you'd like to know?"

Chase, looking sheepish, opened his mouth to answer and then closed it, at a loss for words. But Laurel was completely unruffled. Delicately, she took a sip of coffee. She did not speak until she had returned the cup to its saucer. Then, looking innocently at Devon, she said, "Well, we must do everything we can to be hospitable to Mr. Alexander, mustn't we?"

Devon simply nodded and smiled at her mother.

Really, thought Chase, women were supposed to be subtle but sometimes, he had learned, they could be most outspoken. It was quite disconcerting.

Devon was pleasantly surprised to discover that John rode truly well. Not that the ability was particularly important to her, much as she enjoyed it; it was simply that, like most good riders, Devon disliked people who claimed to ride more skillfully than they actually did. Both the horse and the rider were ill-served in such cases, Devon believed.

"You were too modest, Mr. Alexander! I think you're more than ready for Sirocco," Devon exclaimed. John had suggested that he warm up on a more gentle horse. He had led one of the Richmonds' geldings through a series of intricate jumps in the riding ring and impressed Devon with his skill. She opened the gate to the riding ring so John could exit and change mounts.

"But don't *you* want to ride Sirocco when we go out on the trail?" John asked.

"I can ride him whenever I like. Besides, I'm going to ride him in the hunt on Saturday. Has Mr. Magrath asked you to join us for that?" As Magrath was master of the hunt, and Alexander's host, it was appropriate for him to invite Alexander to participate.

"He did." John dismounted and handed the reins to a groom. "And I'm hoping you'll show me a bit of the countryside today, so that I won't be taken completely unawares."

Devon liked the fact that Alexander respected the hunt tradition. And she liked the modesty he displayed by not assuming he would be able to handle whatever occurred on Saturday. The Tri-County Hunt was known throughout the world for the expertise of its members and the variety and difficulty of some of its courses.

"Well, let's get you on Sirocco and then we'll go," said Devon. She held the stallion's bridle and spoke to him soothingly while John mounted him.

John settled himself in the saddle and expertly manipulated the reins so that the stallion stopped prancing. Meanwhile, the groom helped Devon into the saddle of the gelding John had ridden earlier. She thanked the groom, then led the way out of the paddock area.

"I've been looking forward to this," said John when they were under way.

Instead of giving him a coy reply, Devon simply said, "I have too."

Devon liked the way John gently talked to the stallion in order to calm him. And she couldn't help remarking to herself that riding clothes made her companion look even more handsome.

When they had cleared the area immediately surrounding Evergreen, the two urged their horses into an easy canter.

"Be careful of the stone wall ahead!" cried Devon. "The other side is lower, so when the horse lands, you'll get a jolt if you're not prepared." The two horses and their riders sailed gracefully over the wall, then, a little farther, over a white rail fence. The crisp November air and the bright sunshine spurred them on, and soon the horses were racing over the countryside.

Devon's hair slipped out of its ribbon and flowed behind her in a silvery black stream. Despite John's absorption with the riding, he could not help but admire the young woman's unself-conscious beauty. Her riding attire showed off her graceful legs, long and shapely, and her tiny waist. She was slender but curvaceous, exactly the kind of figure John found most appealing. He noticed from the length of her stirrups that Devon was not as tall as he had originally presumed when he had met her at the Magraths'. He estimated that she was perhaps five foot four, but her horsewoman's erect posture and her innate dignity made her appear several inches taller.

They slowed their horses to a walk as they approached a wooded area.

"We're lucky to have the warm weather today," said John. "I don't normally have picnics in November."

"Novembers are all up and down in Virginia. One day it snows and the next day the flowers start to bud because the weather turns so warm. Februarys here are more like winter."

As they talked, they came to a small meadow where orange, red, and yellow leaves floated through the breeze to land on the grass, still as green as in midsummer.

"This is a pretty clearing. Shall we stop here?" John asked. He was impatient for the opportunity to sit and talk to Devon. To be completely alone with her.

"I have someplace even better in mind," said Devon, with a secretive smile. They rode in silence for several minutes. Soon John heard the sound of burbling water.

"Here!" Devon cried victoriously. John, coming up behind her, suddenly spotted a pristine miniature waterfall, perhaps four feet high. The entire width of the brook was only fifteen feet. By its side, in a clearing, was an immaculately painted white gazebo furnished with white wrought-iron chairs and a table. But most amazing to John was that the table was fully set for a meal, complete with linen tablecloth, china, and crystal. Also on the table was a silver bucket containing champagne.

"What a wonderful surprise!" said John. "However did you manage it?"

"The grooms rode out with it earlier." She laughed, delighted that her surprise had had the desired effect.

Devon slid out of the saddle and indicated that John should do the same. She walked to the table and pulled one side of the tablecloth up, revealing a chest beneath it. Devon opened the lid and removed a platter of fried chicken; a bun warmer containing steaming homemade biscuits; potato salad; coleslaw; several cheeses; and, for dessert, purple grapes and a pecan pie.

"These are all my favorites!" John exclaimed, regarding the feast with appreciation. "I'm glad I worked up an appetite."

Devon smiled at his enthusiasm. "Will you open the champagne while I serve?"

John did as Devon asked while she neatly arranged the food on the plates. When they were seated, he asked, "May I propose a toast?"

"Please do," Devon replied, wondering what he would say.

"To Devon Richmond,
Beauty, horsewoman, hostess extraordinaire:
May this be the first of many such occasions
Which I have the privilege to share."

"I didn't know you were a poet," said Devon, with a laugh. "I hope you won't think it rude of me to drink to that toast, even if it *is* me you've toasted. Consider that I'm drinking to the last part. The part about many more such occasions." Devon found it difficult to meet John's eyes as she said this. His effect on her was heady.

"Devon — may I call you Devon?" John asked, his voice dropping intimately.

"Of course," she said in a soft voice. Suddenly the two were no longer laughing. Devon could hear her pulse pounding in her ears.

John covered her hand with his, but the contact was not enough for him. He stood up, walked to her side of the table, and pulled her to her feet.

Her legs trembled so that she felt she could barely stand without his support. She knew he was going to kiss her. She wanted him to. Breathlessly, she waited. His lips touched hers, tenderly at first, then more urgently as he drew her close and pressed the length of his body against hers. She could feel his excitement, his heart beating against her own. Her arms went around his waist and she felt his hard muscles beneath the fine linen of his shirt. She could smell the maleness of him, his soap mixed with sweat. And the smell of the horse on him. It was the most purely erotic scent she had ever experienced. Overwhelmed with the intensity of her feeling, she pulled her mouth away from his and buried her face in his chest. She was dizzy with desire. He put his hand under her chin. She lifted her eyes to his. They were drowning in each other. The smell, the touch, the taste. She wanted to taste him again. He lowered his lips to hers. She opened her mouth as he gently slid his tongue into it. She couldn't get enough of him. She pulled his head even closer. Pressed even harder against him. His arms tightened around her in a fierce embrace. Their bodies were melded together.

Then, slowly, reluctantly, he released her. She swayed against him, grasping his arms for support.

"Devon . . ." he whispered. He buried his face in her sweetly scented hair, the perfume of it setting him on fire. He knew he should go no further despite his overwhelming desire. He was aware that, because of her inexperience and her enjoyment of the moment, she might allow him to make love to her, but he didn't want to take advantage of her innocence. To betray her trust. "Devon, I must apologize," he finally said, pushing her gently away.

"Don't. Kiss me again instead," she said with a devilish grin.

"Don't tempt me. I can't be responsible for my actions if we keep this up. And I want to be responsible where you are concerned," he said softly, tracing the outline of her lips with his thumb.

"Where I am concerned? Have there been many others?" asked Devon seriously, regretting the words as soon as they escaped her lips. "No . . . I didn't mean to pry. I'm sorry," she said, looking at the ground in embarrassment.

John was touched by her obvious desire to know more about him. He was tempted to tell her that he had never felt about another woman the way he felt about her. Somehow, though, he wasn't quite prepared to say those words. He had known her such a short time. He did not want to say such a thing until he was sure he meant it. He did not ever want to hurt her.

"I'm thirty-two years old, Devon. There have been women in my life, but —"

"Of course there have been women," said Devon, cutting him off in embarrassment. She was afraid to hear the rest of his sentence. Afraid he might say something he did not mean. Something she would want to believe. Something that might later wound her if it turned out to be nothing more than gallantry.

"It was an absurd question," said Devon, the spell now broken. "Let's concentrate on this delicious picnic and forget I ever asked."

Devon's parents sensed that something had happened between the two young people when they saw them together at dinner. The interest that John showed toward their daughter seemed more personal than before, while Devon was uncharacteristically quiet and distracted.

She had little to contribute to the conversation between John and her parents. She was content to watch and listen. She noticed that her father seemed to enjoy talking to John. Devon thought that John seemed older when he spoke with her father; not because he was trying to impress Chase with his intelligence, but rather because of the quiet confidence with which he spoke of business matters. Indeed, John had more business experience than most men his age and had made a substantial fortune, apart from that which he had inherited.

While the men had brandy and cigars in the library after dinner, Devon and her mother retired to the main salon. They settled on a down-filled couch in front of the fireplace. Laurel picked up her needlework and stitched quietly for a few minutes while Devon nibbled absently at the contents of a crystal dish filled with cashews.

Finally, Laurel broke the companionable silence. "Did you enjoy yourselves this afternoon?"

"Yes," said Devon softly. She felt the color rise in her cheeks and looked into the fire so as not to meet her mother's eyes. It was not that her mother would not understand a kiss . . . just a kiss, after all, Devon thought. It was that the feelings John stirred so exceeded that simple physical act that she was embarrassed at the possibility that her mother would read the emotion on her face. For a moment she envisioned how it had been that afternoon. She had never experienced anything like the heart-stopping, searing desire that John aroused in her. Had it been special for him, too? The thought nagged at her. He seemed so knowing. When he took her in his arms, it was with none of the tentativeness of the young men she knew. He was used to having his desire reciprocated. Used to women saying yes to him. Was he also used to women falling in love with him?

Laurel's voice broke into Devon's reverie. "How long will Mr. Alexander be in Virginia?"

"I . . . I don't know. He has business with Mr. Magrath. I suppose whenever that's finished . . ."

Laurel thought she detected a note of sadness in Devon's voice. "Will you be sorry to see him go?"

"Yes," said Devon without elaboration. There was no point in concealing from her mother how much she would like John to stay. "I wonder when I'll see him again. Of course, we'll be in New York in the spring. But that seems like a long time."

"I wonder if he has any . . . attachments in New York," said Laurel, studying her daughter for her reaction. Again she saw Devon blush uncharacteristically.

Devon did not want to admit that the same question troubled her. She did not want her mother to become alarmed. "I have the impression that he is . . . uncommitted," she finally said.

"Well then," said Laurel, with a small sigh of relief. That was good. But of course she would make inquiries.

Loretta Morgan reflected carefully before turning down the dinner invitation from Whitney Ross. He was rich. He was handsome. He was married. Normally, she thought of these as the perfect combination of traits in a man. But now she had John Alexander, who had the first two attractions without the third encumbrance.

Before, when Loretta's only dream had been to become a star on Broadway, she had been willing, even happy, to form attachments with married men. She had, in a coolly methodical way, chosen men who would be helpful to her career. That a man was married meant that he would not demand she give up her ambitions in order to make a home for him. And she had no intention of giving up the stage.

Now that her public was beginning to wonder about her single state, however, her press agent had convinced her that she must marry. He worried — and made her worry — that her fans would think there was something wrong with her. So she knew it was time. If only John Alexander would demonstrate something more than lighthearted enjoyment of her company. Though he showed hearty appreciation for her physical charms, John was clearly not emotionally entangled with Loretta. But of one thing she was certain: he would sever their relationship if he ever suspected she had been with another man. Not out of jealousy, but out of pride. At times she felt that he had maintained their relationship for fifteen months only as a matter of convenience. At other times, however, such as when they made love, she could almost believe that he would one day fall in love with her. Otherwise, she thought, how could a man be so . . . wonderful, so skilled at giving pleasure.

"Come on, Loretta, you know you want to," said Whitney, looking at her reflection in her dressing room mirror as he stood behind her. Really, it had not been wise to invite him here, she chided herself. Particularly when she was wearing only a flimsy silk wrapper. Whitney slipped his fingers beneath the wrapper where it made a *V* at her collarbone. Looking in the mirror again he saw her physical reaction to his touch through the thin material that strained across her full breasts. The wrapper had slid open slightly, exposing her long, white legs from the knee down.

"Please?" he said winsomely. "Just a little supper?"

Loretta was tempted. What if John did not want to marry her? Whitney Ross was one of the richest men in New York. He could give her many, many things. In addition, it would not hurt her career to be linked with such a glamorous figure. Or would it? There it was again. The question of her age and when she would marry. That she was physically attracted to Whitney meant nothing to Loretta. It was as easy to become attracted to one man as another. What counted for her was his ability to help her.

"No," she said firmly, standing up and drawing the wrapper more tightly around her. "And now it's time for you to go."

"Go? But it's only eleven-thirty, darling. The night is still young! Don't tell me you're going home to bed?" he asked suggestively.

"To sleep," she said, laughing to soften her words. No point in offending him for good. Better to keep him dangling in case something went wrong with John.

She gave him a friendly peck on the cheek. "Good night, darling." She headed toward the screen in the corner where she kept her street clothes. "Close the door behind you on your way out."

John Alexander did not sleep the night of his dinner with the Richmonds. Images of Devon kept him awake. He envisioned her as she had been that afternoon, her hair shining in the sun as it cascaded behind her. He remembered her warm lips — her body straining against his.

And he remembered her question about his involvements with other women. There was Loretta, of course, but that was just an amusement. He wondered if he was ready for anything more — for he knew that Devon was decidedly more than an amusement. Devon had many of the traits he considered desirable in a woman. But he was not certain he was ready for a serious commitment. He enjoyed single life. He enjoyed Loretta and women like her. He intended to marry, of course. Sometime in the distant future. But now?

Still, if he could describe the perfect woman, she would have all of Devon's characteristics. Devon had beauty, intelligence, self-assurance, spirit, and wit. He liked to be with her.

Why, then, was he so apprehensive about the feelings she aroused in him? he asked himself. It made him uncomfortable that she inserted herself into his thoughts, even when he was discussing business. He did not entirely like the feeling, he realized.

He tried to remember if he had felt as strongly about the two other women he had loved. It didn't seem so in retrospect, but surely he must have. And those incidents had not turned out well for him. That meant, he decided, that he must not allow himself to lose control again. He needed to be apart from Devon. Or he would be helpless to fight the irresistible lure of her.

CHAPTER

6

THE morning of the hunt was cold, with the first brisk snap of winter in the air. Sirocco snorted and pranced as the groom led him from his stall for Devon to mount. Devon's dark chignon and the horse's sleek black coat made a striking contrast to the bright scarlet of Devon's hunt coat and her white breeches. Devon was proud of the jacket, which bore the hunt colors on the collar, for it indicated that she had been promoted from subscriber to member of the Tri-County Hunt.

Although she had ridden with the hunt for years as a subscriber and her father was a longtime member, it had been a great honor for the master of the hunt to finally award her the right to wear hunt colors. One had to earn the right to go from subscriber to member, an honor that had been bestowed on her only three years before. To earn one's colors, it was usually necessary to have hunted faithfully with the Tri-County Hunt for five years and to have proved oneself a sportsman in ability and spirit.

Devon was proud that John would see her in this light. As Devon waited for her father, she thought of the two days that had passed since she had last seen the New Yorker. She had missed him. And she had hoped that he would call on her, but he had not. It puzzled her, and she found him dominating her thoughts.

Of course he had sent a polite thank-you and a bouquet of flowers to Laurel for the dinner. And he had included Devon in his best wishes. But there were no romantic missives, nothing to indicate that their time together had been as special for him as it had been for her.

As Devon and her father trotted closer to the Magrath estate, just fifteen minutes away, she tried to pick out John's figure from those of the rest of the riders. Since he was not a member of the Tri-County Hunt, John would not be wearing a scarlet coat, known as a pink, but rather a black or gray one.

As protocol dictated, Devon and Chase first went directly to the master of the hunt, Hamilton Magrath, to greet him. Beside him was his daughter Helena, unsuccessfully trying to control the prancing of her mount.

"You're looking beautiful as always," Magrath said, peering appreciatively at Devon. He wished his daughter Helena sat her horse even half as well as Devon. Helena had not yet been invited to be a member of the hunt, a fact which rankled her, since she had been riding for the same number of years as Devon. But, as master of the hunt, Magrath could not show any partiality in extending the privilege of wearing the hunt colors.

Helena noticed Devon's eyes searching the crowd, and asked cattily, "Are you looking for someone?"

"No," said Devon evenly. Where was John? He had been invited.

"Did you hear that Mr. Alexander went back to New York?" asked Helena with barely concealed glee. She smiled to herself as she saw Devon grow pale. She had noticed the attraction between Devon and Alexander the night of the dinner party.

It took all Devon's strength not to burst forward with a torrent of questions. She did not, however, want to give Helena that satisfaction. "He mentioned that he would return home as soon as his business was concluded," Devon replied with dignity.

"He left very suddenly," said Helena, looking probingly at Devon. "I know he and Daddy didn't finish their business."

A pregnant silence hung in the air. Devon did not respond to Helena, but simply looked at her, a polite mask of serenity on her face. I'd like to slap the nosy fool, Devon thought to herself.

Helena, growing uncomfortable, broke the silence. "He probably had an urgent matter to attend to. I mean, he left so sud—"

Helena was cut off by the sound of the huntsman blowing the horn signaling the beginning of the hunt. It was the huntsman's job to handle the hounds and to interpret the noises made by them.

Sirocco responded immediately to the signal. His ears perked forward and he snorted impatiently. Had Devon not been such an excellent rider and Sirocco so responsive to her, he might have been an unsuitable mount for the hunt. In the past, Devon had believed that the best mount for a hunt was not necessarily the best-looking. High-strung beauties often created havoc on the field. They could shy at sounds and unexpected movement, often throwing even the most experienced riders. In addition, Thoroughbreds often had the wrong kind of stride for the high jumps and narrow spaces of the hunting field, and could be uncomfortably bouncy mounts. But Devon loved Sirocco and felt in control.

She politely waited to move in line behind the more senior members of the hunt. Devon knew it was important to observe the protocol of hunting, for a breach of protocol could cause serious, even deadly accidents. For this reason, those whose horses sometimes hesitated at jumps were taught to move to the rear. And when taking a fence, experienced hunters would try to leave at least two horses' lengths between riders, so that if there was a fall, there would be less danger of trampling the victim or injuring surrounding riders.

Soon the hounds picked up the scent — the line, in hunt terminology — of a fox. The huntsman sounded several short notes on his horn, signaling that the line had been detected. As the hounds grew more excited, the hunt picked up speed, and the riders galloped across a hilly meadow sprinkled with fences of modest height.

Someone spotted the fox as it broke cover, and he cried, "Tallyho!" and pointed in the direction of the animal. It scampered in a rusty blur into some woods bordered on one side by a small creek. The hounds, wildly baying, chased after it.

Bent low over her horse to avoid being slapped off by the branches overhead, Devon hurried along in the middle of the group. The ground was somewhat muddy along the banks of the creek, causing the riders to slow their mounts. Helena, however, was having trouble controlling her horse, who was eager to follow the hounds. Several times Devon noticed the animal slip then regain its footing on the muddy earth. After every stumble, the horse sped up again, impervious to Helena's tugs on the bridle. Devon suspected that Helena did not really like riding but rather considered it a link to the two most important men in her life, both superb riders. Devon recalled several occasions when Helena had bowed out of a hunt because of illness only to make a miraculous recovery for the ball that followed.

Thoughts of Helena fled Devon's mind as the horses broke into a gallop over a field punctuated by stone walls and split-rail fences, many of them quite challenging jumps. Sirocco sailed over them, his Thoroughbred blood taking him easily to the front of the group of horses. Brent Hartwick, Helena's husband, saw Devon go by and shouted an admiring comment. Hartwick urged his mount on, catching up with Devon and sailing with her over a small fence.

From her traditional position at the rear of the hunt, Helena observed the exchange. Inflamed beyond rationality, she used her crop to speed her horse forward. The horse, used to Helena's attempts to restrain him, surged forward at this unaccustomed liberty. Helena knew immediately that the horse was running away with her, but she did not have the strength or the ability to stop him. The horse sped past one group of riders and began to approach the duo formed by Devon and Brent. Helena drew closer, until she was directly behind Devon's horse. Devon turned and saw Helena, but was not concerned because she knew that Sirocco did not kick. She assumed that Helena was trying to catch up to them. Brent, intent on the wall ahead, did not turn. He was unaware that the rider closing fast upon Devon and himself was his wife. He, like the others, was accustomed to her being in the rear of the hunt.

"I . . . can't stop!" Helena cried. She wanted to shout for help, but despite her fear, Devon's presence inhibited her, so she satisfied herself with the milder warning and hoped that her horse would slow after the jump. But Devon and Brent, turning at the sound of her voice, saw Helena's distress. Instinctively trying to help, the two reined in their horses, forgetting for a moment the approach of the wall. But Brent's old hunter, with the wall in sight, did not break stride. Sirocco, always responsive to his mistress, momentarily slowed before Devon realized she had given the wrong signal. With sudden horror, she saw that she was too close to the jump to stop her horse safely. Helena's horse, with or without his mistress, had every intention of taking the jump. To try to slow either horse now would endanger both women. Recovering herself in a split second, she allowed Sirocco to resume the rhythm he had almost imperceptibly lost.

Helena's horse, still in a mad gallop, brushed dangerously close to Sirocco and made for the wall. The two horses were neck and neck. The jump was wide enough to accommodate them simultaneously, but a glance at Helena told Devon that the other woman was paralyzed with fear. She was no longer even attempting to control her runaway mount. Instead she wore a blank expression and clutched the horse as hard as she could with her legs.

"Helena!" Devon cried. "Get into position or you'll fall!"

With relief, she saw the young woman obey, as if in a trance. Now, Devon told herself, I just have to make sure we don't collide going over the jump. Collision was a danger, Devon realized in alarm, because although brush and trees had been cleared so that the hunters could use the wall as a jump, the cleared area was only about eight feet wide.

Helena, gripped with terror, was oblivious to Devon. Her only goal was to stay on her horse. She could see that Brent had stopped. He was just on the other side of the wall, ready to catch her reins as she rode by. If only she could reach him, Helena felt she would be safe.

It was Devon who saw what was happening even before Sirocco did. Helena's horse, completely beyond the control of his mistress, headed squarely for the center of the jump, cutting into Sirocco's space. Helena, panicking at her proximity to Devon's horse, jerked the bridle to the left with all her might, and the horse's head with it. Devon was on Helena's right, so far over that it seemed she would collide with a bordering tree. But she did not. Instead, Helena's horse, rebelling against the sudden jerking motion on the bridle just as he was taking a jump, pulled his head and body to the right, slamming into Sirocco's head and side. The anguished cry of the wounded animals screamed through Devon's consciousness as she tried to maintain control of her horse, reeling from the painful collision with the other creature. With the slow-motion awareness that so often accompanies an accident, Devon noticed the strange angle of the trees. The impact of Helena's horse had tilted Sirocco in midair, so that his right side was lower than his left. The delicate balance necessary to launch the powerful animal over the four-foot wall was irretrievably destroyed. With the dizzying feeling of a roller-coaster ride, Devon felt Sirocco's legs slip from under them as he landed. In a blur, she saw Helena's horse land upright, stumble for a moment, and gallop on. Then Devon felt herself slam into the hard ground with an impact that knocked the wind out of her. In terror, she saw the black mass of her horse block out the daylight as he fell on top of her. The impact knocked her cold, so she did not hear the sickening crunch of broken limbs.

CHAPTER 7

LORETTA rolled over languorously, reaching her hand toward John's warm body. She caressed his lean, athletic stomach, then slid her hand lower. Although he was asleep, she felt him respond to her touch.

She smiled to herself. Last night had dispelled any doubts in her mind about John Alexander's passion for her. It seemed that he had missed her even more than she had missed him. He had made love to her in a frenzy. She shivered with the delicious memory of it.

But Loretta had not correctly interpreted the night's lovemaking. John had hoped that seeing the actress again would drive Devon from his mind. Indeed, Loretta still had the power to physically arouse him. It was just that every time she cried out, he imagined it was Devon. And regretted that it was not.

He had fled Virginia hoping to escape the disruption that Devon promised to bring to his life, but he had found her absence, and the possibility of losing her, as distracting as her presence. Since he'd met Devon, the vague prospect of marriage had been transformed into an idea that tugged at him against his will.

Marriage, to John, had always meant curtailment of freedom, dull routine. But he knew that Devon would not be a clinging, dependent creature, mindful only of her place in society. She was an interesting, independent woman — one he thought could make him happy. And that scared him. It scared him to know that if he married Devon she would be the most important thing in his life. That he would be devastated if anything happened to her. In loving her, he would give her custody of his heart and his mind. His happiness would come to depend on her. It was a frightening notion, yet one to which he was beginning to surrender.

The evening with Loretta, though a physical release, had convinced him of at least one thing: he no longer wished to continue their affair. The question was when to tell her that. He was too much of a gentleman, and felt too kindly toward Loretta, to sneak away at night immediately after making love to her. But he did not want to delay the unpleasant task. He would tell her in the morning, he resolved. Face to face. Honestly, but tactfully.

Then, in a few weeks, if he still felt the same about Devon . . . he had not quite decided what he would do.

Loretta, reveling in memories of the night before, thought that perhaps the time was right to broach the subject of marriage. But John was breathing regularly in a deep sleep. Maybe she should let him sleep. Maybe he'd be more willing to discuss marriage if he were fresh and rested. And after they'd made love again.

She slid from the bed and went into the bathroom to furtively reapply her makeup. She wanted to look her best. When she returned, she sidled back under the covers as quietly as she could. She lay on her back and snuggled close to John. She closed her eyes, but found that she couldn't sleep. Her mind was too busy planning what she would say to him. She silently rehearsed the scene dozens of times. And every one ended with a marriage proposal from John. Loretta convinced herself that no other outcome was possible.

That settled, she opened her eyes. She looked around at the white and gold furnishings of her bedroom. It was a woman's room, no sign anywhere of a man in residence, she thought with some dissatisfaction. Well, no more, she promised herself.

She turned on her side and put her arm around John, who had his back to her. She lightly ran her fingernails over his torso. He moaned sleepily, but his body responded to her touch. He turned over so that he was flat on his back and looked at Loretta with sleepy eyes. She expected him to reach for her. Instead, he stretched, then eased himself to the edge of the bed. He sat there for a moment, getting his bearings, then hoisted himself up and went toward the closet. He wanted to be dressed when they had their conversation.

"John?" Loretta's voice registered her surprise.

"Yes . . ." He stopped and looked over his shoulder.

"Are you getting ready to go?"

"Soon. But let's have a cup of coffee first," John said, keeping his tone casual. He was not looking forward to the task ahead of him.

Loretta picked up a telephone that connected her with the kitchen and told the maid to bring in coffee and rolls. Placing the phone back in its cradle, she sighed. "Last night was wonderful, don't you think?"

John emerged from the closet, wearing his slacks. His shirt hung open and his tie was slung around the collar. "Sure . . . wonderful," he said, not really paying attention.

Loretta stood up and slowly came toward him, wrapping a shimmering white silk robe around her as she did so. She put her arms under his shirt and softly ran her long nails across his back.

"We spent hours making love. I guess you missed me, didn't you?" She rubbed her silk-covered breasts on his bare chest.

John patted her arm affectionately in reply, then gently released himself from her embrace. He went toward the bed and stooped down to pick up his socks.

"Well . . . didn't you miss me? Answer me!" said Loretta impatiently. She planted herself in front of him, arms akimbo.

John stood up. "Loretta, I've only been gone a week," he said, a slight edge in his voice. He sat on the bed and put on his socks.

"You acted like you missed me." Loretta smiled suggestively and moved closer to him.

John was never intentionally cruel, so he kept silent. He reached for his shoes.

Infuriated, Loretta demanded, "Did you or did you not think of me while you were gone?"

John lifted his head. "Loretta, I was in Virginia on business. There was nothing there to make me think of you."

"But you told me you didn't finish your business, that you left early." Loretta's voice was accusatory. "Why did you do that if you didn't miss me?"

"Oh, for God's sake, Loretta," John said with visible irritation. He stood up and rapidly started to button his shirt. "Why are you asking me all this? What possible difference could it make?"

He turned away from her and headed toward the bathroom.

"It makes a difference because I want to marry you!" Loretta shouted at his back, forgetting herself. John spun around to face her, mouth open in surprise. Loretta saw the shocked look on his face and immediately regretted her words. She had raised the subject of marriage before — in a jocular sort of way — but she knew her shrill, deadly serious tone now was a tactical mistake of immense proportions. She should have known better. Men were always blurting out such things to her. She knew how *she* greeted such admissions: with condescension. How stupid to put herself in the same position.

The shock on John's face turned to understanding, then pity as he realized that Loretta regretted the admission. Loretta, observing the change, felt a hot fury grip her. Pity! He pitied her! Men begged for a smile from her and John dared to feel sorry for her!

"You!" she screamed. "You should be grateful. You don't understand how men want me, you don't —"

"Of course I do, Loretta," he cut in, trying to placate her and avoid an ugly scene.

How dare he humor me, Loretta fumed. She knew that tone of voice. It was the tone the wardrobe designer used when she demanded changes. Or the hairdresser when she insisted on a more elaborate hairdo. It was the tone of a man who wished to smooth things over so that he could get on with his own life. It was not the voice of a man who loved her, or was even interested in her! He was indifferent to her!

"How dare you use that tone with me!" She was sobbing now. "You think I've been sitting around this place waiting for you? Well, I haven't! Whitney Ross has promised to divorce his wife and marry me," she lied desperately, wanting to humiliate him as he had humiliated her.

"Loretta," John cut her off, recognizing the lie and wanting to save her from making a fool of herself. He looked at the wreckage of the beautiful blond star before him. Her carefully applied makeup was a messy smear, mixing with her tears. She looked older than thirty-four. She looked desperate. Soothingly, John said, "Loretta, I understand that you're angry. I enjoy being with—"

"Enjoy? What do you think I am, your maiden aunt?" She laughed hysterically, babbling on. "Don't you dare patronize me! I'm not waiting around for anyone. I've waited around too long for you. Now get out. *Get out!*" she cried. She grabbed his arm and shoved him toward the door. Then sank to the floor in a flood of tears.

John hastily headed for the door—then stopped. He did not want to leave Loretta in this state. Turning, he approached the sobbing woman. "Loretta. Let me help you up," he said gently.

No words could have inflamed her more. There it was again: pity. Lifting her head, she stopped crying for a moment. She wiped her eyes with the cuff of her robe. Then she looked at John with such pure hatred that he recoiled.

"I hate you, John Alexander," she said fiercely, in an ominously quiet voice. "I hate you and I'll never stop hating you."

The two stared at each other for a few seconds.

"Get out," she said in a voice that, in its very quietness, was more threatening than her screams.

John had no choice but to obey.

CHAPTER 8

THE first sensation of Devon's return to consciousness was not pain but rather darkness. She tried to open her eyes and realized with horror that they were already open. Then she felt the pain. It was like a mummifying wrap covering every inch of her body, leaving no part of her untouched.

"She's awake, I think." Devon heard her mother's voice, anxious, but at the same time calming because it was her mother. A warm hand covered hers. Her left hand. Her right hand was encased in something. She did not know what. She did not know because she could not see. Her stomach clenched in fear as she tried to speak.

She heard a creaky, guttural sound. Her voice, barely recognizable, whispered brokenly, "I . . . can't . . . see."

"Devon, I *thought* you were awake!" her mother said with great relief.

"Thank God. Thank God." Devon heard her father, murmuring hoarsely to himself.

"Don't try to talk," said a gruff, firm voice. Dr. Hickock. She had known him since childhood. But she could not obey him. She had to talk. There were things she had to know.

"I . . . can't . . . see." Even though Devon's voice rose barely above a whisper, the imploring quality of it was impossible to miss.

"You've suffered a severe concussion, Devon," said the doctor. "Your head is bandaged. We've covered your eyes, but it's just temporary," he said reassuringly.

"I . . . hurt," she said in a fractious voice, stronger now. She was bewildered. She did not remember why she was in such pain.

The doctor smiled in victory at Laurel and Chase when he heard the peeved quality of Devon's voice. Your daughter is strong, his look told them. She is already fighting. She'll be fine. He had been reluctant, until now, to be overly encouraging because he had feared the Richmonds would be disappointed by the slowness of Devon's recovery. And it would be slow, no doubt about it. In addition to the broken bones, she had suffered internal injuries.

39

REGRET NOT A MOMENT

He was surprised that she was already awake, since it was only the second day following her accident. That was a good sign. He was relieved. He had treated all the Richmonds since he had been old enough to join his father's medical practice thirty-five years before, and he felt tremendous affection for the family.

He was also surprised that Laurel had shown so much more strength than her husband throughout the ordeal. Chase Richmond was usually a congenial, back-slapping man's man; a family man, of course, but not one given to displays of emotion. Yet he had wept like a baby as he waited outside the doctor's office while his daughter was being treated. Laurel had been much more stoic, her anxiety evident only in the sickly paleness of her face and the handkerchief she had wrung and wrung until it was no more than a tight wrinkled little ball of linen.

Once Devon had been transported home in a makeshift ambulance devised from the Magraths' Bentley (for the nearest hospital was fifty miles away in Washington, D.C.), Dr. Hickock had expected Chase to return to normal. Instead, the doctor and Laurel had listened, with a feeling of helplessness and sadness, to Chase's broken-voiced entreaties to God to spare Devon's life and make her whole again.

Laurel found herself hugging Chase close to her and cradling his head against her shoulder, as she had once done with their children. She murmured soothing words of comfort.

Dr. Hickock could not help but interject his own words of comfort into the highly personal scene. "She won't die, Chase. She's strong and she's young. She'll recover. It may take a while, but she'll recover," he had said quietly.

Laurel and Chase had looked at him gratefully upon hearing those words, but had not for one minute relaxed their vigil since that conversation, almost forty-eight hours ago. Now, as Devon's eyelids fluttered against the bandages, and her mouth worked to form words, the three bystanders looked at one another with elation.

Devon was unaware of the intensity of emotion in the room, but she heard a long sigh of relief. A sweet smell, like orange blossoms, followed the sigh. Her mother's scent. Mixed with it was the tweedy, tobacco smell of her father. The familiarity of these things comforted her.

"Do you remember what happened to you, Devon?" asked her mother.

"No," she croaked.

"You had a hunting accident, darling, but you're going to be fine. Sirocco fell on you. Not squarely, thank the Lord. But you have a broken arm and leg and several broken ribs."

Devon was silent for a few seconds, trying to remember the accident. Then an agonizing thought crossed her mind. "Sirocco . . . ?" She wanted to say more, but didn't have the strength. Her beautiful Sirocco. Was he dead? She had raised the horse from a foal, then trained him herself. They had a special bond. If anything had happened to him . . .

"He's fine," said her father soothingly, recovering himself now that he saw that Devon was well enough to talk. "He landed on his side, so he didn't break any legs. He's bruised, but the vet says he'll recover nicely."

"Laurel, Chase, Devon needs her rest," said the doctor firmly.

"Go back to sleep now, darling," said Laurel, lifting Devon's good hand and kissing it. Devon squeezed her mother's hand feebly. Her father gently stroked the blanket over her ankle, as though afraid he would cause her pain if he touched her. She could feel the blanket stir and she moved her foot slightly so as to make contact with his hand. It was the only form of acknowledgment she could muster. She wished she could summon more energy, but the foggy world of sleep beckoned her.

In that indistinct half-conscious world between sleep and wakefulness she lingered for a moment — just long enough to feel a new twinge of pain. It came from inside and she did not know its cause. It had something to do with . . . she could not remember. A blurred image swam into her consciousness, then dispersed, as though it were smoke blown away by the wind. She fell asleep trying to grasp the image that she knew, somehow, was causing her a pain deeper than that caused by her broken limbs.

Devon hastily put down the silver hand mirror she had picked up only seconds before, shuddering at the reflection she had glimpsed there. Although two weeks had passed since her accident, she was still severely bruised and in considerable discomfort. She had two black eyes and a myriad of cuts and scrapes on her face. But the worst, she thought, was her hair — what was visible of it beneath the gauze that circled her skull. Her head was too tender to allow her hair to be combed, so the once shining black locks hung in a tangled rats' nest on her shoulders. Her frilly white batiste nightgown provided an incongruous touch of daintiness against which rested the already graying cast on her arm.

Devon's maid, Alice, entered the room, carrying a bowl of broth on a small silver tray.

"Here's a snack for you, Miss Devon," she said, drawing up a silk-upholstered armchair to the young woman's bedside.

"Thank you, Alice. You know, if you would put it in a cup, you wouldn't need to sit here and feed me."

"True, but if I put it in a cup, you won't drink as much, and you need to build up your strength." And with that Alice took a spoonful of the hearty-smelling liquid and brought it toward Devon's mouth. Devon swallowed it without further argument.

Alice took that as a good sign and decided to broach the subject on her mind. "Miss Helena has asked if she could call on you today," said Alice, in a studiedly conversational tone.

Devon stiffened at the words, but said nothing. As she had regained her memory of the riding accident, she had grown more and more furious at Helena Magrath Hartwick. Now she was tempted to tell Alice to send the young woman away when she next called.

Alice, as though reading Devon's thoughts, said, "She's been here every day since your accident, Miss Devon. She's been frantic with worry." At each visit, Helena had asked to see Devon, but Dr. Hickock, sensing that an unpleasant scene might occur, had put her off. He did not want his patient's strength taxed. Today, however, he had told the Richmonds that Devon might begin receiving visitors, knowing full well that Helena would be among the first. That was fine. Devon was out of danger.

"Helena worried!" said Devon cynically. "Feeling guilty, you mean." She slipped a finger inside the cast on her arm, trying in vain to scratch a spot just beyond her reach. Her forced inactivity and her discomfort grated on her nerves.

Alice did not reply, knowing that Devon's better nature would finally make her agree to see Helena. Indeed, the young woman's Southern upbringing was such that she could not commit a deliberate act of rudeness.

"All right," Devon told Alice, in a tone that indicated she was girding herself for an ordeal, "ask her to come up when she gets here."

Alice nodded approvingly, pleased that she had judged Devon correctly. "She'll be here in fifteen minutes," said Alice, trying hard to keep a touch of smugness from her voice. She rapidly propelled a spoonful of broth toward Devon's mouth.

Devon stared at Alice as she swallowed, eyes wide with pretended outrage. "Rather sure of yourself, weren't you?"

"Not at all, Miss Devon. I was sure of your good breeding," Alice answered virtuously. Devon laughed at her tone of righteous innocence.

"You know me better than I know myself," Devon said wryly.

"I've known you longer, Miss Devon, since before you were born." Again, both women laughed at this silliness.

"Stop making me laugh," Devon cried, "it hurts!"

Still chuckling, Alice stood and put the empty bowl back on the silver tray. "I'll send Miss Helena up when she arrives."

After Alice departed, Devon lay back in the bed and closed her eyes. She was tired again. She wished she had not said she would see Helena, but it was too late.

Her mind wandered back to the day of the accident. Before the hunt began, she recalled, she and Helena had talked. Now she remembered the conversation clearly. It had been about John Alexander. He had left Virginia suddenly. Thinking of it, Devon experienced a sharp twinge of pain in her throat. She had hoped for something to come of their meeting. He had seemed so right for her, so attracted to her. Why had he left? Was there someone else in his life? she wondered.

Then she shook her head, as if to clear it. Maybe his leaving had nothing to do with her. Maybe it had been a business matter. It was self-centered, she chided herself, to believe that she influenced his actions. In any event, perhaps he would return. Helena had said that John's business with Mr. Magrath was not finished. That gave her hope.

An image of their afternoon by the brook came to her. Even in her injured state, a flush of warmth suffused her body. She felt a physical longing for his touch. What promise it had held for her! Was it possible that she loved him? He had so many of the qualities she admired in a man, but when she thought of him, she did not think of those qualities; she thought only of his lips on hers, his hands on her body. She ached with the memory of it.

What if he did not return? Would her longing for him fade? Worse yet, what if the feeling did *not* go away and he did *not* return for her? Return *for her* — that's how she thought of it. How could anyone live with such persistent yearning? she wondered. She had almost tasted its fulfillment. Could almost guess what her married girlfriends giggled about in hushed conversations, quickly stifled when she appeared. But did only married women know such pleasure? Could she ever be like those women she read about in the novels buried in dusty corners of her father's library? Women who were men's *mistresses*. Of course not, she told herself, it was unthinkable that she should ever commit such an act without marriage. But the alternative — never knowing the pleasure of lying with a man, never knowing the feeling of a strong body against her softer one — seemed equally unthinkable.

The feel of the linen nightgown against her bare breasts as she thought of such things aroused her. They wanted to be touched. She wondered how John would touch them. Would he kiss them? She had read of such things. The idea filled her with unspeakable desire. Tentatively, she reached her good hand to her breast and cupped it. She imagined it was John's hand. Between her legs, she was wet with the heat of her imaginings.

Then she heard the door open ever so quietly. She quickly dropped her hand and tried to push herself into a more upright position, wincing at the pain in her side as she did so. With irritation — both at the pain and at the interruption — she saw Helena edge into the room cautiously, like a soldier expecting to be ambushed. Her pale redhead's complexion grew paler still when she saw Devon. Devon could not help but be amused by the look of horror on Helena's face as she took in the extent of her injuries, but Devon held her smile in check. She knew that the moment was agony for Helena, but she could not bring herself to make things easier for her.

"Devon?" Helena sounded as though she were uncertain that the person in the bed was indeed the beautiful young woman of whom she had been so jealous just two weeks ago. Her voice quavered apprehensively.

"Helena." Devon uttered the word in a neutral, reasonable tone, but one devoid of warmth.

"Devon . . . you're sitting up. You must be . . . better?" Again she concluded her sentence with a question mark in her voice.

She wants to be reassured, Devon thought. She wants me to convince her that I'll be fine and that she's forgiven. But Devon was too angry for that.

"I'm better than I was two weeks ago, if that's what you mean," she snapped.

So far, Helena had remained just inside the door. Devon had not invited her to sit in the armchair beside the bed, the only chair in the room other than the round, skirted little seat in front of her vanity. But she could not continue to withhold common courtesy. "Please come in and sit down, Helena," she said, in the tone of a school principal inviting in a truant.

Reassured by the familiar phrase, if not the tone, Helena expelled her breath in a long sigh and quickly took the seat. She reached her hand toward Devon's, then stopped, as though uncertain whether the gesture would be rebuffed.

Devon felt a twinge of pity for Helena. She could read in her face many sleepless nights fraught with anxiety and guilt. So — much less harshly than she had originally intended — she said, "Helena, what in the world got into you that day?"

"Oh, Devon, I don't know, I just lost control. I'm so sorry. I'm so sorry. I was stupid. I never want to get on a horse again. I've never been a good rider." The words came in a torrent. All the suppressed emotion, all the tension of the past two weeks found an outlet in the river of words rushing from Helena's lips.

Devon could not deny the truth of Helena's words, but the other young woman's humility was disarming. How could she flog someone so intent on self-mortification? "Helena, I'll admit you're not the best rider I know, but you usually show good sense. You don't ride horses that are too hard for you to handle, you stay in the rear of the hunt. Why were you up front that day?"

Helena blushed at the question. She did not reply. Her eyes were cast down, as though studying the fluffy comforter on Devon's bed.

"Helena?" Devon asked again, this time more sternly. She wanted an answer.

"I was jealous," said Helena in a small voice.

"Jealous!" Devon repeated the word more in surprise at Helena's honesty than in disbelief. She knew that Helena had always been jealous of her, from the time they were children.

She remembered an incident that had occurred when the two little girls, then ten years old, had received their first horses. Prior to that time, they had had ponies. The parents had given the girls the horses at the same time. They thought their daughters would be good company for each other as they learned to jump. Both girls had perched proudly on their new mounts, feeling very grown-up in the smart new riding habits that had come with the horses.

Devon remembered all four parents, indulgent expressions on

their faces, encouraging the girls to take the horses through various paces around the Magraths' riding ring.

Helena went first, diligently walking, trotting, and cantering her new horse. She performed the exercises correctly, if rather ploddingly. Polite applause greeted the girl as she returned to where the adults stood leaning against the whitewashed enclosure that marked the riding ring.

"Very good, Helena. We may just make a rider of you yet!" Magrath said. He did not mean to wound; he was simply insensitive to the impact of his words on his daughter. But Helena's hurt was evident to Devon. Magrath found his daughter lacking in grace, and both girls knew it.

"Now you, Devon," said Magrath, oblivious to his daughter's pain.

Because she pitied Helena, Devon made no attempt to show off. But her natural athletic ability, combined with her love and understanding of horses, made her a joy to watch. Helena, sitting astride her horse near the adults, could not help but overhear the words of praise for Devon's skill.

"You've got a natural there, Chase. Don't know where she gets it," Magrath teased. As Devon drew nearer, she heard the good-natured ribbing of her father, and laughed, but Magrath's next sentence silenced her. "Now if she were *my* daughter," he joked, "I would understand her being such a horsewoman."

Devon quickly looked at Helena to see the effect of the words. Helena worshipped her father and wanted so much to please him. As Devon expected, her friend wore a strange, pinched look, as though she were trying to suppress a deeper emotion.

Devon knew Helena could see her watching, but the redhead stared stonily ahead, refusing to meet her eyes.

"What's wrong, dear, why did you stop?" Laurel Richmond asked. Devon was so distracted that she hadn't realized she had stopped.

"I just . . . don't feel well," she said. She didn't want to continue riding. She couldn't bear to see the other girl's humiliation.

"Well, you've both had a great deal of excitement for one day. Why don't you give your horses to the groom and then we'll go inside for lemonade and cookies," said Rosalind Magrath, blind to her daughter's distress.

The two little girls quietly walked their horses to the stable.

Without exchanging a word, they dismounted and handed their horses to the groom. As they headed toward the house, Helena uttered two sentences Devon would never forget.

"I don't need you to feel sorry for me, you know. My father loves me better than anyone in the world," she said with quiet vehemence.

Devon, embarrassed for her friend, did not know how to respond.

"He does!" Helena cried insistently. It was the tone that struck Devon. Helena seemed to be trying to convince herself, not Devon, of the truth of what she was saying.

The sad thing, Devon thought now in retrospect, was that Magrath probably *did* love his daughter more than anyone on earth, but had no idea of Helena's need for reassurance.

Devon, remembering the event, knew that riding was a sensitive subject for Helena, but since Helena had brought it up herself, Devon decided to continue the conversation. She hoped it would clear the tension between them that had started with that long-ago ride and grown worse in recent years.

"Are you jealous because your father hasn't invited you to become a member of the hunt?" Devon asked, sure that this was what Helena meant.

Helena looked at Devon blankly. "The hunt?" she asked, as though she did not know the meaning of the words.

"You said you tried to ride to the front because you were jealous," said Devon, exasperated at having to explain Helena's own words to her.

"Not of that!" Helena said in surprise.

"Then what?"

Helena stared at Devon incredulously. "You really don't know?"

"Know what?" asked Devon impatiently.

"Brent."

Devon recoiled as though she had been slapped. "You must be joking! I've never indicated any interest in Brent. Not since long before you were engaged. And even then . . ." She let the sentence fade away as she realized it would be impolite to admit that she had never found the other woman's husband overly attractive. He was a good friend. She liked him. They had enjoyed each other's company for a time, but on Devon's side at least, the relationship went no deeper than that.

"I know," Helena said with quiet dignity. "You have always behaved properly. It's him. He still . . . admires you. I'm not certain —

and I really don't want to know for sure — but I think he may still love you."

Devon became alarmed. She could not bear the thought of Brent actually being in love with her. "Surely you're imagining things. People gossip so. You mustn't listen," said Devon warmly, covering Helena's hand with her own. For a moment she forgot that Helena was one of the worst gossips in the county. As on that day fifteen years before, Devon wished only to reassure her, to see her confidence bolstered. It was odd; she and Helena had been neighbors all their lives and they were regarded by others as friends. But their relationship had never developed into real friendship. Helena's insecurity prevented her from giving Devon the trust necessary for friendship. Helena had always felt like a failure in comparison with Devon and had thus behaved at times with hostility, at times with prickly defensiveness. Devon, not the sort to tolerate unfriendly behavior, was simply indifferent to Helena. But sometimes, when events occurred that reminded her of Helena's insecurity, Devon felt sorry for her.

"Don't," Helena said in a pained voice. "Don't feel sorry for me. You always have and I can't bear it."

Devon, embarrassed, was silent. She groped for words that would give Helena confidence without sounding condescending. Studying the redhead, whose downcast eyes were brimming with tears, Devon realized that she was quite attractive. Marriage had allowed her to adopt styles of hair and dress that were somewhat bolder than those appropriate for a single woman, and the change suited her.

"Helena, there's no reason anyone should pity you. You're very attractive. And there's no reason for Brent to look outside his marriage for . . . anything. Believe me, he has never, in any way, indicated to me that he is not perfectly happy with you. Of course he still likes me. We've been friends all our lives. But I'm certain I would know if he loved me. Don't forget, his relationship with me ended months before he began to court you."

"I know. But some people said there were . . . reasons . . . reasons other than love that he married me."

"As I said before, it's foolish to listen to gossip. No one can know more about Brent than you, his wife. Isn't that right?"

"That's right, I suppose," Helena said, with hope in her voice.

"And has he ever been anything but loving toward you?"

"No . . . I suppose not." Helena hesitated a moment, then went on. "Except the night of the dinner party at our house. The way he talked to you . . . and that day . . . the day of the hunt . . . you and he were riding together."

"Helena, if you'll pardon me for saying so, I think you're allowing your own doubts to make you see things that aren't there. Brent is a natural flirt, but I don't think he treats me any differently from any other woman, now does he?"

Devon saw that Helena was reflecting on the question. After a few moments, the redhead's face cleared, as though she had just learned a piece of good news. "You know, Devon, I think you're right! I think Brent does treat everyone that way. I never really paid attention before. I was always so concerned with your . . . previous . . . relationship."

"You see!" Devon said excitedly. She had forgotten her anger at Helena and was happy to have found a solution to the other woman's problem.

Then Helena's face fell. "But at the hunt," she said, "he looked at you with such admiration. He wanted to ride with you. Oh, Devon, you just don't see —"

"I see that you're being silly, Helena," Devon interrupted in a stern tone. "I see that Brent looks at my father with admiration when he takes a jump particularly well. He admires my riding. Maybe he even admires me. But he is married to you and I'm sure he loves you."

Tears of emotional release, as well as remorse, were streaming down Helena's face. "Yes . . . yes, I see what you mean." She paused a moment and dabbed at her eyes with a handkerchief. When she lifted her face again, it had cleared. "I think you must be right," she said, her tone tremulous but more cheerful. "Oh, Devon, will you ever forgive me for being so stupid . . . and for causing your accident?"

"Of course. If you promise to keep those silly notions out of your head for good," said Devon gruffly. She was touched in spite of herself. The other woman was exasperating, maybe foolish, but she had bared her soul to Devon and Devon could only respond with kindness.

In her elation, Helena did not measure her next words. She did not mean to hurt Devon. Helena thought of Devon as a superior being and did not realize that she was even capable of inflicting pain on her. In her excitement, she simply spoke the words that entered her head:

"And I really have no reason to be jealous of you," said Helena. "Now I have something you don't. I'm married and you're not. I'm married to a man who used to court you."

Devon was startled by Helena's bluntness, but the real shock came from the words themselves. "You're right," Devon said in a stunned voice. After all, Helena did have something Devon wanted. Each night when Helena went to bed, she slept beside the man she loved. They had done things Devon could only imagine, only long for. In addition, Devon knew that some people pitied her because she was still single. Helena's place in society was ensured by virtue of her marriage. She could attend any event she wished, whether or not she was escorted by her husband, simply because she was married. Like a swift blow that took the wind out of her, the realization that her good looks and self-confidence meant nothing to the outside world shook Devon to her very core. She did not feel pitiable. She was not pitiable, yet society was making her so. Society and her own desires, which she saw no means of assuaging.

"I just won't be jealous anymore," Helena continued decisively. Then, laughing in relief, she said, "It's created an awful mess, hasn't it? Besides, I do have Brent. He's mine now and I don't suppose I need trouble myself beyond that." Helena had new resolve in her voice.

"No . . . no . . . you should never worry about that," replied Devon, but her voice was vague, as though her thoughts were far away.

"And I've been selfish taking up so much of your time when you're still recovering. Why, you seem positively exhausted!" With a new briskness to her movements, Helena leaned down, kissed Devon on the cheek, and bade her farewell.

Alone again, Devon burrowed deep into her pillows and tiredly pulled the covers up around her neck. She felt drained. She needed to rest. But she could not rest because replaying itself over and over in her mind was the realization that life's vivid promise, its glories, could remain closed to her. It was a possibility she had never before considered.

CHAPTER 9

GRACE Richmond Des Rochers had a first name which suited her not at all. Devon's older sister had none of the cool serenity implied by her given name. She was all vivid theatricality and prankishness. She was not a relaxing person to be around, as her nonstop chatter came in a steady stream of witticisms that could easily slip by listeners who were less than alert. In fact, there were many who had warned her husband, Philip, that she was "too chatty" for the role of diplomat's wife. But she had used her talent with words to grasp quickly the languages of the countries to which her husband was posted and, with her ability to converse with anyone on any subject, had proved an asset after all.

Devon and Grace were the best of friends and kept in constant touch with long, self-revealing letters to each other. Both regretted that the career of Grace's husband made their visits so infrequent, yet both knew that Grace was perfectly suited to the life of constant travel and new faces.

But when Grace heard of Devon's accident, she rushed home from Paris as quickly as possible, and now, after a train ride, an Atlantic crossing, and another train ride, she descended on Evergreen in a whirlwind.

After embracing her parents and inquiring after their health, Grace demanded to see Devon. The Richmonds were eager for a reunion of the sisters, certain that Grace's presence would act as a tonic to the convalescent. They worried that Helena's visit, two days before, had sapped Devon of her energy. She had seemed in low spirits ever since. But when they asked if she was feeling well, she insisted that she was. Dr. Hickock had reassured them that her injuries were healing even more rapidly than he had hoped, but he also noticed her quiet distraction. He attributed it to her being bedridden for so many days and, grateful for the physical progress she was making, thought no more about the matter.

"We haven't told her that you're coming," Laurel said in a conspiratorial whisper, leading Grace up the sweeping staircase to the second story. "We wanted it to be a surprise." Her voice had a happy lilt. She was thrilled to have her eldest daughter home and was certain that Devon would benefit from the visit.

"Good. Will I be shocked when I see her?" Grace asked lightly, not really meaning the question. Almost nothing shocked Grace.

"Well . . . yesterday we were able to wash her hair, and that's a big improvement, but she's still black-and-blue," said Laurel.

"You don't recover overnight from a fall like hers," Chase said gruffly. Grace looked sharply at him. For all her appearance of frivolity, she missed very little. Her father did not look well, she thought; he had lost the comfortable girth that had been with him for as long as she could remember. She knew that he was very close to Devon and realized that he must be terribly worried. She'd try to pull him out of it later, she decided. For now, she wanted to see her sister.

Grace didn't bother knocking on the door but simply rushed into her sister's room, a dervish swathed in a flowing red silk Paris original.

"Devon, get out of that bed at once! You've made your point. You've got my attention. Now let's go dancing," she said in a tone of pretend sternness.

Devon could not believe her eyes. "Gracie?" she said incredulously.

"The same," said Grace, folding her sister in a warm embrace, then plopping down beside her on the bed.

"Ouch!" cried Devon. "My side."

"Oh!" Grace jumped off the bed. "I'm so sorry! Are you all right?"

"Oh, Gracie, I'm so happy to see you. I'm fine. I just can't believe you're here. It's wonderful! You look gorgeous." Devon grabbed her sister's right hand in her left one and pulled her into the chair beside the bed. She noted, with a connoisseur's eye, the beautiful cut of her sister's flaming scarlet dress. She didn't need to ask if it was a Schiaparelli. No other designer was so bold with color and line. Yet its very simplicity of design prevented the color from appearing vulgar. Grace's perfectly manicured nails wore the same vivid shade. A chic black cloche with a net veil was seductively tilted to one side on her head, while black kid gloves and matching shoes completed the ensemble.

"Well, *you* look perfectly awful," declared Grace, "but not as bad as I thought you'd look, I must confess."

"I feel better now. But, tell me, when did you get here? How long are you staying?"

"I don't know how long I'm staying yet. That partly depends on you."

"Well, if it depends on me, then stay at least until Christmas. Can't Philip and the kids come here for the holidays?"

"Possibly. We'll see about that later. Tell me how this horrid thing happened to you. I hear that idiot Helena caused it."

"Oh, Gracie, she's not so bad. She didn't do it intentionally. Anyway, it's a long story. I'll tell you about it later." At the mention of Helena's name, a small frown creased Devon's brow. She was still depressed by her conversation with Helena. Reflecting on her life as she lay immobile in bed had caused her to despair for the future. She had realized that, with her sister far away, she would be quite alone in the world if anything happened to her parents. She had friends, of course, but they were mostly married. Where would she fit in? she wondered. If she moved, she was certain she would be even more alone. The prospect was frightening. And the feeling of fright was alien to her. The very newness of her emotions filled her with malaise.

Grace, observing the quiet trouble of her sister, was disturbed. "What's wrong with you?" she asked, keenly studying Devon's face.

Devon jumped a bit as Grace's voice intruded on her reflections. She had almost forgotten her presence. Laughing lightly in an attempt to hide her mood, she replied, "Nothing's wrong. I just was thinking how much I miss having you around to talk to."

Grace looked at her skeptically, but let the matter rest. "Well, as you know, I'll talk your ear off while I'm here. Enough to compensate for all the times I'm not here," she said self-mockingly.

"Tell me everything about Paris, Grace. Do you love it? Your letters always make your life sound so glamorous!"

"There is a certain glamour to life there, but it rains a beastly amount," said Grace with a laugh. "Almost as bad as London."

"But you seem to prefer it to London," said Devon.

"Oh, yes. I like the freedom of Paris. I like the way Frenchmen look at a woman. I like the way Frenchwomen dress and behave. I've rather adopted the French outlook, I'm afraid. I'm not certain how well I'll do when we have to move on," said Grace, with a sigh of regret.

"What do you mean, the French outlook?"

"Well, you've been there. It seems that women are regarded as desirable until they are really quite old. As I grow older, I find that trait very endearing. Then, there's always such scandalously juicy gossip. It seems that love affairs are, if not exactly accepted, at least not too harshly judged. Mind you, I would kill Philip if he ever . . . well, you know . . . but it does lend a certain piquancy to social gatherings. And there's something else, too. Many of society's intellectual leaders in Paris are women. Women are valued for their intelligence. I find that refreshing, don't you?"

"Yes," said Devon, with more intensity than she intended. "It sounds quite ideal. I guess I wasn't there long enough to find out much about how the society works. And I was there as a tourist."

"Wouldn't you like to come for a visit? You know we'd love to have you." Smiling warmly, Grace took Devon's hand in hers and squeezed it.

Devon squeezed back, loving her sister so very much. How she wished Grace lived closer! "Maybe when I'm back on my feet again. Of course, that won't be for months. It would be fun to travel back together on the ship though, wouldn't it? But I don't suppose you can stay that long," said Devon with disappointment.

Grace, concerned at her sister's uncharacteristically low spirits, attempted to tease her out of her mood. "Well, I'll certainly stay until you get your looks back. If I leave before then, I'll have no memory of what the beauty of the family is supposed to look like." Grace was not a beauty like Devon. Her round face was nothing like Devon's high-cheekboned one, nor did her coloration have any of the drama of Devon's. Whereas Devon had startling aqua eyes with shining ebony hair, Grace had more mundane brown eyes with curly auburn hair. But Grace had a sparkle that made men flock to her. With her dramatic style of dressing and her theatrical gestures, she had never had cause to envy her younger sister's looks. Instead, she took great pride in Devon's beauty.

Devon frowned at the mention of her appearance. "My looks? Fat lot of good they've done me so far," she said ruefully.

"What's this? Self-pity. That's something I've never heard from you, Devon," said Grace, going from gay to serious in a split second as she sensed her sister's depression.

"It's not self-pity exactly. I guess I'm just cranky from being in bed all this time," said Devon, ashamed that she had succumbed to such an unworthy emotion within minutes of her sister's arrival. But Grace was so sympathetic, so comforting. And Devon had always shared her deepest secrets with her.

"You're not just cranky," said Grace sternly. "Tell me what's bothering you. I know something is."

Devon did not respond immediately. It was difficult to articulate her emotions. There was fear . . . of loneliness, of emptiness. There was longing for John Alexander. There was bewilderment at his hasty return to New York, at his failure to appear for the hunt. There was depression that she might never know love. There was even a certain — she hated to admit it, even to herself, but there was a certain desperation in the way she felt. As though she would never find someone to love. As though she was being punished for refusing the many offers of marriage that had come her way.

"Grace . . . I'm scared," Devon said, silent tears beginning to make their way down her bruised face.

"Scared? Of not getting better?" asked Grace, bewildered.

"Not that," said Devon, reaching for a handkerchief and gingerly blotting the tears from her sore face.

"Then what? Are you afraid to ride again?" Grace could not imagine such a thing, but she could not imagine anything else that could evoke such sadness in Devon.

"Gracie . . . it's something else. Promise you won't tell Mother and Father?"

"Of course, if you don't want me to." She made the cross-my-heart gesture they had used since childhood.

"I'm afraid I'm never going to know what it's like to be in love — and have a man love me."

"Devon, that's ridiculous!" exploded Grace, surprise jerking her body erect in her chair. "How could you think such a thing? You've refused so many men. You could have any man you want."

"Not any man," Devon said quietly, trying to hold back the tears. She would not meet her sister's eyes. Instead, she looked down at the comforter and picked at it in a childish gesture of nervousness.

"Are you talking about someone in particular?"

Devon knew that confession would be painful, but she needed the release. "Yes, I mean someone in particular," said Devon, raising her eyes to meet Grace's. "I don't know if I'm in love with him. I don't see how that's possible. I've only known him a few weeks."

"What are you saying? That there's no hope with this man?" asked Grace, leaning forward in her chair in an attempt to hold Devon's gaze.

"I don't know. But, Gracie, it's not just him. I'm afraid I'll die without ever having known . . ." Devon could not finish her sentence, could not look at her sister, she was so ashamed.

Grace looked at her sympathetically. She understood what her sister meant. Grace was an extremely sensuous woman and could not imagine life without love — or without lovemaking. "You don't ever have to resign yourself to . . . that," said Grace softly.

"But I've never been in love. I've never wanted to marry any man I met, except this man."

"Who is he?"

"His name is John Alexander. He lives in New York. He was here on a visit." Devon went on to explain the circumstances of their meeting and his subsequent courtship of her.

"Do you want to marry him?"

"How is that possible? I've known him such a short time. All I know is that I want to . . . he makes me feel . . ." Devon paused, too embarrassed to describe the physical longing he aroused in her.

"You mean you would like to make love to him, whether or not you marry him?" asked Grace bluntly.

"Grace! How can you say such a thing!" Devon exclaimed, shocked that her sister could discern the very idea she was unable to stifle in her own mind.

"Don't be priggish, Devon. It's done all the time in Paris. Women make love with a lot of men who aren't their husbands. Some of them do it after they marry, some before. It's perfectly natural to desire a man. In fact, I'm surprised you're still a —" Grace did not finish the sentence, but raised her eyebrows questioningly.

"Grace! Of course I am! Mother and Father would die if they could hear you."

"Well, they can't, so it doesn't matter," Grace said dismissively, scooting her chair closer to the bed. "Look, my dear. You are almost twenty-five, and you've been much too sheltered. You've got to grow up and face the facts of life. If you want this man for a husband, try to marry him, but if you just want him, you should satisfy yourself. It's positively unnatural that a beauty like you has never made love. There, I've said it. Don't look at me with that shocked expression. And one more thing. It *is* possible to fall in love with someone in a week, or even a day. I know plenty of happy couples who knew each other only a short time before marrying. And I know some divorcées who had long courtships and engagements. Time has absolutely nothing to do with love."

"Grace, you're the one who's being unrealistic. It's fine for you to sit there and tell me to make love to a man, but what about the consequences?"

"What consequences?" demanded Grace. "If you mean pregnancy, there are ways to protect against that, as I'm sure even you know. If you mean your reputation — just make sure you don't do it here. This John Alexander, for example, lives in New York, doesn't he?"

"Yes . . ." said Devon vaguely. She was not thinking about such mundane things as addresses. She was trying to envision the audacious act of beginning a love affair. How did one go about such things, she wondered. Unconsciously, she picked up the hand mirror by her bed. She peered into it, as though expecting to see a change there. But no, her face was the same. Talking about an illicit love affair had not transformed her in any way. Was it possible then, that committing such an act could go undetected?

"New York is perfect," declared Grace. "It's a big city. You can be relatively anonymous. Paris would be better yet," she concluded breezily.

"But Grace, if I did want to marry him, wouldn't doing something like that ruin everything?" What Grace was saying flew in the face of everything she had been taught. A husband's respect was contingent upon his wife's being a virgin, wasn't it?

"Devon, I barely recognize you," Grace scolded. "Where's your old sass? Where's your sense? If you want to marry this man, you should certainly try to do it. In which case, you wouldn't want to drag him off to bed a few weeks after meeting him. But if a man truly loves you, and you make love with him, that should not end his love for you." Grace looked Devon squarely in the eye and nodded at the end of her sentence, as though to underline the truth of her words. "If he doesn't love you, and you desire him madly — well, Devon, you're twenty-five years old. I think it's time you acted on your desires! There, you're looking shocked again. Would you please take that wide-eyed expression off your face."

Devon tried to comply, but her mind was reeling from her sister's words. Could a life-style such as Grace was describing really make her happy? She didn't think so. Devon reached her hand out to Grace's and clung to it tightly. "Grace, if I never marry, I'll be so lonely."

Grace shook her head in denial. "Marriage has nothing to do with loneliness. There are women who live for years with men without ever marrying. Sometimes they grow old together. Sometimes not. On the other hand, there are women who are married for thirty years who grow old alone when their husbands die. Or who get divorced. Sometimes, if a marriage is unhappy, it's worse than being alone. Believe me, marriage is no insurance against loneliness."

"But if you marry, you have children, and that helps."

"Sometimes, but not always. Anyhow, there are women who have children without marriage."

"Grace! I could never do that!" said Devon, quickly withdrawing her hand from Grace's as though she had been stung.

"You never know what you can do until you are faced with the situation," said Grace quietly. "Devon, I'm very upset by this conversation. Something has happened to your confidence. You've never had all these fears. You've always been the bravest person I know. Why are you doubting yourself?"

Devon leaned back wearily against the pillows and in a slow monotone told her sister of her recent conversation with Helena. "And it made me realize," Devon concluded, "that no matter how beautiful or how smart everyone says I am, I might have to spend my life alone!"

Grace was uncharacteristically quiet as she digested the story. She could see how the behavior of Alexander followed by the accident and the conversation with Helena could have demoralized any ordinary woman, but her sister was not ordinary. Devon was special. Exceptional.

Devon, who had closed her eyes at the conclusion of her story, was rudely brought to attention by her sister slapping the arm of the chair with the palm of her hand.

"How dare you?" Grace demanded. "How dare you let these picayune events change your whole way of thinking about yourself? You've always been independent. You've traveled all over. You've said and done what you wish. Now, you're letting that idiot Helena, who can't even compare to you in any category, make you feel small. You're letting a man you've only known for a week make you feel hopeless. You're acting like a puling coward. But Devon, you've never been a coward! If your face wasn't so sore, I'd slap some sense into you!" Grace finished hotly.

"A coward? What do you mean by that?" Devon raised her voice to match her sister's.

"You're worried about everything! You're worried about defying Mother and Father. You're worried about defying society. Well, Devon, a third of your life is probably over, and you're just sitting here wishing, like a convict wishes for freedom. Only you're not in jail. You're free to go after what you want and it's high time you did it! I'm surprised and, I must say, disappointed, that you haven't done so before now. Since when have you been such a shrinking violet?" Grace asked mockingly, fury still evident from the flush in her face.

"I am not! I have to live my life here. I can't just do crazy things. That may be what women do in Paris, but they sure don't do that in Virginia!" Devon retorted hotly.

"But you don't have to live your life here! That's my point. You like to travel. You have a trust fund. You can live your life wherever and however you want. Furthermore, if you *do* want to live your life here, then you shouldn't let that stop you from going after what you want. Just be smart about it. You don't take out an ad in the paper," said Grace sarcastically.

Devon had no response. It was difficult to imagine defying the conventions of a lifetime.

"Devon, you have a choice to make here. Something that could determine the whole course of your life," said Grace, reaching for Devon's shoulders and holding them firmly when her sister tried to pull away. "Listen to me. You have always been special. You can choose the coward's way of life. That would mean you don't take anything unless someone offers it. You don't satisfy your longings. You let other people tell you how to live your life. And, because you're a woman, you resign yourself to either marriage or spinsterhood. Nothing in between. But, Devon, you've never exactly fit the society mold. You've always been more outspoken, more independent than is conventional. Your very nature demands that you break away. If you try to stifle that impulse, you'll be a very unhappy person, far more unhappy than any scandal could possibly make you."

Grace lifted the hand mirror and held it in front of Devon's face, forcing her to look in it. "Devon, look at you. You were meant for love. You were meant for adventure. That's your destiny; not sitting here lamenting your lost youth like some shriveled-up old maid."

Beneath the bruises and cuts, Devon saw the beauty to which her sister referred. She saw it objectively, as though studying a painting. To waste it? To waste her desire, so ripe, so perfectly ready for expression? It seemed sinful, more sinful than any illicit act of love. Grace was right, she thought. She must make a choice. She could succumb to the role other people assigned her, or she could make her own way in life. She had never been passive before. Why allow an odd confluence of events to make her so now? Grace was right in pointing out that Devon's thoughts had limited her, not her situation. In reality, nothing in her life was any different now than before, when she had been happy. Events had demoralized her, but she had brooded long enough. It was time to get on with her life!

Sitting up straighter in bed, Devon placed the mirror facedown on her lap. Turning to her sister, she simply said, "Grace, thank you so much for coming." Then, in a gesture of the most delicate tenderness, she took her sister's hand, raised it to her lips, and kissed it.

CHAPTER 10

JOHN Alexander heaved a sigh of relief as he signed the last letter in the pile his secretary had left on his desk. It had taken him almost two weeks to clear up the work that had accumulated while he was in Virginia, and he was finally finished. He pulled out his gold pocket watch and grunted in irritation as he saw the time. Eight o'clock. It was not difficult to lose track of time when the sun set so early, as it did in late November in New York. But that was not normally John's habit, because although he liked his work, he was not compulsive about it. As an extremely wealthy man, he felt that his work was neither a means to prove himself nor a way to earn money; he regarded it simply as useful and interesting.

Normally, John would bid his secretary a cheery good evening at no later than six o'clock. From there he would go to his men's club for a drink, or possibly a game of squash. Afterward, he would stop at his fashionable Park Avenue duplex to change for supper or the theater. Most often such evenings would end at Loretta's, but of course he had not been to Loretta's in almost two weeks and had not been inclined to find someone new.

He still felt a bit guilty about the way things had ended, but he had convinced himself that Loretta was tough enough, and selfish enough, to find herself a replacement for him in short order. After all, the tantrum she had thrown had probably just been a bit of theatrics. Actresses were high-strung and they seemed to enjoy such scenes. He would never forget the time the actress lover of his friend Charles Wittingham had emptied an entire bottle of vintage champagne in poor Charlie's lap. In front of everyone at "21." And that quarrel had been about whether she and Charlie should take the train to the mountains for the weekend or drive instead. He tried to picture Devon doing such a thing. She was high-spirited certainly, outspoken even, but he could not imagine her doing anything undignified.

Devon. Always Devon. John sat back in the tufted leather chair and rubbed his weary eyes as he conjured up her image. He could see her face clearly, radiant and laughing as it had been on the day they had gone riding. He savored the memory of her soft lips, so sweet, so caressing as they brushed against his. And her body. So pliant, so expectant, so . . . willing. In his mind, he followed the curves of her full breasts, her small waist, her gently swelling hips. He imagined the silky smoothness of her skin in the palm of his hand. He remembered her arousal at his touch, and teased himself with the thought of arousing her further. Following the graceful lines of her neck with his lips. Making a hot trail to her inviting breasts. Taking her nipples in his mouth and, ever so delicately, running his tongue over the hard points. He could envision her, head thrown back in sensuous abandon, ebony hair spread on white linen sheets. He grew unbearably excited at the thought of seeing her again.

Now that he was finished with his work he could go back to Virginia. He picked up the telephone to call Hamilton Magrath, then remembered, with irritation, that Magrath refused to have a telephone. "I won't let that confounded contraption destroy the peace of my home," Magrath had declared.

John decided the quickest way to get in touch with Magrath was by wire. He lit a Havana cigar and sat back to compose the telegram.

> HAVE LOOKED INTO PURCHASE WE DISCUSSED STOP WOULD LIKE TO DISCUSS OFFER IN PERSON STOP MAY I IMPOSE ON YOUR HOSPITALITY AGAIN STOP PLEASE ADVISE CONVENIENT TIME STOP ALSO INTERESTED IN HARTWICK PROPERTY STOP BEST REGARDS TO YOU AND FAMILY STOP

It would be at least the day after tomorrow before he received a reply, he calculated. He was impatient to be off, but knew he could not visit Magrath without an invitation. Well, he would just have to wait. He wondered if he should contact Devon before his arrival, but then remembered that she did not have a phone either. He chuckled to himself as he reflected that some of the wealthiest people he knew lived without telephones. He couldn't imagine not having one, but he knew that many people considered them invasions of privacy, especially the conservative old Southern aristocracy.

No, he would surprise Devon. But what would he do when he saw her? he asked himself. Would he ask her to marry him? He did not feel quite ready for such a step, yet he could not escape the conviction that she was the perfect woman for him. He was confused. Confused by the ease with which he had fallen in love with her. Confused by his inability to get her out of his mind. He wondered if, when he saw her again, she would appear as ideal to him as she did in his imagination.

John gathered up his papers and left the room. As he waited for the elevator, it occurred to him that he felt in the mood for a bit of fun. Normally, that would mean female companionship, but he realized that he had no desire for any woman . . . except Devon.

"You've got it bad, boy," he said to himself, but he said it cheerfully, with all the hope and confidence of a handsome, wealthy, somewhat spoiled young man.

Devon blew out the candles on the huge chocolate cake alight with twenty-five tiny flames. It was the day after her conversation with Grace and, restored by her sister's no-nonsense talk, Devon had been determined to make her way downstairs for her birthday celebration. She had chosen to wear a floor-length, full-sleeved burgundy satin brocade dress for the occasion, thus mostly concealing both her casts. The opulent cloth set off her shimmering hair beautifully in the candlelight, but she still bore several black-and-blue marks on her face. Nonetheless, her friends — most of whom had been prevented by the doctor from seeing her since her accident — were jubilant that Devon was up and about and in her usual high spirits. All but Grace were unaware of the depression that Devon had succumbed to, then conquered.

"Devon's indomitable," said Brent Hartwick with admiration as he helped her father ease her from a chair at the dining room table to a soft armchair in the main salon.

Devon glanced quickly at Helena to see if she was bothered by Brent's remark, but Helena gave her a humorous look of commiseration. Devon gave her a dazzling smile in return, glowing with the warmth of finally having made a friend of her insecure, defensive neighbor. Good, Devon thought, I'm glad she's decided not to let things like that bother her. Indeed, Brent's manner toward Devon was one of joking bonhomie rather than yearning romance.

Devon laughed happily as she sat forward and glanced around the room. How foolish she had been, she thought, to be so depressed. She was surrounded by the love of her friends and family and she had her whole life to look forward to. Her best girlhood friend, Letitia Brooks, placed a small, round pillow behind Devon and gently urged the convalescent back in the chair.

"You know, this accident has been a horrible influence on Marianne," said Letitia jokingly, referring to her six-year-old daughter.

"Now she wants to start jumping more than ever so she can be a romantic figure like her godmother."

Devon chuckled as she glanced over at the little girl. Marianne was a special favorite of Devon's, more because of the child's lively personality than because she was Devon's godchild.

"Well, I was going to offer to teach her, but I suppose you're not going to want me to now," replied Devon with a laugh.

"Oh, I don't think Marianne would have it any other way," said Letitia. "At least you can show her how to take a serious fall and survive," she kidded as she patted Devon's shoulder affectionately.

"Time to open your presents!" said Grace merrily as she wheeled over the bar cart piled high with gay packages.

Devon exclaimed in delight as she opened present after lovely present. Marianne had insisted upon a present of her own to Devon, rather than a family effort. She had made, with the help of Letitia's cook, a batch of deep chocolate fudge.

"Marianne, this is my absolute favorite!" said Devon, hugging the little blond girl to her with her good arm. How sweet the child was, Devon thought. For a moment, she reflected on how wonderful it would be to have a little girl of her own. She would have one, she told herself, she knew she would one day. Glancing over at Grace, Devon once again silently thanked her for helping her through her dejected mood. Now, all her old optimism, all her faith in the future was back.

"Grace's present next, please," Devon said. Grace silently handed her a large box wrapped in flowered cotton material and adorned with pink satin ribbons. Inside was a gleaming box bearing the name of the great couturiere Vionnet. The women who were gathered around Devon let out a uniform "Aah!" of recognition and admiration even before she opened the box. To a one, they admired the famous French designer who had pioneered the bias cut and brought women out of corsets. And even the men gasped when Devon pulled out the dress that was couched in white tissue paper. The gown was of heavy, luxurious satin lined with silk crepe de chine. But the gown's most striking feature was its dramatic silver color. It shimmered like mercury in the glow of the fireplace. The dress bore two of Vionnet's trademarks: the bias cut and the halter top, plunging to a daringly low back. The expert eyes of the onlooking women could see that the dress would cling provocatively from the high neck to the bottom of Devon's torso, then softly flare to fall in soft, Grecian folds to the floor. The neck was fastened in the back with three natural pearls.

63

REGRET NOT A MOMENT

"I don't know what to say, Grace. It's so beautiful!" said Devon. Tears came to her eyes as she realized the thought and planning that must have gone into so beautiful a gift. It was custom-made, of course, so Grace must have contrived to obtain one of Devon's dresses or her measurements from her seamstress in New York.

"Well, you'll be craving something to show off in once you're back on your feet and your bruises have gone," said Grace, laughing.

"I can't wait to wear it," said Devon fervently. Indeed, the better she felt, the more she chafed at her confinement.

Devon continued to open her gifts: a new riding habit from her parents to replace the one torn and bloodied in her accident, a beautiful pair of kid evening gloves from Letitia, the racy Chanel No. 5 perfume from her friends Ted and Suellen Willis, and a variety of books, scarves, and handkerchiefs from the many other neighbors and relatives who had flocked to the Richmonds' to celebrate Devon's birthday. Finally, from Helena and Brent Hartwick there was a pair of beautiful leather riding boots. From the way Helena shyly presented the gift, Devon could tell that the gift was a peace offering from the heart.

"I know the ones you were wearing . . . that day . . . I know they had to be cut off. I'm so sorry," said Helena, baring her soul in front of the crowd.

"Oh, Helena, they're exquisite. I can't wait to break them in," said Devon graciously. Her heart went out to the young redhead, who was blushing profusely at the awkwardness of the situation. Devon, anxious to let those assembled know that she had forgiven Helena, reached for the young woman and pulled her down for a hug. "I'll treasure them, Helena . . . and Brent," she said, bestowing her friend's husband with a warm smile.

Devon observed the many happy couples that sprinkled the room. Her parents, of course, bustling around to see that everyone was cared for, Hamilton and Rosalind Magrath, the Hartwicks, her college roommate Margaret Larson and her husband, Mark — they all seemed comfortable and in love. Devon noticed Ted Willis lean toward his wife Suellen and whisper to her. As he did so, he put his arm around her and caressed her neck in a gesture of intimate knowledge. Suellen looked up at Ted with a soft, loving smile. In an unconscious movement of acceptance, she leaned against him, then reached up and pulled his face closer to hers so she could whisper her reply. There was something so heartbreakingly lovely about the tableau that it caused a small ache in Devon's throat. It was not an ache of envy, though, but one of impatience, for she knew that she would one day have what they had. That she would one day make just such a gesture to a man she loved.

CHAPTER 11

"MISS Devon, you have a gentleman caller," said Alice.

Devon was reading in the plant-filled conservatory in a fat yellow-and-white-striped armchair, her cast resting on an equally plump matching hassock. The winter sun pouring in the floor-to-ceiling French doors cast gleaming reflections on her hair as she looked up, startled.

"I'm not expecting anyone," said Devon in surprise. She looked down at her lavender-sprigged woolen lounging dress trimmed with frothy lace at the throat, hem, and sleeves. A wide lavender satin ribbon drew in the waist, but the garment was otherwise full and floor-length, worn to cover her casts. She found that by keeping the cumbersome objects concealed she was less likely to dwell on the discomfort they caused her. Although she knew she looked fresh and feminine, she felt she was too informally dressed to receive guests.

"Who is it?" Devon asked Alice.

"A Mr. John Alexander," said Alice, with a twinkle in her eye.

"John? I mean, Mr. Alexander?" she corrected herself, blushing. "Alice, I can't receive him like this. I have to go upstairs and change!" In distress, Devon closed her book and tried to lift herself out of her chair with the aid of her crutches.

"Now Miss Devon, you just sit right there," Alice ordered calmly. "You look perfectly proper to receive guests. Everyone knows you've had an accident. And with those casts, it will take a good half hour to get you changed. You don't want to keep Mr. Alexander waiting all that time, do you?"

"I suppose not," said Devon reluctantly. "But, oh! I just look so awful. And my face still has bruises. . . . Oh, Alice, bring me that mirror there," Devon commanded.

"Miss Devon, it's hanging on the wall!" Alice protested, but she moved toward it just the same. Struggling with the old hook and wire — the mirror had hung in the spot for over a century — Alice finally freed the antique looking glass and hastily brought it to her mistress.

Devon looked at her reflection in despair. "Thank heavens the bruises on my jaw are gone, but look . . . oh no . . . I still have a black eye!" moaned Devon.

"It's not black, exactly, Miss Devon. More like yellow and green," said Alice soothingly.

Devon looked up at her maid and saw that she was quite serious in thinking those words comforting. Looking at Alice's earnest expression, Devon burst out laughing. "Alice! You should see your face!" said Devon, gasping for breath as she laughed and talked at the same time. "I suppose you think that green and yellow is an improvement over black and blue!"

Alice, realizing the absurdity of her own remark, also succumbed to the hilarity of the moment. "Well . . ." she gasped. "It is really . . . I mean . . . you don't look as bad . . . oh never mind!" she said, trying to compose herself.

"I suppose I'll just have to do," said Devon firmly, regaining her calm. "Tell Mr. Alexander that I will see him. Oh, and Alice? Ask Meg to bring us some tea and cakes, please."

Alice nodded her assent and turned to go.

"Alice . . . one more thing?"

"Yes, miss?"

"Would you please hang the mirror again?"

Alice looked at the heavy gilt-edged object propped against the armchair, reflecting light from around the room. "Why? Do you think Mr. Alexander would notice it there?" asked Alice facetiously.

"Oh, Alice, you're awful!" said Devon, breaking into giggles again.

Devon smoothed her hair nervously as she waited for John's arrival. Why was he back in Virginia? she wondered. Could it be because of her or was it simply business? Should she be angry at him for not showing up at the hunt or should she pretend that she did not remember that he was supposed to be there that day? Really, she did not feel angry at him. Anger seemed petty in light of all that had happened since. Yet she knew that his failure to appear had been rude. Rude or not, though, her heart was pounding violently at the thought of seeing him again.

"Devon!" John's voice startled Devon out of her reverie. Devon looked into his eyes, even bluer than she remembered because of the strong sunlight in the conservatory. She felt a flush of heat rise in her at the sight of him. He was so handsome, so . . . male!

Devon quickly cast down her eyes, not out of modesty, but because the intensity of feeling when she looked at him was almost too overwhelming.

"It's so nice to see you again," Devon said. She hesitated to use his first name. She did not feel as familiar toward him as she had before his departure. "Please sit down," she said calmly. She resolved not to let him see that he disturbed her.

John sat in the armchair opposite Devon and studied her closely, saying nothing for a few seconds. He noted the injuries that Hamilton Magrath had told him about. But even with her bruises, she glowed with life and intelligence. Her quality, her vivid beauty, shined through the surface disfigurement. Devon wanted to squirm at his intense scrutiny, but forced herself to remain still and to meet his eyes.

Feeling the need to break the silence, Devon finally spoke. "I'm quite a mess, aren't I?" she said with a forced laugh.

"I was just thinking how lovely you are. I've thought of you so often. Now I see that my memory did you an injustice," said John warmly.

Devon fought not to appear flustered. Although he sat a few feet away from her, she could feel the heat of his body. She could smell the subtle aroma of his cologne, a scent that reminded her of a crisp morning in the mountains. Her senses vibrated in his presence. And his magnetism made her painfully aware of how unlike her usual self she looked. "I . . . I'm surely not beautiful now . . . with all these bruises."

None of that mattered to John. Impatiently, he leaned forward in his chair. "Devon," he said hoarsely, "I've been a fool."

Devon, startled, simply stared at him.

"Are you angry with me?" he asked sheepishly.

"Should I be?" asked Devon, trying to buy time with the question. She knew exactly what he was referring to, but she did not want to admit that his absence at the hunt — and his subsequent silence — had been of great importance to her.

"Yes," said John seriously. He wanted to touch her, to take her hand, but he did not dare. He could not read her mood. She was polite, of course, but there seemed to be a barrier around her emotions. He wanted to speak directly, to get at the heart of the matter, but he realized that he had appeared virtually out of nowhere. He had been preparing himself for this moment, had spent hours debating what he would say to her. She, on the other hand, had had no idea he was coming.

"Devon, I have to speak plainly because what I have to say has been burdening me for some time now."

Devon said nothing, but nodded for him to continue. He looked at her large aqua eyes, ever so slightly slanted upward at their outer corners. They were an exotic touch in her otherwise classically beautiful face. How he loved that face! Even though bruised, it radiated all the luminescence he remembered from their first meetings. Her beauty seemed to come as much from her inner sense of self-worth as from her outward attributes. Looking at her now, John was sure that the decision he had made about her the day before was a good one. All doubt was gone from his mind. He patted his breast pocket discreetly to see if the box he had brought with him from New York was still there.

"Devon, do you know why I've returned?"

Devon did not know how to answer. By his tone, she could tell that Alexander's call was more than just a polite one. She could see the admiration — and perhaps even more — in his eyes. Yet she did not want to risk making a fool of herself by assuming too much. Finally, she asked, "You're buying some land in New York from Mr. Magrath?"

"Not exactly," said John.

"You're not buying land from Mr. Magrath?"

"I am buying land. That part is true, but . . ."

"Then . . . what?" asked Devon.

"The land I'm buying, it's not just the New York property I originally talked to Magrath about. I'm also buying property from his son-in-law."

Devon's eyes widened as she tried to gauge the significance of John's words. He grinned at her, but gave nothing further away. Well, then, nor would she. "Oh," she murmured hesitantly, "I had heard Brent Hartwick was trying to sell his family's place near Middleburg. Now that he's living with the Magraths, it's only a burden on him. He lost so much in the stock market."

"It is precisely the Hartwick place that I am considering," said John. He leaned even farther forward in his chair and locked his eyes on hers. "What do you think of it?"

"Well . . ." Devon hesitated, trying to read the meaning behind his intense gaze. A little thrill of hope rose in her. Could it be . . . could it really be that he intended to settle in the area? Was it because of her? Oh, but he had once before led her to believe that she meant something to him. And in the end, he had left her feeling bereft. So she stifled the thrill and forced her expression to remain cool and steady. "The house is one of the loveliest in the area. The land is very good. And it has an excellent stable. I think it would be a good buy," she concluded, in her usual decisive way.

"Would it be the kind of place you would like to live?"

The question assaulted Devon's hard-won composure. She felt her cheeks burn as she tried to think of an answer. She wanted to admit giddily, I would live anywhere with you! But how absurd! Alexander had not proposed marriage. Perhaps he was simply interested in her opinion because she had lived for many years in the area. She took a deep, calming breath and studied his face. Unused to obliqueness in her dealings with people, Devon wanted to see his eyes. To see if what she thought she understood was indeed what he meant to convey. John moved to the hassock at Devon's feet and took her good hand in his. The electricity of his touch made goose pimples spring up on her arms and the back of her neck.

"Would you like to live there?" he repeated. His face bore an intense, determined expression. His grip on her fingers was tight.

"I . . . I think I should like it very much," she replied. Embarrassed at her eagerness, she pulled her hand away from his.

"Don't pull away," he said soothingly, reaching out again and grasping her hand tightly in his. "Devon, I—" For a split second he hesitated. He stared into her aqua eyes. Despite the sunlight, her pupils were dilated, two black pools pulling him in. They were hypnotic, her eyes. He had no power to fight against their pull. Didn't want to fight it. And he whispered the words he had been holding back for weeks: "I love you."

Devon's head was spinning. How often she had dreamed of hearing those words from his lips. And yet, once before when she thought he had been on the verge of uttering them, he had left suddenly. Left her bewildered and hurt. But the touch of him seemed to break down all her defenses. It seemed right somehow that he should be here.

Sensing her confusion, John sought to explain himself in a rush of words. "Devon, I've been a bachelor for longer than most of the people I know. When I met you, I knew immediately that we were right for each other, but the feeling scared me. I was afraid to change my life. Afraid to make my happiness dependent on you! So, I fled. But, Devon, I now see that I was an idiot to think I could ever enjoy my life without you. I may have enjoyed it once, but now that I've met you . . . Can you ever . . . Do you understand?" His eyes implored her to say yes.

"I . . . I don't know. All this is so new for me too. It is scary, isn't it?" she asked with a shaky laugh.

"So you *do* love me too?" John asked with elation.

Devon wanted to think sensibly. To hold herself back. To catch her breath. But somehow she couldn't. She couldn't seem to make her head stop spinning, her heart stop racing. She was afraid to utter the words. To lose herself. But, oh, the promise of it all! The joy! He loved her! Her daring spirit urged her on. Caution wasn't in her nature. And her emotions cried out to be heard. "You know it, don't you?" she said, almost crying at the blissful release she felt. "You know I love you."

John's tensed mouth broke into a huge grin. His face wore the unbelieving happiness of a young boy whose most unobtainable dream has come true.

And, looking at him, any doubts remaining in Devon were swept away in the rush of love she felt. It didn't matter that she had known him only a short while. Nor that he had once fled. All that mattered was the overwhelming feeling that filled her whenever she saw him. She was giddy with it. Giddy with love, with excitement, with happiness!

John, seeing her expression, knew the time was right. He took a blue velvet case from his pocket and slowly opened it. Devon gasped at the beauty of the ring within. It was a perfect five-carat oval-cut diamond set in a band of sapphires. Devon stared down at the ring, then up at John. For a moment they were both motionless, lost in each other. Then John plucked the ring from the case. He lifted Devon's hand and paused. The ring sparkled gaily in the sun, rays of colored light shooting out in every direction.

"I'm glad your left hand is the one that is unhurt," John whispered solemnly as he slipped the beautiful ornament on her finger. Then he lifted Devon's hand to his lips and kissed the silken ivory flesh.

She turned her hand over and tenderly stroked his face. "John . . ." she whispered, overcome by emotion.

John once again took her hand. "Then you *will* marry me?" he asked urgently, wanting to hear the promise from her own lips.

She dimpled at his question. Wasn't it obvious? Of course, of course, *of course* she would marry him!

He read the answer in her eyes, but it wasn't enough for him. "I want to hear you say it!" he commanded.

It was barely more than a sigh. "Yes."

John half stood from the hassock and leaned toward Devon, moving his face close to hers. He could feel her warm, sweet breath; then his lips alighted on hers as gently as a butterfly. She returned his kiss, welcoming his lips. He could feel her readiness, the beckoning of her body to his. Bracing his arms on her chair's he leaned even farther into the embrace. He increased the pressure of his lips and ever so delicately opened Devon's mouth with his tongue. Like a child welcoming a delicious treat, Devon accepted him, instinctively meeting his tongue with her own, lighting a wild fire in him. Her kiss had a more intoxicating effect on him than his most erotic sexual escapade of the past. He sat on one arm of the chair and moved her scented hair back from her ear, then he leaned down and gently took the lobe in his mouth. Just as he had done in his imagination, he ran his warm tongue teasingly down her neck. He savored the salty, spicy taste of her. His fingers itched to unbutton the prim lace collar of her gown. He wanted to release her breasts, hold them in his hands. They would be milky white, satiny. He wanted to remove her petticoat. To tear through the lace barrier that hid the most secret recesses of her body from his touch — and his tongue. He wanted to immerse himself in her, become one with her. He could feel his insistent hardness begging for release. But of course, there could be no release . . . not yet.

Devon felt John draw back, leaving her breathless. She was dizzy, trembling. A yearning in the moist, secret part of her cried out for fulfillment. Instinctively, she caressed the nape of John's neck with featherlike touches, sending shivers down his spine. John rested on the arm of Devon's easy chair and kissed her even more deeply.

A discreet knock at the door fairly catapulted John from his perch back to the hassock.

"Who is it?" Devon asked in a voice that sounded shaky even to her ears.

"It's Meg, Miss Devon, with your tea."

"Come in, please," said Devon, hurriedly smoothing her hair.

The young maid entered with a tray, causing an uncomfortable silence in the room.

Recovering herself, Devon pretended to pick up a conversational thread. "In any event, we shall have to have you to dinner, Mr. Alexander," she said in her usual cool, clear voice. She gave the maid a nod. "Thank you, Meg, I'll pour," said Devon.

Meg withdrew, discreetly closing the door behind her. But as she later told the other servants, "They didn't fool me for a minute. As if they could! What with Miss Devon sporting a diamond as big as the moon!"

CHAPTER 12

GRACE studied her sister's fiancé across the dinner table and could find no fault with him. Not only was he handsome, intelligent, and amusing, he was also quite obviously head over heels in love with Devon. Grace sighed with contentment as she contemplated her sister's renewed good spirits. It had been just a short time ago that Devon had been in the depths of depression. Now she was glowing with happiness.

"John has decided to buy Brent Hartwick's farm," Devon chattered happily, "and we'll breed racing Thoroughbreds, although I really don't know much about horseracing. But the farm used to have one of the best reputations around for that and it would be a shame to dismantle it, so I'll just have to learn."

"You mean you intend to be involved?" asked Chase. "I shouldn't think that would go over too well with — what's that fellow's name — he's supposed to be one of the best trainers around."

"You mean Willy O'Neill?" said John.

"That's the fellow. I understand he runs the place with an iron hand," said Chase.

"Well, he'll just have to learn to get along with me. Or I with him, if you prefer it that way," declared Devon.

"Hmmm," Chase said, reflecting, "a woman taking charge of a Thoroughbred breeding and training operation. I don't believe I've ever heard of that." He looked questioningly at John. He wondered what his daughter's fiancé thought of Devon's plans. He wasn't sure what he thought of them himself. It was a most . . . unwomanly occupation, he thought.

"I have complete faith in Devon," John said, with a warm glance at his fiancée. "Although I'll admit it's an unorthodox arrangement," he added diplomatically, turning back to Chase.

"Don't you think I can handle the job, Father?" Devon asked with a teasing look at him.

Chase turned to Laurel, hoping she would say something to rescue him from Devon's question, but she just looked at him, eyebrows delicately raised. Sometimes he felt positively outnumbered.

"Well . . ." Chase mumbled, "I think you'll have a difficult time of it." He couldn't imagine a strong trainer taking to a woman boss. Chase thought it extremely likely the man would quit.

"I think you're right," said Devon thoughtfully, "but I like challenges."

Chase knew that. He admired Devon for it, but at the same time was sometimes afraid for her. He often wondered why his favorite child always seemed to be doing things that were . . . well, unconventional. It made him uncomfortable, although he could not quite say why. Unconsciously, he shrugged his shoulders, then changed the subject.

"Are you going to rename Willowbrook? Its reputation is still pretty decent, even though everyone knows they've fallen on difficult times," said Chase.

Devon turned to John questioningly. "I don't think we've thought of that yet, have we?" Devon loved the sound of the word *we,* loved the vision of a couple, a family, that the word conjured.

"As you say, the Willowbrook name is still good. It's not called Hartwick's Willowbrook, so there's nothing to particularly identify the name with that family. I think we should keep the name if we're to make a go of the business," said John.

"When do you close on the deal?" asked Chase, helping himself to another serving of rack of lamb being offered on a silver platter by Meg.

"We'll close in about a month, I should think," said John. "Meanwhile, I was hoping that you and Devon would agree to come to New York for a visit. My parents are most eager to meet you all. Besides,

Devon will surely have shopping to do for the wedding, not to mention for Christmas."

"Silly! How can I go to New York with my leg in the cast? It will be several weeks before it's off. And Christmas is only three weeks away! I have to spend Christmas at Evergreen and . . . and I thought we would invite your parents to come here." Devon's look appealed to the others to come to her aid and convince John that her plan was best.

"I have to be in Paris for Christmas," said Grace quickly, "so I can go up to New York with you for a week and leave from there. I'm sure I'll be able to help you with whatever you need. And, of course, we'll take Alice."

"But I thought you were going to stay through Christmas," Devon protested.

"Philip can't get away, so I have to go back to be with him and the kids," said Grace with emphasis. Devon studied her a moment. It seemed Grace was trying to send her a message, but she didn't quite understand what it was. "Why don't all of you spend Christmas at the town house?" Grace asked, directing her question to her parents.

"I thought I should wait until both my casts are off to go to New York. That way I could be fitted for some new clothes," Devon said.

"Not to mention your wedding dress," said John, with another warm look at his fiancée.

"I wish you could come to Paris for the wedding dress. Then you could have one by Vionnet!" said Grace, certain that no one could compare to her favorite French designer.

"But we're coming there for the honeymoon!" Devon said jubilantly. She loved Paris and was looking forward to spending the month of June there.

"That part is wonderful, but I still don't see why we have to wait more than six months to get married," John half grumbled.

"Of course you see why!" exclaimed Laurel. "Your mother would be heartbroken if we didn't have a proper wedding and so would I."

"By 'proper' I think Mother means big," teased Grace.

"Certainly not! But we *do* have many friends, as do John and his parents, and I'm certain that you'll enjoy having them at your wedding," said Laurel with slightly ruffled dignity.

"Devon, you still haven't said you'll come to New York with me next week," John coaxed. "In fact, why don't you take Grace's suggestion and all come. You can open up your town house or you can stay with my parents, whichever suits you best." He was so proud of Devon that he was eager for his parents and friends to meet her.

"Well . . ." Devon hesitated. She knew it would be a cumbersome task to travel, but she could not imagine being separated from John. And she was so eager to meet his family. As she hesitated, she saw Grace trying to catch her eye. Looking at her sister, she saw her nod almost imperceptibly.

Devon suddenly understood the message in Grace's eyes. Now she had John's obligations as well as her own to consider. She could not very well insist that he spend Christmas away from his family when her own family had a home in New York, she realized.

"I think it would be a good idea to go to New York," said Devon decisively. "Mother, you always say that Christmas is the nicest time of the year in New York. Why don't we spend it there with the Alexanders? And then, next Christmas we can all come here!"

Laurel and Chase — understanding Devon's wish to accommodate her fiancé as well as her new family — agreed.

"It's decided then!" cried Grace, eager to visit the exciting city she loved. She could not quite understand Devon's affinity for country life.

"Then you'll all come?" asked John.

"Of course, dear," said Laurel. "We look forward to it."

"Wonderful!" said John. "I'll be sure our engagement announcement appears in the papers while you're there. And I promise you the best time you've ever had. Why, we'll be able to bring in the New Year together!"

Everyone toasted the impending New Year, certain that it would be the best ever.

CHAPTER

13

LORETTA stared at the newspaper announcement unbelievingly, fury rising in her like poison.

"That lousy bastard!" she spat.

"Which one, sweetheart, your director or your wardrobe designer?" asked Whitney Ross sleepily, reaching for Loretta's soft white arm and pulling her down to where he lay among her pink satin pillows. But Loretta impatiently shook him off. Whitney sighed lazily and rolled away from her. Although their affair was only a month old, he was already used to her rantings. She was always complaining about her co-stars, or her script, or a myriad of other daily annoyances that he had quickly learned to tune out in order to better concentrate on the sexual satisfaction he invariably derived from her perfect body.

He squinted at the clock on the mantel. It was four o'clock in the morning. That was the problem with having an affair with an actress. One didn't have supper until at least midnight. That meant no bed until one, which left only a few hours until dawn. Whitney Ross was very strict about reappearing at home by dawn. Or rather, his wife was. She did not mind the relief from her wifely duties that Loretta afforded her, as long as their children did not miss Whitney at the breakfast table. They must never know about his affairs, she had warned him, for if they did, she would be forced to divorce him. She would not allow them to think that she tolerated the humiliation. Well, he certainly did not want a divorce on the grounds of adultery. The woman would walk off with a fortune.

Four o'clock. He had to be home by six. That meant he had time for one more . . .

"Loretta, my love," he said, rolling back toward her. He slipped his hand under the sheet and tickled the inside of her thigh.

"Don't bother me now!" she snapped, slapping his hand away.

"What have we here?" he asked sardonically.

"That bastard friend of yours is engaged!" she almost screamed.

"That . . . who?" he asked, knowing immediately who she meant.

The one thing that bothered Whitney about Loretta was the knowledge that it was John's rejection of her that had allowed him to have her.

"I suppose I wasn't high class enough for him," Loretta growled, forgetting, in her anger, her claim that she had dropped Alexander. "He wanted some innocent little fool!"

"Loretta," moaned Whitney, grabbing the newspaper from her hands and throwing it over the side of the bed, "forget about all that. I have to go soon. And before I go . . ." He completed his sentence by lightly pinching one pink nipple between his index finger and thumb.

"Look, I'm not in the mood," said Loretta irritably.

"You know, darling, the word 'mistress' is truly a misnomer. It implies that you have some sort of authority over your lover. In fact, the opposite is true. I say we fuck," he said, deliberately using the vulgarity for its shock value.

"I don't need you!" she said scornfully. "I can have anyone I want!"

"Anyone you want in show business. And certainly your pick of nouveau riche types who want a glamour girl on their arms. But you want society. And that, my dear, you don't just run across every day," he said mockingly as he spread her legs apart with his knee. Her resistance excited him. "You think that if you're seen with enough society types, eventually one of us will marry you. And you may be right." He could feel her resistance slipping away with every word he spoke. He risked releasing one of her arms so that he could reach between her legs and caress her. "But you'd better hang on to the one you've got while you're looking for the one you're going to marry."

Loretta was dumbfounded. She was an actress, but Whitney Ross, who had never shown any interest in her thoughts, never asked her opinion of anything, had seen right through her as easily as if she had confessed her plan to him. In a way, it was a relief to have someone know the truth. As long as that someone was her friend.

"You bastard!" she said, but her tone had a rough affection to it and she rubbed herself against him invitingly.

"There . . . that's more like it," said Ross, lowering his head to her breast and sliding his tongue over her nipple. And when he slipped his erect member into her, he met no resistance.

"There's a . . . woman . . . here to see you, Miss Devon," said Truitt, the Richmonds' butler at the New York town house. The vine-covered Georgian Revival residence was in the trendy neighborhood known as Sutton Place, popularized only ten years before by Anne Vanderbilt.

The Vanderbilts, like many other wealthy families — including the Richmonds — had sold their huge Italian Renaissance–style mansion on upper Fifth Avenue in favor of the more compact quarters.

Devon looked up from her book inquiringly. She was sitting in the main salon of the house, where she and her mother often received afternoon callers, but it was January 8, and most of their guests had already streamed through the house during the holidays.

"Who is this . . . woman?" Devon was disturbed that Truitt had carefully avoided using the word *lady* to describe the guest. It alerted her to the fact that the caller was not one of her friends. Indeed, Truitt's demeanor told her that it was someone of whom he disapproved. She could not imagine why such a person should wish to see her.

"A Miss Morgan. She says she has a personal matter to discuss with you." Truitt sniffed derisively, certain that no such woman could have something personal to discuss with Miss Devon. Devon thought for a moment. She trusted Truitt's judgment implicitly. The dignified mulatto had worked for the Richmonds since he was a fourteen-year-old stable boy. He had been promoted to the post of butler by the time he was twenty-eight, so now, after forty years of greeting people, first at Evergreen then in the New York town house, Truitt was not mistaken about the person calling, Devon knew.

"A personal matter?" she said, racking her brain as to what it might be. "Well . . . I suppose there's no use speculating. Send her in please, Truitt." Devon's arm cast had been removed but she still wore the cast on her leg so she did not stand to receive the guest. Seated before the large, white marble fireplace, she made a lovely picture in a floor-length, blush pink dress of the finest cashmere. Her hair was brushed straight back from her forehead and tumbled gracefully to her shoulders in shimmering waves. Her face was no longer marred by bruises.

Devon had a shock when she saw the woman who followed Truitt into the room. She recognized her as the Broadway star she and her parents had seen just two nights before in the most successful play of the season.

"Why, you're Loretta Morgan!'" she blurted out, pleased and surprised to meet the actress face to face. "I just saw your play two nights ago. You were wonderful!" she said.

Loretta, momentarily disarmed by the warm reception, stood awkwardly staring at Devon. She had dressed with care, wishing to look every bit the successful star that she was. Her ermine coat stunningly highlighted her platinum blond hair. She had not wanted to give the fur to Truitt at the door, preferring to wear it when she first met Devon. Now she shrugged it off and handed it dismissively to the butler. At a nod from Devon, Truitt retreated from the salon, leaving the two women alone.

Loretta stood before Devon in an expensively cut yellow silk dress which, though high-necked and long-sleeved, enticingly flattered Loretta's curvaceous figure. She wore high-heeled black shoes that emphasized her long legs, a black suede beret, and matching suede gloves, which she now removed. Her lips were painted a bright red, the same as her fingernails. Devon thought she looked smashing. But she understood with amusement the reason for Truitt's disapproval. Never had a visitor to the Richmond home been quite so . . . colorful. Yet Loretta Morgan's glamour was undeniable. She did not look ridiculous, just a bit larger than life.

"Miss Morgan, I didn't know that my parents knew you," said Devon, not noticing the other woman's silence. "I wish they were here, but I'm afraid they're out. Won't you sit down anyway?"

Loretta looked uncomfortably around the delicately furnished room. Although she had every luxury in her own penthouse, the understated elegance of the Richmond home bespoke generations of discerning taste. Two long Palladian windows that overlooked the street allowed even the meager winter sun to fill the space with light. The walls were covered with an eggshell silk brocade that had mellowed to a rich cream color. Eighteenth- and nineteenth-century French paintings of museum quality were hung casually about the room. The salon was not overcrowded with furnishings, but rather featured damask-covered divans and chairs in airy pastels, strategically placed to promote conversation. Dominating the space was a large Aubusson carpet in subtle shades of cream, rose, and pale blue.

Loretta, somewhat awed by an elegance she knew she could never duplicate, settled uneasily into a straight-backed Louis XV chair opposite Devon, but she stood up again almost immediately.

"This isn't a social call," she said tersely, pacing in front of the fireplace. "I have something to tell you about a mutual friend." She stopped and stared into the flames as she uttered the words, not wishing to look Devon in the eye. The warm reception Devon had given her was unexpected and she was not sure how to react. She had come to the Richmond home filled with venom and a wish for revenge, but she now realized that Devon had done nothing to hurt her. Seeing the young woman sitting helplessly, her broken leg propped up, she understood that her grievance was against John, not Devon. For a moment, she softened.

But the innocent questioning look that she encountered in Devon's eyes exasperated her. Why had he picked this well-bred virginal girl? She could never satisfy his passion as Loretta had!

Suddenly Loretta wanted to wipe the innocent look off Devon's face — wanted to make her feel the pain that *she* had felt at John Alexander's rejection. It was obvious to Loretta that Devon had been cherished and protected all her life. The idea galled her.

"Your fiancé," snapped Loretta. "You don't know what kind of man he is."

Devon's face changed immediately. The light of innocence in her eyes was extinguished and replaced with understanding. Then a cool mask fell over her beautiful features. Loretta was shocked at the transformation. Was it possible that she had misjudged Devon's ignorance? She was quick, Loretta had to admit, and perhaps not as innocent as she seemed.

But Devon only half understood the nature of John's relationship with Loretta, and she didn't really want to know more. The logistics and emotions involved were completely foreign to Devon. What was clear to her, however, was that the woman intended to create unpleasantness. Devon had been brought up to avoid unpleasant confrontations at all costs. So although she was dismayed, she did not show it. Instead, she tried to disarm Loretta and forestall her confidences. "I know all that I need to know about John. Whatever he was to you has nothing to do with me," she said evenly.

"You don't know everything you need to know," retorted Loretta, angry that her words had had so little effect. "All of last year, John and I had a love affair. He used to wait for me every night to finish up at the theater. He was like a panting dog, he wanted me so much!"

Devon was shaken by the vision Loretta's words conjured. Hands tensely clasped in her lap, body perfectly still, Devon studied Loretta as the blond woman glared challengingly at her. There was a blatant sexuality about the actress. The sexuality had been evident two nights ago on stage, but was even more pronounced now that Loretta was standing before her. There was no doubt that she was ragingly attractive. And yet, John had ended the relationship. The woman was admitting as much by her very presence. Would she be standing here now if she were not desperate? No. Clearly John was lost to her, and she knew it. With that thought, Devon no longer felt threatened by Loretta. After all, John had chosen to marry her, not Loretta.

Devon's gaze coolly met Loretta's. "The situation has obviously changed, hasn't it?" she asked in a carefully neutral tone. She did not want to incite Loretta further by using a mocking voice.

"It changed because I got tired of him!" Loretta cried, moving closer to Devon so that she stood directly in front of her chair.

"I don't believe you," Devon said stonily. "If that were true, you wouldn't be here."

Loretta stamped her foot, frustrated by Devon's poise. She groped for a response, but in her excitement, she could only think to say, "I'm here because I want you to know what you're doing before it's too late!"

"An act of charity?" Devon said, raising one eyebrow in marked disbelief. She was feeling quite sure of herself now. It was obvious that the woman was being eaten alive by jealousy. John had never denied the fact that he had had women before Devon. Well then, she told herself. This was one of them. So be it. She refused to let it touch her. It had nothing to do with their love.

"You think someone like you can hold him? What do you know about pleasing a man like John?" said Loretta scornfully.

"Miss Morgan, I don't see the point of continuing this discussion any further. Whatever interest Mr. Alexander had in you is gone. It doesn't matter why or how. I'm going to marry him. I suggest you reconcile yourself to that," said Devon, reaching for the bellpull to summon Truitt. But before she could do so, Loretta bent over and grabbed her wrist.

"Just remember this," she hissed, hating Devon for her unruffled demeanor, for her privileged birth, for everything she represented that Loretta could never become, "when he goes to bed with you at night, he'll be comparing you to me. You won't be able to live up to that! You won't know how to please him. And he'll come running back to me then!"

Devon angrily jerked her wrist from Loretta's grasp and rang the bellpull. "Don't wait for him, Miss Morgan," she said, pronouncing each word with deliberate iciness, "you'll be wasting your time."

Truitt appeared immediately, indicating that he had been hovering worriedly outside the closed door.

"Miss Morgan would like to leave now, Truitt. Will you please show her out?" said Devon, in a voice that was so pleasant and calm that an observer would have supposed that a routine social call was coming to an end.

Truitt looked at the red-faced blonde angrily making her way toward him, then at his mistress, straight-backed in the armchair, a tight little smile on her face. Impassively, he turned and led Loretta from the room. Loretta did not wait for Truitt to help her on with her coat, but snatched it rudely from his hands as she hurried out the door.

Devon did not change for dinner that evening. Instead she sat quietly thinking by the fire until John was announced. He dined at the Richmonds' several times a week now.

"Darling," said John. He stood behind Devon's chair and leaned down to kiss her after hastily looking around the room to be sure they were alone. "Don't you look beautiful. I love that pink dress on you." He caressed her silky hair, relishing the feel of it in his fingers. His hands drifted down to her shoulders and Devon reached behind her to grasp them lovingly in her own hands.

"I know it's one of your favorites," said Devon warmly. "That's why I didn't change. Besides, it's just family tonight." Devon turned and pulled John gently around her chair so that she could look at him.

"I thought tonight would never come," said John with a big grin, sitting on the hassock in front of her and leaning forward for another kiss. This time his lips lingered on hers as she put her hands up to encircle his neck. At the sound of a door closing in the hallway, he backed away from her, sighing with regret. "I missed you today. What have you been up to?"

"Oh, the usual thing," said Devon casually.

"I saw Bart today. He said Sydney might call on you. Didn't she stop by?"

"No," said Devon. "No visitors at all today."

CHAPTER 14

MARRIED to John, truly married — Devon could not believe how happy she was. Their state room on the luxury ship was crammed with friends wishing them bon voyage on their honeymoon trip. Just a week ago, most of the same people had crowded into the little church in Middleburg, Virginia, for Devon and John's wedding.

It had been so beautiful. Devon still grew misty-eyed as she thought of it. Her gown, though not a French design as Grace would have liked, could not have been more perfect, in Devon's view. The long, straight lines of the dress had been carefully cut to mold Devon's slim figure, its long-sleeved, off-the-shoulder style showing off the lovely roundness of Devon's neck and shoulders. It was of rich ivory satin entirely covered with alençon lace, ending in a long train. The veil — her mother's — had been almost as long. It began with a coronet of pearls, then flowed into an expanse of lace-trimmed tulle.

John had looked so handsome in his gray morning coat that Devon had been afraid her face would betray her longing for him — and in front of the minister! She glanced at him now as he clinked his glass against that of his best friend, Charles Wittingham. Her heart fluttered as she remembered their wedding night. It had been all she had hoped for, yet all so new and unexpected! They had spent their first night as man and wife in a guest room at Evergreen, since their new estate, Willowbrook, was undergoing renovations. Laurel had tactfully placed them in a secluded wing of the house, knowing that they would cherish the privacy. They had entered the room following the afternoon-long reception, and had not left the luxurious old canopied and curtained bed until twenty-four hours later. A supper had been sent up on a tray but it had remained largely untouched, as John and Devon's hunger for each other had been far greater.

At first, Devon had been nervous. She had managed to push Loretta's taunting words from her mind for months, but suddenly, faced with the threat of not pleasing John, they replayed themselves in her mind over and over, as though Loretta were standing by her side, mocking her. Would she please him? she wondered. She had been told to expect some pain — would it ruin their pleasure?

But all her worries had been dispelled as soon as John had taken her in his arms. He had hugged her to him for several minutes, kissing her and whispering endearments, then he had turned her around and slowly undone the long row of tiny pearl buttons down the back of her dress.

Cold and excitement made her shiver as he slipped the luxurious material off her shoulders and ran his warm tongue up her spine to the nape of her neck. From behind, he took one of her firm breasts in each hand, sensually massaging them until she ached with desire.

He turned her around then and knelt before her where she stood in nothing but transparent lace-trimmed panties, frilly garters, and white silk stockings and shoes. With teasing feathery kisses, he encircled each nipple in turn until they were both erect, straining for more attention. Devon could feel his touch vibrate through her body. With excruciating slowness, he slid the panties down her satiny legs, helping her to balance as she lifted first one leg, then the other, to remove them.

The sight of her long legs clad in nothing but her stockings and shoes almost made him lose control of himself, but he knew not to hurry her. Still kneeling before her, he hugged her to him, laying his head against her stomach as he ran a hand lightly over her thighs and buttocks. Oh, how she wanted him to touch her . . . there . . . between her legs where her body cried out for relief from the exquisite tension. Her desire was so great that she actually reached for his hand and brought it up to her. An act so bold as to be almost unthinkable!

But John was delighted that her desire overcame her shyness and, tentatively and oh so gently, slipped a finger inside her as he massaged her on the outside with his thumb. She was unable to stand any longer. Her knees simply buckled, sending her into his arms. It was so erotic to be naked against him while he was still fully dressed. Somehow it seemed he knew that, because he simply laid her down carefully where she was and, spreading her legs, inserted his tongue where his finger had been earlier. She could not believe he was doing such a thing! She knew about the act of procreation, but had no idea that people did . . . this. At first she recoiled, but the pleasure was too great and it was beyond her control to stop it. Then it happened for the first time. That strange, dizzy feeling as sweet release flooded her. And while she was still so wet and open to him, he undressed and, unable to contain himself any longer, entered her. The pain was not so great. The pleasure was greater as they began to move together in an instinctive, ancient rhythm that was perfectly . . . right. And, in a few seconds, she felt that sweeping pleasure rise in her again. That tension that made her limbs stiffen, her muscles strain around him. She enfolded him in her. Drew him deeper and deeper, as he moved more forcefully with each stroke. Then she felt him shudder. He moaned as he thrust into her and the motion drove her over the peak until she, too, was moaning with the sheer ecstasy of it.

Later that evening, when she had had more time to study his body, she marveled at the beauty of him — the long muscles rippling in his arms, legs, and shoulders. His small waist and flat stomach, with its line of dark hair leading downward. The sight of him aroused her to the extent that she wanted him again, although he was lying sleepily in front of the fire, spent from their love. So she had done to him what he had done to her earlier. He had been surprised, perhaps even shocked, that she would take him into her mouth in that way. At first she had not known exactly what to do, but with subtle movements he had indicated his pleasure, and when he was hard again, she had wrapped her legs around him and drawn him into her. And there had been no pain this time.

"I love you, Devon. You excite me beyond my wildest dreams," he told her afterward.

She thought of Loretta no more.

Now, as she watched him talking to their friends, she had a desire for him that was so strong that she felt herself grow moist. Suddenly it seemed as though the spacious suite was too small, too hot, and she could barely restrain herself from ushering their guests out. Feeling her stare, John looked up and caught her eye. For a second they stood riveted, locked in each other's gaze.

Somehow, John and Devon managed politely to hasten their good-byes. As soon as the door closed behind their last guest, they turned the lock, and without even bothering to lead Devon to the bed, John began to undress. Devon's impatience matched his, and breathless with desire, she almost tore the buttons from her lavender silk traveling suit as she hurried to remove the jacket. Naked now, John knelt and pulled Devon's skirt over her ankles. She began to unfasten her underthings, but he stopped her, unable to wait any longer. Shoving her loose silk panties to one side, he bent his knees and slid his erect member into the warm space between her legs, pleased to find that she was as ready as he. Using the door as a brace for her, he lifted her slightly as she encircled his back tightly with her legs. Moving together in dazzling unison, flesh upon flesh, explosive with waiting and wanting, the contact drove them over the edge. Both of them lost control almost at once as their knees buckled with sweet release.

"You look ecstatic, Devon," Grace said. It was a warm, sunny day and the two women were lunching at a sidewalk café. The sisters drew many appreciative stares as they spoke across the tiny table in confidential tones. Grace had managed to capture the unmistakable high style of the Parisienne, from the figure-hugging severity of her white piqué Chanel suit to the coquettish tilt of her veiled straw hat. Accessories were the key to Grace's look, and today her choices were a striking pair of harlequin-patterned white-and-black kid gloves along with matching shoes. These small but important deviations from her white ensemble added an intriguing flair to her chic. Devon, softer in her look, evoked visions of romance in the men who beheld her. Her dress was also white, but the material was a soft and billowy cotton organdy that flowed provocatively with each step and enticed with hints of transparency. With it she wore a large white picture hat with streamers of pale blue chiffon.

"I am ecstatic," said Devon with a happy sigh. She cut into her grilled steak before continuing. "Do you know that today is our third anniversary?"

"What?"

"John and I have been married exactly three weeks today. Oh, Gracie, I wish you could have been at the wedding. It was so beautiful!"

"Me too, but I knew I'd be seeing you here and you'd tell me all about it. By the way, does John mind spending his honeymoon with his in-laws?"

"Don't be silly, Grace. Besides, we're not spending our honeymoon with you. We're at the Ritz."

"Still . . . I'm stealing you away from him today," said Grace.

"He's probably relieved he doesn't have to go shopping with me," Devon said with a knowing half smile. "Anyhow, he and Philip get on so well together. And he loves the boys."

"Good, then I won't feel guilty," said Grace. "By the way, where will you live when you get back to the States?"

"Mostly at Willowbrook, I should think. After all, if we want to raise racehorses, we have to be there. At least at first. You know, this is delicious, Grace, how do they do the potatoes like that?"

"I'm not sure. No one at the American embassy has ever been able to duplicate them." Grace laughed. "But what about John's work? Won't he mind living at Willowbrook?"

"I suppose not, since he bought it," said Devon casually.

"Perhaps he bought it as a country home, not full-time living quarters," Grace speculated. "You really haven't discussed it?"

"Not at length."

"Would you mind living in New York?"

"Certainly! You know I love Virginia. It's my home. Of course, we'll go up to New York for weeks at a time. We have a lot of friends there and I've made some wonderful new ones since meeting John. I'm sure John can look after his business that way."

"Won't John want to live in New York?"

"Well, I know we'll return to New York after our honeymoon. But we'll stay only a few weeks. I'm dying to tell Sydney Howell-Jones — you remember her, that wonderful strawberry blonde who's always so amusing — all about the honeymoon. But then we'll go home, I imagine."

"You know, Devon, your home is where John is," said Grace seriously.

"Of course I know that! But from the very first day I met John, I told him I would never want to spend all my time in New York. He's never brought it up, but I'm sure that's why he bought Willowbrook."

"I'm not so sure," said Grace skeptically. "I have the impression he wants to spend most of his time in New York."

"Grace, I'm certain it won't be a problem," said Devon with a dismissive wave of her hand.

"How is it that you two have never had this discussion?" Grace asked curiously.

"Well, as I said, he's always known my opinion on the subject and . . . I don't know . . . a conflict has never come up. We've just always gone back and forth when we needed to."

"That was before. You were planning a wedding and there were plenty of reasons for you to go to New York. Are you going to be as willing to go just because John wants to?"

"Of course . . . within reason."

"Devon, I think you've lived too long as an only child," said Grace bluntly, as she signaled to the waiter to bring them coffee.

"What do you mean by that?" asked Devon, offended. "Are you saying I'm spoiled?"

"Not exactly . . . I mean, Mother and Father never denied us anything, but I think they were careful to teach us to value what we have. I'm not talking about that kind of spoiled. I just mean that you seem very set in your ways. I'm not sure you always consider what John might want. You call Virginia 'home.' It's true that it's where you were brought up and where our parents live, but you don't live with our parents. John's home is New York. When you marry, it *is* customary to live in your husband's home."

"I know that!" said Devon in an exasperated tone. "But Willowbrook is his home too," she insisted.

"He bought it for you. And I'm sure he intends to spend time there. But it may not be as much as you like."

"Oh, Gracie, you worry too much!" Devon said with a small laugh, trying to lighten the mood.

"Now, you know that's not true. In fact, I almost never worry. I just couldn't help noticing from your conversations with John that you hadn't quite addressed the question of where you would live. I can tell you two have very different ideas of how it will all work."

"We love each other too much to fight over something like that," said Devon, smiling at the thought of her husband.

"I hope so" was all Grace said.

Paris had always been Devon's favorite city and she enjoyed showing John all the obscure little places she had discovered when roaming about on previous visits. John had been to Paris only once before and it had been a brief, guided affair, not at all like his discoveries with Devon. They had spent the last three weeks exploring the city, yet she still showed him something new every day.

"This *pâtisserie* has the best lemon tarts in Paris," said Devon, leading him into a tiny green shop hidden along one of the winding cobblestone streets that characterize the Left Bank.

"Now how exactly do you know that?" John teased as they waited for the woman behind the counter to wrap up four of the small yellow confections.

Devon looked at him in mock incredulity. "Why, I've tasted them all, of course."

"You don't expect me to believe that, do you? Not when you're so slim," he said, putting his hands around her waist. Indeed, they almost encircled her, she was so slender. His pride in her, and his love, sometimes seemed so full that it overwhelmed him. John was amazed at the things she had discovered in her wanderings around Paris and it seemed as though each new place she showed him revealed something wonderful about her.

"Believe it or not, I've tried them all. And all the chocolate truffles and almond croissants and *tartes Tatin* — all of them!" she said, biting into the lemony cream and buttery crust as soon as they were outside the shop.

"Hold on a minute! I thought we were saving those for tea." John laughingly took the package from her and hid it behind his back before she could extract a second tart.

"How do you expect me to wait until then? It's only ten-thirty in the morning. Besides," said Devon, as she pretended to lunge for the package behind his back, "I'm eating for two now." Devon plopped down on a bench under a tree and pretended fascination with a nearby fountain as John stood dumbfounded before her, digesting the news. Devon looked up at him and playfully pulled him down beside her. She was bubbling over with excitement and was waiting for John to get over the shock so that he could join her celebratory mood.

John was silent for a few seconds, then he said, "Devon, are you sure?"

"Well, not absolutely, but I'm several days late," she said. "Of course, it could just be all the excitement, the travel . . . all of that." Devon had dropped her joking tone. She was completely serious now. She hoped so much that she was pregnant, but she did not want to be disappointed if she was not. That was probably what he was feeling, too, she thought. That was why he was so restrained.

"But haven't you been using the —"

"Yes, but I didn't get it until the day before we left New York to come here. Remember? You wanted me to see a specialist instead of Dr. Hickock." Devon was puzzled. Didn't he believe she was pregnant?

"Yes, but before that I was very careful to —"

"Obviously not careful enough, I suppose," Devon joked. "Besides," she said in an intimate tone, snuggling closer to him, "you may recall that your incredible love for me prevented you from always showing the proper . . . um . . . control." She whispered in his ear, "Especially on our wedding night."

John said nothing, but reached for her, enfolding her in his arms.

She put her head on his shoulder. "You're happy, darling, aren't you?" she murmured into his chest.

"Of course . . ." he said, but his tone was not convincing.

Abruptly Devon pulled away from him so she could see his face. "You're not pleased!" she cried, astonished.

"It's not that, Devon," he said hastily. "It's just that I was hoping for a little time to ourselves. I didn't want to start a family quite yet. Do you know what I mean?" He grasped her shoulders, imploring her with his eyes to understand him. He loved her completely and fully, but marriage had been a major change in his life. When he had first realized his love for Devon, he had not been certain that he was ready to undertake the commitment and responsibilities inherent in marriage. He had overcome those misgivings and was now wondrously happy he had done so, but a child was a different matter . . . an encumbrance of sorts.

Devon thought she understood. "Darling, a child will only add to our love. It won't come between us," she said, thinking of how much she loved her goddaughter. Her love for her own daughter — or son — would be even deeper.

"It's not so much coming between us that I worry about," said John, sitting beside her. "It's just that we've talked so much about the things we'd like to do together. Getting Willowbrook back on its feet. Traveling."

"Why can't we do that with a child? When I was a child we all traveled with our parents. Alice took care of us a lot of the time, but we were with them. I don't think we acted as encumbrances," said Devon reasonably.

"I'm not so much worried about logistics as I am about . . ." He didn't know how to finish. The responsibility? He didn't want to say that. It sounded . . . immature somehow. "I suppose I enjoy our freedom. I can't think of myself as a parent yet," he finished lamely.

"I wonder if anyone does until the time comes," said Devon, turning away from John to settle back on the bench. She stared straight ahead, trying to envision what life would be like with a child. She could imagine only joy, not the problems John was so vaguely articulating.

"Maybe if we had more time . . ." said John pensively.

"Maybe? What do you mean by that?" asked Devon, turning her head sharply to look at him once again. "Don't you want children? You've always said you did."

"I meant in the future, after a few years," John explained. He was not even sure why the idea disturbed him so. His parents had left him largely in the care of a nurse when he was small, a tutor when he was older, and boarding school when he was an adolescent. All his friends had grown up similarly. Parents spent time with their children and enjoyed them, but mostly saw the best sides of them. The pleasures of children without the pitfalls. What was so frightening about that? John asked himself. Was he afraid of growing older? Afraid he would not be a good father? He was not certain. He felt only that he was not ready for fatherhood.

"Well, we haven't much of a choice," said Devon sadly. She felt like crying, but she restrained herself. She didn't want to become more upset than she already was. How was it possible that her overwhelming joy was not shared by her husband? She felt betrayed and irreparably hurt.

With remorse, John realized the blow he had dealt her. "Darling, I'm sorry. I'm being a brute. Of course, once the child is born, we'll laugh at all my misgivings. I'll love it. And . . . it's done now . . ." he said, trying to keep the regret from his voice.

"Oh, John, you say that as though it were something bad!" cried Devon. "How can you be that way?"

He put his arm around her and hugged her to him, but she pulled away. "It's not something bad. It's just that I'm not used to the idea."

"I don't know what to say," she said, standing up. She felt as though all her happiness had turned to ashes. It wasn't just his attitude toward the child that troubled her. It was a deeper fear that she sensed in him . . . something she couldn't quite define. And it seemed as though her love for him, so full and complete, had suffered a damaging blow. She studied his face, so handsome, so exciting to her with its vivid blue eyes. But the face did not seem to be the face of her beloved. Suddenly, it was just a handsome face. A coldness gripped her, making her afraid. She did not want to stop loving John.

John, sensing something of her mood, also grew afraid. "Devon, you're looking at me so queerly," he whispered, pulling her back down next to him. She said nothing, only continued to look at him. She was looking at him as though she did not know him, he thought. He could almost feel her love — which always seemed to enfold him — slipping away. At the thought, the beautiful Parisian scene around him seemed transformed into a harsh, alien landscape. He could not allow her love to die, he thought in panic. She must love him!

He reached for both her hands and squeezed them reassuringly between his own. "Devon, I'm just going through a few jitters." He gave a nervous laugh. "Why, I'll be the happiest and proudest father you ever saw!" he said with false joviality. He wanted to believe the words. Perhaps when he saw the child . . .

Devon allowed herself to be comforted. She wanted to love him. Loving him had made her happier than anything in her life. The idea of not loving him left her desolate.

Both of them wanted to believe him. Both of them knew he was lying.

CHAPTER 15

"IT'S quite daring! Very Parisienne," Grace said admiringly as she observed her sister's reflection in the gilt-edged cheval glass. "I've never seen you wear anything like it."

They were in the ornate lounge area adjacent to the guest powder room at the American embassy in Paris. The large room was decorated in Louis XIV style, with crimson silk brocade wall coverings, intricately modeled crystal chandeliers suspended from twelve-foot ceilings, and gilt-edged mirrors. A uniformed maid stood discreetly in the corner, assembling the items she would need for the evening ahead: a sewing kit, a lint brush, linen hand towels, bottles of French perfume and lotions, tortoiseshell combs and hairpins, powder, and the countless other items ladies used to beautify themselves for a gala evening.

Grace sat on a delicate antique love seat, intricately carved and upholstered in white-and-red-striped silk, as she puzzled over her sister's daring black satin evening gown. Not that there was anything inappropriate about it. It was clearly expensive, and because of its simplicity, it retained its elegance. But it hugged Devon's gracefully slim figure in an indisputably provocative way. The halter-topped bodice was cut into a deep V, so that it pulled her breasts close together to form an intriguing cleavage. From there, the dress curved in again, lovingly clinging to every contour of her body, loosening only when it reached the knees, and there flaring out slightly in a graceful flowering of the silken material.

"Turn," Grace commanded, making a spiraling motion with her index finger.

As Devon slowly made a 360-degree turn, Grace took in the deep *U* in the back; a *U* that plunged dizzyingly to the curve of Devon's waist, drawing attention to her perfectly shaped buttocks. Devon's black hair gave the effect of more satin, falling in soft waves to just below her creamy white shoulders. The contrast of Devon's white skin against the black satin textures of her hair and dress was mesmerizing — and highly erotic.

"What's come over you?" Grace asked the question in a joking tone, but she was truly curious as to why her sister had selected a dress so out of character for her. Devon was always elegant, usually quite stylish, and sometimes even subtly sexy in her clothing selections, but she had never before worn something so blatant as the daring creation she had chosen for the dinner party at the American embassy that evening.

"Doesn't it look like something Jean Harlow would wear?" Devon asked with a wicked sparkle in her eye.

"Frankly, yes," Grace replied with a skeptical shake of her head.

"You disapprove? Is it indecent?" Devon asked, tilting her chin upward defiantly.

"No . . . but Martha is probably turning over in her grave," Grace replied in mock seriousness.

Devon looked puzzled. "Martha?"

Grace gestured offhandedly toward the portrait on the wall. Like all the mirrors, it was edged in gilt. "Washington," she said. The oil painting dominated even the large sitting area, which was empty except for the sisters and the maid.

Grace was usually called upon to arrive early at embassy functions, as she was the wife of the third ranking diplomat in Paris and well liked by the wife of the ambassador. The ambassador's wife knew that she could count on Grace to ensure that the last-minute touches were carried out correctly while she and the ambassador dressed for the evening ahead.

Devon glanced away from her reflection toward the portrait and let out a merry peal of laughter. "Ha! That's all you know. I'll bet Martha Washington had to be a pretty exciting woman to keep a man like George Washington interested."

"Well, she never wore anything like that, I'm sure. Even in bed," Grace said with a smirk.

"I just felt . . . I don't know. Like being a femme fatale for a change," Devon said in an offhanded fashion, walking toward the marble vanity table covered with cut-crystal perfume bottles. She picked up one of the delicate containers. Lifting the stopper, she took a whiff of the scent, then, without using any, replaced it on the table. She picked up another bottle, still avoiding Grace's eye. Devon didn't feel like being studied and questioned because she herself did not know why she had chosen such a dress. She only knew that ever since her conversation with John about her pregnancy a few days ago, she had found herself doing little things to annoy or anger him. That had included flirting an unusual amount with their dinner companions the previous night, a duo of old school friends of John.

One was living in Paris as a correspondent for an American newspaper, while the other was simply using a small portion of his inheritance to sample the pleasures of the Continent. The latter was a handsome man, in a dissipated way, but Devon knew he was one of society's takers, not a contributor, as John and his reporter friend were. Nonetheless, she had found herself smiling warmly at his extravagant compliments, and even encouraging them. And when they had danced together, she knew she had allowed him to hold her a bit too close. It had all ended harmlessly, with John appearing not even to notice, but Devon was at a loss to explain her own uncharacteristic behavior.

Actually, John's response — or lack of it — had disturbed Devon. He had been pensive and absentminded since he had heard the news of her pregnancy, and she could tell that his mind was often far away, even when they were engaged in conversation. Although the couple went through the motions of enjoying their honeymoon to the hilt — packing each day full of activities — it seemed to Devon as though they had somehow lost contact with each other. John had not tried to make love to her once since hearing the news, and Devon, for reasons she could not explain, felt reticent about initiating sex, although she had done so at other times since their marriage.

"Devon, is something wrong?" Grace asked, startling her from her contemplation. Devon quickly replaced the bottle she had been distractedly holding and turned toward her sister.

"Of course not," she said with a nervous laugh, "what could be wrong? Come on, we'd better go downstairs."

"Oh, yes. I have to check the place cards and see to it that the martinis are properly chilled. I don't know what the French have against cold drinks. It seems things are never . . ."

Devon did not hear the rest of Grace's words, so lost was she in her own ruminations. She looked down as they walked, smoothing the dress over her perfectly flat stomach. She wondered when she would begin to show. Why didn't she tell Grace she was pregnant? They had never kept secrets from each other. Yet if she did tell her, Grace would surely make some reference to John. And Devon was afraid that her shock and disappointment would spill out of her. Somehow, even though John was the cause of those feelings, she felt it would be disloyal to reveal them to a third party — even to her own sister. Devon was sure that if she told Grace of John's reaction, Grace would say something harsh about her husband. She did not want to hear any criticism of John, though. And she did not know what she could say to defend him if Grace did criticize. She had not even justified his reaction in her own mind. She had tried simply to push it into her subconscious and accept John's reassurances that he had only been reacting to the initial shock — that he was indeed happy that she was pregnant. But, like a tiny pebble in a shoe, John's reaction kept poking into her consciousness against her will. And it was crippling her ability to love him as fully and unreservedly as she had done before.

But I love him, she insisted to herself. He's my husband. I've got to get over this. So will he. I *do* love him. . . .

"What?" said Grace, turning to face her with a puzzled look on her face.

"Did I say something?" Devon asked, startled and embarrassed.

"You whispered something."

"I must have been talking to myself," Devon murmured.

Grace stared at her a moment, her face a mixture of skepticism and concern.

Devon smiled and took her sister's arm. "Why don't we go and have a nice *cold* martini? Although, I must say, it won't be nearly as good without the forbidden aspect to it." Prohibition was still in effect in the United States, though it rarely affected the wealthy, most of whom had ample wine cellars, as well as the connections necessary to obtain harder spirits.

John, Philip, and Ambassador Long turned away from the antique wall map they were studying as the women entered the salon. They were enjoying cocktails and a few moments of quiet conversation, knowing that the room would soon be filled with guests. It was a room made for entertaining on a grand scale. On the walls hung ancient tapestries, their colors faded but still magnificent. At each end of the vast room was a fireplace as tall as a man and wider than ten men. They were impressively set off by white marble mantels dating from the Empire period, elaborately chiseled with carvings in a swan motif. On this warm June evening, however, there were no fires. Indeed, on the wall opposite the entranceway, six sets of French doors stood open to let in a gentle breeze. Outside, lit tapers illuminated a seemingly endless marble terrace. The space was punctuated by a small fountain sending a cascade of water over a giant seashell that held a three-foot-high Venus.

The men's conversation died away as Devon and Grace approached them. Grace looked smart in a Grecian-style dress of pure white silk chiffon, the soft draping of the skirt moving gracefully as she walked. But it was Devon who drew the eyes of the men. The play of light against the sleek black cloth of her dress cast a hypnotic spell over the group; each man enjoyed the sight of Devon in silent admiration.

John, far from being annoyed by the daring black gown, had felt an almost irresistible desire to make love to Devon from the first moment he had seen her in it. No, not to make love, but to take her — without the caution or patience. The feeling of desire was welcome, for he had inexplicably felt no urge to make love to Devon since learning of her pregnancy. He did not know why, did not even fully acknowledge the feeling to himself. Yet it was there — an invisible barrier between him and his wife, where once there had been nothing but unreserved love.

But Devon's entrance in the black dress drove away any feelings of reserve that had been troubling John. It was not that the dress was any more revealing than a thousand others he had seen in the past. It was Devon herself. She gave off an aura of wantonness, while at the same time saying and doing only the appropriate and polite thing. To John, this wantonness was something new in his wife. He did not understand its source, but he recognized it as something that had always lain deep within her; something he had discerned the first evening they had met.

John's eyes swept over Devon appreciatively and he grinned. A crooked, unconscious grin that sent a frisson of anticipation down Devon's spine. For a moment she forgot about the hurt he had inflicted — she felt only love. Not just love, but also pure animal attraction that made her, without her realizing it, move with even more languor than before.

Suddenly, John thought of Loretta. Loretta had that sheer animal sexual appeal that Devon was only now displaying for the first time. But Loretta lacked Devon's refinement; that utter correctness that ensured that Devon would always be accepted in any society. A burst of pride filled John. Pride and happiness that Devon was his wife.

He took a step toward her and gently lifted her hand to his lips. Not releasing her eyes, he gave her one small whisper of a kiss, then drew her to his side. His arm went around her slim waist, and as she turned to make a remark to Ambassador Long, he felt his fingers brush the shiny material over her stomach.

Then he remembered. For a moment — no, several hours — he had forgotten. But now, much to his dismay, his ardor died within him. Devon did not look like a mother. Was it really possible that she would soon be one? Just a few moments before, he had compared her to his former mistress, and he had found their similarities — and their differences — immensely exciting. But Devon would no longer be like a mistress to him once her child — *their* child, he reminded himself — was born. She would have another person to consider before him.

What John wanted was more time alone with Devon — both as companion and lover. More time to mine fully her hidden sexuality. Each time he tried something new with Devon in their marriage bed, she was at first shocked, then compliant, then an enthusiastic participant. Her innocence allowed him to hold the exclusive key to her sensuality, and he enjoyed slowly unlocking door after door to the most secret depths of her. He could not imagine that it would be the same after the child was born.

John reflected for a moment on his own mother. How to describe her? Well . . . *matronly* was the only word. It seemed she had always been the formidable, gray-haired dowager she was now. Had she ever been young and eager for love, like Devon? Yes, she had. At least if his parents' sepia-tinted wedding photograph was any indication. She had been a curvaceous, ash blond beauty, ample of bosom and slim of waist. Her lips had been generous, her eyes sparkling. She had been desirable once. But even if John reached back for his earliest memories of her, he could not recall an image of a blossoming young woman. Instead, he saw a kind but rather strict lady who never raised her voice but when angry compressed her full lips into a tight little line. He saw a woman who always wore high collars and never wore any perfume except a rather insipid lavender water.

Nor had John's father ever shown any sign of spontaneity or youthfulness. Would John become like that after the baby was born? John felt that he was too young to have a child. Once the child was born, however, was he not too old to continue the amusing, glamorous life-style he had envisioned for himself and Devon? He felt old and weighted down when he considered the inhibiting element the child would impose on their lives.

Of course, there will be a nanny, he told himself. But he knew Devon well enough to understand that she was not one to turn over the upbringing of her child to another woman. His and Devon's freedom would completely vanish. Was vanishing now, as her responsibility to the child overpowered her responsibility to him.

Devon, sensing John's withdrawal, reached for his hand, all the while nodding politely at the white-haired ambassador's monologue on the beauty of the French Riviera. When her fingers met John's, however, he simply gave her hand a quick squeeze and withdrew his own. Looking away briefly from the ambassador, Devon turned her head just enough so that she could see John's profile. Instead of meeting her look, John stared fixedly ahead at the ambassador. Devon, not wanting to draw attention to herself, turned again toward the older man. But a cold stab of anger filled her, for Devon was discerning enough to sense, if not to articulate fully to herself, the reason for John's withdrawal.

Of course she was too well schooled to show her anger in front of the others. John, though, was aware of it. The evidence was there in the tight little line into which she had transformed her usually generous lips.

The Marquis de la Brisière was entranced to find himself dining beside the enticing dark-haired American who spoke such fluent French. A connoisseur of women, he had been drawn to her immediately upon entering the room. And since then his eyes had not left Devon for more than a few moments at any point during the evening.

Now he found that the happiest of coincidences had placed her to his right at the dinner table. The woman to his left, the soignée blond wife of one of France's leading industrialists, was also charming. It was not difficult to spend the requisite amount of time conversing with her. But he savored the moments, at the end of alternate courses, when etiquette allowed him to turn once again to Devon.

"You are even more beautiful in close proximity," he told her in English too perfect to be anything but a second language.

"Ah, you speak English?" Devon asked, surprised that he had not told her so earlier.

"Yes. But like most Frenchmen, I prefer my own language," he said with a smile.

Devon noticed his straight white teeth, something not always found in Europe, where dental hygiene was not taken as seriously as in America. He's not exactly handsome, Devon thought, but he's lethally attractive. Indeed, women found his sharp, predatory features exciting, for they gave him a devilish air. But the marquis was not at all evil. He was a wealthy, pleasant man whose passions in life were women and winemaking. In that order. His manner of wooing the objects of his desire — and they were many and varied — had become a fine art. And his artistry almost never failed.

"I notice," he continued in English, "that you speak French exceptionally well. So many Americans have trouble with our vowel sounds." But not this one, he thought to himself. When she spoke, she moved her mouth with all the mobility of a Frenchwoman, forming each word perfectly, uttering each sentence in the singsong melody that made French such a seductive language. The marquis enjoyed watching her crimson-rouged lips as they spoke his language. He could easily imagine himself kissing those lips. Kissing them, nipping them, and inserting his own tongue between them.

"My mother always believed that one should be fluent in a second language. So I had a French tutor from the time I was five years old. I used to resent it terribly," said Devon with a laugh.

"Yet you learned beautifully," replied the marquis.

"Only after my tutor discovered the secret to teaching me," said Devon with a mischievous grin.

She is even more sublime when she smiles, thought the marquis. He smiled back out of sheer enjoyment of her comeliness. "The secret?" he asked, pleased that she was revealing secrets so soon. She would reveal many more to him later, he promised himself.

"That the best way to teach me was on horseback. Luckily, Monsieur Lamarque knew how to ride."

"That is a secret I shall remember, for I intend to make use of it at some point in the future," he promised.

The air was thick with undercurrents of sexual tension while the fish course — a meltingly delicious sole Véronique — was served.

"I look forward, with unprecedented anticipation, to the poultry course," the marquis said with a sly grin, turning back to the lovely blonde on his left, as etiquette demanded.

Devon, too, found herself reluctant to turn to her other dinner partner, though politeness dictated that she do so. The ruddy banker was an important friend of the ambassador, but he drank a great deal and spent most of his time discoursing on how he managed to be one of the few profiting from the Depression. Devon was eager to return to the marquis.

As the footman placed the smoked pheasant in wild currant sauce before her, Devon scolded herself for her inappropriate attraction to the marquis. But as she turned toward him, an involuntary smile lit her face.

"So . . . we are reunited," he said.

He has that absolutely deadly way that Frenchman have of looking at you — like a visual caress, Devon thought. And he's a master at it. Wherever the marquis looked, Devon felt a warm tingle, until her entire body felt flushed with heat.

The heat was palpable to the marquis, who, though accustomed to such reactions, never failed to be delighted by them. Ah, this one will be delicious, he told himself. She is seductive, but seems unaware of it. She still has a refreshing innocence about her. "Are you newly married?" he asked, trying to solve the mystery of her.

Devon looked toward John, who was on the opposite side of the table and several chairs away. Suddenly, she was stricken with guilt. How could she have allowed herself to feel such attraction for a stranger? She loved John. Loved him with all her heart.

The marquis realized immediately that he had made a tactical error in bringing up Devon's husband, yet he was amused by her reaction. She is very young, he thought to himself, suddenly feeling quite old at age forty-two. For a moment, his thoughts dwelt on his own wife. She was an entrancing brunette his own age who still had the power to intoxicate any man she wished. The marquis knew that she spent many lively moments without him on the French Riviera and in Italy. He did not mind, for it kept the piquancy in their marriage. They enjoyed each other on the occasions when their paths crossed. Had there ever been a time in their marriage when his wife had chided herself for being attracted to another man? He had certainly seen no sign of it. Yet here was a seemingly sophisticated woman, of potent desirability, who was still innocent enough to be embarrassed at her attraction for a man not her husband. Intriguing. Intriguing but dangerous to his own strategy, he realized. He had to immediately reassure her that she had not made her feelings toward him obvious.

"You seem to be very much in love with him," said the marquis in an indulgent tone.

"Oh, yes. Very much." Devon was glad to have the opportunity to say it. The marquis should not misunderstand — just because she had been friendly . . .

"But you did not answer my question. Are you newly married?"

"A little less than a month, actually," said Devon. Again she glanced nervously at John. This time he was looking at her. She smiled at him, forgetting, in her guilt, her earlier anger.

The marquis also turned toward John and met his gaze. He very slightly raised his wineglass in a subtle toast. It was a polite gesture. A fairly commonplace gesture of greeting. But something about the marquis's manner drew John's attention.

John returned the gesture, smiled once more at his wife, and turned back to the lady on his right. But he found himself trying to observe Devon out of the corner of his eye. Every time he reached for his wineglass, he turned his head a bit more than necessary so that he could have a better view of Devon and her dinner companion. Now he took a sip and noticed the rosy glow that seemed to emanate from his wife. Even just one glass of wine had the ability to give her pale complexion more than a hint of pink, but tonight the glow seemed to come from within as well. The look she gave the marquis as the footmen served the meat course — and she was forced to turn to the gentleman on her other side — disturbed John. There was a familiarity about their demeanor that John would have expected from two people who knew each other well — yet they had just met.

John studied the Frenchman. He was distinguished, in a vulpine sort of way. He had an aristocratic bearing, but it was not affected. Rather, the man had about him an easy charm of manner that John could see would be very attractive to women. He laughed and chatted easily and seemed truly interested in the conversation of the lovely blond woman beside him. He flirted with her a bit, but John could see that the woman, though enjoying herself, was not as affected by his charm as Devon was. She seemed amused, but not enthralled. Devon, John realized, had concentrated on the man with an intensity he had previously seen her focus only on himself.

John picked rather halfheartedly at his beef Wellington as he listened in distracted silence to the small talk of the woman beside him, a kind-faced American matron who had apparently attended the Lancaster Academy for Young Ladies with his mother.

"Of course, your mother was two years behind me," she was saying, "so I was not well acquainted with her. But she was a perfectly lovely girl . . ."

John didn't have to concentrate on what she was saying. He could just nod politely and pretend to listen, which left his mind free to think about Devon. About Devon and the marquis.

As the salad was served, he watched his wife turn back to her seductive dinner partner. She was glowing. Positively glowing. And she was extraordinarily lovely. It was no wonder the marquis was taken by her.

John watched her tilt her head sideways and laugh at something the marquis was saying. She looked enchanting, John thought, with her hair spilling over her shoulder, her smile lighting up her face. A wave of jealousy and desire such as he had never known swept over him. He wanted her in his arms right at that moment. Wanted to kiss away the misunderstandings of the past few days. To fill the rift that had grown between them with the warmth of his love for her.

Just at that moment, Devon caught John staring at her. The desire in his face was unmistakable. She felt her heart turn over in response.

He has that effect on me, she thought to herself, and I suppose he always will. She gave him her most beautiful smile and lifted her glass to him in the same toasting gesture the marquis had performed earlier. John grinned back, feeling heady with relief and euphoria. It was wonderful to be in love. Wonderful to have the most beautiful wife in the world. He was the luckiest man alive!

The marquis, observing the exchange, sat quietly back in his chair and said nothing. It was clear to him, in that moment, that he could not hope to compete with the young man who was Devon's husband. Devon would never agree to that final, most sublime surrender.

He sighed to himself and turned toward the blond industrialist's wife. She was, after all, extremely alluring.

It was not until Devon retired thirty minutes later to the ladies' room that she discovered that the warm moisture between her legs was blood.

CHAPTER

16

WILLOWBROOK reminded Devon of the magnificent Greek Revival plantation houses that she had seen during her family's voyage to Louisiana ten years before. Indeed, the Hartwicks, from whom John had bought the estate, had originally come from Natchez, Mississippi. Willowbrook, built in 1845 by Brent's great-grandfather Beauregard Hartwick, had been intended to approximate the Hartwick estate in Natchez, and he had tried to transplant as much of its ambience as possible.

As the Alexanders drove up to their new home in the twilight of the midsummer evening, Devon thought that the only thing missing from Willowbrook to make it a replica of a Deep South plantation was the Spanish moss that draped the giant live oaks along the delta. But Willowbrook had the live oaks. They flanked the long, straight, gravel-covered drive that led from the main road to the house.

"The Hartwicks were so proud of this house," Devon said wistfully, thinking back to the days before the Depression.

"I loved it from the first moment I saw it," John said softly. "I'm glad you do too," he said, taking his right hand from the steering wheel and giving Devon's hand a squeeze.

"Oh, stop here for just a minute!" Devon cried as she spotted the white Corinthian-pillared portico of the mansion through a frame created by the overhanging branches of the grand trees.

"It looks very imposing, doesn't it?" John asked.

"Very. I guess the exterior hasn't had time to get run down, even though I know Brent hasn't had anything to spend on upkeep," Devon said. In the last two years, she had noticed that some of the house's delicate interior wall coverings had grown worn and the furnishings and paintings severely depleted as piece by valuable piece had been sold in an attempt — not always successful — to meet debts and maintain the productive capacities of the farm.

"Well . . . I had the outside painted," John admitted with an excited smile. "And everything's been whitewashed and the garden brought back. Other than that, everything was in pretty decent repair. Old Mr. Hartwick apparently kept the place up until he died."

"Oh, yes. There was always work being done. But it looks more splendid than ever!" Devon responded happily. "I can't wait to see it up close. Let's go on!"

The gravel drive ended at a vast Kentucky bluegrass lawn that featured a small brick-edged fish pond surrounded by flowers and flanked by eight venerable magnolia trees. A brick walkway led from the pond to the front staircase, a graceful, wisteria-covered affair of black wrought iron that swept down to ground level in wide, converging arcs.

As John and Devon approached the stairway, he picked her up to carry her over the threshold. "I think I should be commended for including the stairs in this ceremony," he joked.

"Commended and rewarded," Devon replied, giving him a feather-light kiss.

The massive Corinthian columns that extended to the second story of the house created a spacious porch that wrapped around three sides of the house. The perfect symmetry of the building was punctuated by the four French windows that flanked each side of the front door. The main entrance to the mansion, a shiny black door surrounded by narrow rectangular panes of beveled glass, was topped by a similar door at second-story height, which opened onto a balustraded balcony.

"Can you open it for me?" John asked. "It's not locked. Your mother arranged for someone to make things ready for us."

The door was large enough for John to walk through without turning sideways to avoid hitting Devon's outstretched legs. Once inside, he placed her gently on her feet and turned her toward him for a long embrace. But they were both too eager to inspect the house to linger.

After a thorough look around, Devon decided that as impressive a facade as Willowbrook presented, her favorite vantage point was from the rear, where the second-story veranda spanned the whole width of the house, and French doors created another large living area of the outdoor space. From there, Devon could enjoy the vista of green lawn gradually sloping down to a small lake surrounded by weeping willow trees. The willows partially screened the view of the barn and stables, painted white to match the house, and the white-fenced paddock beyond. It was a scene of perfect bucolic splendor, a peaceful and inviting setting for Devon and John to begin their new life together.

* * *

"I barely know where to begin," Devon said to John the next morning as they stood in the thirty-foot-wide center hallway and examined the scuffed floor.

"The first thing to do is rehire the staff the Hartwicks had to let go. Many of them are still out of work, I imagine, with times as they are," said John, looking up at the Regency chandelier, which was badly in need of polishing. "I thought about hiring them for you when I bought the place," John continued, "but I thought you would want to take charge of the hiring yourself."

Devon turned toward John with the dimpled smile he loved, and joked, "We've been married less than two months, but you already know me too well!"

"Let's just say I know my place," John said with a chuckle, leaning forward to give Devon an affectionate kiss.

In response, Devon wrapped her arms around his neck and drew him to her for a more prolonged embrace. Their tongues intermingled as the heat from their bodies inflamed their passion.

"Shall we go upstairs again?" Devon asked breathlessly. "Since we don't have any servants yet to be scandalized by our behavior."

"We just got up!" John laughed. "I thought you were anxious to see the stables." But his halfhearted objection was contradicted by his actions. With one easy motion, he swept Devon into his arms and, in a replay of the threshold ceremony of the evening before, carried her up one of the curving staircases that flanked the entrance hall. The master bedroom lay in the middle of the gallery that overlooked the foyer, and John carried Devon there now, kicking the door closed behind them and throwing her playfully onto their still-unmade bed. As Devon sunk into the soft goose-down mattress, her pink silk robe fell open, exposing her long white legs and the dark triangle that lay at their apex.

John hesitated a moment at the edge of the huge carved four-poster bed, enjoying his wife's beauty. Then he leaned over and slowly pulled off the pink velvet tie that encircled Devon's waist, causing the robe to fall open entirely. Devon slid out of the robe and threw it toward the foot of the bed, reaching to pull John down beside her as she once more reclined into the pillows. John removed his own navy silk robe and let it drop to the floor, eager for the touch of Devon's body against his.

He lay beside her and rubbed his hands over her soft body, sinking his lips into the crook of her neck. He felt Devon's tongue slip into his ear, her warm breath sending shivers down his spine. He trailed his hand up the length of her body and softly covered her breasts, teasing the nipples until they stood erect.

Devon gasped with pleasure at John's touch, spreading her legs wider to invite him into her. They found each other's lips, and with a long kiss, John eased his way over Devon until his own legs were between hers, his erection at the mouth of her sex.

Devon tried to draw him into her, but she felt John resist.

"What is it?" Devon mumbled, her voice thick with desire.

"You're not protected, are you?"

"No . . ." she moaned in reply. "But it's a safe time." Devon tried to pull John back to her, but still he resisted.

"Darling, there's never really a safe time," John said patiently.

Devon was tempted to argue further, but a memory stopped her. The memory of John's face when he'd learned of her supposed pregnancy. For a few days it had seemed as though their love were doomed. Devon could not forget the rift that had briefly existed between them. John was simply not ready for children. Things had been so perfect since the moment at the American embassy dinner party when their eyes had met across the table and John's desire had been rekindled. Then, later, when he'd learned that she was not pregnant, it had been difficult for him to hide his relief. Oh, everything he'd said had been properly regretful, but it had been easy for Devon to see that there was no genuine regret. At first, it had bothered Devon that he should be so relieved. But the happiness of the ensuing days of their honeymoon had almost obliterated the hurtful memories. And it reassured Devon, in her inexperience, to learn that they could weather a crisis in their marriage and emerge with their love intact. Her anger at John had passed like a summer storm, leaving behind it the fresh, giddy feelings that had existed before, made even more poignant by the threatened loss of them.

Devon was certain that John would one day want to have children. In the meantime, she could understand his desire to have some time on their own. With a sigh, she reached toward the bedside table and withdrew the small rubber device that the doctor in New York had given her. She slid off the bed, put the pink robe around her, and went into the bathroom. As she inserted the device, she glanced outside the window at the bright, sunny garden behind the house. Beyond that, horses grazed in a field. As far as she could see, the land was hers. Hers and John's. It gave her a wonderful feeling to know that she and he formed a unit.

Exiting the bathroom, she impatiently threw off her robe and jumped back into the bed.

"There now, that wasn't so bad, was it?" John teased.

Devon gave him a mischievous look as she felt his body against hers. "I can see that the wait didn't dampen your ardor."

John covered her mouth with his and pushed her back onto the pillows. Devon could feel herself growing aroused again, almost as though there had been no interruption. She closed her eyes and felt herself sink into the sensuality of the moment, enjoying the salty taste of John's skin against her tongue, the feel of his fine brown hair against her breast. He skimmed her arm with feather-light kisses, stopping at the pulse inside her elbow. Then he shifted his attention to her torso, running his tongue from her breastbone to her navel. Devon felt chills of desire spread downward. He moved lower, teasing the insides of her thighs with his tongue. Then, with exquisite languor, he moved upward until she was writhing with impatience for him. He slid his lean, muscled body gracefully on top of her. She could feel his arousal, and she twined her legs around him, pulling him snugly against her. Unable to wait any longer, he entered her. They moved together in pleasure like two perfectly matched dancers. Their movements grew more urgent, breathless, dizzying. Devon's muscles locked as she felt herself approach a shattering climax. John quivered within her as he tried to contain himself until she had attained her pleasure. When he sensed that she was ready, he resumed his long, steady strokes in and out of her, driving her into a frenzy with the sweet friction. He felt her open herself fully to him, and then they abandoned themselves to the sensations that swept their bodies. At that moment, it seemed as though their love was a palpable entity unto itself. An indelible bond that would never be broken.

"She's gorgeous, there's no denying," said Willy O'Neill, head trainer at the Willowbrook stables. He pronounced the word "gau-jus," more than a remnant of his Irish brogue still evident, despite more than thirty years in America. Willy's leathery, wrinkled face looked like a gnome's. He had a bulbous nose, a wide, thin-lipped mouth, piercing blue eyes recessed under fuzzy caterpillars of graying eyebrows, and two tufts of hair above his ears that stood straight out from his balding head like wings. The phenomenon was a result of his nervous habit of putting on and removing a battered green baseball cap that inexplicably bore the insignia BROOKLYN DODGERS. As far as anyone knew, Willy had never been anywhere near Brooklyn. But no one teased Willy about the hat. Willy was not a man that people teased. He was over fifty, but he had about him an air of vigorous pugilism that discouraged familiarity. His short stocky body was pure muscle, and he was secretly proud of the fact that he had no paunch despite a ration of Irish whiskey each afternoon and each evening before bed.

Willy was the undisputed king — dictator, really — of Willowbrook's stables. His word was law, had been law since the Hartwicks had hired him twenty-five years ago, when he had been the wunderkind of the horse-training world. And it was only thanks to him that the farm had managed to retain a measure of its good reputation despite the loss of the Hartwick fortune. The Hartwick horses were not seen as often as they had been prior to the stock-market crash, but those few that competed performed impressively, and past champions were still in demand for breeding. But even Willy's best efforts were not able to make the vast estate profitable. Willowbrook Farm, which had the capacity to house eighty horses, was down to only thirty horses since the reversal of the Hartwick fortune. Of that thirty, however, only five were currently racing. Seven were being trained for racing, and the rest were allowed the more leisurely routine of breeders.

All that was forgotten, though, as Willy studied the filly before him. He knew everything there was to know about horseflesh and what he saw now pleased him. The smile on his face was a rare sight to those who worked under him. His smiles were almost never bestowed on people, only horses, and then usually only when Willy was alone with the animals.

Now Willy straightened up and released the leg of the chestnut filly before him.

"Gau-jus! And the leg's as good as new." He nodded an acknowledgment to sixteen-year-old Jeremiah Washington, the exercise rider who had helped to work the filly through her temporary lameness. Although Willy's reticence had never allowed him to express it, he recognized in Jeremiah a kindred spirit. A true horse lover. One who had a special feeling for the animals, a link of understanding with them that was not a learned skill but a natural gift.

Willy patted the horse on the flank and nodded again to Jeremiah, a signal that the filly should be put back in her stall. The rigid hierarchy of Willowbrook Farm was second nature to Jeremiah, so rather than return the filly to the stall himself, he handed her to a groom, who in turn checked to see that the stable boy had properly cleaned the spacious enclosure and had spread enough fresh straw on the floor. The routine was not designed to satisfy egos; rather, it had grown from need. Willy needed the exercise boy at his side as he checked the legs of each horse. Jeremiah, in turn, needed to see what Willy was seeing, so that he would not be surprised by weaknesses that might turn up during training. Furthermore, Willy and Jeremiah tailored the routines of each horse according to its strengths and weaknesses. Grooms attended the horses, each day picking their hooves clean, currying their manes and tails, brushing them, and ensuring that their tack was cleaned after each use. Stable boys fed the horses and kept the stable immaculate.

But it was Willy himself who checked to see how the horses were eating. Now he looked into the tub of the filly's feed bin to check its contents. It was empty. Good. When a racehorse didn't eat, it meant trouble. The first thing Willy did in such a circumstance was take its temperature. As a result, Willy's morning routine, which began every day at five o'clock, consisted of examining each horse from head to toe, then checking each horse's feed bin. Later, he would ask Jeremiah and the other exercise riders to jog the horses.

"You do it when they're dead cold, first thing in the morning," he had instructed Jeremiah upon his promotion from groom to exercise rider. "That way you can see if he's nodding."

Nodding occurred when a lame horse hit the bad foot at a jog. The head would bob up or down at that point, depending on whether the injury was in a rear or front leg. A sound horse's head, in contrast, would remain straight throughout the exercise.

Despite cutbacks in staff and horses, the white-painted building, an L-shaped structure with eleven-by-fifteen-foot stalls on both the outside and inside, was absolutely spotless. Aisles that ran the length of the building were fifteen feet wide, meaning plenty of light and space in which to attend to the horses. Tack was kept in a meticulous state in a small rectangular building a few yards from the stable.

The employees, Willy included, lived in a small white dormitory a few hundred yards from the stables. But Willy never socialized with the men who worked for him. His quarters — consisting of a one-room living/dining/kitchen area, a bathroom, and a bedroom — bore no mark of his personality except for the bottle of Irish whiskey that was always present on the kitchen table. There was no hint of Willy's past, why he had come to America, or who his parents were. If he had ever been married, he never spoke of it.

On this morning, there was particular tension in the air, for all the stable workers knew they would be meeting the new owners of Willowbrook. Willy had, of course, made no concessions to this occurrence, not deviating from his routine one iota. Jeremiah wondered how the older man felt about the change. He wondered if the new owner, a Yankee, would understand the way things were done in horse country. Would he know that the trainer was the law in the stables? Would he know that people usually worked for the same employer for their entire lives? Family loyalties between servant and master intertwined in a synergistic hodgepodge common in the South, but rare elsewhere.

"What're you dreamin' of, boy? Take the bandages off his legs." Willy's impatient voice interrupted Jeremiah's reveries.

Startled, Jeremiah focused on the colt whose lead rope he was holding. Gently, he unwrapped the bandages on the colt's legs. The colt had placed second in a race the week before, something the new owners would undoubtedly be happy to learn, and it was customary to bandage the legs for some time after a race.

"Looks like the swelling's gone down," Jeremiah noted.

Willy's response was a grunt that could have meant anything, but which Jeremiah knew meant satisfaction.

After a moment of running his calloused hands over the horse's flank and withers, Willy asked, "The burning?"

"Better. Almost gone. 'Cause it's been so dry, I guess." Racing on sand tracks usually burned the hair off the back of the horses' fetlocks, then irritated the skin underneath. Infections could result in wet weather because the wound never really dried.

"Yeah. You're a good old boy, ain't you." Willy patted the horse's flank and nodded for him to be rebandaged and put back into the stall.

"A beauty."

Willy and Jeremiah turned quickly to see who had uttered the words. Standing several yards away in the doorway of the barn were the new owners of Willowbrook. Both were wearing riding clothes, jodhpurs and boots and plain white shirts. Neither wore a jacket. They were a dazzlingly handsome pair, Jeremiah thought. He had seen both of them before, of course. Mr. Alexander had spent considerable time in the stables prior to buying Willowbrook, and Miss Devon had been a frequent visitor of Mr. Hartwick.

Now Devon walked toward them and said, "Hello again, Mr. O'Neill, Jeremiah."

The adolescent nodded back shyly. "Ma'am," he said.

Willy stood up straighter, but just nodded in acknowledgment of the greeting.

"We've met before, Mr. O'Neill," said John, walking toward the older man and extending his hand. Willy took it, shook it as briefly as possible, then dropped his own hand back to his side.

There was an awkward moment of silence as the members of the group studied one another.

"We'd like to take a look at the stables. Have you go over which horses are running," said John. John had no intention of becoming involved in the stables on a day-to-day basis, but he wanted to restore the business to its former stature. With fewer horses running, the operation had been losing money. More horses would cost more money, but prize purses could offset the additional cost. In addition, winners always created more business for the breeding operation.

Willy looked from John to Devon and back again. "You can finish the rounds with me if you like. You can watch the exercise. Then we can go to the office," said Willy in a grudging voice. He didn't like interruptions during morning rounds. The Hartwicks had always been careful not to disturb him in the morning.

Devon sensed O'Neill's annoyance at being interrupted and accepted it philosophically. She was eager to learn about the world of horseracing and believed that O'Neill could teach her a great deal, but she knew that he would resist doing so. Racing was a man's world. There were few women breeders. Certainly no women trainers. Trainers of O'Neill's stature were highly valued. She did not want to get off on the wrong foot and risk losing him to another farm. An angry departure of a good trainer could ruin the reputation of an owner in the racing world, making it impossible to recruit another equally qualified trainer.

It gratified Devon that John recognized her superior skill with horses and was thus willing to turn the racing operation over to her while he pursued his career in New York. Both agreed that her skill in breeding and training hunters, and her natural ability with horses, would make it easy for her to grasp the essentials of raising racehorses. Still, she knew that Willy O'Neill would not be eager for her presence on a daily basis. She would have to handle him with the utmost tact. For now, she resolved, she would keep silent.

Devon and John watched Willy examine every horse, unwrapping the bandages around their legs, checking their hay racks and feed buckets. The Alexanders were impressed by his thoroughness. Then it was time to watch the horses exercise.

The group went to the private racetrack that lay behind the barns in a flat area surrounded by gently rolling green hills. Of course, horses scheduled to run in the near future would be taken to the track at which the race would be held.

"This filly here is Ginger Snap. Okay, Jeremiah, take 'er slow," Willy said. When the horse had worked enough for Willy to determine that she had no injuries, he instructed Jeremiah to pick up the pace.

The filly had a particularly large stride, so even when Jeremiah galloped her, it felt as though he were going slower.

Devon noticed the characteristic and mentioned it to Willy, who grunted an acknowledgment. He was aware that she had bred a couple of good hunters, and that she was highly thought of in the Fauquier County horse world. But as far as he was concerned, she was a dilettante. A pretty, spoiled dilettante.

Now the filly was galloping at high speed around the track.

"Gettin' ready to prop," Willy mumbled.

Devon knew the term. It meant the horse was getting ready to stop short in an attempt to shoot the rider forward off her back. Jeremiah obviously had observed the same thing because he snapped his crop briefly, causing the horse to keep moving.

"It was her ears, wasn't it?" Devon asked Willy. The filly's ears had moved in such a way as to indicate that the ploy was forthcoming. Devon had seen it many times in hunters.

Willy nodded in response to Devon, but refused to be impressed. Any experienced rider should be able to recognize such a signal, he told himself.

"Pull 'er back a bit!" Willy yelled as Jeremiah rode by. He didn't like his horses to exercise too fast. He preferred to save it for the racetrack.

After a few more minutes, Willy signaled Jeremiah to bring the horse to a walk. A groom ran to the horse and rider and waited for Jeremiah to dismount, then proceeded to walk the horse for several minutes around an adjoining paddock. Later, the horse would be washed, as would its tack.

Jeremiah mounted another horse but kept it off the track while another exercise rider took his mount through its paces. Devon and John were impressed by the military precision of the stable's organization. Willy O'Neill was obviously a very important asset.

"Willowbrook is lucky to have you," Devon said quietly.

Willy did not reply, simply followed the galloping horse with his eyes. But he heard the comment and was gratified that the woman recognized the quality of the operation. A lot of people didn't even know the difference.

"We'll go to the office after this." Willy directed this remark to John. "You'll want to look at the books. We've been winnin', but . . ." Willy completed his sentence with a shrug.

Later, as John sat at Willy's scarred oak desk and carefully read the ledgers, he realized the cutbacks in personnel that Willy had had to contend with.

"No money. Can't afford jockeys. Can't afford hot walkers. Can't afford enough exercise riders. Can't afford to race," Willy explained in his usual staccato fashion.

"I commend you for what you've been able to do," John said, leaning back in the old captain's chair and pushing the ledger away from him. Willy stood beside him, while Devon sat on the only other piece of furniture in the room, a green leather love seat with one cushion that had been torn, then carefully taped. As everywhere else under Willy's jurisdiction, the office was spotlessly clean, strictly utilitarian. "I hope you'll want to stay on," John continued.

"As long as I have a free hand, no reason not to," Willy declared, looking John coolly in the eye.

"You'll have that," John assured him, careful not to look at Devon. He knew she wanted to learn about the racing operation, but he would have to persuade her to approach Willy gently and to defer to him on all matters.

Willy looked at Devon for a moment, but he said nothing. Then he turned back to John. "A free hand would mean that I'd hire back the boys we laid off."

"Fine," John agreed.

"We'd probably want to buy a few mares. Give the brood operation a pickup."

"Just tell me how much you'll need."

"Won't be cheap," Willy answered. "Then there's travel to auctions. We've had to cut back on that. In any event, I'll have to be gone a bit. Keeneland's this month." The famous Kentucky sale took place each July. It was universally considered to offer the highest quality horseflesh on the market.

Devon was tempted to say that she could fill in for him at Willowbrook during his absence if he would only teach her how, but she was afraid to alienate him at this crucial point in the negotiations.

"That's no problem," John said. "Go wherever you need to go. Hire whomever you need."

"Well, then. If there's nothing else, I'll be gettin' back to the barn," Willy said, putting the green Brooklyn Dodgers cap back on his head.

Devon stood up and gave Willy her most winning smile. "Thank you for showing us around, Mr. O'Neill. It appears that your reputation is well earned. I know it's been difficult for you since the cutbacks." She was tempted to put out her hand to him, but was oddly apprehensive that he would not accept it.

"Ma'am," he replied, touching his fingers to his cap. Then he turned and walked out, closing the door behind him.

For a moment, Devon and John stared at each other, saying nothing.

"Seems like a very able fellow," John finally said, "though he's a bit of a chatterbox."

Devon burst out laughing and went to sit on John's lap, giving him a warm kiss.

"I don't think I'm going to have an easy time with him," she said.

Within a week Devon had assembled a household staff. In addition, Alice was permanently ensconced as her lady's maid, while John's manservant, Wilkes, settled into his Willowbrook quarters, knowing he would be called upon to travel with his master between his homes.

Meanwhile, Willy O'Neill acted quickly to rehire the stable staff previously let go by the Hartwicks.

"It's good to be back operating at full force again, isn't it, Mr. O'Neill?" Jeremiah asked.

"Not there yet," Willy responded gruffly as they walked together to the barn. Though it was still dark, the weather was already balmy, promising a scorching day of high temperatures and equally high humidity. Willy lifted his cap up, ran his hand over his bald scalp, then replaced the old green hat. "There's still the auctions," he added.

Jeremiah wished that Willy would ask him to go along on the trip to Kentucky. His secret ambition was to be a jockey, then later a trainer. But there were no black jockeys in the racing world, and it seemed an impossible dream. Yet in the period from 1875 — the first year of the Kentucky Derby — to 1911, black jockeys had dominated the sport, and there had been several black trainers as well. But for some reason that was no longer the case.

In any event, as far as the auction was concerned, it was not usual for trainers to be accompanied by their exercise boys. Still, Jeremiah was certain that he could learn a great deal from Willy.

As though reading his thoughts, Willy said, "You'll be needed to look after things here while I'm gone."

Jeremiah nodded, proud at the trust implicit in Willy's comment.

"Mr. O'Neill." A cultured feminine voice came out of the darkness, startling the men. Willy spun on his heels to see Devon in riding clothes walking rapidly behind them, trying to catch up. He would have liked to continue walking, but knew that the young woman had done nothing to warrant such rudeness. Somehow, though, she irritated Willy. Threatened him, really. It was not that he feared her authority over him. He simply did not want his meticulous routine disrupted. And it was clear that Mrs. Alexander, who thought she knew quite a bit about horses, wished to be involved in the running of the stables. Oh, she had done nothing to infringe on Willy's prerogatives; she carefully asked questions rather than issued orders. Always stood quietly observing the exercising rather than chattering on about inanities. In sum, she conducted herself as the perfect owner. But in the week since she had returned from her honeymoon, it seemed she was always *there*.

Jeremiah, in contrast, liked the young Mrs. Alexander. She was beautiful in a way that melted his sixteen-year-old heart. And she was kind. She treated him with respect and often asked him questions about his work. She seemed to appreciate his skill with horses, a skill that she also possessed.

Politely, the teenager said, "Morning, Miss Devon."

"Good morning, Jeremiah," said Devon with a warm smile. She liked the fact that he called her Miss Devon rather than Mrs. Alexander. He used the more familiar term because he had known her before, as a friend of Brent Hartwick, but it made her feel accepted in the current situation. Willy O'Neill was another story. It was clear he did not welcome her presence.

"Mr. O'Neill, I'd like to accompany you on your rounds this morning," Devon said evenly.

"You're the owner," the trainer responded with a shrug. He turned then and walked quickly into the barn, Devon and Jeremiah trailing behind him.

The first horse they approached was named Winning Spurs. The three-year-old had placed fourth in the Kentucky Derby, a severe disappointment for Willy.

"If we could've hired Kurtsinger to ride 'im, he would've placed," Willy had told Jeremiah. But the skilled jockey had previously committed to another trainer and had piloted the winning horse, Twenty Grand, with a time of two minutes one point four seconds. The purse had been $48,725. The owner had been a woman, Helen Hay Whitney. Ownership was quite acceptable for a woman, but the day-to-day running of a stable was thought to be man's work.

"I understand you decided against running him in the Preakness," Devon commented.

"Couldn't get a good jock. Your husband was away and I had no authority to offer the kind of pay I needed to get Kurtsinger or Sande, or any of the top guys."

"Well, that won't be the case from now on," Devon promised.

"So your husband said," said O'Neill. His agreement had been with *Mister* Alexander, his tone told her.

"Will you run Winning Spurs anymore this year?" asked Devon, leaning back against the stall opposite the colt's.

Willy grunted an assent as he bent down to examine the horse's left foreleg, turning his back to Devon in the process.

Devon's eyes met Jeremiah's where he stood holding the horse's halter. She read there a mixture of sympathy and amusement, and she gave him a wry smile in return.

"You're going to exercise him today?" she asked no one in particular.

"No, ma'am," Jeremiah responded, "Bertie is."

"Well, I'd like to do it myself," Devon said firmly. She might as well make her desires known to O'Neill because no matter how diplomatic she tried to be, he behaved as though he were offended by her very presence.

Devon almost laughed at the expression on Willy's face as he stood. His caterpillar eyebrows were drawn together in a frown of puzzlement, and his thin, mobile mouth was a grim line. He was confused as to how to respond, Devon saw. She was glad she had turned the tables on him for once.

"We have hands for that," Willy said.

"What are their qualifications?" Devon asked coolly.

"Weight. Riding ability. Knowledge of Thoroughbreds," Willy barked.

"Good. Then I'm perfectly qualified. I weigh one hundred and ten pounds, I've ridden for twenty years, and I've bred and trained Thoroughbreds for hunting. I doubt if you have an exercise rider as experienced as I," Devon said defiantly.

Like a bystander at a tennis match, Jeremiah turned his head back to Willy to see how he would respond.

"You want to be an exercise rider?" Willy asked, mock incredulity filling his voice.

"Not as a career, no," Devon answered. She would offer no more. Why should she? He never offered more than the minimum in his responses to her.

"Well, hell," Willy said, wanting to shock Devon and daring her to upbraid him for the language. Let her object. He would walk right out on her. Here and now. An interfering woman was a handicap he didn't need. But Devon did not respond as he had expected.

"Indeed," Devon said, an amused gleam in her eye. "Please don't let me hold you up. Continue your rounds. I'll just follow a few paces behind you." She had won her victory. Now it was time to let him reestablish his dominion over the stables. Continuing with his routine would help him do that, Devon knew.

Willy turned and signaled impatiently for Winning Spurs to be put back into his stall. Then, without looking again at Devon, he walked to the next stall, Jeremiah behind him. As Willy turned toward the next horse, the black youth gave Devon a small nod of encouragement. Congratulations! it seemed to say.

CHAPTER 17

"THE first thing we must do is have a telephone installed. I won't go along with this ridiculously old-fashioned opposition to an instrument that is so convenient," John declared, placing his napkin on the long mahogany dining table and pushing back his chair.

"I've never minded not having one," Devon said, not really protesting. She took a last sip of her morning coffee and rose from the table. In her royal-blue-and-white-striped cotton dress she looked as fresh as the unseasonably cool morning. Through the open French doors, the scent of roses wafted in.

"Well, I need to keep in touch with my office. And what about when we're in New York? Won't you want to check on things here?"

Devon waited until they had found their way into the sunlit conservatory before replying. She did not speak until she had closed the set of glass doors that separated the green and white room from the rest of the house. "I trust the staff to look after Willowbrook," Devon said mildly, "but I imagine that a telephone will come in handy when you're in New York without me. We'll enjoy being able to speak to each other."

"In New York without you?" John looked puzzled, stopping in the middle of the checkerboard-patterned, white-and-black-marble-tiled floor. "That doesn't sound very appealing."

"Nor to me, darling," Devon said, sitting on a nearby love seat, "but with your business there and my interests here, it does seem that some days of separation are inevitable."

"Why? Why can't we divide our time between the two places? Why can't you accompany me wherever I go?"

"Well, I'm trying to learn the Thoroughbred business. There will be times when I won't be able to leave. Like when an important race is coming up."

"But that's why you have O'Neill, isn't it?" said John impatiently, pacing back and forth before Devon.

"I want to be more involved, though. I don't want to just turn over every decision to O'Neill. I'd like to help him train a couple of horses. Learn from him."

"He said he wanted no interference. I won't risk losing him." John's voice sounded a warning. "This is, after all, a business."

"I've been exercising the horses for two weeks now and he hasn't left yet," Devon said defensively. "Do you think that I'm so offensive that he won't be able to endure my presence?"

"It has nothing to do with you, per se! And I know it seems foolish that a trainer should dictate to his employers, but these men are a breed apart. Good ones are hard to come by. You know that," said John, trying to assume a tone that would appeal to Devon's reason.

"Well, if I learn enough from him, maybe he won't be able to dictate to us. Maybe I won't need him at all!" Devon said in a show of bravado.

"Don't be absurd!" John retorted, his voice growing heated. "Even the most knowledgeable owners have trainers."

Devon's eyebrows shot up at the rebuke. She struggled for a moment to suppress her rising anger. Then, in a quiet but unsteady voice, she said, "I do not propose to fire Mr. O'Neill. I recognize his value. On the other hand, I don't enjoy being dictated to by anyone. I am extremely careful not to get in his way. But I insist on undertaking tasks of which I am capable. And I've done very well so far. Why, yesterday I clocked the best time ever on Firefly. She's ready for Saratoga!"

"Does O'Neill say that?" John stood still before Devon, curiosity overtaking his anger.

"He does," Devon replied, with a lift to her chin. "And I'm going with her!"

"We'll both go!" John said excitedly, cheered by Devon's news. "I can't wait to see how she does."

"We'll be taking Winning Spurs, too. And Home Run!" Devon said, caught up in John's excitement and relieved that the tension between them had eased.

"Why, that's wonderful news!" John reached for Devon's hands and pulled her up beside him, wrapping his arms about her in a bear hug.

"You see? Everything is fine!" Devon exclaimed.

"Better than fine," John murmured, giving her a lingering kiss.

Devon returned his embrace warmly, but then pulled back. "Come down to the barn with me," she invited. "I'm due there in half an hour."

John was disappointed. The embrace had kindled in him the desire to return to their bedroom. "Can't I divert you for just an hour?" he asked with a winsome grin.

"Well . . ." Devon was reluctant to refuse him. She had never before done so, and did not believe that it was a good thing to do. On the other hand, Firefly each day surpassed her own time. And today was the day that she would actually race against some of the colts in the stable to see how she responded to the competition after her weeks of intense training.

John could see the conflict on Devon's face. "Go on, I can tell you're dying to get down there," he said with a good-natured smile.

"You're the most understanding husband in the world, darling. And I'd like a rain check," said Devon, standing on tiptoe to kiss him once again.

CHAPTER 18

"WHO'S that beautiful woman over there?" Devon whispered to Sydney Howell-Jones. Sydney's husband, Bart, was a close friend of John, and the two women found themselves equally drawn to each other. Both couples had horses running at Saratoga that day, as did their other friends the Whitneys, the Vanderbilts, the Astors, and the Dukes.

They were sitting in the rarified section reserved for owners, each woman smartly decked out in crisp linen and a flirty hat. But even among the sleek, well-cared-for women of America's elite, the young blonde whom Devon had indicated stood out.

"You've never met her?" Sydney chuckled knowingly, her husky voice rich with innuendo. "That's Marion Davies."

There was no need to explain who the film star was. Her fame in the movies had several years ago been eclipsed by her notoriety as the mistress of William Randolph Hearst. "Of course . . . I thought she looked familiar. And that must be Mr. Hearst beside her. I haven't seen him in years. He and Father did some business together and he visited us at Evergreen, but that was at least ten years ago. I didn't immediately recognize him, though I must say he doesn't look much older."

"Well . . . having a young girlfriend helps, I'm sure." Sydney laughed. "But you know, he's close to seventy."

"And she's only about thirty, isn't she?"

"That's right," Sydney said with a wicked smile. Sydney had no malice in her, but she adored scandalous gossip and could resist neither listening to it nor repeating it. A stunning strawberry blonde with lush cupid's-bow lips, Sydney exuded an aura of cynical sexuality that acted as an irresistible lure to the opposite sex. In reality, she was steadfastly faithful to her husband, Bart, who seemed not to notice the harmless flirtations she enjoyed so much.

Devon looked again at the blond woman, Marion Davies, who was discreetly dressed in a white linen suit with navy blue piping, white gloves, and a navy blue straw hat that set off remarkable blue eyes.

"She doesn't look at all like someone's mistress," Devon noted.

Sydney raised one auburn eyebrow expressively, smirked, and said, "Take my word for it."

Devon broke into peals of laughter at her friend's expression. "Oh, I know it's true. It's just that she looks so sweet and . . . I don't know . . . clean-cut, I guess." Devon, somewhat naively, expected mistresses to proclaim themselves by wearing too much makeup, too much jewelry, and loud colors.

"Well, they're more faithful to each other than a lot of married couples I know," Sydney said thoughtfully. "I suppose you've seen the photographs of that place he built in California." Sydney was referring to La Cuesta Encantada — or Enchanted Hill — known commonly as Hearst Castle.

"It's amazing, isn't it?" Devon said in awe. Devon, like all of her group, was accustomed to the estates of the wealthy, but no one had ever seen anything like Hearst Castle, or the Ranch, as the newspaper magnate called it.

"The place has the most incredible swimming pools," said Sydney. "One indoors and one outdoors. The outdoor one is surrounded by columns and looks like a Roman temple. He calls it the Neptune Pool. In fact, he has part of a Roman temple right there by the side of the water. It must be at least fifteen hundred years old."

Devon shook her head in wonder at the extravagance. Her parents were wealthy, but they were not extravagant.

Sydney continued, "The indoor one is made entirely of tiny glass mosaic tiles from Venice. They're partly filled with eighteen-carat gold, so the whole room glitters."

"Sounds breathtaking!" said Devon, looking again at the world-famous newspaper tycoon.

"The whole place is," Sydney assured her. "But you'll probably visit it yourself. He and John know each other. You know, John used to be a very active investor in motion pictures — and not just in those produced by Mr. Hearst's studio either."

Devon stared at Sydney, surprised by this news about her husband. "Motion pictures? He's never mentioned any interest in those."

Sydney laughed huskily, indicating to Devon that the topic somehow pertained to sex. "Many men are investors in film or stage productions, you know," Sydney remarked. "John apparently gave that up when he fell in love with you. And that's good." Sydney gazed directly into Devon's eyes, trying to see if her friend understood her innuendo.

Devon blushed furiously as she suddenly grasped the import of Sydney's words. "Oh, I see what you mean," she murmured, avoiding her friend's eyes.

Sydney was half amused, half disconcerted by her friend's distress. "That's all over with now, you know," she reassured her.

"Of course," Devon said, regaining her poise. She tilted her chin up and smiled what she hoped was a cool, woman-of-the-world sort of smile.

"In any event," Sydney said, anxious to avoid delving further into the sensitive topic, "Mr. Hearst invites hordes of people to the ranch every weekend. I know John has been there before and I'm sure you'll be invited soon."

As if on cue, the formidable William Randolph Hearst tipped his hat to the occupants of their box and raised his champagne glass in salutation. John returned the greeting, then signaled for Devon to join him as he went over to pay his respects to the older man.

"How are you, John!" the big man boomed, trying to make his voice heard over the crowd surrounding them. "It's been too long. You remember Marion, of course."

"How could I forget the lovely Miss Davies." John smiled, taking the young woman's hand briefly before turning to Devon. "And you haven't met my wife." John beamed proudly at Devon as he made the introductions.

Devon and Marion Davies shook hands and smiled at each other, then Devon turned to Hearst, whose large hands swallowed her smaller one in their grasp. He studied Devon approvingly, obviously enjoying the sight she presented in her white-and-pink-sprigged organdy dress and matching picture hat. Hearst was a man who appreciated classical beauty and he recognized it at once in Devon.

"You're a lucky man, John," Hearst said quietly. The tone of sincerity in his voice transformed the clichéd phrase into a genuine compliment. "Won't you join us for a glass of champagne?" he continued.

"Oh please do," Marion chimed in with a hospitable smile.

Devon took the seat Hearst vacated next to his mistress and greeted the others in the box. She was excited to meet Gloria Swanson, whom she found ravishing, and Clark Gable, who seemed to have enthralled every woman around him. In addition, she recognized two of her acquaintances from New York and the publisher of a Boston newspaper who was a former schoolmate of her father.

"I understand you have a horse running in the next race," Marion commented to Devon.

Devon looked at her in surprise, suddenly realizing that she and John had been a topic of conversation. She wondered what had been said about them.

"I've been trying to learn more about horseracing," Devon said, "and I have very high hopes for my filly Firefly. But, you know, fillies don't usually do too well against colts."

"Well, there's always a first time. And I'll root for you. I'll even bet on you," Marion said, laughing at nothing in particular.

Devon found the young woman's laughter contagious and laughed with her, without knowing why. Marion Davies seemed to be the kind of person who had a perpetually sunny outlook on life. Devon liked her immediately.

Devon had never before met people in the movie industry and she discovered now that they were a wisecracking, pranksterish group. She felt a little reserved and stiff in comparison to them. They were all so vivid and glamorous.

Despite the joviality of the group, none of the pranks or wisecracks were actually directed at Hearst — whom Marion called W.R. The entire party seemed respectful and a bit afraid of him, as though he were a parent in a group of adolescents. Only Marion treated him with the same casual good cheer that she showed everyone.

There was great excitement in the box when it was Firefly's turn to run. Devon was gratified by the support of the group, especially as the

Whitneys, in an adjoining box, were running a colt in the same race. The Whitneys were truly the First Family of the American turf, highly regarded for their stables, their trainers, their jockeys, and their sportsmanship. Willowbrook Stables had just three years before rivaled the Whitney family's Greentree Stables, and Devon intended to restore her farm to its former glory. Devon recalled that it was, in fact, a Whitney horse that had been the only filly to win the Kentucky Derby. Harry Payne Whitney's Regret, run in 1915, had proven that a filly could indeed win the greatest of all American horseraces.

As though reading Devon's thoughts, Marion leaned toward her, put her daintily gloved hand over Devon's, and said, "I'd like to see a filly win."

Devon squeezed the tiny hand in hers and smiled nervously, glad to have the support of the lovely woman. She was not quite satisfied with the outcome of Willy O'Neill's search for a jockey to rival the great Linus "Pony" McAtee, who worked for the Whitneys. She looked at the number-six position at the starting line — Firefly's position — trying to reassure herself that the less experienced Slim Bocaso would serve her as well. Willy had hired him just two weeks before, but with reservations at his comparative lack of experience. He was comparing him, though, to McAtee, who had worked for Willowbrook before being wooed away by the Whitneys.

Picking Bocaso out of the crowd on the track, Devon was glad she had redesigned the Willowbrook silks so that they were now her own choice of colors. She had debated with herself the wisdom of tampering with a respected, if somewhat faded, image, but she had ultimately decided that a signal of change and progress would be good to send to the racing world. As a result, she had discarded the blue and green colors that had been the Hartwicks' and designed a bolder uniform — scarlet torso and sleeves with a black diamond on the front and back, rather like a playing card. The jockey's cap had scarlet and black quadrants and a scarlet bill.

The start of the race came almost too soon, despite Devon's impatience. Like a shot she was out of her seat, silently praying as she held the binoculars glued to her face. She was oblivious to John as he came behind her and placed his hands on her shoulders. Oblivious to the noise of the crowd. For a moment she could not find Firefly, then she saw her.

The filly had started quickly — often the case with fillies. The question now was whether she would maintain her lead once the colts pulled alongside of her. It went against every instinct of a filly to do so, but there were exceptions to the rule.

Firefly was holding her lead, Devon observed excitedly. Now it was Firefly and the Whitneys' colt, Dance With Me. Bocaso was maneuvering Firefly toward the inside of the track, leaning to the left to bring her in — and away from Dance With Me. That was a good move, Devon thought with approval, but she was dismayed to see the Vanderbilts' Hip Hip Hurrah gaining from behind.

Suddenly, Dance With Me surged ahead until he caught up to Firefly. McAtee tried to move his horse closer to Firefly in a perfectly legal attempt to intimidate the filly and cause her to slow down. Meanwhile a fourth horse, a gray with the name of Court Order, had pulled past Hip Hip Hurrah and seemed to be gathering strength for a final surge ahead. His jockey, too, was trying to ease closer to Firefly.

With jubilation, Devon saw that Firefly refused to be cowed. On the contrary! "Look, she's pulling ahead!" Devon cried to no one in particular. She could hear the roar of the crowd, now caught up in the drama of the little-known Willowbrook filly winning a race that offered a good-sized, if not impressive, purse.

With only an eighth of a mile to go, Firefly was holding her lead. Holding it, but not by any significant distance. Then, in a split second, Dance With Me took the lead. He was ahead by a nose. Devon heard John groan behind her as his grip tightened on her shoulders. But Firefly stubbornly refused to be defeated and, with one length to go, she reached her legs as far as she could, edging past the colt.

In a blur, Devon saw the filly cross the finish line. Cross it first.

"We won!" John hugged Devon from behind and lifted her off her feet. In a dizzy rush, Devon felt herself being led out of the box. Shouted congratulations bombarded her and John as they made their way through the crowd. She felt her heart bursting with pride; her mind stunned with disbelief. It had been so easy! Her first race! And a filly! Devon thanked the endless stream of well-wishers in her path.

Finally, she saw Willy. He was holding the reins of a lathered Firefly, Slim still astride. A reporter was shouting questions at the trainer, who answered them in his usual monosyllabic fashion. Devon rushed toward the group, ignoring the photographers' requests for a picture. She wanted to hug Willy and jump up and down with him in celebration over their victory but as she drew nearer to him, his habitual dour expression inhibited her.

Devon approached Willy quietly and stood facing him. "Well?" she said, unable to restrain an elated smile.

"Well what?" he asked brusquely, ignoring the questions shouted at him by the reporters.

"Well, what do you think?" Devon asked, a wide smile still on her face.

Willy lifted his Brooklyn Dodgers hat off his head, then replaced it. He looked down at the ground and, scratching his cheek, mumbled, "It's a start."

Devon put out her hand for Willy to shake, almost afraid that he would ignore it. But he didn't. He raised his eyes to her and shook her hand firmly, the clicking of cameras accompanying the action.

"We did okay," he added.

Devon wanted to lean over and kiss his weather-beaten cheek. She thought seriously about it, then decided that Willy had made enough concessions for one day. Instead, she turned to congratulate the grinning Slim Bocaso, relieved that she had found a jockey for Willowbrook Farm.

CHAPTER 19

LA CUESTA ENCANTADA rose like a fairy-tale castle out of the sun-browned California hills, its white stucco walls and tile roofs providing the only textural variation in the endless fields of parched grass that surrounded it. But as amazing as the apparition was, what always hypnotized Devon was the breathtaking panorama of the Pacific Ocean from the vantage point of the ranch itself.

Though it was Devon and John's fifth visit to the ranch, and many of the other visitors in the convoy to the hilltop were either too jaded or too engrossed in conversation to remark on the view, Devon turned all the way around in her seat to gaze out the back window of Hearst's chauffeur-driven Packard at the dawn light glimmering on the sea.

The entire party of thirty-six, including Marion Davies and Hearst, had left Los Angeles in his private railroad cars at 8:15 the previous evening. The train had arrived in San Luis Obispo at approximately 4 A.M., where a fleet of cars awaited them for the drive to the ranch. From San Luis Obispo to San Simeon, the tiny village where the Hearst ranch lay, was a drive of a little under two hours. But to travel from the entrance of the ranch to the top of the hill where the houses stood took about another half hour. Sometimes more, depending on whether wild animals were blocking the road.

Devon thought that some of the most fascinating features of the ranch were the exotic animals that Hearst had imported from obscure corners of the earth. Many of the herd animals, such as the zebra, were allowed to roam free. The apes and big cats, however, were kept in Hearst's private zoo. Devon always felt sorry for the magnificent felines who paced back and forth in the small spaces, their tails twitching restlessly at the confinement.

Devon and John enjoyed their visits to La Cuesta Encantada. They were times of uncharacteristic abandon, where it seemed that every fantasy could be fulfilled. The gay Hollywood group that made up the majority of the guests always seemed to loosen the inhibitions of the smaller coterie of East Coast society folk and politicians. Devon and John found themselves dancing more, drinking more, and relaxing more than they usually did at gatherings closer to home. It was not a life-style Devon coveted on a permanent basis, but she relished the interludes. John, on the other hand, seemed most relaxed in California, and often spoke of buying a home there.

The limousines discharged their passengers at the bottom of a set of curving marble stairs that led around the Neptune Pool to the main house and the three equally lavish guest houses.

"Devon and John, you'll share Casa del Mar with Sydney and Bart," Marion announced with a warm smile, referring to one of the elaborate guest cottages that stood apart from the main building. "I know how you love the view of the ocean," she murmured in an aside to Devon. It was one of Marion Davies's most endearing traits that she tried hard to accommodate the likes and dislikes of her favorite guests while never being overbearing.

Illicit lovers, however, were never assigned the same bedroom, for Hearst was quite prudish, despite his own situation.

"Breakfast in half an hour," Marion called after her departing guests.

"I think we should skip breakfast and take a nap," John said to Devon, with a yawn and a stretch. Like most of the other guests on the train, he and Devon had spent the evening drinking champagne and playing cards.

Devon hesitated, tempted to agree. "Well . . . W.R. wants to show me his new colt after breakfast," she said. Devon was one of the few female guests that Hearst actually sought out. He found her quiet intelligence a pleasant contrast to the frivolity of most of his other guests and he respected her knowledge of horses.

"All right, but don't blame me if you collapse of exhaustion," John teased.

"Are you going to have breakfast or take a nap?" Devon asked, opening the door to the magnificently furnished cottage. Casa del Mar was Hearst's favorite cottage and the most ornate. Devon and John had been given one of the upper suites, notable for its carved ceiling decorated with gold leaf imported from a palazzo in Venice, its red silk walls, and the Italian marble pilasters at each entranceway.

As they climbed to their room, Devon could feel the weariness creep into her body. A nap would be wonderful, she thought, entering the bedroom. The bed had been turned down in anticipation of just such needs, and Devon stared hungrily at the crisp linen sheets.

"Sleepy?" John wheedled, following her gaze.

Devon nodded.

"More sleepy than hungry?"

"Well . . . they always have the best waffles . . ."

John turned the key in the door and began undressing. Despite her fatigue, Devon could not help but admire the play of his muscles as he removed his clothes. My husband is deliciously attractive, she thought to herself. As though of their own will, her hands moved to the collar of her traveling suit and began to undo the buttons.

John, naked, slipped between the cool sheets, but left the corner of the bed turned down invitingly.

"Ahhh," he sighed, snuggling into the soft bed, "this feels wonderful." His eyes, full of mischief, met Devon's. "Are you sure you don't want a nap?"

Devon felt irresistibly drawn to the bed, to her husband in it, to the idea of cool linens on her body. Removing her underclothes, she walked toward the bed and slid into the warm cup into which John had curled his body. The comforting feeling of his arms around her combined with the clean, lavender-scented freshness of the sheets lulled her almost immediately into a deep, dream-free sleep.

Devon awoke to the sun streaming full strength through the large picture window overlooking the ocean. She stretched languorously, then turned to face John, rubbing her body against his in a catlike fashion. She looked down at him, still fast asleep. His long eyelashes curled against his sun-browned cheek in an endearing fashion. His strong profile silhouetted against the pure white pillowcase aroused in her tenderness, admiration, desire — all the ingredients that added up to love. She felt very lucky to be so in love with her husband — and so sure of his love for her — when she considered the number of divorced people she knew.

With a smile, she quietly eased her way out of the bed so as not to awaken John. She used the bellpull to signal Alice that she wanted her bath drawn. Alice always traveled with her to the Hearst ranch, for a lady's maid was necessary for all the clothing and hairstyle changes required of those who sojourned there.

By the time Devon had bathed and dressed in riding clothes, it was noon. Lunch would not be served until two-thirty, so Devon decided to go for a ride.

Hearst always had a fine selection of mounts, and Devon found that her favorite, a huge white gelding named Eskimo, was available. Eskimo was far more calm and gentle than the mounts she was accustomed to at home, but it was not uncommon for the roars and screeches of Hearst's wild animals to cause the horses to shy or bolt, so Devon preferred the stolid Eskimo to more easily spooked mounts when she was riding solo. Although riding was prohibited in the area where wild animals roamed free, the roars from the zoo could be heard for miles around. On one occasion, Devon and Sydney while horseback riding had encountered a rattlesnake baking in the heat of the afternoon sun. Eskimo, in the lead, had stopped, then slowly backed away from the deadly creature, but he had not panicked.

Since then, however, Devon always rode with a revolver in a hip holster. She would have preferred a shotgun, but had ultimately decided that the revolver, while less lethal, would be easier to handle in an emergency.

As she had foreseen, Devon could hear the screeching of the big apes that Hearst kept not too far from the human residences. The caged animals were accessible by horseback and by foot, and the small zoo was a favorite stop for Hearst's guests. On this particular morning, the apes seemed to be screeching even more than usual, and Devon found the noise disturbing. As she drew closer, she also heard the sound of human laughter, but a curve in the trail prevented her from seeing what was happening.

Then another round of earsplitting shrieks from the apes pierced the air, followed by the sound of clanging metal. The people laughed even more loudly. Devon wondered what the noise was about. As she rounded the bend in the trail, the cages came into view. In front of a family of chimpanzees — male, female, and a baby — she saw several people she had met on the previous evening's train ride: four men, two of them actors, one of them a studio head, and one of them a director. With them was an alluring young woman whom Devon did not recall meeting. She showed off her marvelous figure with a pair of white shorts and a white halter top. All her companions seemed enthralled with her. None of the group was aware of Devon's presence behind them.

The five revelers were standing directly in front of the chimpanzee cage, close enough to disturb the animals but too far away to endanger themselves. On the ground were two empty bottles of champagne and an ice bucket containing a third bottle.

"More champagne, Bebe?" yelled one of the actors, reaching for the bottle in the ice bucket.

The young woman held out her glass for the refill. The other actor slid his hand around the girl's waist, then down to her firm buttocks. She did not acknowledge the contact but went on pointing to the animals and talking.

Bebe. The nickname was familiar to Devon. She wondered if the girl was Bebe Henley. If so, Devon was slightly acquainted with the girl's family in New York and recalled the girl's debut two years before. Since then, she knew the girl had been classified as "wild" by New York society. As though to confirm this, Bebe turned to the director and gave him a long kiss, rubbing her body against his invitingly. The actor who had been holding her did not show annoyance but simply leaned against her rear, resting his head on the back of her shoulders and rubbing the backs of her thighs and buttocks.

Devon started to urge her horse onward, not wishing to intrude on the boozy, wanton scene. Suddenly, the sound of agonized screeches from the chimpanzees stopped Eskimo in his tracks. Devon turned to face the group. The studio head, probably annoyed at being ignored by

Bebe, was picking up a stone and preparing to throw it at the cage. Apparently a previous stone — the cause of the screams — had hit its mark, because the baby chimpanzee had a cut above its left ear and the mother was frantically screaming while the father rattled the cage with his strong arms.

Bebe pointed at a sign affixed to the cage. DO NOT TEASE THE ANIMALS, it said. She laughed and threw her champagne glass at the sign, but it missed its mark and shattered against the iron bars. Most of the glass fell harmlessly on the ground outside the cage, but some fell inside. The furious male chimpanzee picked up a handful of the stuff and threw it at his tormentors, who raised their arms to shield themselves. Now the ape screamed in pain at the cuts on his palm, jumping up and down as he vocalized.

At first the entire group, unhurt by the flying glass, stared in stupefaction at the ape, then Bebe let out a peal of laughter that seemed to act as a signal for the others. Appalled, Devon watched as one of the actors mimicked the movements of the injured animal. The other actor, wanting to go him one better, approached the cage and kicked it, backing away quickly as the chimpanzee rushed toward him.

Fury and disgust took hold of Devon. Charging on Eskimo into the middle of the drunken group, she yelled, "Stop it!"

The group scattered at the vision of the avenging woman, black hair gleaming around her shoulders as she flew at them astride the big white horse. She brought the animal to a halt so abrupt that he reared up on his hind legs before settling down in a cyclone of dust.

"You are disgusting!" Devon spat at no one person in particular. "How dare you torment an innocent animal."

The shocked group was silent for a few moments. Bebe regained her composure first and, glaring up at Devon, said challengingly, "How dare you tell us what to do?"

Devon turned toward her, contempt radiating from her aquamarine eyes. "I dare because I'm right! You should be ashamed to torment something that can't defend itself!" Devon let her eyes travel from one member of the group to the other as she said this, forcing them to meet her eyes. One by one, the men dropped their gazes before Devon's implacable one. She could see that they were indeed ashamed of their behavior, or at least ashamed at being caught.

Bebe, on the other hand, refused to drop her gaze. "I don't have to do what you say," she taunted childishly. She picked up another rock and turned toward the animal cage.

Devon turned to the men, each of whom was staring at the ground.

"Gentlemen," she commanded in a tone that brooked no contradiction, "either you control your companion or I will."

The men looked up at Devon. They saw her gun. They saw her riding crop. Devon made no move to use either, but something in her attitude convinced the men that she would do whatever was necessary to stop the destructive girl. They had no doubt that she would win this battle, one way or the other.

The studio head gently took Bebe's arm. "C'mon, honey, let's cool off with a swim." The young woman started to shake him off in irritation, but the director came to the other side of her and grasped her elbow forcefully, leading her toward the dirt path.

Devon stood in front of the chimpanzee cages, watching the group go. Just as Bebe reached the path, she turned and faced Devon. She didn't say anything to her; rather, she seemed to be trying to memorize Devon's face. Then, with a contemptuous toss of her head, she turned back to her companions and strutted up the path.

John stretched and opened his eyes. For a moment, the sight of the crimson and gold brocade canopy above the bed disoriented him, and it took him a few seconds to remember that he was at the Hearst ranch. The space beside him was rumpled but empty. Devon must have gone riding, John concluded. Rolling over to look at his pocket watch on the bedside table, he saw that it was one-thirty in the afternoon.

"Good, almost time for lunch," he murmured to himself.

He decided to forego bathing because he intended to have a swim. He pulled on a pair of cream-colored linen slacks and a blue shirt and made his way to the Neptune Pool. In the cabana, he chose a new swimming suit from the selection Hearst always kept on hand for his guests, slipped a terrycloth robe over it, and handed his clothes to the valet who manned the dressing room.

Emerging into the pool area, he squinted at the bright sunlight and looked around for someone he knew. He spotted Sydney and Bart, apparently asleep on lounge chairs, and walked toward them. Quietly, so as not to awaken them, he eased onto a lounge chair next to Bart, took off his robe, and closed his eyes. But a few moments later, the sounds of an argument caught his attention.

Coming into the pool area was one of the most stunning women he had ever seen. She was accompanied by four men, one on either side of her, two lagging slightly behind. Taller than either man at her side, she had endlessly long legs, which made her appear even taller. Thick, wavy blond hair spilled over her shoulders almost to her waist in a style that was not strictly fashionable, but which suited her to perfection. Her white shorts and halter top revealed a figure that was curvaceous but not so full that it could be called voluptuous.

The woman was heatedly berating the men at her side. "You should have defended me!" she said angrily.

A short fat man, who John thought he recognized as the head of Crown Studios, replied in an exasperated tone, "Look, forget about it. It's not important."

John saw one of the two stragglers go over to the barman by the side of the pool and place an order. Meanwhile, the group settled at a table underneath a blue and white umbrella.

The woman was apparently unwilling to let the dispute drop. Even after the barman had filled five champagne flutes with the chilled wine and brought them over to the table, she continued.

"There were five of us and one of her. But you all caved in like a bunch of little boys! What kind of men are you anyway!" she said scornfully.

John put on his sunglasses so he could observe the group without appearing to. He was often intrigued by the dramas that played themselves out at the Hearst ranch. Guests there, insulated from the real world, seemed to lose their inhibitions. They were like a group of teenagers away at camp: hungry to experience everything, to play, to act wild, and to suffer none of the consequences for doing so.

The woman looked vaguely familiar to John, but he could not place her. He smiled to himself as he realized how he had changed since his single days. As a bachelor, he would have surely remembered the details of a meeting with someone as attractive as the blonde.

Suddenly she scraped her chair back from the table, stood up, walked to the water's edge, and jumped into the swimming pool. Doing an angry crawl, she swam down the length of the pool toward John and his friends. Reaching his end, she placed her hands on the edge of the pool surround and hoisted herself out of the water. She stood for a moment directly before John, the flimsy white cloth of her shorts and halter top clinging to her, revealing every detail of the firm body underneath. Her pert, pink-tipped breasts pointed out through the transparent fabric, erect from the coolness of the water. The girl lifted her arms to push her long hair away from her face, closing her eyes and turning her face to the sun. She turned back toward the pool, holding her hair over the water and squeezing. He had a perfect view of her tight buttocks, visible through the wet material.

She turned to face John again. Handsome, she thought. "Hello," she said.

"Hello." John looked over at Bart and Sydney. Bart was snoring now, fast asleep under the noonday sun. Sydney had not moved since John's arrival. The sight of his friends made him think of Devon and he guiltily averted his eyes from the young woman's body.

"Bebe Henley," she said, walking toward him with her hand outstretched.

"Bebe Henley?" John, startled, politely scrambled to his feet. "But I remember you as a little girl!" He smiled broadly, taking her hand and shaking it heartily. "I'm John Alexander. Your father and I had some business together a few years back. You probably don't remember me."

"John Alexander!" said Bebe with a laugh. "I won't believe it's you until you take off those awful sunglasses. I remember you had the most devastating blue eyes. I had a mad crush on you, I want you to know."

John obediently removed the glasses. Bebe took a step closer to John, not releasing his hand. He was disconcertingly aware of her naked body through the thin cloth.

"Yes, it's really you. And your eyes are more devastating than ever," she purred.

John was torn between wanting to flirt back and the realization that he should stop. The last time he had seen Bebe, she had been an awkward adolescent, much too tall for her age and with a slight case of acne. Five years had vastly changed her.

Before he could respond, Bebe asked, "May I join you?"

"How rude of me not to have offered. It would be a pleasure," John said, feeling clumsy and a little flustered. He realized that he had not really flirted with a woman since his engagement to Devon. He hadn't been particularly interested in flirting. But there was something exciting in the idea that this woman — girl, he reminded himself — clearly found him attractive. He knew it was a game he should immediately end, but he enjoyed it. I'm not actually *doing* anything, after all, he told himself.

As graceful as a cat, Bebe reclined into a chair, stretching her hands over her head. John sat down next to her.

"How is your father?" John asked, feeling obligated to channel the discussion in a more serious direction.

"Angry at me all the time, I'm afraid." Bebe sighed.

"Oh?" answered John noncommittally.

"I stand accused of ruining the family name with my antics," she said sardonically.

John vaguely remembered hearing some gossip about his old acquaintance's daughter, but could not recall its content.

"I can't believe you would do such a thing," he said with a laugh that showed his startling white teeth against his bronzed skin.

"Oh, I'm guilty as charged," she admitted playfully. She turned on her side, once more giving him a full view of her body.

John did not reply. He had an uncomfortable certainty the game had gone far enough.

He replaced his sunglasses, though he knew it was impolite to do so. She's just a child, he told himself, heady with her power over men. And you've seen too many like her to take her seriously. "If you'll excuse me, I believe I'll go and change for lunch," John said formally, gathering up his terrycloth robe from the table that separated his lounge chair from that of the still-snoring Bart.

Bebe immediately sensed John's mood change and, slightly piqued, rose abruptly to leave. "I'll just rejoin my friends," she said, and coolly put out her hand for John to shake.

John jumped up and took her hand, shaking it more warmly than necessary because he felt guilty for his sudden change in tone. After all, he told himself, I don't need to be rude. Before he could complete the thought, Bebe had turned and walked away.

John put on his robe and tied it. He glanced at his snoozing friends, somehow glad that they had not witnessed his encounter with Bebe.

As he passed Sydney's chair on the way to the cabana, a low suggestive voice followed him. "Careful, honey, that little kitty has big claws."

John turned in surprise and stared at Sydney. She looked asleep; she didn't move from her prone position on the lounge chair.

John wrapped his arms around Devon, admiring her reflection in the mirror. As was often the case, Marion Davies had decided to organize a theme costume ball, and Devon and John had thrown themselves into the spirit of it. The theme of the ball was ancient times. Easy enough for the men, who had mostly chosen to wear togalike garments that they hoped approximated ancient Greece. A bit more difficult for the women, who seemed split between ancient Egypt and ancient Greece.

Devon had chosen ancient Egypt, and was wearing dramatic eye makeup in the style associated with Cleopatra. Alice had devised a headdress using a gold band to encircle Devon's head; from the band hung gold lamé so fine that it floated behind her like a veil when she walked. Her strapless dress was of the same material and it wrapped around her in a way that showed off her tiny waist and full breasts. Gold sandals and two thick gold cuffs completed the ensemble. With her shining black hair and her light golden tan, Devon looked convincingly exotic.

"I feel absolutely ridiculous in this getup, but you look gorgeous," John said. He lowered his head to her shoulder and teasingly nipped it. "I missed you today," he murmured as he slid his hands over her breasts, cupping one in each hand. He lightly stroked Devon's nipples until they stood erect, clearly visible through the gold cloth.

"Stop that!" she said throatily, but she made no move to disengage herself. She could feel his hardness against her buttocks and she leaned against him.

"Please," John moaned, "I'm not sure what this toga will or won't reveal, but I feel quite vulnerable in it."

Devon turned to face him. She reached up and drew his head to her, giving him a lingering kiss. The movement of his tongue inside her mouth sent erotic shivers through her body. "It's tantalizing to think that you're almost naked under that," she said breathlessly. "All I have to do is reach up . . ." She lightly ran her fingernails up his muscled thighs, eased his underwear down, then sank on her knees in front of him.

John gasped as she enclosed him in her warm mouth. "We don't have time . . ." he said in an unconvincing attempt to stop her.

Devon drew away from him for a moment. "You don't need much time," she replied with a smirk. She found the easy access to him afforded by the costume incredibly exciting. She swirled her tongue around his member, enjoying his helplessness in the face of her seduction.

He closed his eyes and abandoned himself utterly to the pleasure she aroused in him. She cupped his buttocks with her hands, pulling him into her. As his excitement rose to a climax, he half opened his eyes. In the mirror, he saw their forms reflected. The image drove him over the edge until he felt his knees weaken and the hot juice come spurting out of him.

Devon cradled him in her hands until she heard his breathing return to normal. Then she stood and straightened their clothes. John drew her to him tenderly. "I love you so much," he said.

"I love you, too." Devon kissed him lightly, then stepped away from him, moving toward the bathroom. "But we'd better finish getting ready."

A knock on the door interrupted them. "Come in," Devon called.

Alice entered with a wreath of eucalyptus leaves. "I wove these for Mr. John," she said with a smile. "I thought they'd set off his costume very nicely."

"Alice, you are a she-devil," John accused her with a broad laugh.

"I?" replied Alice, in a tone of complete innocence.

"I think I should refuse to wear that."

"As you wish, sir," said Alice, playfully sinking into a deep curtsy. "Pay no attention to the labors of those who serve you with devotion."

"Get up, you wench, and send my valet in to help me with this ridiculous contrivance."

Devon beamed from one to the other. She was glad that Alice and John enjoyed each other's sense of humor so much, for she loved them both dearly. She sighed in perfect contentment.

When Devon emerged from the bathroom, she found John alone in the room holding the wreath on his head and looking in the mirror with a frown.

Well, don't spend forever preening," Devon joked, "or we'll be late for the ball."

"Better yet, let's sneak out of here while Alice is fetching Wilkes. That way, I won't have to wear this blasted thing." So, giggling like two children, Devon and John quietly slipped out of Casa del Mar.

Light and music poured out of the open windows of the assembly hall in Casa Grande. The huge medieval-style room was lit with giant *torchères,* the flames adding romance and mystery to the surroundings. The immense carved wood ceiling provided a dramatic counterpoint to the lustrous tapestries that lined the walls. The effect was one of grandeur, further emphasized by the priceless paintings, sculptures, and other treasures that filled the room.

"In the daytime this room seems gloomy, but it absolutely shines at night," Devon said dreamily. John nodded his agreement and took her hand as they joined the group of partygoers. It seemed that more guests had arrived during the day, so that the room, much too large to be actually crowded, was abustle with dancing and merrymaking.

"Even Gary Cooper looks silly in a toga," John commented wryly.

"Well . . ." said Devon in mock hesitation. "Okay . . . I'll grant you that."

A passing waiter offered the couple glasses of champagne, which they took.

"Shall we get a bite to eat?" John asked Devon. She nodded in agreement and followed John as he made his way to the adjoining room. They stopped numerous times to greet fellow revelers before they reached the huge banquet hall, with its three long tables almost hidden under an extraordinary array of delicacies, along with more pedestrian fare. William Randolph Hearst enjoyed entertaining and was pleased to offer his guests the most exotic dishes, but he preferred more simple food himself. As a result, mixed in with the smoked quail and the medallions of venison with truffles and port wine sauce were meat loaf and potato salad. And, as always, bottles of ketchup were placed at regular intervals along the length of the table.

"Devon, John, how are you?" Their host greeted them heartily as he balanced a plate filled with ketchup-covered meat loaf, coleslaw, and lima beans.

"Wonderful party, W.R," John said. "Where's the lovely Miss Davies?"

"Oh, she's around here somewhere. Look for a Roman slave girl."

After a few more greetings and some sampling from the delicious buffet, Devon and John returned to the assembly hall, drawn by the sound of the band. A lindy hop left the couple breathless, but their heart rates slowed to normal after a soothing waltz. There was a pause between melodies and John and Devon each took another glass of the proffered champagne.

Devon was facing John, talking to him, when she heard a voice coming from over her shoulder.

"John? Once again I almost didn't recognize you."

Devon turned with a smile, but her expression froze when she saw who had spoken. It was the tall, blond girl who had been teasing the chimpanzees. In contrast to her earlier coarse behavior, the blonde's breathtaking face was aglow with a charming smile. She was clad in a white satin toga that set off her tan and her silken blond hair. A golden belt at the waist was the only adornment she wore, and it was all she needed; in that way, nothing detracted from the perfect shape of her breasts and hips. Devon noticed that like many of the other women present, the girl was braless, her erect nipples highlighted by the shimmer of the white cloth.

Devon's gaze traveled from the girl to John. She noticed that he was beaming at the vision before them and that the girl was looking up at him with an expression that was a mixture of respect and coyness.

"Devon, have you met —"

"We've met." Devon cut John off, her voice icy. John turned to look at his wife, puzzled.

The young woman, her face a mask of innocence, looked questioningly from Devon to John. "Have I intruded?"

"Not at all," John said with a heartiness that he hoped would gloss over Devon's inexplicable hostility. "I'd like to introduce you to my wife, Devon."

"Your . . ." The woman raised one eyebrow, and, after a pause, uttered the word, "Wife? Well," she said, seeming to recover from her surprise, "how nice to meet you. I'm Bebe Henley." She put out a hand to Devon.

For a split second, Devon thought about refusing the gesture, but it went against her innate good breeding to do so. She took the young woman's hand and shook it as briefly as possible.

"How do you do," she said flatly.

"Lovely, thank you," said Bebe, her voice honeyed.

John turned toward Devon and said, "Bebe's father is an old friend of mine." He felt terribly uncomfortable, though he was not quite sure why.

As the band struck up a romantic Cole Porter tune, Bebe turned to Devon and said, "Would you mind terribly if I stole your husband . . . just for this one dance?"

"What was I supposed to do? Refuse to dance with her?" John demanded, slamming the door to their Casa del Mar suite in exasperation.

"Don't slam that door. There are other people here," Devon said coldly.

"Screw the door," John said, deliberately using the profanity to vex his wife, who he felt was being unreasonable, "and answer me."

"It was not the dance that I objected to. It was the fact that you allowed her to plaster herself against you while you were doing it."

Devon hated herself for showing the jealousy she felt for Bebe Henley. But there was something disturbing about John's reaction to her. Other women had flirted with her husband since their marriage, but John had always appeared oblivious to them. That had not been his attitude toward Bebe, however. He had obviously enjoyed the young woman's admiration — seemed stimulated by it. Devon knew he cared nothing for the girl. Still, every factor in the equation added to her fury.

After the initial dance, the band had gone on to play a waltz, then a tango. Altogether, John and Bebe had shared four dances as Devon looked on and fumed. She had concealed her anger in front of their friends, but had avoided John as much as possible for the rest of the evening. And it seemed that every time she looked up, Bebe was beside him. It was only on their way back to Casa del Mar that Devon had the opportunity to explain to John the basis for her dislike of the young woman — a dislike that in a few short hours had blossomed into something akin to hatred. The passion of her anger disturbed her, made her feel weak.

"Look," said John in a conciliatory tone, "I can certainly understand why you're disgusted by Bebe's behavior this morning. I would have been too. But you can't judge someone by just one incident. Maybe she had a bit too much to drink."

"How can you say that? What circumstance justifies cruelty to animals? You always speak out against it. Why are you now excusing it just because it's Bebe Henley?"

"I'm not excusing it. I'm just trying to say that there may be an explanation. She seemed perfectly well behaved this evening."

Devon found the forced reasonableness of John's tone particularly irritating. "Please don't speak to me as though I'm a mental patient that has to be humored," Devon said coldly.

"I didn't say anyth—"

"I'm talking about your tone," she snapped. Taking a deep breath, she began again, speaking deliberately and calmly. "I find your behavior toward this woman offensive because it's different from the way you've treated other women who have flirted with you. I'm not stupid, John, I could see that you enjoyed the attention she gave you. But most of all, I don't appreciate that you would excuse behavior in her that you would condemn in anyone else."

"That's ridiculous!" John lost control again, his voice rising in anger. "She's nothing to me and I don't excuse anything. I'm just not so judgmental as you are."

Devon turned her back on John, trying to keep her anger under control. She already regretted the fact that she was showing jealousy over someone she knew was of no importance. It was probably wise to drop the matter, or to act nonchalant about the small flirtation. It was just a *small* flirtation, after all. Yet she found it abhorrent that she and John could disagree so violently on their opinions of another person's behavior.

"I guess I expected you to share my opinion of her now that I've told you what she did," Devon said bitterly.

"I agree that the act was terrible, but that doesn't mean that the whole person is."

"Well, I just don't see how you can separate the two, but I suppose there's no point in discussing it further since it's apparent that we disagree." Devon picked up her silk peignoir and went into the bathroom, closing the door behind her.

John stared at the closed door, tempted to knock on it and demand that Devon come out and give him a chance to respond. But what can I possibly say? John asked himself. I *did* flirt with Bebe. I *did* enjoy dancing with her. She's an enticing woman. I love Devon, but that doesn't mean that I never notice other women. Anyhow, he told himself, it would be best if I just avoided Bebe in the future.

But that would prove to be a more difficult task than he had anticipated.

CHAPTER 20

LIKE all racing Thoroughbreds', Firefly's birthday was officially January 1. She would be three years old, which made her eligible to enter the Kentucky Derby.

"Fillies don't win the Derby," Willy insisted. He and Devon were in Willy's small office, standing almost nose to nose arguing. The room was chilly, but Willy and Devon, both concentrating on keeping their tempers under control, were oblivious to the temperature.

"Firefly was our biggest money-winner last year," Devon pointed out. Willy was overgeneralizing, Devon thought. It was true that fillies were not usually the champions that colts were. Fillies had a tendency to deliberately slow down when challenged by colts, a timeless instinct originating from life in wild herds, where a stallion always took charge of a harem of mares. But such was not the case with all fillies, and Firefly was proof of that, Devon believed.

"Aye, she won a lot. But mostly in all-filly races."

"But not always. She won a race at Saratoga last summer against colts. And one at Pimlico."

"That was different and you know it. We weren't really challenging her, we were just testing to see how she'd do."

"And she did marvelously!" Devon said victoriously.

"Look, Miz Alexander," Willy said, fixing Devon with a baleful glare, "only one filly has ever won the Derby in all these years."

"Well, this year will make it two," declared Devon.

"I happen to think that we've got a better chance with Fearless Leader. But maybe you don't care what I think," Willy harrumphed.

Devon glared back at him. She was exasperated, but afraid of saying anything to antagonize him further. She knew that in the past several months she had pushed the limits of his tolerance. He had flatly stated when they had bought the farm that he would brook no interference from owners in the day-to-day handling of the horses. Well, he had put up with more involvement from Devon than many trainers would have, she admitted to herself. At the same time, Devon's input had been of value. She had served well as an assistant trainer and exercise rider, and Willy knew it, though he would never admit it aloud. Still, Devon knew he knew it. And that he had developed a certain grudging respect for her.

"I tell you what," Devon said in a more conciliatory tone, "let's see how they do this spring. We'll let the Blue Grass Stakes be the deadline. We can decide after that. It's only February, so we have some time. But let's treat them both as though they were going to the Derby."

"I've got no problem with that," Willy conceded, his tone still gruff. "But I only want to put one horse in the Derby. The operation's just getting up to speed again and I don't want us to spread ourselves too thin."

Devon knew that many of the top racing farms often entered more than one horse in the same race. In such cases, a bettor on one horse would win — even if his horse lost — if the other horse from the same stable placed in the race. For the owner, it heightened the chances of winning purse money. Sometimes an owner's stock would place in more than one winning position, thus winning not only first-place prize money, for example, but also second- or third-place money. On the other hand, many owners considered dual entries a waste of horsepower and money because only one horse could win first place.

Although there were pros and cons to entering horses in the same race, Devon on this occasion could see Willy's point. It would be the first Derby for the renewed Willowbrook Farm, and it was important to regain the racing world's faith in the name. For only with that faith would the farm become once again a viable breeding operation. And it was breeding, not racing, that provided the steady, predictable income vital to a profitable racing stable.

"I agree to those terms," Devon said, "and I have another proposal." For the first time since their conversation had begun, a smile played around Devon's lips. "I'll be the lead trainer on Firefly, you on Fearless Leader."

Willy, riled again, barked, "I can't have that!"

"Why not?" Devon asked innocently.

"Because I'm the trainer!" he almost shouted.

"Are you saying I'm incapable?" Devon's voice rose.

"I'm not saying anything about you! It's a question of authority in the paddock."

"Do you think this will lead to defiance on the part of the men here?" Devon asked in a tone that implied that the notion was ridiculous.

Willy suddenly quieted down. He pulled hard on the bill of his baseball cap so that it pushed his ears out in a comical way. But Willy's stormy demeanor firmly stifled any amused reaction from Devon. In a deadly serious tone he said, "I think it will lead to divided loyalties. I can't operate that way."

Devon stared at him a moment, trying to think of a response. Once again, she could see his point.

"I see what you mean," she acknowledged. Then she had an idea. "Look, suppose I commandeer just one exercise rider. Until Kentucky he'll work just with Firefly and some of the other horses, but not with

Fearless Leader. That way, there won't be two people putting demands on him."

"I still think this is a recipe for trouble. That makes it look like if anyone here has a problem with something I tell them, they can go to you. You told me I was the boss of the day-to-day operation here. I don't see how the men can believe that if you're over there running a separate little training operation."

Devon mulled this over for a moment. She needed Willy. She was beginning to see that one day they might have a showdown, but it would be disastrous if that occurred now, before the Derby.

Finally, she said, "Then I have another idea. If we choose to run Fearless Leader, I'll step out of the picture for a few weeks. Go to New York. You'll have your man back full-time and it will be clear that I'm no longer involved in the Derby training."

"What if it looks like Firefly should run the Derby?"

"We collaborate on her training."

The challenge intrigued Willy. Though there were many variables other than training that went into the making of a racehorse, the exercise would primarily be a chance to pit his training skills against those of Devon. He felt that she had a talent for training. He respected her skills even more than she knew, which was the only reason he was able to tolerate her daily presence at the stables. At the same time, he was eager to prove that his horse was better, so that once and for all, Devon would be forced to admit to either his superior mastery of the horses or his superior judgment — Willy didn't care which. He only knew that he wanted her to withdraw to the same comfortable distance that most owners maintained from the daily workings of their racing operations.

Now she was offering him a chance to prove beyond any doubt that he was the authority on the racing operation. She was less experienced than he and had a further handicap in that she was choosing to back a filly. He could think of only one real objection to the arrangement, and he could see many advantages if his horse turned out to be the better one, as he was certain that it would.

He brought up the point that was bothering him. "I'll do this under one condition," Willy said, indicating by his tone that there would be no negotiation on the condition.

Devon raised her eyebrows expectantly.

"I choose which horse runs," he said in the tone of one who anticipates trouble.

Devon thought for a moment. It would be an act of considerable trust to allow Willy to choose between a horse she trained and one that he trained. But to give him that authority would help to assuage his doubts about her involvement in the racing operation. Furthermore, she did not believe that he would allow his ego to control his professional responsibility. He wanted Willowbrook Farm to win the Derby, and it didn't matter which horse did it.

"All right, I agree," Devon said finally. "And as to my exercise rider, I pick Jeremiah."

"Jeremiah! But he's my best man!" Willy objected.

"And you'll still have him. For every horse except Fearless Leader. Look," Devon added, "I have a handicap in that I've chosen a filly. You've already acknowledged that. I know you believe in fair play, so you should give me a chance to even it out by loaning me Jeremiah."

"I can't do that. Anyhow, you've acted as your own exercise rider until now. Why not go on?"

"I've acted as *your* exercise rider," Devon corrected him. "You know I can't be Firefly's head trainer and exercise rider all at once. How can I watch what she's doing if I'm on her?"

"Oh, all right." Willy threw up his hands in exasperation. "Take Jeremiah! I'll use Henry on Fearless Leader."

"Good," Devon said calmly.

"Fine," said Willy in a frustrated tone.

"See you later," Devon said, her hand on the doorknob. She exited and closed the door softly behind her.

"That's the problem," Willy mumbled under his breath.

John was proud of Devon's capability with horses. But it annoyed him that she often refused to go to Manhattan with him because she did not want to leave her activities at Willowbrook. It was a source of frequent arguments between them, and John was beginning to find himself almost jealous of Firefly and other aspects of Devon's life in Virginia, although he told himself he was silly to feel that way.

"It's only until the Derby," Devon often assured him. But he knew that she was hooked on racing, and that she would always find more satisfaction in life at Willowbrook than in New York City.

"Don't you miss the opera and the theater, all our friends?" John would ask wistfully.

The fact was that Devon did not. She loved the country, John loved the city. She had many friends in Fauquier County. But John found them staid in comparison to the faster New York set. Many of their New York friends, in fact, owned farms in the Virginia countryside, but none of them insisted, as Devon did, on spending more than a few weeks at a time on them.

"If you don't miss New York, I at least hope that you miss me," said John one night during a long-distance telephone call from his office.

"Of course I do," Devon assured him. And she did. Very much. But she had many activities to fill her days and she had her family and friends to fill her evenings. She missed John's warm touch beside her in bed. She missed his advice and companionship. But she was too busy to dwell on his absences for long — and John sensed it.

"Devon, I'm lonely for you," John said.

"Me too. When can you come home?"

"*This* is home, too. Home is where we are. Together."

Devon had no reply. She had never thought of New York as home.

"Devon, are you still there?" John asked, exasperated.

"Yes . . ." Devon thought for a moment of her parents, her friends. Of Grace and Philip. In every successful marriage, it seemed that wives followed their husbands, centered their lives on them. Devon's independence more closely resembled her actress friends' — whose marriages usually ended in divorce. She thought about the few New York friends who lived separately from their husbands. There were a handful of such liaisons, but those were loveless marriages that also ended in divorce more often than not. Devon did not want that for herself and John. Yet she could not think of a woman she knew who led a life independent of her husband's and yet still managed to sustain a loving, viable marriage. Devon realized that she would have to make a choice: adhere to the role society had dictated was hers or risk losing her husband because of her refusal to do so.

"John, I understand your frustration and I believe that you're right to feel that way." Devon sighed.

John heard the disappointment in his wife's voice and it hurt him. Why wasn't he enough for her? How could her interests in Virginia be more important than he was? He understood that Devon would capitulate to his wishes, but he felt that it could prove to be a hollow victory if she was unhappy doing so.

"Darling, don't be sad. I won't insist that you join me here before the Derby. All I ask is that afterward you put all that aside for a while and just spend some time with me and our friends."

"You don't want to spend summer in the city, do you?" Devon asked, incredulous. None of their friends ever summered in New York. Most went to Newport in June and July, then to Saratoga for the August racing season. Some went to Europe, and a handful went to their estates in Virginia. But not New York City in summer!

"Of course not. I'd like you to come to New York in May after the Derby. Then we've been invited to the Vanderbilts' for the last two weeks in June and to Sydney and Bart's for July. You don't have any objection to accepting those invitations, do you?"

"No . . ." Devon hesitated. "But won't we spend any time this summer at Willowbrook? There's so much I need to do here and—"

"Darling, I have no intention of renouncing Willowbrook and I never meant for you to get that impression. I simply enjoy spending time with our friends and I don't want to miss the entire Newport season on account of Willowbrook."

"Oh . . ." Devon sighed, this time with relief. "Could we spend the first two weeks in June here?"

"Of course," said John warmly, happy now that Devon had agreed to his plan. He looked forward to a summer filled with long days of sailing, tennis, and golf and the nights of sumptuous dinners and parties. He was a gregarious man who enjoyed his friends. He often felt restless when Devon and he spent quiet evenings at home, whereas Devon could go weeks on end without socializing with anyone but family and the most intimate friends. He resolved to see to it that Devon had the most amusing summer of her life.

Devon knew that Firefly had the breeding, the gait, and the physical ability to win races. These factors were already established and beyond Devon's control. But there were two very important factors that she could, to a great degree, control: training and surveillance of Firefly's health. Finally, Firefly had the handicap of being a filly, a variable that Devon could not control but *could* manipulate.

Because Devon did not possess many hard-and-fast beliefs about Thoroughbred training, she was free to let her imagination explore unconventional possibilities. What she decided was to train Firefly to win by having her become accustomed to winning.

As Devon had pointed out to Willy, Firefly had won several races the previous year, but Willy had not entered her in any top competitions because it was important to his pride to resurrect Willowbrook as a revenue-generating enterprise. He had thus entered her in races that he believed she had a good chance of winning, rather than those in which she would be challenged.

But Thoroughbred training involved challenging horses to the utmost. Willy and most other experts trained their horses by a combination of running them alone and running them against challenging competition. Devon's training theory, however, was based on her knowledge of horses in the wild. She knew that horses survived by staying close to the herd; thus the winner of a horserace was most often an animal that has stayed in the middle of the pack, or close to it, until the end, when the whip of the jockey urged him forward. A natural pack leader, though, would try to pull ahead of other horses; it was his instinct to do so. And in the wild, stallions were pack leaders. A filly's instinct, especially as she aged, was the opposite. Devon concluded that Firefly could only become a Derby winner through careful reconditioning — by competing against and beating colts on a regular basis. Devon hoped that Firefly's victories the previous year would provide a good foundation upon which to base future training. So, instead of urging the colts Firefly competed against to run faster, Devon would place Firefly in a field of three colts, surrounding her, and she would instruct the exercise riders to hold their colts back to the degree that Firefly would remain part of the pack but still win.

While Firefly, like all racehorses, was kept in her stall almost all day so as to conserve her energy, her competitors were allowed to run free over the vast Willowbrook acreage. Firefly would emerge from her stall each day explosive and ready to vent her suppressed energy. The colts, on the other hand, were free to do so all day. Almost from the first, the tactic worked remarkably well. Her time was better than that of Fearless Leader's no matter what distance was run. So much so that Willy did not know what to make of the phenomenon.

"Fearless Leader is a mudder," Jeremiah commented one day as he slowly walked Firefly around a corral to cool her down, Devon in step beside him. Normally, a junior stable employee, called a hot walker, performed the task, but Jeremiah and Devon preferred to handle almost every aspect of Firefly's training themselves. They were afraid that the hot walkers would shortchange Firefly's cool-down time, and as a result leave her stiff and sore. "That was fine when the weather was so wet last fall, but it's been dry most of this winter and Firefly, she likes a dry track."

"But what are we going to do when the spring rains come?" Devon asked.

"That I don't know, ma'am. It's not that Firefly can't run a muddy track. It's that Fearless Leader loves it."

"After all," Devon said, "Fearless Leader is my horse too. It really doesn't matter if he does better. As long as one of them is Derby material."

Jeremiah gave her a sidelong look with his intelligent brown eyes. He smiled sympathetically and said, "Yes, ma'am."

Devon could not resist laughing out loud at his careful diplomacy, and the young man responded with a handsome flash of white teeth against chocolate skin.

"Jeremiah, I want you to know that I'm very grateful for the hard work you've put into helping me with Firefly," Devon said in a more serious tone.

"Firefly's the long shot, ma'am. It's always good to see the long shot win," Jeremiah said with equal gravity. "If she wins, the payoff could be mighty sweet," he added reflectively. "With two strikes against her, the odds'll be high."

"Two strikes?" Devon asked, puzzled.

Jeremiah nervously looked away from her and pretended to concentrate on taking Firefly's pulse.

"Two strikes?" Devon repeated, forcing the young man to turn and meet her penetrating aqua eyes.

"Well, she's a filly and . . ."

"And?"

"And her trainer is a . . . a . . ." Jeremiah bent over Firefly's right front hoof, studying it carefully.

Devon put her hands on her hips and said in a tone that was half mocking but demanding all the same, "Young man, you stand up and look at me and tell me what you mean."

"Well . . . you're a lady . . . I mean, a lady trainer," Jeremiah blurted out.

Devon's dark brows came together, forming a furious scowl in her smooth alabaster forehead. Jeremiah bowed his head, awaiting her wrath.

"Jeremiah, do you think you ride as well as any man in this place?"

"Ma'am?" The young boy looked up, startled at the seeming change of subject.

"You heard me."

"I guess I ride as well as just about anyone," Jeremiah said tentatively.

"Then why aren't you training to be a jockey?" Devon asked.

Jeremiah looked at his employer, startled. "Well, ma'am, there haven't been any colored jockeys in years."

"Why not?"

Jeremiah searched for an answer, trying to arrive at one that he thought would be inoffensive to Devon.

Growing impatient, Devon said bluntly, "For no reason other than that you're colored, right?"

"I . . . I guess so . . . I don't rightly know, ma'am."

"Well, I'll make a deal with you, Jeremiah," Devon said. She waited a few seconds until he raised his brown eyes to meet her determined gaze.

"Ma'am?"

"You help me get Firefly into the Derby. I'll help you become a jockey."

A vivid smile spread over Jeremiah's face like sunshine. "Yes, ma'am!" he said excitedly.

Devon smiled broadly in return, then signaled for them to go to the paddock.

"And one more thing, Jeremiah."

"Yes, Miss Devon?"

Devon stopped in her tracks and turned once more to look squarely at Jeremiah. "It's no handicap that you're colored and it's no handicap that I'm a woman. Only fools think like that. And so much the better for us if they do. Because that makes our victory that much sweeter. And that makes them feel like even bigger fools when we do win."

CHAPTER 21

IT seemed as though a thousand dancing lights shone from the long Palladian windows that graced the front of the elder Alexanders' Fifth Avenue mansion. The air bore just a trace of warm weather on it, reminding visitors that spring would officially begin soon, despite the fact that it had snowed just two weeks before.

"Isn't it a perfect evening?" Devon sighed to her mother-in-law, who was carefully inspecting each dish to be set out for the vast buffet that would be served at midnight.

"We're lucky," said the elder Mrs. Alexander, smiling at her daughter-in-law. "But the most wonderful birthday gift for John will be your presence here."

Devon looked away guiltily at the words. Her mother-in-law's serene voice betrayed no hint of criticism, nor did her expression, but Devon's own discomfort with the subject led her to wonder if indeed gentle criticism had been intended. With an uncharacteristic lack of poise, Devon plucked at her crimson chiffon Schiaparelli gown. Victoria Alexander's absolute serenity sometimes unnerved her. It was difficult to tell what lay behind her sweet expression. She had always demonstrated great kindness toward Devon, and the younger woman knew that the Alexanders were pleased with their son's match. But lately, it seemed as though they, too, thought it wrong of her not to accompany her husband on all his travels.

Devon bit her tongue to keep from explaining the pact she had with John. After the Kentucky Derby, she kept reminding him.

Smoothly, Victoria Alexander changed the subject as she glided across the spotless white tile floor of the huge kitchen, delicately holding the sweeping skirt of her gray silk dress in one hand. "Do you think that John has guessed this is anything other than a family dinner?"

"I'm not certain. He seemed to be fishing for information this afternoon," Devon said with a significant look, "but I didn't give anything away."

"We've never done anything like this for him before. He probably would think it very out of character for us."

Devon suppressed a giggle. Indeed it was out of character for the staid Alexanders to host a surprise party and midnight supper for John's birthday. Their brand of entertainment usually consisted of dinner parties for no more than twelve; cocktails at seven, dinner at eight, home by the stroke of eleven.

Even the menu for John's birthday was completely different from that usually served at the Alexanders'. Well, Devon said to herself, Victoria *did* ask me what all John's favorite dishes were.

It was an odd question, Devon thought, for a mother to ask, and it demonstrated the remoteness that she had observed in the Alexanders' relationship with their son. It was clear that they loved John, but that they felt so far removed from the daily occurrences of their son's life that they did not know how to communicate with him. John had not lived with them, except during holidays, since he had been sent to boarding school at age twelve. As a result, they often treated him like a much-loved but distant relative.

Devon surveyed the lobster in brandy cream sauce, the rack of lamb, and the salmon *en croute*. Never had she seen any of these dishes served at the Alexanders'. Their dinner parties invariably featured a standing rib roast or a Virginia ham. Devon was touched by the effort her mother-in-law had put into John's birthday.

"I am absolutely certain John will be thrilled," Devon said with a glowing smile.

Victoria glanced up from her inspection of the delicacies and caught the look of genuine affection in Devon's eyes. She smiled back at her daughter-in-law, a slightly tremulous smile that — just for a split second — seemed to acknowledge her need for help when it came to her relations with her son. But the look of vulnerability was gone in a flash, for Victoria had been schooled all her life to hide weakness.

"What reason did you give for meeting John here rather than coming with him?" Victoria inquired, indicating with a gesture that it was time for them to depart the kitchen.

The butler held the door open for them, then followed the two ladies up the gracefully curved staircase to the third-floor ballroom. "I told him I was having cocktails with Sydney. You know she's leaving for Paris the day after tomorrow?" At a nod from Victoria, Devon continued. "She's my best friend here, so John knows I would want to catch up with her before she leaves."

"What a shame you are spending only a week here, my dear. We receive so many inquiries about you," said Victoria, again with no hint of admonishment.

This time, Devon felt compelled to explain. "I've promised John to accompany him everywhere this summer once the Kentucky Derby is run, but, of course, it's most unpleasant being separated so often until then."

Characteristically, Victoria did not answer. The rustling of their skirts as they climbed the stairs suddenly sounded very loud to Devon. But she too had been trained to maintain a calm facade, and she withstood the silence with no outward show of her discomfort.

The two women automatically stopped at the closed double doors that marked one of the two entries to the ballroom, waiting for the butler to open the doors for them.

"Thank you, Parker," Mrs. Alexander murmured as they stepped into the huge room, empty except for a row of small gilt chairs along each of three walls, and four long tables covered in white linen. Each table was punctuated by two-foot-high vermeil candelabra. The walnut-stained parquet gleamed like a mirror, reflecting the starry twinkle of the room's four massive crystal chandeliers. Hothouse jasmine was draped in garlands along the walls, imparting an exquisitely heady fragrance.

"It's absolutely splendid!" Devon breathed.

Victoria turned to her, a happy flush beginning to rise on the pale skin of her cheeks. "Do you think he will be pleased?"

Impulsively, Devon reached for her mother-in-law's hand and gave it a reassuring squeeze. "Of course he will!" She promptly released the hand, not certain if Victoria liked such contact. They had never touched, other than to give each other polite little pecks of greeting. But Devon knew it was no condemnation of her that this was so, for the Alexanders never touched one another, except in the same perfunctory way.

This time, however, Devon was surprised to feel Victoria's hand reach for hers and squeeze back. "Thank you," Victoria said quietly, though Devon was not sure why she was being thanked.

"Oh, there you are, Victoria." The cultured voice of John's father echoed through the expansive chamber. The two women turned and walked toward the gray-haired gentleman, a man as handsome as John but with none of his son's charismatic sexuality. "Aren't the guests scheduled to arrive soon?" he asked, pulling a fine gold watch from the waist pocket of his vest.

"I expect so," said Mrs. Alexander. "I just hope that John doesn't decide to come early, before all the guests are here, or it will spoil the surprise."

As if on cue, the front-door chimes sounded and the three Alexanders made their way to the gallery at the top of the stairs overlooking the main foyer. There they would receive their guests. Parker, meanwhile, had already stationed himself in the entrance foyer so that he could direct both staff and guests to where they should go. Three of the staff were assigned to relieve the ladies of their sumptuous furs and the men of their dark coats of cashmere, alpaca, or mohair.

Another retinue of servants, crisply uniformed in black and white, was ready to circulate among the guests with trays of cold hors d'oeuvres and champagne. The family's baronial dining hall would serve as the permanent station for the predinner buffet of hot appetizers. They were meant to ensure that no guests suffered from overintoxication while awaiting the heavier meal to be served at midnight.

Devon and her in-laws greeted wave after wave of guests. Many of them were young, so Devon knew they were John's friends, yet she had never met most of them. She was relieved when she spotted the familiar faces of Sydney and Bart.

"Who are all these people?" Devon whispered wryly to her friend.

"Your husband's friends," Sydney replied in a pointed fashion.

Even Sydney, modern-thinking Sydney, was critical of her long separations from John! Devon realized.

"Thank you so much for your help, dear," Victoria said to Devon's friend. Devon realized that Sydney must have compiled the guest list, since Devon, who had also contributed, did not know many of the people there.

Suddenly Devon spied a familiar face — a blond woman accompanied by a distinguished older gentleman.

"Horace, how are you?" said John's father, shaking the other man's hand heartily. Devon could tell that this was someone that the elder Alexanders had invited themselves. When the man stepped toward her, Devon had an unobscured view of the young woman — Bebe Henley!

The older gentleman was speaking to Devon now. "Horace Henley, my dear. A pleasure to see you again. You were only a girl last time I saw you and your parents."

Devon quickly focused her attention on him. He was a tall man whose blond hair was turning to white. In his stature and fine bone structure, Devon could see the marked resemblance to his daughter.

Now it was Bebe's turn to stand before her. Devon realized why she had not immediately recognized her. The young woman's long blond hair was pulled back into an intricately woven chignon at the nape of her neck and was covered with a diamond-studded snood. The hairdo made her look older, but more elegant. The intricacy of her hair decoration was offset by a starkly simple ivory silk gown, long-sleeved and perfectly straight. It was clear that Bebe Henley was a much more subdued person when her father was present, Devon thought.

"How do you do, Mrs. Alexander," Bebe Henley's voice rang out. The question was the socially correct one, but Bebe's eyes were defiant, as if to say, I know you detest my presence here, but there's nothing you can do about it.

Devon refused to react to the look, instead fixing the younger woman with the usual blandly welcoming expression of those faced with a long receiving line.

"How nice of you to come," she replied coolly, waiting the proper second or two before turning to the next guest. She would not give Bebe the satisfaction of snubbing her, for that would be to reveal that she felt some emotion toward her.

"Marion!" Devon exclaimed in surprise a few moments later, recognizing her hostess from La Cuesta Encantada. "I didn't dare hope that you would be able to make it."

"How could you even think for a moment that we would miss John's surprise party?" Marion chided, with a flash of her laughing blue eyes.

"How kind of you!" Devon said, enfolding her friend in a warm embrace.

Just as it seemed that all the guests had arrived, Parker came to inform Mr. Alexander that it was almost time for John to appear. Devon asked Sydney and Bart to help quiet their guests and direct them into the main salon and adjoining dining room, then Parker closed the carved mahogany double doors behind them so that John would not be alerted to the presence of the two hundred people there.

Devon, meanwhile, went downstairs to the white marble foyer to await her husband. As always when Devon knew she would see John, she felt an excited fluttering in her heart. She wondered idly if all her friends felt the same way about their husbands, or if the feeling was due to the very separations that were a subject of such criticism.

"Mr. Alexander has arrived, madam," Parker said in his rather haughty voice. Parker's absolutely immutable correctness sometimes tempted Devon into deliberately doing things that were just a bit *in*correct by his strict standards.

"I'll open the door for him, Parker," said Devon. And then I'll kiss him right here in front of you in the foyer, she added silently with a mischievous grin.

Hurrying toward the door, she threw it open so that the night breeze lifted the gossamer chiffon of her dress in a cloud around her knees.

"What a beautiful sight," exclaimed her husband.

Devon wrapped her bare arms around his neck and kissed him. John kissed her back until a movement at the corner of his eye alerted him to the presence of Parker. Gently disengaging himself from Devon, he stepped inside, closing the door behind him. Parker came forward to relieve him of his coat and hat.

"Well, are you ready for a delicious birthday dinner?" Devon asked.

"Let me guess," he whispered. "Standing rib roast, Yorkshire pudding, and, for dessert, English trifle."

"Close," Devon said, laughing, "very close."

"At least I can always count on some good claret," John said with a resigned sigh.

"Now behave. Your parents want very much for you to enjoy this evening."

"Who else have they invited?"

"Well, let's see, there's Mrs. Whitney, Mr. Stanhope-Carruthers, Sydney and Bart."

"Sounds fine so far."

"There's Charlie Wittingham, of course."

"Fine."

"And . . ." By now they had reached the double doors that led to the salon. Parker, always nearby, opened them with no more expression on his face than he wore for any other occasion.

"Why aren't the lights — " John began, but no sooner did he utter the words than a roar of "Surprise!" went up from the crowd.

John turned to Devon, a look of shock on his face, as his friends crowded around him to wish him happy birthday. Then the guests parted to make room for John's parents as they came toward their son.

In typical Alexander fashion, John's father shook his son's hand warmly, saying, "Many happy returns."

His mother, her usual placid smile intact, said, "Happy birthday, dear," and gave him a light peck on the cheek.

Devon looked from her in-laws to John. It was odd, she thought, Victoria had shown her, Devon, more emotion about the event than she was now showing her own son.

"Thank you, Mother, Father," he said in the usual formal tone he used when addressing his parents.

They shyly withdrew, letting his friends move to the forefront. Ladies surrounded John, each kissing him in turn. Suddenly, out of the crowd, Bebe Henley appeared directly in front of John. Pulling him toward her, she kissed him on the lips — a kiss that lasted just a second longer than those of his other female friends.

"How nice to see you again so soon, John," she murmured with a familiarity missed by no one immediately surrounding them.

John threw Devon a worried glance, then answered in the same formal tone he had used for his parents, "Thank you for coming."

Devon noted the short dialogue with no change of expression. She would not let this forward young woman create trouble between her and her husband and spoil her evening. She was not going to let her imagination arouse her jealousy.

After all, I trust John completely, she told herself.

At dawn, after Devon and John had danced through the night, after he had opened his multitude of gifts, after they had made love, all thoughts of jealousy or concern were completely eradicated from Devon's mind.

With John sleepily rubbing her arm where it lay on the crisp linen sheet, Devon's head on his naked chest, the couple knew one of those moments of complete harmony, ease, and love that occur between happily married couples.

"I'm glad you're my wife," John said to Devon, giving her a lingering kiss.

"You certainly proved that to me last night . . . this morning, I mean," Devon said with a sly smile. She rolled over so that she lay on his stomach, her breasts pressed into his broad chest. She squirmed until she found a position that was comfortable, both her legs between his, her head resting on his shoulder.

"Then you must be very, very glad that I'm your husband, you brazen woman," he teased, running his hands over her firm buttocks.

Devon moaned. "I've missed you so much these past few weeks," she said, her voice husky.

John rolled over so that Devon was pinioned under him. He lifted her arms above her head, holding them there, then roamed over her breasts with his tongue. Devon arched her back, loving the sensations he was arousing in her. She was moist between the legs from their previous lovemaking, and she needed no further foreplay to prepare for him. She pushed against him until he was once more under her, then she mounted him, her legs on either side of his body. She swayed her hips to and fro lazily, clasping him inside her. He reached for her breasts, teasing her nipples with a light touch. Then he encircled her waist with his hands, moving inside her more urgently. Devon threw her head back and closed her eyes, reveling in the sensuality of their lovemaking. Now she altered her rhythm so that she rose and fell on him, controlling the timing and pressure of his penetration. The wetness inside her dripped onto him as she moved closer to fulfillment. Then spasm after spasm shook her, and she collapsed forward onto John's torso as a wild tremor vibrated through his body.

They awakened slowly a few hours later, neither able to summon the energy to leave the bed. Devon smiled to herself as she thought of their passionate lovemaking in the gray dawn light. It had felt terribly decadent to make love in the house of her in-laws, slightly drunk, wildly uninhibited, completely blissful. And at just about the moment that the elder Alexanders normally arose to begin their day.

It was usually the time she, too, awakened to visit the stables. But John enjoyed sleeping until at least eight-thirty, usually not arriving at his office until ten. He was a night owl, while Devon was the opposite. She blinked at the bright sunlight that spilled through a crack in the drawn drapes, then closed her eyes again. She put her head on John's chest and asked sleepily, "Were you surprised by your party? The truth."

"The truth?" John paused for a moment. "Well . . . yes, mostly."

"Mostly?"

"I was surprised that my parents hosted it, but I rather suspected something might be afoot."

"Who gave us away!" Devon demanded in a tone of mock anger, pushing herself up on one elbow so that she could study John's face.

"I'm not sure I remember . . ."

"Who?" Devon insisted.

"Someone at a dinner party last week."

"What did they say?"

"Just 'See you next week.' "

"Why should that alert you to anything?"

"It was Bebe Henley," John said in an offhand way, "and I, of course, knew that I had nothing on my schedule that would cause us to see each other this week." John was not a good liar. And by telling Devon the truth, he felt he proved he had nothing to hide.

There was a moment of silence during which John waited for Devon to erupt in anger. He knew that his wife despised Bebe, and that the knowledge that the secret had been revealed by her would infuriate Devon.

Instead, though, Devon simply replied, "Oh, well, at least you were a little surprised." She closed her eyes so that he could not read her expression. She refused, absolutely refused, to allow John to think she suffered from petty jealousy. And she was glad that he had told her the truth, rather than lie in order not to mention Bebe's name. She would let the matter pass without comment.

But with a woman's true instinct, she knew beyond a shadow of a doubt that Bebe Henley intended to create trouble at Devon's expense. Or at least to try.

CHAPTER 22

THE light-headed feeling would not leave Devon. She had, as usual, eaten a hearty breakfast. She had drunk an extra cup of the cook's strong Creole coffee. But still the feeling would not leave her.

"I'll just ignore it," Devon told herself firmly, tossing her napkin on the table and heading out the French doors to the paddock.

It wasn't even light yet, but already the chill of the night had dissipated. The blue-black sky was cloudless, the moon still a distinct silvery crescent. It would be a beautiful April morning, as Jeremiah had predicted the day before.

Devon smiled as she thought of her assistant. They worked well together and had become fast friends. Seemed to have the same faith in Firefly, too. Once Jeremiah had become accustomed to Devon's training methods, he had developed confidence in the ability of both Devon and Firefly to win.

Devon knew that despite herself she had made the racehorse owner's biggest mistake — she had come to love her horse. Willy had warned her against developing such emotions on the first day she had begun training Firefly.

"I know all you pleasure riders think your horses are pets. These ain't pets. You don't run a pet injured. You don't keep a pet cooped up in a stall all day. Racing is a business, and I aim to see that this one is profitable," he had declared.

Devon understood, in theory. Racehorses were meant to be moneymaking machines, and like anything driven to its limit, they had a tendency to get hurt, or even die, for their efforts. Most trainers tried their best to avoid developing personal tenderness for animals under their jurisdiction, but there was often one steed that had such heart, such courage, and such a good disposition that it won the love of even the most jaded trainer. And Devon was no jaded trainer. Firefly had all the traits of a winner and something more — a delightful personality, calmer than many of Willowbrook's horses, yet high-strung enough to guarantee quick reflexes. Firefly had grown to trust Jeremiah and Devon, and the filly displayed toward them the affection of an overgrown puppy, much as Devon's pleasure horses had done.

Yet Devon was certain that it was not just her love for the horse that made her believe that Firefly could be a major stakes winner. Firefly was impressive, and Devon believed that Willy would have to admit it. The Blue Grass Stakes would be run in two weeks. It was the last major race before the Kentucky Derby. It was used by many odds makers as a gauge to predicting Derby winners. And it was the deadline for Willy's decision on which horse to run in the Derby.

As Devon drew closer to the paddock, she saw Jeremiah enter the door closest to Firefly's stall. As usual, they would undo the bandages on the filly's legs to check for any swelling or other injuries.

"Good morning, Jeremiah," Devon said as she caught up with him outside Firefly's stall.

"Miss Devon," he said with a nod and a smile.

"I think we should take it a little easy with her today. We ran her pretty hard yesterday," Devon said, bending down to examine the horse's left front leg. Suddenly, as she was about to rise, the feeling of wooziness caused her to lose her balance. She staggered a bit, leaning against Firefly's warm side for support. Just as she thought the spinning feeling would stop, she tasted the spicy sausage she had had for breakfast in the back of her throat.

"Oh, my! I think I'm going to be ill." Devon bent over, holding her stomach. "Help me . . . help me outside," she said, reaching out to grab Jeremiah's arm.

Alarmed, he caught his employer by her tiny waist, eased her weight onto him, and hurried outside with her. The smell of horse manure — a smell Devon normally loved — caused her to gag and, before she could stop herself, she felt her breakfast rise in her throat.

"Leave me!" she cried to Jeremiah as she gratefully kneeled in the dirt and emptied the contents of her stomach into one of the large tin buckets used for chores around the stable. After the spasm had subsided, she slumped back into the dirt, her back propped up by the side of the barn, her legs, in their white breeches, stretched out before her.

Jeremiah reappeared around the corner of the barn with a clean, water-soaked rag. He knelt down beside her and pressed the cloth to her forehead.

"Miss Devon . . ."

"I know!" she groaned, in a voice filled with despair.

"That's the third time this week. That I know of," he said with a searching gaze.

She was too weak to do more than nod.

"You've got to tell Mr. Alexander. A man's got a right to know when his baby's on the way," Jeremiah said with conviction.

"Then . . . then, you know?"

"Any fool could guess, ma'am. Anyone who spends every morning with you, like I do."

"I suppose so," Devon said in a defeated tone. "But . . . he may want me to stop riding. He may even want me to stop training." She was in despair at the thought.

Jeremiah reflected on this a moment. White folks were like that, thinking that a pregnant woman was sick. Every woman he'd ever known had worked almost until the moment of childbirth. His own grandmother had been born while her mother had been picking tobacco in a Virginia field.

"You got to do what your husband says, Miss Devon. It's his baby too."

"No!" she burst out. "Not with the Blue Grass Stakes so close. And then what if we go to the Derby?"

Jeremiah's expression told her that he disagreed, but he held his tongue. Still, Devon understood. It's odd, she thought to herself. Here I am discussing the most intimate matter possible with a seventeen-year-old who works for me. And his opinion matters.

"You're right." She sighed with resignation. "I'll have to say something."

What she couldn't tell Jeremiah, of course, was that she wondered whether John would even be happy about the news. At the same time, she was certain he would use the pregnancy as a pretext to insist that she withdraw from the racing operation.

Suddenly, she caught herself. I'm thinking of him as though he were an enemy, she said. Someone that I have a right to deceive. Someone who doesn't want for me what I want. Why would I think he would try to use the pregnancy as a "pretext" for anything? If he wants me to stop racing, it will be because he's truly concerned for my health, she insisted to herself. When did I start thinking otherwise? When did it become what he wants versus what I want?

Devon wearily made her way to the main house, looking forward to a hot bath and a cool lemonade. Her clothes were filthy, not only from her sprawl in the dirt during her morning sickness, but from a fall she had had later in the day when Firefly had been spooked by a blacksnake in the middle of the track. Aside from a sore elbow she was unhurt, but she was bone-weary.

"Aren't you a filthy thing!" exclaimed Alice when her mistress entered the bedroom.

"Aren't I though," Devon agreed with a tired smile.

"I don't know how you get so dirty out there. Just like when you were a little girl," Alice chided, taking the clothes that Devon handed to her.

"I had a fall today. That's why I'm so dirty."

"A fall!" said Alice, in an alarmed voice. "In your condition!"

Devon's eyebrows went up in surprise. "What do you mean?"

"You know exactly what I mean, miss, so don't be acting like you don't," said Alice in her no-nonsense voice.

"How do you know?" asked Devon in wonder.

"How could I not? You suddenly start taking naps every afternoon, when you usually complain about there not being enough hours in the day to do what you want. And then, there's the changes in you . . ."

"You've noticed?"

"I've known you for twenty-seven years, Miss Devon. I would have to be a pretty dim character if I hadn't noticed."

"I thought everyone would think I had just gained a little weight."

"Well, it's not very evenly distributed, if you know what I mean," said Alice with a mischievous grin.

Devon laughed out loud at the sly expression on her maid's face. "I know what you mean; I can barely fit into some of my undergarments anymore."

"Yes, miss, I've noticed."

"Well, I believe that if I don't have my bath right away, I'll be tempted to put my dirty body on those nice clean sheets without it," Devon said with a yawn.

She went naked into the bathroom and sank into the hot, sudsy water.

"Will you be needing anything else, Miss Devon?"

"No, thank you, Alice," she replied, pouring a generous measure of shampoo into her palm.

A few minutes later, she emerged pink and glowing, wrapped herself in the thick white towel that rested on a brass stand beside the bath, and dried herself quickly.

She crossed the white marble floor for one last look out the window at the stables and track. She surveyed the activity below with pride and a sense of accomplishment. Feeling content, she went to the bed and slipped between the cool white sheets. She drifted off to sleep thinking of the Blue Grass Stakes.

"Sleeping Beauty." The familiar deep voice awakened her just as John leaned down to kiss her.

"John!" Devon exclaimed, excitedly throwing off the sheets and jumping to her knees so she could put her arms around her husband.

"Darling," he said, giving her a long, warm kiss.

"What a surprise!" she said breathlessly. "Did you just get in?"

"About a half hour ago, but Alice ordered me to allow you to nap a bit."

"I'll thrash her!" Devon declared in mock anger. "Imagine not letting me see you immediately."

"I'm teasing. But she did tell me that you had just lain down and that you were exhausted, poor girl."

"Well, I'm perfectly rested now, but I would like to return to bed, if you please," said Devon suggestively.

"Good idea. I could use a nap."

"Oh, you!" Devon said, throwing a pillow at him.

John, laughing, quickly undressed and slid into bed with his wife. "Mmm . . . delicious," he said, drawing her close.

"You too." Devon sighed.

John's hands slid over her breasts. For a moment, Devon held her breath, waiting to see if he would comment on any difference, but he simply went on caressing her. Devon relaxed and returned his caresses, enjoying the feel of the down on his strong brown arms.

They made love rather hastily, both eager after ten days of separation. Once they were finished, Devon closed her eyes and felt herself drifting off to sleep again. John snuggled close, turning her so that her rear end was encased in the cup formed by his bent body. His arm went around her waist. They slept in that position for almost two hours, awakening after dark.

John rolled away from Devon and stretched, reaching for the small porcelain clock on the bedside table. He squinted in the dark.

"Seven o'clock!" he murmured in surprise. He replaced the clock and turned to his wife, burying his face in the curve formed by her neck and shoulder.

"Wake up, darling," he whispered, kissing her warm rosy skin.

Devon moaned and turned on her back, reaching for her husband and kissing him.

"I'm sleepy," she protested.

"I know, but it's time to dress for dinner."

Devon pushed herself up on one elbow. "Already?"

"Already! From what I can tell, you've spent all day in bed. How much more sleep do you need?" John teased. He rolled out of the soft bed, pulled the sheets gently off Devon, and lifted her from the warm cocoon.

Here was the perfect opening for Devon to tell John her news, she thought. But how would he react?

"Actually, John, about that . . ."

John kicked open the bathroom door and set Devon down on the fluffy white area rug adjacent to the bathtub. He leaned over to put in the stopper while Devon turned the brass fixtures until she had achieved just the right mix of hot and cold water.

"Yes?" he queried absentmindedly. " 'About that,' you were saying."

Devon sat down on a small tuffet covered in crisp black-and-white-striped polished cotton. She wound her long black tresses into a bun, using hairpins from a Lalique crystal box on a shelf near the tub.

"You look beautiful with your hair that way," John said softly, looking down at his wife. "In fact, you look particularly beautiful today," he said, really examining her for the first time since his homecoming.

Devon smiled back, but feeling a sudden urge to cover herself, she went to the mirrored closet next to the pedestal sink and put on one of the monogrammed terrycloth bathrobes she found there.

She turned abruptly back to John and blurted out, "John, I love you."

"And I love you," he said automatically, leaning down to test the water in the bathtub. He sat on the tuffet and swirled the water about with his hand in an effort to mix the hot with the cold. "It's almost full."

Devon came toward John and stopped directly in front of him. She put one hand on his shoulder, causing him to look from the water up to her.

"What is it?" he asked, reading the serious expression on Devon's face.

"I have some good news," Devon said in a voice so quiet that it was difficult to hear her over the running water.

John turned the brass knobs and stepped into the tub, motioning for Devon to join him. Instead, she sat on the tuffet. Trailing one hand in the water near John, she looked into his eyes. He was so dear to her. And she knew that he felt the same way about her. Yet he had been so disappointed at the idea that she had been pregnant two years ago. Since then, she had faithfully used the device her New York doctor had given her. Except on a few occasions, the most recent one being the evening of John's birthday. Sometimes their passion had been too great, sometimes the moment too precious for Devon to interrupt.

Now she wondered if John would berate her for her carelessness — berate himself for his impatience. If he would regret those unions.

He was looking questioningly at Devon now. Wondering what her news could possibly be. His first thought was of the racing operation.

Devon had been completely enthralled by it for the past several months. Surely her news pertained to that.

"What is it?" he urged.

Devon raised her head and looked John straight in the eye. She tried to brace herself for any reaction, hoping for the best but expecting the worst. Always forthright, she could think of no way to cushion the shock she knew he would feel.

"John, we're going to have a baby." She said the words evenly, but with a touch of defiance. She wanted this child. And, though she would be disappointed if John did not feel the same way, she would not let his attitude spoil her joy in her pregnancy.

John's face was transformed. With a huge grin of delight and surprise, he leapt to his feet and, though soaking wet, engulfed Devon in his arms. "What wonderful news!" His voice resounded in the huge marble bathroom.

Devon, giddy with relief, hugged John's slippery body to her. No response could have made her more ecstatic. A rush of love for him filled her heart. "Then, you're happy?" she asked breathlessly.

"Happy. Proud. Overcome. Oh, Devon, this is wonderful!" He squeezed his wife even more tightly to him, then suddenly pulled away as he reached to her waist to untie the robe. Slipping it off her shoulders, he pulled her into the tub with him.

It had come off just as he had practiced it. She had been convinced. Now, lying beside his wife in the dark, listening to her deep, regular breathing, he could allow himself for the first time to reflect on his true reaction to the news.

It had not been as unexpected as he had let on. Each time that he and Devon had made love without contraception, he had worried afterward that this might be the result. And, inevitably, their carelessness had caught up with them. As he had known it would.

He could recall one occasion when he had been alone at their New York town house on a quiet Monday evening. There hadn't been anything of interest on his social calendar. He had found himself thinking about the possibility of Devon being pregnant. He knew that he could not, absolutely could not, react as he had the first time. Two such reactions would seriously damage their marriage, he had concluded. So, he had put his book down, gone into his dressing room with its full-length cheval glass, and practiced assuming a surprised and delighted expression to such news.

He would hug her first, in order to give himself time to compose his features. He would then grin broadly. Like this, he practiced. No, too phony — like this. Yes, just like this, he said to himself, as a charming dimple played around the right side of his mouth. He would raise his eyebrows, widen his eyes, and grin. He would hug her and appear to be overcome with joy. Like this, he demonstrated to himself in the looking glass.

He practiced for some time because he knew that it was vital to his marriage that he do so. He knew Devon would be apprehensive about telling him she was pregnant, and he could not bear the thought of hurting her as he once had done. Even more frightening was the thought of losing her.

But, he thought to himself, he had, in effect, lost her now.

"She won't be the same." He was surprised to hear the words actually come out of his mouth. Quickly, he looked at Devon to see if she stirred in her sleep. No, she slept the deep, addictive sleep of the mother-to-be.

She wouldn't be at all the same. She would grow heavier and heavier. He could already feel his physical attraction to her waning. He turned once more to look at her. His eyes, wide open for more than two hours in the dark, could easily see her features. She was beautiful. Still beautiful.

I'm being absurd, he said to himself. She'll always be beautiful. Why should she change? He could think of many wives of friends who had remained alluring after childbirth.

Our child. Hers and mine. A product of our love. I should be happy. It's perfectly normal. Everyone wants children, don't they?

He pulled down the crisp linen sheet just far enough to expose her breasts as she lay on her back.

"Beautiful," he murmured almost soundlessly. He leaned toward her and put the tip of his warm tongue on one of Devon's exposed pink nipples. Although she remained unconscious, the nipple hardened at the contact. He took more of her breast into his mouth. He felt simultaneously comforted and stimulated.

Soon her breasts would flow with milk, he thought. Soon there would be no place for him there. They would belong to the infant.

Suddenly he felt ashamed of himself, as though he were furtively doing something wrong. As though he were sinning. His hardening member at once lost its rigidity and he drew away from his wife.

He wondered if his lust for her would ever rise again.

CHAPTER 23

"COME with me to Kentucky," Devon begged, "it's just for a few weeks."

"Darling, I can't. I'm negotiating the sale of the Thirty-sixth Street development and I have to be in New York."

Devon paced back and forth in front of John's huge Chippendale writing table. Sometimes she felt that his study was the only room in which John felt truly at home at Willowbrook. It was a typical man's room, with deep green leather furniture, and bookcases lining two walls.

"But Firefly and Fearless Leader are going to run in the Blue Grass Stakes. And we're going to the Keeneland auctions. This farm is your business too."

Devon stopped directly in front of John and turned to face him, her hands on her hips, her entire posture one of frustration. "Everyone will be in Kentucky until the Derby. The Whitneys, the Coopers . . . everyone."

John smiled indulgently. "Some people will be there, I grant you. The horsey set."

"That's everyone we know," Devon said emphatically, resuming her pacing.

"Do sit down, dear. It's very distracting for you to be shuttling back and forth like a wooden duck at a shooting range."

Devon and John both laughed at the comparison, easing the tension between them.

"You say the funniest things sometimes," Devon said, sinking into a leather chair in front of her husband's desk.

John picked up a cigarette and put it to his mouth.

"I wish you wouldn't do that in here, John. It's such a filthy habit and it leaves an odor in the room," Devon said with exasperation.

"I won't smoke in any other room then, Devon, but this is my study and I choose to smoke here," John said firmly.

"Oh, fine. It doesn't matter anyhow. What we were discussing was more important than smoking. I don't understand how you can always have time to go off and visit one of your friends in Oyster Bay or some such place, but when it comes to devoting some time to the racing operation, you never seem to be available."

"You know the racing operation is really yours," John said.

"By default! You don't show an interest." Devon sat on the edge of her seat, leaning toward John as she made her point.

"To be frank, my interest is not as keen as yours," he said, leaning back and exhaling a stream of blue smoke. Devon watched the smoke break apart into curly wisps then waft toward an open window.

Fixing her eyes on John again, she said, "I'll be in Kentucky almost six weeks if Firefly does well at the Blue Grass Stakes."

"Then you'll be busy training her every day, so my presence will just be a burden, won't it?" John challenged.

"How can you say that?" cried Devon, coming to her feet and moving around the desk to sit on John's lap. Once settled there, she put her arms around his neck and murmured, "Your presence could never be a burden. I miss you so much when we're apart." Then, pulling back a little, she added, "Besides, you know all about racing. I could use your advice."

John threw back his head and laughed. "What a romantic argument!"

Devon studied John. There was something wrong between them and she did not know what it was. He was withdrawn, preoccupied most of the time. On some occasions he was as affectionate as ever, but he had not initiated sex since she had told him about the baby. Yet he had seemed so happy about the news.

Devon wanted to ask him what the matter was, but she was afraid to broach the subject. Afraid to discover something that would upset her. It was easier to just gloss over the matter and hope it would go away.

CHAPTER 24

JOHN studied Devon beside him in the owner's box. For the Blue Grass Stakes she had dressed with special care, and John realized that it had been some time since he had seen her clad so formally. Usually she wore riding breeches or dungarees. Her concession to the dinner meal was to change into a clean pair of slacks or a simple frock. Now, however, she wore a splendidly cut white silk dress that flowed gracefully around her legs thanks to a myriad of tiny pleats. A fitted navy bodice emphasized her still-tiny waist and full bosom, while a length of stiff white organza swept dramatically from a high collar in the back to an off-the-shoulder effect in front. She wore pale silk stockings and delicately strapped sandals of white kid with heels so high that she gained three inches in stature. An extravagant picture hat of navy straw lined in white organza and trailing two long white streamers of the same material made Devon's aqua eyes appear to be a shade of celestial azure.

"What are you staring at?" Devon asked with a grin.

"You look wonderful," John murmured softly.

Devon, happy, returned to her conversation with Marion Davies. Their other guests in the box included W. R. Hearst, Sydney and Bart, and John's and Devon's parents.

John studied his mother. She looked as she always had for as long as he could remember. Serene. Poised. Matronly. Utterly sexless. He turned his gaze to his father. Strict. Judgmental. Unaffectionate. Also utterly sexless. He shifted his scope of vision to encompass Devon's father, Chase. Portly, kindly, but a bit pompous. Boring.

John realized that he had probably always been afraid of what age and maturity might bring. Perhaps that was why he had remained single until his thirties, and why also he had been so reluctant to admit to himself that he wanted to marry Devon. Growing older meant commitment and responsibility to others. Had those burdens sapped his parents of their vitality?

Is that what's bothering me so much about this pregnancy? he asked himself. The idea of encumbrance? A child was a fearsome responsibility. More so than a wife. With a wife, mistakes could be ameliorated. Many of his friends were divorced, though his family would be horrified if John did any such thing.

I don't want a divorce, of course, he emphasized to himself. At the same time, the option was there, wasn't it? That was the difference. Even if divorce were not an option, he knew many married couples who led lives completely independent of each other. They took lovers. They stayed together for the sake of convenience. Or for the children.

That was it. A child was an immovable, unavoidable, irrevocable burden. And try though he might, illogical though it was, John could not forgive Devon for imposing it upon him.

Just at the moment that this strong wave of resentment engulfed John, Devon took his hand and squeezed it with anticipation.

"Let's go down to the paddock and check on the horses, John," she whispered. "I have a few things I want to go over with McClintock."

It had been a concession of Devon's to allow Fearless Leader to have their house jockey, Slim Bocaso. On the other hand, McClintock, though younger and less experienced, raced only in Kentucky and knew the track better than Bocaso. It was difficult to say which was the greater advantage. Often in a tight situation the older jockey with responsibilities would try to avoid danger, while a younger jockey still making a name for himself would take the kind of daredevil chances that could result in a spectacular win — or a tragic loss. Devon felt that with the odds stacked against her as they were, she wanted her filly to be ridden as aggressively as possible.

Devon and John made their way through beautifully dressed well-wishers and rivals in the owners' boxes, then down to the seedier back side, the part of the racetrack where the work really took place. John observed that almost every male that Devon passed interrupted his work to stare at the lovely vision she created, her white dress wafting around her shapely legs on the light breeze.

Devon's gasp of surprise brought John out of his reverie. And he also gasped when he saw the cause of his wife's distress. Fearless Leader was standing by his stall, his front leg buried in a bucket of ice.

"What's wrong?" Devon demanded of Willy, who remained staring down at the leg, a look of disgust on his face.

"Not sure. Track doc says cannon bone's swelled up. He was favoring it this morning."

"Oh, no!" Devon cried. The cure for an inflamed lower leg was rest and lots of it. To force Fearless Leader to run with the discomfort, as some owners would, might cause a severe injury that could spell the end of his racing career.

"You're going to have to scratch him from the race?" Devon asked. She was close to tears at the thought of all the time and effort they had put into preparations for this race. It was their first chance to show the blue bloods of the racing world that Willowbrook's three-year-olds were prime stock. It was important to the future of the stable to feature as many of their horses as possible. Firefly and Fearless Leader had performed well as two-year-olds, but the secret was to demonstrate staying power. The potential for long racing careers was what brought high stud fees and what sold brood mares from a particular farm.

"If we don't scratch him, he may not be able to run again this season. Then we'd have to train him all over again next year," Willy grumbled. "It's just better to sit this one out."

Devon's shoulders slumped in dejection. John put his arm around her. But no sooner had he made the gesture than he felt her straighten her spine smartly and raise her head.

"It's a good decision, Willy," she said firmly. "We'll just have to count on Firefly to make a good showing for us."

Without a backward look, she strode down the long center aisle of the paddock to the section where the fillies were stabled. Rick McClintock, wearing Willowbrook's scarlet and black silks, was engrossed in conversation with Jeremiah.

"Gentlemen," Devon said crisply, nodding to the two young men.

"Ma'am," said Rick, removing his cap.

"How's she doing?" she asked, indicating Firefly with a gesture of her chin.

"Top form, Miss Devon," said Jeremiah, with a broad grin.

"You heard about Fearless Leader, I suppose?"

Both men looked down and shifted their feet uncomfortably. It was a blow to everyone who worked for Willowbrook to have Fearless Leader scratched from the race. Although Jeremiah and Devon had faith in Firefly, they both knew that racehorses were unpredictable. It was possible that she would fare badly. It would have been better to have had two chances to show off their new operation.

John drew alongside his wife and watched the exchange. He was amused to hear Devon discussing the upcoming race in the peculiar slang of the racetrack. She had learned it quickly and it seemed like second nature to her now. Still, it was always a surprise to hear the vulgar trainer-to-jockey lingo enunciated in Devon's impeccably well-bred accent. The surprise effect was compounded by her delicate looks. But Devon used it for none of those reasons. She used it because it saved time and because it was most effective for communicating with the men who worked at the track.

"Okay, McClintock," said Devon in a commanding voice, now fully recovered from the news of Fearless Leader, "I want you to come out shooting ducks." That meant that Firefly should be started at top speed rather than held back until the end of the race.

"Yes, ma'am," said McClintock respectfully. He had no resentment of owners, and no hesitancy to accept orders from Devon. He had seen her in training sessions with Firefly. She could ride like a jockey and she was completely fearless. And she had a special rapport with the filly that was impressive.

Turning to John, she put her arm through his and said, "Shall we return to our places?" She was once more the gracious society lady. The race was now in the hands of McClintock — and Firefly.

Back at their seats, Devon looked down at the *Racing Form* in her hand. There were ten entries in the race — nine, now that Fearless Leader had been scratched — and each came from a farm with an excellent reputation. Her horses had not been favored to win. That honor went to the Vanderbilts' colt Rainmaker. The track odds against Firefly had been twenty-four to one the last time Devon had checked. The odds changed from moment to moment as gamblers continued to place their bets. Booming over the background noise, the loudspeaker announced that Fearless Leader had been scratched from the race. Within ten minutes the odds against Firefly had jumped to sixty-six to one. That was because when two horses with the same owner ran in the same race, the odds against them were identical by regulation. The gambler won the same amount no matter which of the two horses placed. Without Fearless Leader driving up the chances of a win, gamblers were not willing to put their money on the lone Willowbrook filly.

Devon could barely contain her excitement when the starting gun sounded. She immediately leapt to her feet and brought the binoculars to her eyes. McClintock was doing just as she had instructed. Firefly was in the lead — flying down the track like a fury. There was a theory that a winning filly ran not toward the finish but away from the pack of colts chasing her. A panic run. But Firefly was in control — that was clear even from the stands.

Rainmaker had started at the end of the pack, but as he passed the first furlong he began to pick up speed. Devon could see the Vanderbilt jockey whipping him now — not frantically, but enough to let him know that it was almost time to exert himself.

"And in the lead it's Willowbrook's Firefly, followed by Tornado and Jungle Girl," said the track announcer. "In the middle of the pack, we've got Rainmaker nose to nose with Salt and Pepper; close behind is Fake It, Now's the Time, and Sugar 'n Spice. Trailing by two lengths is Sassafras."

No sooner had the announcer finished this chant than Rainmaker surged forward. The voice on the loudspeaker raised its pitch in excitement.

"Look at this move by Bob Vasquez on Rainmaker. He's pushing past Salt and Pepper, now Jungle Girl. And Tornado takes the lead, with Firefly in second place and Rainmaker behind by a length. Now moving ahead!"

Devon, oblivious to the screams around her, concentrated all her attention on the three lead horses. As Rainmaker drew nearer to Firefly, he turned his head slightly, looking into the filly's eyes. It was a common form of confrontation in wild-horse packs. Fillies almost always backed down. And, with a sinking heart, Devon saw Firefly falter for a moment as Rainmaker edged past her. It was Rainmaker and Tornado nose to nose.

"It looks like it's not going to be a filly today," said the track announcer.

"No!" Devon whispered to herself. And on cue, Firefly, finding herself falling behind, pushed forward, her competitive spirit apparently overcoming her natural submission to the male. Rick McClintock was whipping her frantically and she was responding with all her heart. She was gaining, gaining . . .

"I can't watch!" Devon heard Sydney cry beside her. But Devon could not look away for even a second.

"It's Rainmaker in the lead as they approach the finish, Firefly neck and neck with Tornado. Now Firefly's passing Tornado!"

Devon could hear the excitement in the announcer's voice as her filly pushed past all the others. All the others except Rainmaker. He was holding his lead.

"We're going to win!" John exclaimed jubilantly.

Devon held her breath. Held it . . . The track announcer crowed, "And it's an amazing finish with Willowbrook's filly Firefly in first place, bringing glory back to a venerable name!"

CHAPTER 25

THE next day Devon appeared at the track, impatient to discuss with Willy the training regimen he had in mind for Firefly's bid in the Kentucky Derby.

She found him on his knees unbandaging the filly's legs, studying them for injuries. His back was to her and he did not see her approach, but a broad grin broke out on Jeremiah's face at the sight of her.

"Miz Whitney's already been down here offering to buy her," Jeremiah announced without preamble.

Willy looked up from his work just long enough to mumble his usual grumpy, "Mornin'."

"Well, I hope you told her she isn't for sale." Devon smiled.

"We told 'er," Willy said, standing upright and facing Devon.

Devon was a little amused. Despite their victory, despite the percentage of Firefly's prize purse that Willy would be awarded as Willowbrook's trainer, he still did not seem able to smile.

"Well, I'm here as threatened," Devon joked.

Willy studied her as if he did not know what she was talking about.

"How do you want to work out our collaboration on Firefly?" Devon asked, more seriously.

"I'm not sure I follow you."

Exasperated by his deliberate obtuseness, Devon said, "To get her ready for the Derby."

"I'm not runnin' 'er in the Derby," Willy said flatly.

Devon stared at him, incredulous. "What are you talking about?"

"Fearless Leader'll be fine by then. It was nothin' serious."

"I'm glad to hear that, but Firefly won the Blue Grass Stakes."

"She faltered."

"She won!"

"I don't want to risk somethin' like that happening for a race as important as the Derby," Willy said. And with an air of finality, he kneeled to examine the filly's rear legs.

With a voice like ice, Devon said, "I would like to speak to you in private."

Willy did not interrupt what he was doing.

"Now."

The tone of her voice made Willy turn and look at her over his shoulder. The expression on her face brought him to his feet.

"Follow me," Devon commanded, leading him up to her empty owner's box. They made the five-minute trek in hostile silence.

Once they were seated, Devon said in a calm voice, "I do not believe that you are weighing fairly each horse's chances for winning."

"When we made this deal, you said it would be my call. I choose Fearless Leader."

"Why?"

"He's run faster in practice than Firefly did yesterday. His injury will be fine. He's a colt. I think he's got the best chance of winnin' the Derby. Firefly, on the other hand, faltered yesterday when Rainmaker challenged 'er. She fell behind."

"For a split second. Anyway, I learned from that. I'll run her with blinkers next time."

"It's a good idea, but fillies don't win the Derby."

"Regret won," Devon said in a reasonable voice.

"Aye," Willy acknowledged. "The only one."

"Firefly will do it," she insisted more emphatically.

"The choice was mine, you said. I made my choice."

"But it's totally capricious!" Devon said. "You're just trying to prove something — to prove that you're the power at Willowbrook. Well, I won't have it! Firefly can win the Derby!"

Willy jumped to his feet, outraged that his objectivity as a trainer had been challenged. "If I thought Firefly would win, I'd run 'er and you know it!"

Devon, just as angry, pushed back her chair with such force that it fell over. She leaned closer to Willy and glared into his eyes, her eyebrows forming a furious line, like dark storm clouds over an aqua sea. "Your reasons for thinking she won't win are absurd. They're based on some rigid rule about fillies and colts. Trainers like you are why more fillies haven't won the Derby!

"Now, I agree that she had a momentary problem," Devon said, her voice trembling from the effort to calm herself, "and I believe blinkers will solve it. Plus we'll work with her in practice on it. But her time beat the track record! Willy, for God's sake, she can win!" Devon stamped her foot to emphasize her last words.

"I'm not convinced of that!" Willy yelled, tearing his baseball cap off his head and slapping it against his thigh in frustration.

"Well, you don't have to be!" Devon yelled back.

For a moment, they were both too taken aback by her furious words to say anything.

Devon took a long, shaky breath and continued in a quieter voice. "I respect your opinion very much, but you haven't worked with Firefly like I have. What it comes down to, Willy, is that I'm the owner. I know we had an agreement, but I can't let you do something I completely disagree with. If you want to run Fearless Leader, fine. He's a great horse. But I'm running Firefly, and that's my final word on the subject."

"Then we've got nothin' more to say, have we?" And without waiting to be dismissed, Willy slammed the baseball cap onto his head, turned, and stomped away from Devon.

The guest cottage of Mr. and Mrs. Cooper Lyle III's estate was so pleasant that Devon was beginning to think of it as home — at least for the time she was in Kentucky. After a long day at the track — more tiring than usual because of her fight with Willy — Devon was looking forward to relaxing with John over a cold drink on one of the white wicker lounge chairs overlooking the cottage's tiny private pool.

She immediately felt the tension slip away from her as she turned into the long, dogwood-lined driveway of her friends' estate. So vast was the Lyles' property that it took her another few minutes to reach the little circular driveway in front of the cottage. Devon closed the door of the borrowed Packard and hurried into the cozy living/dining area calling John's name. The English floral chintzes, cheery brass accessories, and pastel colors acted as a balm on her frayed nerves.

"In here, Devon," John called from the bedroom, a fluffy pink and white affair that looked sunny even on cloudy days.

"Hello, love," Devon said wearily, giving her husband a kiss. Her eyes were immediately drawn to the leather trunk on the floor. It was open and John's valet was carefully folding his master's clothes into it, each layer meticulously lined with tissue paper to prevent wrinkling.

Devon, startled, asked, "What are you doing?"

"Getting ready to go home, of course," John replied matter-of-factly.

"What do you mean? It's still several weeks until the Derby."

"Yes, I know, but you said that if Firefly wasn't to run that you would come to New York with me. I asked Alice to prepare your things as well. I believe she's doing some laundry at the main house."

Devon arched an eyebrow in puzzlement. "But Firefly is running," she explained.

"No."

"No?" Devon was too dumbfounded to think straight.

John turned to his valet. "I can finish up here, Wilkes, why don't you go and prepare your own things."

"Very good, sir," said the manservant, quietly closing the door behind him as he exited.

"I had a visit from O'Neill today," John said, busying himself with some toiletries on the cherrywood chest of drawers.

"How dare he!" Devon cried, furious.

John cocked an eyebrow. "How dare he talk to his employer?" he said sardonically.

Devon moved deliberately so that she stood directly beside John. He was forced to meet her eyes.

"What did Mr. O'Neill have to say?" Devon asked in a tone that was abnormally quiet. So quiet, in fact, that John could tell she was attempting to keep her voice from rising.

"He related your conversation of this morning."

Devon squared her shoulders and fixed John with a glare. "O'Neill related our conversation and now you've decided we're to go home?"

"I have," John said, looking challengingly at his wife.

"On what grounds, may I ask?" Devon enunciated each word sharply in order to ensure that her sentence was coherent. Otherwise, she was afraid she would spew forth a stream of vituperative babble. She was outraged that Willy should have involved John in their dispute, but what absolutely stunned Devon was that her husband was siding with him! Humiliating her! The betrayal almost made Devon feel physically ill.

John straightened and faced Devon, his posture rigid. "On the grounds that I agree with his decision to run Fearless Leader in the Derby. That I agree with him that we should run only one horse in the Derby, and that I agree that Firefly has less chance of winning." John said all this in a reasonable tone, but his fists, jammed into the pockets of his linen slacks, were clenched tightly.

"Well," Devon said, her voice rising in pitch, but growing no louder, "I disagree with his assessment. And I am at the track every day," she added pointedly.

"Yes, I know." There was a pause, during which John clearly transmitted his resentment to Devon. "You are indeed at the track every day. You have, rather unbecomingly, I might add, attempted to usurp the authority of one of the best trainers in the world. We should count ourselves fortunate that he didn't quit over this *ridiculous* dispute."

The words were like a punch in the stomach for Devon. Never had John been so ugly to her. Never had he complained about her involvement with racing, other than to say that he missed her in New York. On the contrary, he had encouraged her in her interest. Now John was like a stranger to her — revealing an autocratic side of himself that Devon had never seen before. His attitude made her more defiant.

Devon placed her hands on her hips and took a step closer to John. "We should be grateful to Willy? To be dictated to by an employee?"

"One of the most competent."

"I agree. But that still does not make him the owner of Willowbrook Farm. If I were a man, he perhaps wouldn't like my involvement, but he wouldn't think of questioning it."

"I don't know if that's true. Nevertheless, you are not a man. You are my wife. And I stand with O'Neill on this issue."

"How can you say that? Yesterday, you said the decision of which horse to run was mine and O'Neill's!"

"That was before I heard his side of things."

"But you haven't even heard *my* side of things yet!"

"O'Neill explained your rationale."

Devon's fair complexion flushed red-hot as the blood pounded in her temples. "So now you're allowing that man to speak for me without even listening to what I have to say," she hissed.

"All right," John said calmly. He sat on the edge of the bed and crossed his arms, a look of mocking expectancy on his face. "Tell me your rationale."

Devon wanted to slap the expression away. Her palm itched to do it, but she controlled herself. Finally, she decided to ignore the sarcasm of his expression and proceeded to explain why she believed Firefly could win the Derby. By the time she had finished, she was a little calmer. "And," she concluded, "if she wears blinkers, I believe we can avoid the problem we saw at the Blue Grass Stakes."

"What you're saying may be true," John conceded, "but I've already made my commitment to O'Neill."

At these words, Devon took a step backward as though she herself had been slapped. "So your commitment to O'Neill is more important than my views?"

"You made a commitment to him, too," John pointed out.

"That is correct," Devon said in a tight voice. "I don't like to break a commitment and it's not something I usually do. However, I believe he is being old-fashioned and superstitious in his idea that a filly can't win the Derby. Firefly proved herself, but he won't admit it. He's just being stubborn."

"So are you," John pointed out. "Dammit, Devon, why are you making this a personal quarrel — it's strictly a business decision. I'm going with the decision of the man I pay to give me his best judgment."

Raising her voice, she cried, "But Firefly won the Blue Grass Stakes! Won! If she had only come in second, I would agree with Willy, but she won! I don't see the dollars-and-cents wisdom of not running a proven winner."

How could she make her husband realize the logic of what she was saying? He seemed so distant. Kneeling next to the bed, she pounded a fist into the mattress near John's thigh. "Don't you see? I trained Firefly. By myself. I'm not the novice at this that I was when I began. Of course O'Neill is one of the best and I don't want to lose him. But I don't want to be controlled by him either. Firefly has all the heart in the world. She can win the Derby. I'm sure of it. She's never had any health problems."

John suddenly softened. "I know you believe that," he said, stroking Devon's hair, "and it may even be true. But I can't let you undermine O'Neill's authority."

"You keep repeating that!" Devon jumped to her feet in exasperation. "I'm not a child who has to be taught my rightful place, but that's how the two of you are treating me," she said bitterly.

What was most hurtful about the men's attitude was that it seemed to indicate that they had no respect at all for her, despite her proven ability. On the other hand, one part of her acknowledged that she had made a commitment to let Willy pick the Derby horse. But that had been before Fearless Leader's injury. Before Firefly's victory. Who could have foreseen such a juxtaposition of events?

"Can't you see, John? This way, you're undermining *me!* Willy should not have come to you behind my back. That was wrong. He and

I work together every day. You aren't involved in the farm. Every time I ask you to be, you say you haven't the time." Devon's voice became more vehement as she went on. "Why now should he suddenly come to you as though you were a higher authority?"

John cleared his throat uncomfortably. He seemed to be searching for just the right words, but there was no way to soften the blow of what he said next. "The fact of the matter is that I bought Willowbrook before our marriage. Willy came to work for me with the understanding that he would be in control of the racing operation. I believe strongly, Devon, in the principle of delegating authority to those I hire for that purpose — and not undermining them on a whim. And let me add, ungentlemanly though it may be to remind you, that I am, in fact, the highest authority at Willowbrook." Devon opened her mouth, angry retort ready, but John interrupted. "And remember, the first day I brought you to Willowbrook, you and I together told O'Neill that he'd have complete control of the racing operation."

Complete control? No, she told herself. She would not let the threat of Willy's resignation prevent her from running a filly that had won the Blue Grass Stakes. A filly that had been the highest stakes winner of Willowbrook Farm the year before.

Calmer now, but full of steely resolve, Devon said, "Things change, John. I respect Willy's knowledge and his experience, but he's not God. He hasn't worked with Firefly as I have. I know her better. I won't give up her chance to run in the Derby."

"What do you mean by 'won't'?"

Devon fixed John with a steady gaze. "I mean that I intend to run Firefly. As I told Willy, he can run Fearless Leader."

John rose to his feet. He stood squarely in front of Devon. "And if I tell you not to?"

Devon's aqua eyes turned icy. "As you so accurately point out, you are the sole legal owner of Firefly. But while we're on the subject of agreements, you will also recall that you agreed that the racing operation was my bailiwick. You may, of course, prevent me from running Firefly in the Derby, since she is your horse. In that case, I have two options. I can buy her from you, or I will set up my own racing operation elsewhere. I don't think that either of us wants that kind of division in our marriage, but it may be that your commitment to O'Neill is more important to you than your commitment to me."

"That's absurd!" John said in disgust. He paced back and forth for a few moments in angry silence. Never had they had a dispute that struck so fundamentally at the core of their marriage. Devon, for the first time, was declaring that if John stood in her way, she could — and would — do what she wished without him.

He could feel Devon's gaze boring into the back of his neck as he stared unseeingly out the window. She said nothing. She had said her last word. The choice was now his. Finally, he whirled around and blurted out, "I don't know why you've made this a matter of such stupendous importance, but obviously you have. The whole thing is absurd and your actions go against everything I believe in, in terms of business. And now you're forcing me to make a personal choice rather than an objective business decision. No matter what I decide, I'm not going to feel comfortable. So run Firefly, if you insist. But I'm not going to stay around to try to smooth things over with O'Neill. I'm going to New York tonight, just as I planned. And don't expect my help in persuading another trainer to come to work for you when O'Neill leaves you flat. Because if he leaves — when he leaves — people will find out why. And then no decent trainer will be willing to work for Willowbrook Farm."

"O'Neill will never get a chance to resurrect a farm like Willowbrook again. It is the challenge of his life. He won't quit. Anyway," she added in a tone of studied indifference, "worse things could happen."

She made an about-face that was almost military in its stiffness. Reaching the door, she turned once more to her husband. "Incidentally," she said coolly, "neither you nor anyone else *tells* me what to do. Do *not* use that particular phrase with regard to me again."

It seemed on the surface like a gift, the deed to Willowbrook that John messengered from New York by airplane the morning following their quarrel. But in a moment of crystal-clear prescience, Devon had the sickening conviction that it signaled an unbreachable rupture in her marriage.

Sitting at her breakfast table with a glass of orange juice, she turned the document over in her hands and, despite her fears with regard to John, a feeling of elation soared through her at the thought that Willowbrook belonged to her — and only her. The deed gave her carte blanche to do with the farm as she wished, to take command with confidence that her word was the final word.

I'll let John cool off for a few days, then I'll fly to New York to try to work things out, she told herself. But now I've got to deal with Willy.

She tried to imagine the effect the change would have on the trainer. He had to be told that Firefly would now run in the Derby; more important, that Devon was now sole owner of Willowbrook. Would he quit? Devon wondered. What would she do if that happened? she asked herself. She was pregnant, but not due until Christmas. She intended to continue working until the baby was born. But could she handle the work load of the entire stable? She did not think so. All right then, who could she hire at the height of racing season? The best trainers already worked for people she knew. She did not think that Willowbrook Farm would attract the top talent for several reasons. Mostly because she was a woman owner who wanted a say in the day-to-day running of the operation, but also because the stable was far less prestigious, at this point, than those of many of her friends. In addition, because the operation was smaller than others' in her set, her trainer would win less money from prize purses.

She had to try to hang on to Willy, she realized, or risk losing the gains made so far by Willowbrook. With a new feeling of resolve, she quickly threw on a pair of fawn-colored riding breeches and a plaid shirt and headed out the door, grabbing her hairbrush on the way. The car left a wake of dust as she sped down the drive, all the while using her free hand to brush her hair without even a glance in the mirror at herself.

Once at Churchill Downs, she set out immediately to find Willy, anxious to settle things between them as soon as possible. She found him standing with both arms on the white fence, one foot on its lowest rung, watching Fearless Leader be ridden by Jeremiah the wrong way around the track. It was always easier to control horses — prevent them from breaking into their fastest gallops — if they were guided around the track clockwise. Willy and most other trainers were against straining the delicate bones and tendons on a daily basis, preferring to exert the horses to the fullest on a controlled schedule.

Willy did not hear Devon approach, so when she spoke his name he turned with a startled expression on his face.

"We had better talk," she said coolly.

He did not remove his arms or foot from the fence, and for a moment Devon thought that he would turn away from her, but instead he gave Jeremiah a signal to bring the horse in. When he was assured that the exercise rider had seen his signal, he wearily pushed away from his perch at the fence and turned to Devon, his hands stuffed into the pockets of his baggy khaki trousers.

"I'm not sure what we have to talk about," Willy replied with grim seriousness.

"Let's go up into the stands," said Devon, ignoring his remark.

Once they were seated, she began. She spoke bluntly, in part because it was her nature, in part because she enjoyed shocking Willy with her news. "Mr. Alexander is no longer owner of Willowbrook Farm." Devon paused. "I am."

A perturbed look came over Willy's grizzled features as his mind processed the information. For a few seconds, he said nothing. Then he stood up. "In that case, I'll pack my things and get out of here." He looked toward the track where the Thoroughbreds pranced and galloped, their coats gleaming in the sun. He seemed to be looking for something, Devon thought, as his eyes scanned the distant figures. Then, turning, he looked toward the corral where hot walkers led the horses around and around until they were cool. A groom was performing this task for Fearless Leader. Willy's eyes lingered on the duo.

Devon suddenly felt terribly sorry for Willy. Sorry for the misunderstandings between them. Sorry that they seemed unable to agree on how Willowbrook should be run.

"Willy . . ." she said softly. He turned cold eyes toward her and waited for her to speak. Her feelings of regret vanished at the look in his eyes. Still, her words were more gentle than she had planned. "I wish you wouldn't leave," she said stiffly.

Willy seemed to consider this a moment. His reply was less gruff than Devon had expected. "I don't think I can work for you," he said, completely straightforward as usual.

Devon realized that was at least one quality that she very much liked in Willy. "Why not? Because I'm a woman?"

"Maybe. Maybe because I never had someone interfere so much with what I was doing before."

"But Willy," said Devon, exasperated by his refusal to look at things in a new way, "my interference has in no way damaged you or Willowbrook. If you could just think of it as a collaboration instead —"

"Can't do it," Willy interrupted her, lifting his baseball cap off his head and smoothing his hand nervously over his balding pate. "Look, you're all right as far as women go. Maybe as far as owners go. But I can't work in a place where any decision I make could be overruled by someone else. Mr. Alexander understood that. What I did — going to talk to him and all — wasn't about you. It was about the promise he made to me when I came to work for him."

"Okay. Now Willowbrook has a new owner. If you could just put aside, for a moment, your agreement with him and look at me as someone you have to negotiate with all over again. Forget about Mr. Alexander. Tell me what you want from me. I can't abide by promises made by him, but I can abide by ones I've made."

"You already broke one promise to me. Two, really, if you count the fact that you were with Mr. Alexander when he promised me a free hand."

Devon flushed. She knew Willy would never respect her, never work for her, unless she admitted the truth. "I broke my promises. I knew nothing about racing when I met you, but as I became more interested, I wanted to have more of a say. You can't blame me for breaking a promise made before I knew anything about what I was promising," Devon insisted.

"I thought all you rich folks had this code of honor. A promise is a promise. The word of a gentleman." He spat out the last words contemptuously.

"I like to think that I am a person of honor. But I'm not a saint and I guess all I can do is apologize. On the other hand, I'm firmly convinced that there are special circumstances here —"

"I don't see it that way. About Firefly, you told me I would be the one to decide whether she ran in the Derby."

Devon was silent. The conversation was getting them nowhere. Finally she said, "Look, let's wipe the slate clean. I can't offer you the final authority on which horses are run. I can only offer to delegate those decisions to you most of the time. But if I believe in a horse, and if I have plenty of facts on which to base that belief, there is no reason why I, as owner, should defer to you, as trainer. That was the case with Firefly. You can't offer me any good reason not to run her in the Derby."

"You gave your word," Willy said stubbornly.

"I trusted you to be fair," Devon said, looking levelly into Willy's eyes.

"You think I wasn't?" Willy raised his voice. "You believe I'd sabotage a race just for pride?" He was outraged at the suggestion.

"If you didn't think a filly could win the Derby, why did you make that bargain with me?" Devon countered.

"I thought she might be our best chance, but now I think that Fearless Leader would be. We've already gone over all this!"

Devon did not respond immediately. After a few moments of silence, she asked, "You believe that strongly in Fearless Leader?"

"I do!" Willy said, a frown of conviction on his face.

"Hmmm . . ." Devon had an idea. "Suppose . . . we run both horses in the Derby?"

"I already said that was a bad —"

"And" — Devon cut him off — "suppose I give you Fearless Leader and the entire purse if he wins."

Willy's mouth popped open in astonishment. Most trainers worked for others all their lives dreaming of the day that they could afford to own a top racehorse. Owning such a horse, however, was well beyond the means of most people. It wasn't just the cost of the animal, it was its care, feed, and training. Then there was money needed for entering races, for silks, and for jockeys. Owning racehorses was a rich man's hobby. Trainers who worked for the wealthy and also owned their own horses had to pay rent and board to stable their horses with their employers', or pay the same fees to a local racetrack.

Reading Willy's mind, Devon added persuasively, "With the prize money, you could afford to buy your own farm."

Willy looked at her shrewdly. "What would I do with one horse and my own farm? You know how expensive it is to have a racing operation. But if I had a prize brood mare . . ." He let the sentence linger between them uncompleted.

Devon pretended to consider this, but inside she was elated. He was going to stay, she thought. There was just one problem.

"The brood mare is reasonable, but if I give you one, then you have to agree that I never have to pay a stud fee to you for Fearless Leader. And —"

Willy grunted in disgust, sitting back down in his seat and crossing his arms.

"And," Devon continued evenly, "I have the option on the mare's third foal. That gives you at least three years to get going."

"In that case, I want the option on Firefly's first foal. You won't need three years to get going," said Willy, leaning forward and placing his hands on his knees.

Devon and Willy had never enjoyed each other's company so much as at this moment. The horse-trading acted as a tonic to them both.

"Firefly?" Devon said mockingly. "You must think very highly of her."

Willy snorted. "She's the only decent nag you've got to offer at this point."

Devon ignored the crack, secretly amused. "Fine. Just so you don't say I broke my word, I have a few other conditions I want to discuss with you."

"What else!" Willy cried, wondering just who was getting the best deal.

"If you win, I need you to stay on for one year. By then my baby will be six months old and I'll be able to return to work full-time."

Willy scratched one graying sideburn. "I believe I'm due for a raise."

"Ten percent," Devon offered.

"Hah! I can do better than that anywhere!" Willy scoffed.

"No one else will give you a Derby winner!" Devon responded in the same tone.

"Twenty percent," said Willy.

"Too much. Fifteen," Devon said crisply.

"Agreed." A smile, barely discernible, played around Willy's mouth.

"Now," Devon said, taking a deep breath as she broached the most difficult topic, "about the day-to-day running of the operation . . ."

"That could be a sticking point."

"I will never overrule — and have never in the past overruled — an order you give to one of the stable hands."

Willy nodded in agreement, then waited expressionlessly for the other shoe to drop.

"But —"

"Ah, I knew there was one!" Willy threw up his hands and looked away in exasperation.

"But," Devon said, ignoring the interruption, "I am the boss. Your only boss for as long as you work for Willowbrook. I have the right to inquire about any matter as I see fit. And I am interested in the top horses. I will have a say in which ones we run and when we run them. You will ask my opinion and we will talk things over, and if we ever disagree, my opinion rules. I will, however, leave breeding decisions to you. I will most likely want to train at least one horse a season and I will use Jeremiah as my exercise rider. There's no reason we can't both use him," Devon said.

"You sound like this is a permanent arrangement. It's only for a year. Then you do whatever the hell you want." Willy shrugged.

Devon narrowed her eyes. "You sound awfully sure of yourself," she said in a low voice.

Willy simply shrugged again.

"Well, that's good. Then you won't mind teaching me everything you know about buying top stock. I'll be with you at Keeneland and Saratoga for the sales. After all, if you're not going to be around . . ."

"Surely you'll hire another man," Willy declared.

"I don't know," Devon said thoughtfully. "I think you may have been more trouble than you're worth. Who says the next one will be any better?"

This time Willy exploded with laughter. Devon had never heard him actually laugh before. She was so happy that they had worked things out that she laughed with him.

Abruptly Willy stopped. Putting his hands on his knees again, he leaned forward. "Okay, what if Firefly wins? Then what do you want?"

"I want you to stay on at Willowbrook for the same amount of time we've already discussed. That's all. You can look for another job after that if you want."

"Sounds okay," said Willy, pushing himself into a standing position. "Well, then, if there's nothing else, I'll be getting back to work."

"I'll be going with you," Devon reminded him.

"Yeah," Willy mumbled.

"And I'll have my attorney draw up our agreement in writing. He should have it to us by next week."

Willy turned to Devon. "I always done business on a handshake. I don't want no crazy lawyer-talk that you can't make heads or tails of."

"You trust me, then? Even after what's happened?"

"You're not a greenhorn anymore. You know what you're promisin'. That's good enough for me."

Devon studied the man who for so many months had been little better than an enemy. She was beginning to feel a certain amount of respect from him, and she appreciated it. She decided to put aside her pride and tell Willy what she was thinking. "I appreciate your giving this another chance, Willy." She put out her hand to him.

He took it without hesitation and shook it firmly, as firmly as he would have shaken the hand of a man.

CHAPTER

26

"CAN'T you sleep?" John asked Devon, who for the fifth time that night had awakened him with her tossing and turning.

"There's no point now." Devon sighed in the dark. "It's almost four-thirty. I have to get to the track soon."

John rolled toward his wife and moaned. "I don't think I've slept more than two hours tonight."

"I'm sorry," Devon said, patting his arm. "I'll go ahead and get up. Maybe you can go back to sleep."

"I'll try," he mumbled, closing his eyes and tugging the sheet over his head.

Devon slid out of the bed and pulled on her robe, shivering a little as the crisp morning air ruffled the curtains at the open window.

As usual, Devon slid into her breeches and a cotton shirt. She would take an hour in the afternoon to come back to the Lyles' farm and change for the Derby. She pulled her hair into a ponytail and tied it with a cotton bandana. On her way out the door, she made a detour to the small kitchen, where Alice had left her some biscuits from dinner the evening before. Devon didn't care that they had hardened. Anxiety had killed her appetite; she ate only because she knew she would have no other chance to do so during the hectic day.

She was barely aware of driving to Churchill Downs, of returning the greetings that came out of the purple darkness as she walked to Firefly's stall.

Firefly snorted softly when she saw Devon.

"There you are, sweetheart," Devon murmured, caressing the filly's nose.

Jeremiah seemed to materialize out of nowhere. "Nervous, Miss Devon?"

"Didn't sleep a wink," she acknowledged with a rueful smile.

"So's Firefly. She knows something's up. She's been restless."

Devon automatically looked at the feed bucket and the hay rack. Firefly had eaten everything, she noted to herself, feeling a brief moment of relief. Peeking over the door to Firefly's stall, she confirmed that the groom had, as instructed, lined the enclosure with bales of straw so that Firefly would not do herself an injury if her nerves caused her to kick the walls around her.

"Everything okay?" Devon asked the exercise rider.

"Fine, ma'am," he replied in a voice that soothed her with its calm assurance.

Devon bent down and examined Firefly's legs. Then, taking her time, she checked over the filly's body from nose to tail. Finally, she turned to Jeremiah. "We'll give her just a little exercise this morning. Very light. I want to save all her energy for this afternoon."

Jeremiah nodded approvingly and signaled the groom to saddle Firefly.

Walking behind her horse, Devon felt a sense of unreality. Was she really preparing her own entry for the Kentucky Derby? A year ago, she had known little about racing; now she was blithely risking her most valuable colt, Fearless Leader, and a great deal of money on her conviction that Firefly could win. How could she have thought she knew better than Willy? Oh, she had been a fool. John and Willy had been right!

Her dismal train of thought was interrupted by the sound of Firefly's whinny. The filly raised her head and snorted, prancing in the morning breeze. How splendid she was, Devon thought. The power of her muscles, her young, sleek body. She had never been injured, never had a day's illness — extraordinary for a racehorse. She would win! John and Willy had been wrong!

Since their fight several weeks before, he had remained in New York, coming down only two days before the Derby. Oh, he had called her faithfully each day. In addition, he had congratulated her on her successful negotiations with Willy, and had graciously accepted her thanks for the gift of Willowbrook.

"Darling, you know in your heart that Willowbrook should be yours. Always, no matter what," he had said.

"What do you mean?" Devon asked, alarmed.

"I don't mean anything," he said smoothly, "just that Willowbrook is yours and that's the way it should be. End of discussion."

All in all, John had behaved as a loving and generous husband. Yet Devon knew that he had not forgiven her for . . . for what? For insisting that Firefly run in the Derby? For overruling Willy? Why should those things anger her husband to the extent that he seemed to have lost all desire for her company? And why hadn't he made love to her when he had rejoined her in Kentucky? They had been separated for almost three weeks!

She had asked him during one of their phone calls if he was still angry with her.

"Angry?" He laughed. "If I were angry would I give you a racing operation and a thousand-acre farm?"

Yes, she said silently. Yes. Because of your pride. Because I stood up to you and wouldn't back down. But how could she say such words aloud? They would only deepen the rift between them.

Instead of confronting him, Devon had been unfailingly cheerful and affectionate. Their conversations consisted of small talk — nothing more. On the surface, everything seemed perfect.

Maybe if Firefly wins, Devon thought, he'll be so happy that things will return to normal. Or maybe if Firefly loses, things will be even better, a wicked voice inside of her said slyly. Devon shook her head as though to banish the ugly thought.

Looking up at the night sky, now streaked with pink and yellow at the edge of the horizon, Devon hurried up to Jeremiah and said, "Let's get this over with before it gets too light."

Many trainers tried to conceal particularly impressive exercise sessions from their competition, and Devon believed in this practice. No need to provide her rivals with clues about what to expect from Firefly. They had learned enough about her from previous races. The exercise timer sat in the grandstand overseeing the morning workouts. The results of his task were printed each day in the *Racing Form*. The fastest workout of the day appeared in this bettors' Bible with a black dot printed beside it, and was appropriately called a bullet workout. Devon tried to avoid such publicity by exercising her horses most strenuously before it was light when she was at a public track. But this was not always possible, as it was the job of the clocker to record times for every contender.

Once Firefly's workout was finished and the hot walker had taken her, Jeremiah instructed the groom to give her a bath and a rubdown. Jeremiah himself, however, wanted to oversee the final currying, hoof-polishing, and brushing. He wanted Firefly to shine, both literally and figuratively.

Devon suddenly found herself with nothing more to do. She felt superfluous. She wondered what Willy was doing. Fearless Leader's stall was not visible from Firefly's, since the colts were housed in a separate section. With a final pat of Firefly's muzzle, Devon strolled down the wide aisle of the barn toward Fearless Leader's stall.

With a peek inside, she determined that he, too, had already been fed, exercised, and bathed, and was now being allowed to rest. She looked into the magnificent horse's big brown eyes, then reached up to stroke his neck.

"I hope I don't lose you," she whispered to him.

"Sayin' your good-byes?" A voice behind her made her wheel sharply around.

Willy almost had a smile on his face, Devon noticed with amusement. He had never joked with her, though his manner toward her had been less strained since she had become owner of Willowbrook.

"Pretty sure of yourself," Devon remarked.

"Only way to be," he grumbled. "Aren't you?"

Again Willy startled Devon. She could not recall his ever asking her how she felt about anything.

"I don't know," Devon replied honestly. "I think I've got the jitters."

"That's natural," Willy said, drawing closer to Fearless Leader and cupping his muzzle in his callused hands. Devon noted the gentle way in which this roughest of men treated the colt.

He loves them, no matter what he says, Devon thought to herself. "Are *you* nervous?" she asked, not really expecting an affirmative answer. Willy would never admit to such an emotion, she was sure.

"Nah," he replied predictably, looking away from Devon.

"You have a lot riding on this race."

"Right. But I don't have nothin' to lose. You do."

"Believe me, I know," she moaned ruefully. She was surprised to note that they were smiling at each other. Willy actually smiling!

As though caught doing something wrong, Willy abruptly turned away from Devon, erasing the smile from his face.

Why, he's embarrassed by the fact that he actually found me likable for a moment, Devon thought.

"Willy . . ." Devon hesitated. She was trying to read Willy's face under the bill of the Dodgers cap, but it was obscured in shadow. "Will it be so bad for you if you lose? I mean, will you look for another position when the year is over?"

Willy was quiet for a moment. "I don't know," he said finally. "I'd have to see how it works out back at Willowbrook."

"You mean, how we work together?"

"Whatever," he mumbled.

"I suppose you've always dreamed of a farm of your own?" Devon sighed.

" 'T'would be sweet," he said, his voice almost wistful.

"Well . . . good luck." Devon put out her hand to the trainer.

"Yeah. You too," he said with a firm shake.

Devon turned to go.

"Miz Alexander . . ." Devon did an about-face in surprise. Willy almost never addressed her by name. "You'll be proud of Firefly today. Of that I'm sure," he said with a nod of his baseball cap.

"I know," she said, raising her chin and smiling at Willy, "but thanks for saying so."

Devon drove home to change, feeling a little less anxious than before her talk with Willy. His assurances meant more to her than she cared to admit. After all, she reminded herself, he knows a good horse when he sees one. Why shouldn't I feel good about what he said? But she knew it was more than just his expertise about horseflesh that soothed her. His confidence in her, too, was implicit in his remark. And why shouldn't he respect my abilities? she asked herself with a smile. He's one of the best trainers in the world — and he trained me. Kicking and screaming all the way, but he *did* train me.

Devon returned home to find John eating breakfast on the patio.

"How's everything?" John asked, looking up from his newspaper.

"Looks good," Devon answered, dropping a kiss on the top of his head.

"Would you like some?" he asked, pointing to the bacon on his plate.

"I couldn't eat a thing." Devon gave a nervous smile. "I think I'll just have a hot bath and start getting dressed."

"You should eat something," John said absentmindedly, returning to his reading.

Devon stood for a moment looking at him. Dressed in tennis whites, with his tan limbs contrasting handsomely with the starched linen, he looked strikingly attractive. She wondered how many other women envied her for being married to him — how many flirted with him, even tried to seduce him, while she remained hundreds of miles away.

After today, she told herself. After today she had promised to spend the summer with him, going wherever he chose. She wondered if he remembered the promise, or cared whether she fulfilled it. Sometimes it seemed they were complete strangers.

If Firefly won the Derby, Devon would enter her in the Preakness and the Belmont Stakes in a bid for that rarest of all horseracing awards: the Triple Crown. But she knew that no matter how much she wanted to be involved in Firefly's training, she would have to delegate it to Willy. Her marriage depended on it.

"Darling," she murmured.

John didn't look up from his newspaper. "Hmmm?"

"I love you, John," Devon said, the vehemence in her voice transmitting her suppressed emotions, her worries.

He raised his eyes, gave her a quick smile, said, "I love you too, darling," then lowered his eyes to the newspaper again.

"No, I mean . . ."

John looked up at her, a politely attentive expression on his face.

Devon did not know what more to say. Perhaps she was imagining things. Her nerves were raw. She was being silly. "I mean," she continued more smoothly, "that I'm looking forward to spending the summer with you, with nothing to do but relax and enjoy ourselves."

"That will be wonderful," he agreed, his eyes drifting back to the article he was reading.

Devon sighed and went into the cottage. After her bath, she carefully applied her makeup, then donned the striking ensemble she had designed especially for the Derby. She wore the same black and scarlet as her racing silks. The dress was made of black silk shantung with pleats that began at midthigh and fell to below her calves. Each pleat was faced in bright scarlet, so that her movements caused the skirt to explode into a dance of black and red. At the waist she wore a red lizard belt. Above the waist, the dress's simple bodice was also of black silk, but the long, full sleeves were pleated in the same lively pattern as the bottom of the skirt. She wore a red straw picture hat piped in black, with a black grosgrain ribbon around the crown. Her open-toed black shoes with red lizard heels had been custom-made in New York for her, and on her hands she wore red gloves of the finest kidskin.

John finished dressing at the same time she did, although he had started forty-five minutes later.

"You look wonderful," he said, genuine admiration in his voice. "You'll be the most beautiful woman there."

Although John had flown his plane to Kentucky, he had also instructed his car and driver to meet him there. The long black Rolls-Royce, gleaming richly from headlight to tailpipe, transported him and Devon to Churchill Downs in grand style. Once John and Devon were at their box, John's driver brought from the car a two-bottle ice bucket filled with Roederer's Cristal and placed it by John's side. Also spread on a large silver tray that sat upon a bed of ice were pâté and small rounds of French bread; caviar surrounded by hard-boiled eggs, sour cream, and minced onions; and huge succulent Gulf shrimp.

John took a small piece of toast and spread some caviar on it, then offered it to Devon.

"No, thank you." She fidgeted in her seat a few seconds, greeting friends in neighboring boxes. Unable to sit still any longer, she stood up abruptly. "I have to go and see Rick McClintock."

"But the race is still hours away!" John protested.

"I know," Devon said with a sheepish smile, "but I'm too on edge to sit here."

"Leave the poor man alone to dress," said John, filling a glass with champagne. "Here, sit down and drink this. It will calm you." He pulled her back into her chair.

Devon took a sip, enjoying the sensation of the ice-cold, tangy little bubbles on her tongue. "That's nice," she said.

John covered her hand with his. Devon was grateful for the contact. It made her feel better. She put her free hand over his and gave it a squeeze.

"Oh, there are Sydney and Bart." John called to the couple, who came toward them slowly, their progress interrupted every few feet by a handshake or a kiss on the cheek from friends and acquaintances. By the time Sydney and Bart reached their box, they were trailing behind them six more of the Alexanders' friends.

Devon embraced Sydney warmly and gave Bart a perfunctory kiss on the cheek. She was glad to see Sydney. Bart was another matter. Devon admitted that he was good company and wonderful to have at parties. Women found him attractive, with his glossy brown hair and deep, almost black eyes. At first, Devon had liked him. But there was a dark side of Bart that made Devon distrust him. He seemed to enjoy needling his friends. Many of his remarks appeared deliberately calculated to create misgivings in the listener. None of his compliments were straightforward.

"You look lovely, Sydney. That's a very slimming dress," Bart often said to his wife. Sydney would thank him, all the while looking anxiously at others in the room. Was she anxious because she was afraid that she might indeed be too heavy, or was she worried that others had observed the backhanded nature of the comment?

Whenever Bart did this, Devon came to her friend's defense."It is lovely, Sydney, but of course you're too slender to worry about whether or not it's slimming," she would say.

"John, old boy," Bart said loudly now. Bart seemed genuinely to like and respect John, Devon thought. He never made him the butt of his little needling remarks. But Devon was not usually spared.

"Missed you the other evening," Bart said, turning to Devon.

"It was a wonderful dinner party, Sydney," John complimented his friend's wife.

"I'm sure you thought so," Bart said slyly to John, "what with the beautiful Bebe hanging on to your every word." He turned back to Devon with a wink. "You'd best keep an eye on this one, my dear," he said, patting her hand.

Forcing a small laugh, Devon said in a tone that she deliberately kept lighthearted, "Apparently I don't need to, since you're doing such a good job for me." She would not let her tone of voice betray her annoyance with Bart.

Instead of turning away from him, as she was tempted to do, she forced herself to go on joking and talking with him for a few more minutes.

"Well, if you'll excuse me, I'd like to go down and check on a few things."

"Ah, our amazonian trainer!"

Bart gave John a sidelong look as he said this, but John only said, "Hurry back, darling."

As Devon made her way to the stables, she pondered Bart's comment about John. Had it come from anyone but Bart, Devon would have taken it more seriously, but she knew that he enjoyed seeing the effect of such disquieting statements on her, so she decided to dismiss it. John had probably confided his annoyance at her long absences to his friend, and Bart was just playing off of that weakness in Devon and John's relationship.

Devon approached Firefly's stall and caressed the filly a few moments. She would have liked to give her a carrot, but it was too short a time until the race. Most trainers believed that horses ran best on an empty stomach. Devon had ordered Firefly's rations that morning cut by twenty percent.

"Are you hungry, sweetheart?" she murmured, kissing the horse's soft nose. She put her arms around the filly, and Firefly nipped her gently on the shoulder, knocking her hat off. Devon let it lay at her feet as she devoted her attention to the horse. She did not even mind when the filly left two wet marks from her mouth on the black silk of the dress.

She bent to retrieve her hat, then wandered over to the small row of white-painted cabins where the workers stayed. The best jockeys did not usually live at a particular track. Many earned a great deal of money and had very comfortable homes of their own. Others worked full-time for one owner, enjoying the benefits of pleasant, free housing on some of the nation's finest country estates. Rick McClintock was of the former breed. He had been assigned a room at Churchill Downs for the Derby, but he actually lived in a magnificent antebellum mansion near the racetrack. He drove a sporty crimson Morgan and had a different beautiful woman waiting for him after each race. He was a typical bachelor jockey. As he had come to know Devon better, he had even begun flirting gently with her, though he was careful not to overstep the bounds of the business relationship.

"Ah, Mrs. Alexander, how lovely you look today," said McClintock as he invited her into his quarters.

Devon gave him a dazzling smile. Jockeys always amused her, with their mammoth egos crammed into pint-sized bodies. But she had to admit that McClintock was attractive. His roguish grin and dancing eyes always lit up flatteringly at the sight of her.

Devon walked to a rickety wooden chair and sat down. Rick sat in a second chair that did not match the first. Track housing was rustic, at best.

"All right." Devon got right to the point, oblivious to her surroundings. "Is there anything we haven't gone over?" Since the Blue Grass Stakes, she had hired Rick McClintock to ride Firefly regularly. Because McClintock did not work for Devon at Willowbrook, he had not known Firefly well prior to the Blue Grass Stakes. But by now he knew her almost as well as Jeremiah and Devon did.

"She's been doing great with the blinkers on," Rick replied. "They were a good idea. Otherwise, it's like you already said. The strategy that works with Firefly is to start out at top speed and just keep at it."

"Well, then, I guess there's not much else to say," said Devon with a shrug and a smile, "except good luck."

They put out their hands simultaneously for a handshake.

"Get ready for the winner's circle, Mrs. Alexander. I am," said McClintock with his reckless grin.

She was. Oh, she was.

Devon felt tears come to her eyes as the crowd sang "My Old Kentucky Home" — a Derby tradition. She was overcome with emotion, not from the song, but from the occasion itself.

Devon's nerves were stretched so taut that she could barely speak. She watched through her binoculars as Firefly was led to the starting line. Fearless Leader was already in. They both had decent post positions, which were assigned through a blind drawing.

"It's going to be fine," Sydney reassured her. But Sydney did not know how much was at stake. No one but John did.

Sooner than Devon expected, the signal to run sounded and Firefly, as at the Blue Grass Stakes, was one of the first to shoot forward.

"It's the filly Firefly in the lead, followed by Battering Ram, Snowball, Sensation, One for the Money, Young Turk, and Boisterous. Fearless Leader breaks behind the field, but recovers and sneaks past Starlight and Henry's Boy to overtake Motherlode and Lollapalooza going neck and neck," said the announcer.

Devon sprang to her feet and leaned as far as she could over the rail of her box, her binoculars glued to Firefly. She focused on McClintock, who looked well in control. Firefly wasn't even running at top speed yet! Devon was so proud of her.

"McClintock's fighting off a challenge from One for the Money, trying to hold Firefly's lead. Fearless Leader now on the inside overtakes One for the Money. It's Firefly, Sensation, One for the Money, and Fearless Leader nose to nose, with the rest of the field a length behind. Bringing up the rear is Henry's Boy.

"Fearless Leader surges ahead now, past One for the Money, Firefly still in the lead by half a length."

Devon saw McClintock hunker as close as he could to Firefly's neck and urge her forward with his crop. She sprang forward like a fury, lather streaming off her neck as she flew down the track. McClintock edged her to the inside of the track. Devon stopped breathing. The turns were tighter at the inside, but also shorter. There was more danger, but it could be the best position on the field if well ridden.

The blinkers seemed to be working. Firefly looked neither right nor left, despite Fearless Leader pounding almost nose to nose with her.

"And it's Fearless Leader losing some ground to One for the Money, Firefly still in the lead," said the announcer.

The gray One for the Money had indeed moved between Fearless Leader and Firefly. He pushed forward. Slim Bocaso, Fearless Leader's jockey, fought the maneuver.

"Bocaso fights back, but he's trapped by Sensation. And One for the Money breaks through the traffic jam and puts the pressure on Firefly. The filly's still leading. She won't give up! It looks like she may set a new track record!"

Firefly was galloping, galloping with all her might; Devon could see the veins standing out on her neck. She was almost a blur, she was going so fast. Her tail was a horizontal line behind her.

Suddenly a horrified gasp went up from the crowd.

"What's happening? Firefly's tumbling! She's collapsing and McClintock can't hold on to her! McClintock's down! He's hit by Sensation. It's a collision and Sensation rolls over McClintock!" the announcer said, the words spilling out of him in an excited torrent.

"My God!" screamed Devon. She pushed past her friends and out of the box, tripping over stairs, people, handbags to reach the field.

Somewhere in the distance, Devon heard, "And One for the Money wins the race, with Fearless Leader in second place, and Young Turk in third. Firefly can't get up. Sensation is up now. She's limping but her leg doesn't appear broken. McClintock's still down, but he's moving. Now he's getting up. He's limping over to Firefly! Firefly is still motionless."

As though in a nightmare, Devon saw the white ambulance roar through the crowd toward the track, the moan of its siren an eerie portent of the hopeless disaster she knew awaited her on the field.

The track veterinarian was beside Firefly now. He was leaning over her, his stethoscope on her chest. Devon ran, ran as hard as she could, to the field, a small figure in red and black.

"Ma'am, I'm sorry, you can't go down there." An arm on her. She brushed it off as though it were no more than a fly.

Sweat poured down Devon's back. She was wet all over. Her silk stockings were in tatters, her legs cut from bumping into people and objects. She kicked off her shoes because her heels sank into the turf, slowing her down. Unnoticed, her hat was lifted off her head by the breeze. For a moment it floated on the air like a red beacon of distress.

"Firefly, Firefly, Firefly," Devon repeated aloud to herself in a singsong chant. "Please, God. Please, God! Let her be all right," she begged.

She was almost on top of them now. Two white-coated men were urging McClintock to get onto the stretcher. His scarlet and black uniform was torn; blood mingled with the red cloth. He was carried away just as Devon reached the field.

Devon saw a cluster of bodies surrounding her filly. Shoving through the group, she reached the horse's side and sank to her knees in the dirt.

"Firefly!" Devon gasped. The filly's beautiful brown eyes stared unseeingly at her.

"I'm sorry, Mrs. Alexander," said a man in black, folding his metal stethoscope into his bag. "I'm afraid . . ."

"No!" Devon cried.

"It was a heart attack, ma'am," he insisted gently. He stood up, his arm reaching down to help Devon up. He wanted to pull her away from Firefly.

Devon refused. She stretched an arm out toward the filly. "I just want to touch her."

"I don't think that would—" began the man in black.

"Fuck off! She's got to pay her last respects." Willy's gruff voice dismissed the veterinarian.

Devon put her hand on the filly's silky neck. "She's still lathered," she said to no one in particular, tears streaming down her face.

Willy knelt down beside her. "She gave you everything she had. She ran a good race. She would have won," he said.

"She gave me her heart. She had so much heart," Devon put her head against Willy's rough denim shirt and sobbed. His arm encircled her and he patted her soothingly on the back.

"She had heart," he agreed. "And that's the best compliment you can pay a racehorse . . . she had heart."

CHAPTER 27

DEVON had never before felt such pain, but when the doctor laid the tiny warm creature upon her chest, all pain was forgotten.

"John?" Devon called weakly, eager to share the moment with her husband.

"Here, darling." He came toward them, mother and daughter, and enfolded them in his arms.

Devon was filled with a sense of perfect love, of renewal, of happiness so overwhelming she thought it would burst from her body like a waterfall. She sighed, cradling her daughter in her arms, "A Christmas baby . . . the best present of all."

"Have you finally picked out the name you prefer?" John teased. They had discussed several names — had settled on names several times — only to have Devon change her mind.

Devon smiled sheepishly. "Morgan, I think. And her middle name will be Victoria, after your mother."

"Morgan Victoria Alexander. I like it. But what about your mother?"

"I'll save that for our next daughter." Devon grinned.

John looked at the wrinkled little body in Devon's arms and was surprised by the feeling of protectiveness that came over him. The helpless little baby had depended for nine months on Devon; now she was his responsibility also.

"May I hold her?" he asked, almost shyly.

Devon looked up at her husband and laughed. "Of course! She's your daughter, you know."

Ever so gently, John lifted the squirming creature into his arms. Her hands, so tiny, were just visible above the clean white swaddling cloth. Little tufts of dark hair — ebony, like Devon's — stood almost straight up on her head. Her small mouth looked like a juicy raspberry, round and red and sweet. John lowered his cheek to hers, and promptly fell in love with her.

"Morgan," he whispered, "I'll always take care of you. I promise."

CHAPTER

28

"IT'S a surprise for you!" John said, placing the large satin-ribboned box on Devon's vanity with a flourish.

"What's the occasion?" She laughed.

"Valentine's Day and your getting your figure back." John grinned with the excitement of a little boy, his blue eyes sparkling.

"Well . . . almost . . ." Devon said ruefully, pinching an extra inch of skin around her waist. She slid the huge pink ribbon off the box and lifted the glossy white cardboard lid. Inside lay a gown of scarlet velvet, absolutely devoid of adornment except for luxuriant black mink cuffs.

"It's gorgeous!" Devon breathed.

"You'll wear it to the ball this evening?" John held it up to Devon, admiring the blush the rich red cloth brought to her cheeks.

"This evening?" Devon looked questioningly at her husband.

John looked crestfallen. "You haven't forgotten!"

Devon looked down in embarrassment. "Well, I wasn't sure we would attend. You know Morgan's been a bit fractious today. She's — "

"Now look here, Devon," John declared, pacing back and forth across the pastel Aubusson carpet in frustration, "we have people to look after Morgan. We haven't been out together since before Christmas."

"That's not so!" Devon protested. "Just last night we went to your parents' house for dinner. And last week we went to Delmonico's with Sydney and Bart."

"That's not what I mean and you know it," John replied impatiently. "I'm talking about social events. Of course, that was natural for a time, but there's no reason to go on behaving as though we live in a cloister!"

"John, I know you enjoy parties. Why don't you go without me," Devon ventured. She had lost her taste for such occasions. First, in the summer, there had been the death of Firefly. It had taken something out of her, had left her bereft for weeks. Despite that, she had dutifully attended all the social engagements she had promised John she would.

They had sailed in Newport, partied in Saratoga Springs, and gone hunting at the Whitney estate in Thomasville, Georgia. She had looked forward to the final days of her pregnancy with relief at the respite from the constant social whirl. Now John wanted to resume their former life as though they had no new daughter at home.

"I don't want to go anywhere without you!" John exploded. "I want you to remember that you have a husband and that you owe me some time and attention, too."

Devon turned away from him guiltily. He was not the only one to sound that lament. Grace, home for a New Year's visit, had warned her not to neglect her husband. Grace had returned to Europe in the first week of February, but her words lingered behind to haunt Devon.

"Remember, you have an extremely attractive husband. And you have neglected him — no, don't argue — just close your mouth and listen," Grace had said in her usual blunt fashion. "You'll recall that I warned you at the beginning of your marriage to remember your duty is to him first — not your parents, not your children, but your husband. Now it turns out that you've had long separations while you've pursued this racing thing."

Devon protested, "But John gave me Willowbrook to make it what it once was!"

"And I understand you have a trainer capable of doing just that —"

"But —"

"Hush! Listen to your big sister. There's something wrong between you and John. I see it. I wouldn't say anything if I didn't love you, but I can't sit by and watch you throw a wonderful marriage down the drain."

"He loves me and he's absolutely crazy about Morgan!" Devon denied her sister's words, but deep inside she feared they were true.

Sensing she had struck a chord, Grace relented. "That's right. Now you have a chance to make everything right between you again. Don't throw it away or you'll regret it the rest of your life!"

"I have no regrets," Devon said coldly, "I haven't regretted one moment that I've spent on the racing, and certainly not one moment that I've spent with Morgan!"

"You're being foolishly stubborn," Grace replied with equal coldness, "and you may not regret it yet, but you will one day if you continue like this. John is admired by many women. I've only been here one month, and I've already heard rumors—"

"Don't be ridiculous! Just because we were apart a lot this spring. John's never been unfaith—"

"Probably not," Grace said in a maddeningly skeptical voice.

"You don't think—" Devon exploded, outraged.

"No," Grace admitted, "but I think he's on the verge and I think that if he does you have no one to blame but yourself."

Stung, Devon argued, "Each person is responsible for his own behavior, and there is no excuse for adultery!"

"There may be no excuse, but there's usually a rationale. And, sometimes, it's a fairly good one."

"Well, I never thought I'd hear you express such old-fashioned views," Devon huffed. "You always went on so about the freedom of Frenchwomen. What about me? What about the things that interest me? Why shouldn't I be free to pursue them? And why should I have to give up everything I enjoy for fear of losing my husband."

Grace looked levelly into her sister's eyes. "I'm not old-fashioned. I'm realistic. Of course, you're free to do as you wish. And it may be that Willowbrook is more important to you than your husband is. Or that Morgan is. If so, then that is your choice. But don't be surprised if that choice offends John. And don't be surprised if you lose him to another woman."

"But that's not fair!" Devon protested like a child railing against the inevitable.

"No," Grace said grimly.

"You can't agree that it's right!"

"No." Grace shrugged.

"Then why should I go along? John works. He spends all day at the office. He could spend more time at Willowbrook, but instead he's always trying to persuade me to come to New York. Well, here I am and you're saying it's still not enough." Devon cut herself short, surprised at her own resentment and hostility. Was her husband less important to her than her own pursuits? she asked herself. How had it happened? There had to be a way to resolve the situation.

As though reading her thoughts, Grace said, "I'm surprised that you seem to care so little for his happiness. For your happiness as a couple. You seem completely absorbed in your own separate world."

"Morgan is his daughter, too!"

"Morgan doesn't need you by her side every minute," Grace said firmly. "I think you're using these things as an excuse to hold John at arm's length. And for the life of me, I can't understand why. But thinking back, even as early as your engagement, it seemed you were reluctant to make the kind of concessions a wife usually makes for her husband. Remember when you didn't want to spend Christmas in New York with him that first year?" Grace asked.

"That has nothing to do with —"

"You're too stubborn," Grace said with finality. "That's fine, of course, if you want to spend your life alone, but if you want to share it with a man —"

"But this is 1935! Women work. We have the vote. We aren't supposed to just be our husbands' appendages!"

Grace burst out laughing, a peal of cynical laughter that was totally devoid of mirth. "Oh, you poor naive child! Where in the world did you ever get such ideas? No wonder you're unhappy. You haven't accepted the truth."

"Which is?" Devon said angrily.

"That no matter how 'modern' our society becomes, a man will always expect to be the number-one priority for his woman. Try it any other way and you're doomed to fail. You can fight it. You can resent it. But if you don't give in to it, you'll lose the man. It's as simple as that."

"Well, I do resist it. I have things I want to do with my life — *my* life, independent of John's, and I intend to do them," Devon said defiantly. She could make it work, she told herself. She would spend more time with John. They would go out more. She would show him that she loved him. But she would not give up her racing. She would not turn over the upbringing of her child to servants. And she would not deny herself the pleasure of achieving something apart from her family.

Grace heaved a sigh of resignation. "I hope you enjoy your other pursuits very, very much. Be certain that they're worth what you pay for them. If they are, then you've made the right choice. But realize, my dear, that you are making a choice, and that you must be prepared to live with the consequences."

It was that conversation that came back to Devon now as she regarded the scarlet velvet dress on the bed. John had specifically had it designed in her racing colors to please her. Now it was her turn to try to please him.

"You're right, John. And anyway, with such a beautiful new dress to wear, I know I'll enjoy going out," Devon said as enthusiastically as she could. She rang the bell to summon Alice.

"Would you please prepare my bath. We'll be going out tonight," Devon told her maid. The look of approval in Alice's eyes made her feel no better. It seemed the whole world disagreed with her.

CHAPTER 29

THE first time Devon placed her daughter, Morgan, in the saddle in front of her, the child cried so much that her parents were afraid she would make herself ill.

"For heaven's sake, Devon, give it up!" John said, reaching up to take the child.

"I don't understand why she's so afraid. I'm holding her, after all." Devon was not mounted on one of her racehorses but rather on a mild pinto mare used for pleasure riding.

"She's only two years old! It doesn't matter why she's afraid. Either she'll get over it or she won't, but there's no use in forcing her to stay up there."

"I know that," Devon said, insulted by the implication that she would allow her child to suffer in order to satisfy a desire of her own. Sometimes it seemed that she was always defending her actions to John. She handed the squalling baby down to her father and then dismounted herself.

"Riding is just not for everyone," John declared.

"Oh, she'll get over whatever's bothering her," Devon said confidently, "it's just a matter of time."

"Maybe," John said, a note of skepticism in his voice.

"Don't you want her to ride?" Devon asked, handing the reins to a groom and walking toward the main house.

"I don't really care," John said mildly.

Devon took Morgan back from John and crooned to her until she quieted. After the child was calm, Devon said to John, "You like to ride. I like to ride. Why wouldn't you want Morgan to enjoy it?"

"Devon," said John, stopping and turning his wife toward him, the baby cradled in her arms, "it just isn't important. That's why."

Devon pulled away from her husband and shrugged as best she could with her burden.

John and Devon had frequent disagreements about Morgan's upbringing. John, though he loved the child, wanted her raised at Willowbrook so that he and Devon could spend weeks at a time alone at their New York home. He did not want the burden of full-time parenthood. He wanted to live freely and as a couple at least a few months of every year. Devon, on the other hand, believed that the child should travel with them. It was a constant source of arguments.

Then again, there were times when they seemed to realize that they were endangering their relationship, and they would make an effort to be especially kind to each other, for there was real love between them.

Now, feeling guilty, John asked, "Would you like me to look after Morgan awhile so you can work in your greenhouse?"

Devon, appreciating John's effort to make peace, said, "Thank you. I'd like that. It's time for her nap, so you can just give her to Penny."

Devon watched them go, the tiny child cradled against her husband's broad chest. She had an overwhelming feeling of love for them both — a feeling that was laced with sadness, though she could not say why.

CHAPTER 30

DEVON and Morgan scanned the vegetable garden for the most select pumpkins. "Can I make faces on them?" Four-year-old Morgan was breathless with excitement.

Devon smiled down at her daughter's eager face. "You can draw the faces, but Daddy has to cut them."

Morgan's face fell. "But Daddy's not here!"

"He's coming home this afternoon," Devon replied soothingly.

"Yay!" Morgan did a little dance of excitement. She wished her daddy were *always* here, but Mommy said he had lots of work in New York. That made his visits very special. But sometimes it seemed like they had to get to know each other all over again every time he came to Willowbrook. At least Mommy was always here. And they did so many fun things! Morgan loved her father, too, but he wasn't as casual and cozy as her mother. He never seemed to get dirty and go in the woods with her like her mother did. Her father, though, could throw her up in the air and catch her by her waist without even hurting her. So that made up for a lot.

"Will Daddy . . ." Morgan hesitated.

"What is it, sweetheart?" Devon kneeled next to her daughter so that their eyes were on the same level.

"Read me a story tonight?"

Devon ruffled her daughter's hair. "I'll bet he'd like that," she assured her.

But when it came time to tuck her in that night, only Penny came. When Morgan asked for her parents, Penny told her they were talking. Morgan could hear them. It was loud. They talked loud a lot, but not when Morgan was in the same room, she noticed.

A few minutes later, though, Morgan received a pleasant surprise. Her mother came to say good night to her looking like a beautiful fairy in a fluffy pink dress. Instead of smelling like hay, as she usually did, she smelled like flowers. She had white sparkles hanging from her ears and neck, just like raindrops.

"Is that ice?" Morgan asked, touching the hard, bright surface.

Devon laughed. "In a manner of speaking, I suppose." Seeing the look of puzzlement on Morgan's face, she clarified her statement. "No, it's not ice. Those are diamonds."

"They look like magic!" Morgan breathed.

"A lot of people think they are," Devon said with a smile, "but they're not."

"When's Daddy coming to read me my story?"

Devon looked at her child, almost a replica of herself at that age. She looked so peaceful, her shiny black hair neatly plaited for sleep, her crisp white cotton nightdress blending with the lavender-scented bed linens.

"Soon. He's getting ready to go to a party," Devon explained softly.

"Are you going to a party too?"

"Yes."

"Together?"

Devon studied her child, surprised at the question. Could a child so young see the discord between herself and John? They tried to hide it from their daughter. "Of course we're going together, sillybilly, why would you ask that?"

The child did not answer directly. Instead she asked, "Are you mad at Daddy?"

"Of course not!"

"Why do you talk loud with him?"

Devon thought a moment. "You know how sometimes you make Mommy angry, like when you hit Leslie or when you won't eat your vegetables?"

"But Daddy likes veg'bles," Morgan declared, sure of herself on this topic, even if she couldn't quite pronounce the word. He had told her so on the many occasions when she had tried to avoid eating the hateful things.

Devon laughed at this. "Yes, he likes vegetables, but sometimes big people disagree on other things."

"Dis-a-gree?" The child grappled with the new word.

"To disagree is like when I say I love peas and you say you don't. It's not the same as a fight. It's not as mean as a fight. It's called a disagreement. It means we don't think the same thing."

"You and Daddy . . . do you . . . dis-a-gree a lot?"

"No, not at all," Devon said. When she thought about it, they didn't disagree on many things. It's just that what they disagreed on so fundamentally affected their lives.

"Then why do you talk loud so much?"

Devon was truly disturbed now. She and John had assiduously avoided arguing in front of their child, but Morgan had obviously still heard them. And the little girl was worried.

"It bothers you when we talk loud?" Devon asked, caressing her daughter's forehead.

Her daughter answered timidly, "Sometimes."

Devon bent down and hugged her daughter. "I don't want you ever to worry about anything like that, sweetpea. I love your father very much and he loves me, but most of all, we both love you more than anything on earth." She tucked in the sheets around Morgan and caressed her cheek. "Daddy will be in to read you a story in just a minute."

But by the time John came in, Morgan had fallen asleep.

CHAPTER 31

JOHN kissed Grace on the cheek as her Pan American Airways flight to Chicago was announced. It was the first leg in her journey from New York to the Hearst ranch to celebrate Devon's birthday. A journey that John was supposed to have made with her, had business matters in New York not delayed him.

"I hope Devon understands," he said, looking into Grace's eyes for absolution. "It's one of the most important packages I've ever put together."

"It's not your fault Henley's been ill."

"Yes, but now that he's better I suppose I could have put him off . . . I'm sure he would have understood."

"You've invested a great deal of time and money in this deal, as I understand it," Grace said reassuringly, "and the other investors have all come to New York especially for these negotiations. Anyway, you'll only be one day late."

"Yes, but I'll miss her party."

"Oh, pooh! Marion has a party every night. Maybe I can persuade her to put Devon's off a day."

John knew that Marion had specifically scheduled Devon's birthday for a Saturday so that their Hollywood friends who were making movies would be able to attend. If she delayed it until Sunday, the actual day of Devon's birthday, it would be a much smaller celebration.

As though reading her brother-in-law's thoughts, Grace said, "Devon's birthday is not really even until Sunday. You'll be there by Sunday afternoon. That's the most important."

"Well, I suppose there's nothing I can do about it now anyhow, so there's no point in worrying about it."

"Right you are," Grace said with a smile. It touched her that John was so worried about missing Devon's birthday.

Grace, however, did not understand the real reason for John's concern. He was afraid that Devon would be offended not because their relationship was so loving, but precisely because it stood on such unsteady ground.

John waved good-bye to his sister-in-law, then exited the airport to where his car and driver awaited him.

"Where to, sir?" asked the driver.

" '21.' " John would grab a steak, perhaps have a drink or two, then head back to his office to prepare for his meeting the next day.

John was greeted warmly by the maître d' of the renowned watering hole and shown to his regular table. Without his asking for it, a whiskey and soda was placed before him. The restaurant treated its regulars well.

"I'll have the usual," he told the waiter, knowing his steak would be prepared perfectly medium rare and his potato would contain both butter and sour cream. John liked gourmet food, but sometimes he just wanted a thick steak and a baked potato.

When the food came, John eagerly sliced into the grilled meat and took a bite. The juicy goodness of it acted as a balm to John's mood. He relaxed, enjoying the meal.

"Well, good evening!" A lively feminine voice interrupted John's solitude.

Bebe Henley, splendid in a strapless gold sequined gown, looked down at John.

John quickly stood up. "How nice to see you again!" he said, dazzled by the play of light on Bebe's gown.

Bebe took one step closer to him before saying, "May I join you for a moment?"

"By all means," John said with a broad smile. He looked around to see who was accompanying her, but she was apparently alone.

Reading his look, Bebe said, "I'm afraid I've been left on my own. You just missed Daddy. He's still not feeling quite up to par. He said he was going to turn in early so he'd be on his toes for his meeting with you tomorrow. Anyhow, it's *much* too early for me," she said conspiratorially as she slid gracefully into the tufted chair.

John had a moment of disquiet. It was one thing to be seen with

Bebe and a third person, it was quite another to be seen *en tête à tête*. He knew she had married since their meeting in San Simeon. But she made no mention of a husband. John wondered about that. His unease grew as Bebe crossed one long, tanned leg over the other and the fashionable slit in the front of her gown dropped open to present a clear — and extremely enticing — view.

Bebe, as though unaware of the effect she was creating, casually searched in her gold mesh evening bag for a cigarette.

"Allow me," said John, politely taking her black enameled Cartier lighter from her and holding the flame to the tip of her cigarette.

"Thank you," Bebe said, relaxing into her chair.

John knew he had no option but to invite her to have a drink with him.

"I'd love a Courvoisier," Bebe said, blowing a stream of smoke through perfectly shaped coral lips.

She had her Courvoisier as John ate his meal, then one with John after he had finished. John found himself relaxing, laughing as Bebe told him anecdotes about herself and her father. He urged Bebe to join him in a bottle of champagne, a suggestion she agreed to with alacrity.

He did not know what they spoke of for three hours. He only knew that at the end of that time — and after two bottles of champagne — he had no desire to go home. For a moment, he tuned out what Bebe was saying and allowed his eyes to roam over her lovely body. Her champagne hair tumbled over her shoulders and rested lightly on the burnished skin of her full breasts — tightly hugged by the bodice of her dress. Her arms and shoulders, sleek and smooth, glowed in the dim light of the restaurant. John had the irresistible desire to peel the shimmering dress off Bebe's lush body to see if the reality was as good as his memory of that long-ago day beside the pool at San Simeon.

Thinking of San Simeon, though, suddenly brought him back to the present. He closed his eyes for a second and tried to envision his wife. Instead of seeing her in all her beauty, however, the image that came to his mind was of their last argument.

"What are you thinking of?" Bebe's husky voice insinuated itself into his thoughts.

John's eyes held Bebe's for a moment. The air between them was electric. And the message in her eyes was clear. Embarrassed by the intensity of his attraction, John looked away. "I think I'd better be getting home."

Bebe surprised him when she said, "Yes, it's late." For some reason, John had expected her to try to detain him at the restaurant. Bebe had behaved seductively toward John for several years, but he had never been around her alone for a sustained period of time, nor had he ever sought her company. But now, as he followed the mesmerizing sway of her hips out of the restaurant, he found her incredibly inviting. Life with Devon was so complicated, so fraught with tension. How marvelous it would be to simply enjoy this young woman's feline sexuality.

"Drop me?" Bebe asked casually as John's driver held the door of the Rolls open for him.

Now he understood her willingness to go home. He had not known that she did not have her own car with her. "Of course," he murmured, knowing that he was making a crucial decision, but too drunk with champagne and sexual heat to care.

Once in the car, however, the full gravity of his current course of action came to him. He had been married eight years. He had never been unfaithful, nor did he condone such behavior in others. How, then, could he be contemplating acting out an old, recurring fantasy that he had blotted from his mind on many occasions for the sake of his marriage?

As the car pulled in front of Bebe's town house, just a few blocks from his own, he heard her say softly, "Would you care to come up for a nightcap? My husband is out of town." She turned toward him, her white fur stole beautifully setting off her honey-tinted skin. In the low glow of streetlights filtering into the car she looked like the embodiment of temptation.

With difficulty John answered, "I . . . I think not, thank you."

Bebe pursed her lips in a playful pout. Then she turned away from him and leaned back against the seat of the car. "Did I misunderstand you?" she whispered.

John, faced with her directness, was at a loss for words. He was glad it was dark so she could not see his color rise. "I . . . I'm not sure what you mean," he finally said.

Without moving her body, Bebe turned her head to the side and gazed into John's eyes. She gave him a sharp, knowing look. "I may have made the mistake of thinking you were ready for this, John, but don't you make the mistake of thinking I'm a fool."

"Of course I don't —"

Bebe cut him off. "Call me when you're ready. I may still be available."

She did not wait for the driver to open her door. She slid away from John and disappeared in a swirl of sparkling gold light.

CHAPTER 32

MORGAN, immeasurably excited, leaned forward and blew out the five pink candles as the assembled group sang, "Happy birthday to you!" Under the watchful eye of Laurel and Devon, she grasped the beribboned knife and, with her plump little hands, awkwardly cut into the chocolate cake.

"Grandmother, look! It's my favorite!" The chocolate buttercream frosting covered a sinfully rich chocolate torte separated by layers of crumbly chocolate praline filling.

"Chocolate, chocolate, and more chocolate. You're just like your mother." Laurel laughed.

Morgan looked happily around her. Willowbrook's sunny dining room was filled with all the people she loved. The shiny mahogany sideboard was covered with gaily wrapped presents. She couldn't wait to unwrap them.

"May I see my gifts now?" she asked Devon.

"Certainly not, young lady," Devon answered with mock severity. "I'm sure our guests would like to enjoy their cake and perhaps have some hot apple cider."

Despite Devon's joking tone, Morgan knew she had said the wrong thing. Her mother would explain why later, she was sure. But Morgan didn't mind. Penny and Alice always told her what a wonderful lady her mother was. Morgan wanted to learn how to be just like her.

Finally, however, the thrilling moment came when she was given permission to unwrap her gifts.

"Daddy, she's so pretty!" Morgan cried as she opened a box containing a beautifully dressed china doll. The doll had silky black hair like her mother's, and she was wearing a long lavender gown that puffed out like a bell.

The little girl ran to her father and climbed onto his lap. "Throw me in the air and catch me," she begged.

"Oh no!" John groaned. "You're much too big for that now. I don't think I'd be able to lift you!"

Morgan giggled at such silliness. Her father was the strongest man in the world, she was convinced of it. "Pleeeease, Daddy!"

"I'll drop you if I do!" But John obliged, standing up and throwing her in the air. Then he caught her and held her close to his chest so that she felt completely surrounded by him. She loved the warm, safe feeling of his arms around her.

Morgan looked up and caught her mother's eye, but her mother was looking at her father. They were grinning at each other. That made Morgan even happier. Then her mother turned back to her.

"Your father and I have another gift for you. A very special one," Devon told her daughter.

"Where?" Morgan asked excitedly.

"Outside," Devon said playfully, leading her to the foyer.

"Put on your coat first." Her father leaned down and held the little red garment up for her.

Morgan buttoned the black velvet collar without having to be told, but she left the rest of the buttons undone as she impatiently ran to the front door and pulled it open.

The sight that awaited her stopped her in her tracks. There stood Jeremiah holding the reins of a glossy brown pony with a cream-colored mane and tail. Around the pony's tail was a big red ribbon.

"It's . . . it's . . . thank you," the child stammered. She was so distressed she could barely speak. It was her worst nightmare come true. She knew she should be happy. CeCe Hartwick had been ecstatic when her parents had given her a pony. But CeCe knew how to ride! Morgan was afraid to ride, except in the saddle in front of her mother. Didn't her parents know that? Oh, she wanted to cry!

Devon and John could read Morgan's thoughts with one glance. They exchanged a worried look and bent down so that they were on a level with their child.

"Darling," Devon said soothingly. "If you don't like it, I can take it back."

But how could Morgan admit to not liking it? Her parents loved horses, and she wanted to be like them.

"You know, Morgan. You don't have to ride him. He could just be your pet. How would you like that?" John asked.

Well . . . the pony was cute and really quite tiny. Morgan screwed up all her courage. "Could I . . . pet him?"

"Of course!" her parents said in unison, leading her toward the little creature.

Morgan tentatively put one small hand under the pony's nose. The diminutive animal was not much taller than she was. She giggled at the feel of his breath on her skin. "It tickles!"

Devon reached into her pocket for the omnipresent sugar cube — almost all her clothes at Willowbrook had sugar cubes hidden somewhere in them. "Here's a treat you can give him. But keep your fingers together and your hand flat so he doesn't accidentally nip you."

The child carefully followed her mother's instructions, and was delighted when the pony put his head near hers as if to ask for more.

After a few moments, her father asked, "Would you like to try to ride him?"

Morgan hesitated. No. Never! That was the answer she wanted to cry out.

"Maybe it's hopeless," John murmured to his wife over the child's head. Devon nodded, her expression downcast. Devon had persuaded John to participate in this final attempt to overcome Morgan's fear of riding. John had gone along with the idea on the condition that if the pony did not interest the child, Devon would never again try to persuade her daughter to ride. Riding, however, was such an integral part of life at Willowbrook — and in Virginia in general — that the Alexanders had agreed that they should at least try to expose their daughter to the sport. And Morgan had reached the stage where she was willing to ride double with Devon. But she refused to ride alone. Devon had reasoned that a small, nonthreatening animal might overcome Morgan's fears. John had seen the logic of Devon's argument, agreeing that the high-strung, rather frightening Thoroughbreds of Willowbrook were vastly different from a Shetland pony.

Now it seemed that the plan had worked only up to a point. Morgan was willing to play with the cute little animal. Riding it was another matter.

CHAPTER

33

MORGAN looked up at her mother astride the sleek chestnut Thoroughbred then back at her pony, Frisky, whom Devon was holding by a long leading rein. The little Shetland was saddled and stood docilely behind the big horse, but Morgan couldn't bring herself to mount it. "Mommy, can't I ride double with you?"

Devon sighed. In the month since Morgan had received the pony, she had petted it, fed it countless apples, and brushed it. But she hadn't ridden it. Several times before, as on this day, Morgan had declared that she would ride the pony. But her courage always failed her.

"Sweetheart, you're getting too big to ride Skylark with me," Devon replied gently. "It's not very comfortable and you don't like me to go faster than a walk."

Morgan looked down at the ground, torn between fear and the desire to please her mother.

Sensing her dilemma, Devon said kindly, "You don't have to ride at all if you don't want to."

Morgan studied Frisky. He was so cute and friendly that she felt, irrationally, sorry for her little pet, as though by not riding him she were rejecting him. And that made her feel guilty, not just toward Frisky, but toward her parents, who had given her the pony.

"I love Frisky, Mommy," Morgan said, almost in tears. She drew near the pony and caressed its neck. Frisky nickered softly and nudged her with his nose.

"I know you do, darling," Devon reassured her. "And so does Frisky."

"I feel sorry for him. We always leave him here alone." Morgan turned and looked at the pony. "Can we take Frisky with us?"

Devon couldn't suppress her surprised laughter, "Why? If you're not going to ride him . . ."

"Just . . . because," Morgan said, giving her mother a look of entreaty.

Devon thought for a moment. "What if we try riding in the ring first, instead of on the trail? I'll stand in the middle and hold Frisky by the leading rein. I won't let him go any faster than a walk. All you have to do is sit in the saddle."

Morgan hesitated.

"Come on," Devon said decisively, slipping off Skylark and handing him to a groom, "let's get you on Frisky. You'll see — he's so short that you won't feel scared at all. It'll be a lot less scary than being all the way up there with me."

For the next few days, Devon helped Morgan grow accustomed to riding Frisky in the ring. After an initial period of trepidation, the child seemed to enjoy the exercise, delighting in Frisky's obedience to her commands. However, she insisted that Devon maintain a hold of the pony with the leading rein. It was about twenty feet long, and enabled Devon to guide Frisky in a large circle around her.

After a week of this routine, Devon urged Morgan toward the next step. "Shall we try the bridle trail?" she asked her daughter as she helped her onto the pony.

"No!"

Devon gave her a puzzled look. "Aren't you getting bored going around in circles in that ring?"

"Well . . ." Morgan *was* getting bored. But a ride in the woods!

"I'll still have Frisky by the leading rein," Devon reassured her daughter. "He'll follow Skylark. Don't worry."

"I'm scared," Morgan whispered, ashamed.

Devon patted her leg soothingly. "That's all right. Everyone's afraid of new things. Just try it. If you don't like it, you can get on Skylark with me."

"Okay," Morgan said, her voice resigned.

Devon was simultaneously amused and moved by her daughter's woeful expression. She's just like Helena Magrath used to be, Devon thought to herself. Her childhood playmate had always been uncomfortable on horseback, yet had persisted in riding simply to please her father. Devon remembered her feelings of pity for Helena as they were growing up. Devon didn't want Morgan to feel that her mother's love depended on her being a good rider. "Darling, you don't have to do this. You can go back to the house and ask Penny to play with you."

"No! I want to be with you."

"Sweetheart, I'll only be gone for a couple of hours. We can be together after that."

"Why can't we ride double?"

"Morgan," Devon said patiently, "you've been riding Frisky alone all week. The only difference is that we'll be on the trail."

Morgan was silent as she thought this over. "I'll try," she finally said, but her voice lacked conviction.

"That's a brave girl!" Devon encouraged her. She handed Frisky's leading rein to the groom and mounted Skylark. Then she took the rein and led the two horses onto the bridle trail.

Morgan was silent as they rode. She was completely absorbed in the dangers that threatened her. Fallen logs cropped up unexpectedly in her path. Scuttling sounds in the forest originated from unknown creatures. Bare black branches reached out to slap her as she passed.

Devon turned in her saddle to observe her daughter. She despaired as she saw the look of misery on Morgan's face. This would have to be a short ride. Just long enough to give the child a sense of accomplishment, Devon decided. "Are you all right?" she asked Morgan.

The child's response was a tense nod.

As they progressed, the path narrowed. The smaller space made Morgan feel safer, more enclosed. She began to relax a little.

The next time Devon turned to check on Morgan, she saw a tentative smile on the child's face. Devon smiled back. "You know, when spring comes, we can bring a picnic with us."

"Can we have chocolate cake?" Morgan cried, delighted.

"What's a picnic without chocolate cake!" Devon laughed happily, pleased with her daughter's change of mood. She turned back around just in time to guide Skylark around a huge mud puddle that blocked most of the path.

"Morgan," she said, looking over her shoulder, "make Frisky go around that puddle if you can." Devon was holding the long leading rein, but it would require Morgan's guidance with the bridle to direct Frisky around the obstacle. Devon stopped her horse and turned it toward Morgan, prepared to verbally walk her through her task.

Morgan began to tug on the pony's bridle as her mother instructed. She was so concentrated on her hand movements, however, she forgot to pay attention to where she was going. With horror, Devon saw she was headed straight for a thick branch at neck level.

"Morgan, look out!" Devon cried.

The child looked up in alarm, only to be slapped across the chest with the thick limb. Devon watched in horror as her daughter toppled backward and landed with a resounding splash in the mud puddle.

Devon leaped off Skylark and ran to Morgan's side, kneeling in the bog.

Morgan lay still, shocked by the icy water and the impact. Then she opened her mouth and began to howl.

Devon scooped up the girl and held her to her breast. She felt Morgan's arms grasp her and was relieved that the child was able to move freely. But Morgan was near hysteria. "Aaaahhh!" she screamed. "Mommy! It hurts!"

Devon cradled her, murmuring soothing words. As she did so, she ran her hands over the child's limbs, searching for signs of damage. She noticed that Morgan's protective riding hat lay in the mud a few feet from them — the chin strap had obviously snapped open from the angle of impact. Worried that the child's head might be injured, Devon lifted the glossy dark locks and searched for cuts. But all she saw was mud.

"Morgan, sweetheart, I don't really think you've hurt yourself too badly, have you?"

At this, Morgan's howls increased in volume.

"Ssh, ssh, you'll be fine," Devon said, kissing the girl's cheeks and hair. She rocked her in her arms until the sobs began to quieten.

"Morgan," Devon said softly, "you're all wet and it's cold. We need to get you home. I'm going to put you down and I want you to stand up." Devon eased the whimpering child from her lap and stood. Then she gently pulled her daughter upright, not letting go of the little hands until Morgan was standing on her own. "That's good. Now we'll get back on and go right home." Devon led Morgan over to Frisky.

"No!" Morgan began to howl again. "I want to ride with you!"

Devon sighed, distressed by her daughter's fear. "You know, sweetheart, you won't feel so scared if you just get right back on Frisky and ride him home."

"No! No! With you!" Morgan cried, holding out her arms to her mother.

Devon couldn't bear to see her child so upset. Morgan was usually such a jolly little girl. But when it came to riding . . . Well, they would tackle that challenge another day. "Okay," she capitulated, "you hold Frisky's leading rein in your hands and we'll ride Skylark together."

Morgan's tears subsided at these words. Devon lifted her into Skylark's saddle and mounted behind her. "Do I have to wear my riding hat?" Morgan asked, dreading the thought of putting the wet sticky object on her even wetter, stickier hair.

Devon smiled. "Just this once you don't. Hold it in your other hand."

Morgan sighed contentedly and leaned back against her mother. She felt safe again.

CHAPTER 34

SYDNEY and Bart were getting a divorce. It didn't seem possible to Devon; they had been a fixture in the Alexanders' lives since Devon and John's engagement.

"I thought what we had was love, but I couldn't understand why he always made me feel so bad," Sydney explained over lunch at the Plaza Hotel's Palm Court. She gazed thoughtfully into space over the rim of her teacup.

Devon had never seen her look better. Her friend wore a beautifully cut suit of rich chocolate-colored velvet with a bright scarf of yellow, red, and brown tucked into the collar. A matching hat with a cotton-candy swirl of a veil gave her an air of mystery, revealing as it did her wavy shoulder-length hair but little of her features. Her nails were lacquered a vivid shade of red and her lips painted the same color. Everything about her was striking, alive, intoxicating.

"I'm sorry to hear about it nonetheless," Devon said softly. It always frightened her when friends divorced. It made her realize how very vulnerable her own marriage was.

"Don't be sorry," Sydney said pragmatically, "unless it's that I wasted so many years with Bart."

"But you never let on that anything was wrong," Devon said, bewildered. The Plaza's rich chocolate mousse — one of her favorite desserts — sat before her untouched.

"Didn't we?" Sydney asked the question with real curiosity. It had seemed to her that Bart was always criticizing her in front of their friends. But had he been so subtle about it that the darts were only heard by her? "Didn't you notice those awful remarks Bart was always making to me?"

"Yes . . ." Devon admitted, "only he always seemed adept at mixing a compliment with an . . ." Devon hesitated, trying to frame her words tactfully.

"Insult. Go ahead and say it. I recognize it now. For a while I thought I was being overly sensitive. That's what he always told me."

"Do you know why he was that way?"

"Well, you won't believe this, but he always had trouble in the . . . well, you know what I mean." Sydney blushed under her veil. "In any event," she hurried on, "he used to blame it on me."

"How awful!"

"More awful still — I believed him. Until I met Douglas."

Devon's eyes widened.

Sydney continued, "It was last summer at Saratoga. You may remember him."

"Your brother's old college roommate?" Devon vaguely remembered a plain-looking, rather quiet man.

"Yes. Not exactly the type one pictures for an illicit affair, is he?"

"Not really." Devon remembered him as a rather tweedy sort, almost professorial. He had a kind face.

"As it turns out, he's been carrying a torch for me since we were kids."

"Did he ever marry?"

"Never. Flattering, isn't it?"

"I think it's absolutely lovely. Very romantic," Devon said warmly, happy that her friend had found someone who loved her so deeply.

"Anyway, we'll be married as soon as I'm back from Reno. Bart and I just wanted to get the holidays out of the way before telling the rest of the family."

"Douglas doesn't live in New York, does he?" Devon asked, worried about losing touch with her friend. She wondered if John would be angry at Sydney on behalf of Bart.

"Vermont, of all godforsaken places." Sydney laughed. She took a long ebony cigarette holder from her handbag, inserted an exotic-looking cigarette with a black wrapper and a gold tip, and lit it with a Cartier lighter inlaid with semiprecious stones.

"It's rather hard to envision you there." Devon gave her friend a sidelong glance that revealed her skepticism.

"Oh, I shall be madly happy. All my little frocks will go straight into a cedar chest and I'll wear nothing but tweeds and walking shoes." Sydney's face wore a sardonic expression, as though she herself did not fully believe what she said.

"Life in the country has more pleasures than you know," Devon reassured her.

"Well, I've always been a city girl, but I'm willing to go anywhere with Douglas." Her voice took on a dreamy quality as she said, "I feel as though I'm seventeen again with my first crush. Only I'm old enough to know that what he has to offer is truly something to be cherished. It's not often someone gives you total, unconditional love."

Devon put her hand over her friend's and squeezed it. "You'll visit us, won't you? I should hate to lose touch."

"Naturally." Sydney smiled. "You're my best friend, Devon. And you're one of a rare breed: a truly good person. You've never been catty or underhanded. You've never revealed a confidence. Even if we're far apart, you'll always be special to me."

"Stop! You're making me cry," Devon said, taking a lace-edged handkerchief from her purse. "I don't know what I'll do without you."

"You?" Sydney laughed. "But you're one of the strongest, most independent women — *people* — I know." Sydney's face became more serious. "Sometimes I think too independent for your own good."

"You're not the first to say so," Devon said wryly.

"Just watch out for yourself," Sydney answered softly.

Devon dropped her eyes, twisting the hanky in her hands. "Let's change the subject," she said, looking up and putting a wide smile on her face. "Let's set a date for when we next get together. What about at the Blue Grass Stakes? I've got a new colt I've been training. He'll be in it. I'll save you and Douglas a place in my box."

"It's a date," Sydney replied happily. By then she would be Mrs. Douglas Silverman.

CHAPTER

35

MORGAN leaned against the banister of the second-story veranda and wistfully watched her mother mount Skylark.

"Miss Morgan, don't lean on the railing." Penny stuck her head out of the glass-enclosed sun room and admonished her. "And it's too cold for you to be standing out there. Come inside and we'll play a game."

"I want to go with Mommy," the child said quietly.

Penny looked at the little girl sympathetically. "I know," she murmured.

Morgan hung her head and came toward her nanny. Penny closed the door behind them as the child sank into one of the down-filled chairs that made the sun room so inviting.

"I wish I was like Mommy." Morgan sighed.

"Your mother and father love you just as you are," Penny reassured her. She sat in a love seat facing the armchair and picked up a piece of sewing.

"But everyone else can ride," Morgan lamented.

Penny couldn't argue with that statement, for all Morgan's friends had ponies and eagerly looked forward to riding them. "Maybe you should try one more time," Penny suggested tentatively. "You really didn't get hurt last week. Just scared. Right?" She met Morgan's eyes with her own brown ones and held them.

There was a pause. "Right," Morgan finally admitted.

They had to start all over again. Morgan wouldn't even consider riding on the trail. But she finally gathered enough courage to ride Frisky in the ring.

"You know, Morgan, I've fallen lots of times," Devon confessed as she stood in the middle of the ring, Frisky's leading rein in her hand, "and I've only really been hurt once. Everyone who rides falls."

"They do?" Morgan didn't know this.

"Yes," Devon said firmly.

"Has Daddy?"

Devon laughed. "*Everyone*."

Morgan digested this in silence for a few moments. "I really didn't get hurt, did I?" she finally asked, remembering her nanny's words.

"That's very brave of you to say that!" Devon praised her.

"I *want* to be brave," Morgan said vehemently.

"Well, you are. Just being on Frisky now proves that."

"It does?" Morgan was wide-eyed. "But I'm still scared."

"Then you're even braver. Because when you do something that scares you, that's braver than not being scared at all."

Morgan grinned in delight at this assessment.

And it was with that thought in mind that she allowed her mother to persuade her to go on the trail again, provided that Devon held Frisky with the bridle trail. Once she knew that it was all right to be scared, she was able to do the thing that scared her most.

"Try to stay out of the mud this time." Devon dimpled at her daughter.

The child giggled at this as the groom lifted her onto Frisky's saddle.

It was a typically bitter February day and Devon saw mist coming from Skylark's nostrils with every breath.

As they entered the canopy of trees, Devon turned in her saddle. "Are you warm enough?" Morgan nodded nervously. Her stomach was all butterflies, yet she was not quite as frightened as she had been the first time.

Devon unconsciously shook her head from side to side at the tense expression on her daughter's face. "Morgan, let go of Frisky's mane and hold on to the bridle." If only she could relax! "See, I'm holding on to Frisky, so he can't trot. We're just going to walk along slowly." A few seconds later, Devon remembered another piece of advice. "And don't forget to duck when you see a branch!"

They continued on for almost half an hour, in silence except for the breathing of the horses and the rustle of leaves.

Devon turned every few minutes to check on her daughter, and each time she did so, she saw Morgan hastily remove her hands from Frisky's mane. Devon smiled to herself, but didn't comment on the child's surreptitious breach of form. It was enough that Morgan had summoned the courage to join her on the bridle trail. Devon was proud of her for trying to overcome her fear. She wondered if her daughter would ever come to love riding as she did. Not that it matters, she told herself firmly, she may never grow to like it. Still, it would be nice . . .

As they ventured farther, Devon noticed that the wind was beginning to rise. Branches, dark and scraggly against the crystalline white sky, swayed and groaned, while whirlpools of leaves rose up and floated through the air. Devon looked up. Gray clouds lumbered overhead, threatening snow.

"Mommy, I'm getting cold!" Morgan cried.

Devon turned. "It *is* getting cold," she admitted. "Maybe we should head back." As if on cue, minuscule flakes of snow began to sprinkle down on them. Devon looked up again. She enjoyed riding in the snow, and had she been alone, she would have continued, the cold notwithstanding, but she knew that Morgan had had enough for one day. "Darling, we're going to go forward for about five more minutes, but then cut back at the fork up ahead. We should be home in half an hour." It would actually take longer at their pace, but Devon knew that to say so would only upset Morgan.

"Half an hour!" Morgan moaned.

"It's the quickest way," Devon said firmly, facing forward and urging her horse on.

"But I — ouch!" Morgan's pained voice pierced the still air.

Devon whirled about in her saddle to see Morgan holding her mouth. "Are you all right?"

"A branch hit me." Morgan started to sob.

"Oh, no! Darling, you have to be careful to duck!" Devon hastily slid out of her saddle and tethered her horse to a nearby tree. She hurried to her daughter's side. "Let me see."

"No, it hurts!" Morgan wouldn't move her hand from her mouth.

"Morgan," Devon said firmly, "I want to see if you're bleeding."

Reluctantly, Morgan lowered her hand, but her sobbing continued unabated. A red welt slashed across a portion of her cheek and her upper lip was swelling. But there was no blood, Devon was relieved to see. "Come here, sweetheart," said Devon, lifting the child out of the saddle. The little girl wrapped her legs and arms around her mother and clung to her, her sobs growing louder. "Morgan, are you really hurt?" Devon asked gently.

"I don't know!" the child said tearfully, rubbing her eyes.

"Well, you can ride with me. And when we get back we'll have a nice hot chocolate."

Morgan sniffled, but looked up at this last. "With marshmallows?" she asked, her voice still mournful.

"With marshmallows." Devon winked at her. "Now, come on."

Devon lifted Morgan onto Skylark's saddle, then mounted behind her. She handed Frisky's leading rein to Morgan. "Now hold this, just like last time."

Morgan looped the leather around her hand and gripped it tightly. She snuggled against her mother, feeling more secure already despite the increasing wind.

"Better?" Devon leaned forward and kissed Morgan's cheek.

"Uh-huh," Morgan said, content now that she no longer had to concentrate on riding Frisky. "Can I take off my hat?"

"No," Devon replied firmly.

Devon squeezed her legs against Skylark's sides, urging him to pick up the pace.

"Don't trot, Mommy," Morgan said.

"Don't you want to hurry? It's so cold!"

"It's too bouncy," Morgan complained. She had a hard time holding on to the leading rein when she was bouncing up and down. She made another loop in the leather thong around her hand for safe measure.

Devon, complying with Morgan's wishes, pulled on the bridle of the powerful gelding and Skylark immediately slowed.

But the little pony behind them didn't respond quickly enough to the change of pace. He drew too close to Skylark's rear and, suddenly, the big horse kicked out its hooves in a violent bucking motion.

Frisky squealed with pain as Skylark's hooves hit him in the chest. The pony reared away from his attacker, and his motion jerked the leading rein Morgan was grasping. Her arm snapped backward, pulling her body along with its momentum. Morgan broke through the enclosure formed by Devon's arms as the leather loop tightened around her wrist and pulled her from the saddle. Devon, horrified, felt the little girl being wrenched from her.

"Mommy!" Morgan screamed as Devon tried in vain to grab her. The child desperately searched for something to hold on to with her free hand — her mother, the saddle, anything — but Skylark's bucking motion caused both mother and daughter to miss. And as Devon tried to bring Skylark to a halt, she had a split-second impression of Morgan hitting the ground.

Even before the gelding stopped, Devon leapt off, anxious to reach her daughter. She tripped over something as she landed. Without giving it a thought, she kicked Morgan's riding helmet out of her way and hurried toward the child.

But a movement by Frisky immediately claimed her attention. He was rearing on his hind legs and his action caused Morgan's arm to jerk upward. Devon let out a cry of distress as she realized that Morgan's limb was still entangled in the leading rein. Devon had to free her before the pony bolted, dragging Morgan behind! Devon ran toward Morgan, placing her own body between the pony and her daughter. She hastily grabbed Frisky's bridle and unhooked the leading rein, releasing the pony's hold on Morgan. Then Devon kneeled next to her daughter, who lay in a pile of leaves. She lifted Morgan's limp arm and quickly disentangled it from the leather thong, cursing herself for not noticing earlier Morgan's dangerous method of holding the rein.

Thank God the leaves broke her fall, Devon thought. She turned her attention to her daughter's face. Why was she so still? "Morgan, did you have the wind knocked out of you, sweetheart?"

No response. Morgan lay motionless. Devon slipped her hand under the child's head to rouse her — and gasped in shock when she felt the wetness there. Afraid of what she would see, she slowly withdrew her hand from beneath Morgan's tumbled black locks. It was covered in blood, and she stared at it in stupefaction. She was pierced by fear so acute, so all-encompassing that she was utterly paralyzed.

Then, instinctively, Devon lowered her head to Morgan's chest, searching for a heartbeat. And there it was! So faint that she had to hold completely still in order to hear it. But it meant that Morgan was alive! Dizzying relief washed over her.

"Morgan?" she said, hoping that her daughter would open her eyes and speak to her. Still no response. "Morgan!" She said the word sharply, an edge of hysteria in her voice. Devon had to suppress the urge to keep yelling her daughter's name over and over in an irrational attempt to force her awake.

She sat stock-still, lost in indecision. Then, a miraculous surge of adrenaline made her move automatically. She slid her arms under Morgan and gently pulled her to a sitting position. Devon looked at where her daughter had been lying. Jutting from the leaves were the lethal edges of a boulder, its pale quartz surface covered in blood. Devon held Morgan's upper body steady then scrambled on her knees until she was behind her.

What she saw made her gag. She clamped her eyes shut and choked back the contents of her stomach. Somewhere deep inside her a voice commanded her to regain control. She forced her eyes open and stared at the obscene mess before her. Morgan's skull was smashed inward, her hair forced into a huge gash at the base of her cranium.

Devon wanted to scream and scream and never stop. She stared at her daughter, willing it not to be so. She looked helplessly at the gaping wound. She had to do something. If only she could stop the bleeding. Then maybe she could see the extent of the injury. Maybe it wasn't as bad as it seemed.

Devon yanked a wool scarf she was wearing off her neck and, with trembling hands, dabbed at Morgan's head with it. Gingerly, she applied pressure to the wound, hoping to staunch the flow of blood. But it was no use. Her scarf was quickly soaked through. Devon had to get help, and quickly.

How long would it take to get back to the stables? If Devon took Skylark at a gallop, maybe twenty minutes. But the trail was narrow and it was impossible to gallop over the entire course of it. And then, once home, what sort of rescue equipment could she and the others bring onto the trail? They could devise a litter. But how long would that take? Meanwhile, Morgan would be lying alone, bleeding. How long did it take to bleed to death? Devon couldn't leave her daughter to die alone in the snow. She sobbed in despair at her helplessness. But she couldn't be helpless — she had to help Morgan.

Devon tied her scarf around Morgan's head like a bandage. She made it as tight as she could, hoping to slow the bleeding. Then, tentatively, she picked up her daughter. She took a few unsteady steps. She looked down at Morgan. The child's eyelids fluttered. Devon's heart surged with hope. If only she could get help in time.

Could she put Morgan on the horse with her? Of course not, she chided herself. How would she balance her on the saddle and guide the horse at the same time? And if she tried to hurry Skylark, there was no telling what the motion would do to Morgan's wounds. Tears of frustration coursed down Devon's face. She had to move. Morgan was bleeding!

Devon held the child tightly against her and started down the path toward home. How long would it take on foot? An hour? She wanted to sit down and sob. Wanted someone to rescue them. But they were all alone.

She tried to gather her thoughts. It was snowing harder and the wind was biting. Making little grunts of exertion and distress, she plodded down the path, her load feeling heavier with each step. She was in agony wondering if her lurching movements were further harming her daughter.

She looked down at the little face. The blood had soaked the arm of Devon's wool coat, and the sweater beneath. She could feel the clammy dampness of it on her skin. She wondered if Morgan was still bleeding as profusely as before. She didn't dare stop to look. Snow landed on Morgan's face. It outraged Devon to have to expose Morgan to the snow and cold, but what could she do?

A long sob escaped her.

Morgan's lids fluttered open. She was conscious! There was hope!

"Oh, Morgan, you're going to be fine. I love you, honey. I'm getting help for you," Devon cried as she surged forward on a new burst of adrenaline. It made Devon frantic to know that there was nothing she could do to ease her daughter's pain. "Hang on, Morgan. We'll get help in a minute."

Morgan's eyes closed slowly.

"That's right. Just rest, darling." Devon's voice was an eerie chant. "Just sleep. Just rest. You'll be okay. Please, God, let her be okay. Please, God . . . Please, God . . ." She was unaware of what she was saying, unaware of even speaking aloud. And she continued to chant as she staggered on, faster than she would have believed possible yet still excruciatingly slow.

Suddenly, in the distance, she saw the stables. "Morgan, we're there! Oh, thank God, we're going to make it!" she cried. She did not know where the strength came from, but she found herself moving even faster. Forward, forward. She was panting and each breath was a trial for her. She had no more strength, yet she tramped forward. She reached the outer perimeter of the racetrack that marked the edge of the developed portion of Willowbrook.

"Morgan, darling, we're there," she gasped. Devon struggled up the long hill. It seemed to go on forever. Her breath was coming in great rasping moans now, but she went on. Because at the end there was help. That thought kept her going. And as she approached the barn, she saw two stable hands working outside. She started yelling for help at the top of her lungs. Yelling and yelling like a woman possessed.

The two workers rushed toward the woman and child. Devon's face was bright red from cold, and blood spotted her cheek. Her nose was running unheeded. Her hair was plastered to her skull, hanging in strings to her shoulders.

But it wasn't her disarray that chilled their blood, or even the sight of Morgan, limp in her mother's arms. No, it was Devon's strange crooning. She was muttering words of comfort and hope, applying pressure to the girl's head, doing something with a bloody scarf, smoothing back the soaked hair from Morgan's pale face.

As if any of it would help. As if she didn't realize that Morgan's large green eyes were staring blankly up at her.

CHAPTER 36

"IT was not your fault, and you have to stop telling yourself that it was." John enfolded Devon in his arms.

Only in the dark of the night, in the shelter of their bed, was she able finally to talk about Morgan's death. For two days after it happened, she had hardly uttered a word. She was drowning in remorse, shock, grief.

Then, the day of the funeral, it had seemed that the presence of her friends and family had reminded her of the existence of the world outside her private nightmare. Although her speech had been stilted and her responses automatic, she had conversed normally under the circumstances. But not until now, the night after the funeral, had she been able to share her grief and guilt with anyone else. Why was she unhurt while Morgan lay dead in the ground? Why hadn't she listened to John and not tried to overcome Morgan's fear of horses? Why hadn't she checked to see that Morgan was holding the leading rein correctly? Done *something* different? She flayed herself endlessly.

Devon did not sob or moan in a way that might have been cathartic. She cried silently, continuously.

"You must hate me," Devon insisted quietly. The voice that told of her grief escaped her in whispers, like poisonous vapors compressed in an underground source.

"Don't be crazy. It was an accident." John did not know how to comfort his wife. There was a part of him — an ugly, hidden part — that agreed that Devon was to blame. But he fought to keep it concealed, even from himself.

"But if I hadn't tried to talk her into . . ."

"Look, if you think that way, you could as easily blame me. I agreed to go along with giving her the pony," he offered.

"No."

"You did what you thought was right at the time."

"I killed her —" Devon's voice broke. "And — she must have been in such pain. She was so scared, but she trusted me to protect her and I let her —" Devon couldn't continue. She choked on her tears, lost in heartbreak and remorse.

"You never forced her to go with you. You were always careful about that." John tried to reassure her, near tears himself. "Don't paint yourself as a monster because you wanted her to enjoy the things you enjoy. Morgan loved you and wanted to be like you. That's only natural for a little girl."

Devon's logic told her that John's words were true, but in her heart she bore a guilt that would never, ever be erased.

CHAPTER 37

THE only relief Devon found from the torments that plagued her was in her work. She immersed herself in it to an unprecedented degree. The time that she spent in New York with John seemed idle by comparison. There she found herself with too much time on her hands and too little to occupy her mind.

The atmosphere at Willowbrook calmed her. The quiet country nights, the warming presence of her parents nearby, the multitude of living things around her — horses, flowers, butterflies, birds, and other country sights — all these she found soothing.

John, in contrast, found that evenings filled with laughter, dance, and champagne took his mind off his sorrow. He was basically a social animal, Devon a solitary one.

Devon also found that there was more and more for her to do at Willowbrook, for over the past seven years the enterprise had grown. Willowbrook was once again internationally renowned as a racing stable and her top stallions now commanded stud fees as hefty as any in the world. Willowbrook had become a profitable business concern, and Devon and Willy regarded as among the most knowledgeable horse experts in the country.

Prior to Morgan's death, Devon had made the effort to participate in the activities John liked, to spend time in New York with him. Now, being with John was a strain. He was always urging Devon to put her grief behind her, to "rejoin the world," as he put it. But instead of rejoining someone else's world, she had created her own, and if she was not happy, she was at least content.

"Devon, have you heard?"

John's voice over the long-distance telephone line crackled erratically through the static.

Devon brushed the dirt from her hands and put aside the spade she had been using to repot her ginger plants.

"I don't know what you mean." Devon spoke loudly to compensate for the static.

"Germany has defeated France!"

"Oh my God! Grace and Philip are in France!"

"Devon, I can barely hear you, but I just wanted you to know that I'm coming down to Willowbrook. I'll fly down tonight after work."

Devon had a thousand questions, but the connection was so full of static that it was no use prolonging the conversation. "I'll see you tonight!" she yelled into the receiver.

No sooner had Devon put down the telephone than it rang again. It was Laurel.

"Devon, have you heard?"

"You mean about France? John just told me. It's awful, isn't it?"

"Yes. Oh, Devon, I'm worried about Grace and Philip."

Devon didn't want to worry her mother even more by sharing her own misgivings. Instead, she said, "Mother, he's an American diplomat! I'm sure there's nothing to worry about. I'll tell you what. I'll call John back and tell him to wire Grace and Philip. It will be much quicker than if we have to go to Western Union ourselves."

"Good idea. And Devon . . . would you come over for dinner this evening? I . . . I would feel better with you here."

"Of course I'll come! John is coming down from New York, but he probably won't arrive until ten o'clock tonight. I'd like to be home by then, though."

"I'll have dinner served at seven-thirty rather than eight, in that case."

Despite their early dinner, Devon arrived back at Willowbrook to find John waiting for her in the sitting area of their vast bedroom. He was reading a book, a glass of cognac on the table beside him.

"John! I thought you'd be later! I was at my parents'. They're frantic about Grace and Philip. Do you have any more news?"

"No," John said stonily.

His icy tone made Devon take a step backward. "What's wrong?" she asked.

"It would have been nice for you to have been waiting for me here when I came home."

"I intended to be. I didn't think you could possibly be here until ten o'clock at the earliest," Devon explained. They had made it a practice since the beginning of their marriage for each to be at home for the arrival of the other.

John did not reply, but returned to the book he had been reading.

Devon, eager to make peace, walked to the down-cushioned easy chair where he sat, and kissed him on the top of his head. "Look, I'm sorry. And I'm glad you're back," she said lightly.

John did not reply. "John!" said Devon, hurt, "aren't you even going to give me a kiss hello?"

John put his book facedown on the table beside him and stood up. "Of course, dear," he said, kissing her coolly on the cheek. He proceeded into the bathroom and closed the door behind him. Devon could hear the sound of water running as he took a shower. She thought about joining him, then decided against it. She was almost afraid that he would reject her.

Such incidents were occurring between them with greater and greater frequency. This time it had been her fault, in a way. But he should have understood her explanation and accepted it. She couldn't have anticipated that he would arrive earlier than usual. Surely he could see that, Devon thought.

The more Devon thought of John's reaction the more it annoyed her, so that by the time he emerged from the shower, Devon was ready to confront him.

He reentered the room casually drying his hair, his monogrammed terrycloth robe the only garment he wore.

"You know," he said, his earlier pique soothed away by the time alone and the steamy, relaxing shower, "I heard an interesting rumor on Wall Street today. The war is —"

"John, I have something I'd like to say," Devon interrupted, standing up.

He raised his eyebrows in a signal for her to go on.

Devon paced in front of the love seat. "When I explain why I've done something and I apologize for it — even if it's something that you don't like — I expect a little more gracious a response than you gave me tonight."

"Well," John said, moving to his armchair opposite her. He sat down and crossed his legs, staring into the cold fireplace. "I had intended to put that incident behind us, but since you insist on resurrecting it . . ." John began bitingly.

Devon turned to face him. "I 'insist' because it is the type of behavior that seems to engender more of the same . . . on both our parts, I'll admit," Devon said evenly. It wasn't just tonight. It was the lack of understanding that was now a thick concrete wall between them.

John stood up and poured himself another glass of cognac from the cut-crystal decanter that rested on the table between the two easy chairs. Standing before the fireplace, his back to Devon, he said, "I don't see that I was responsible for any aggravating behavior tonight. Even if you didn't know what time I'd arrive, it wouldn't have hurt you to stay here and wait for me. You know we've always tried to do that for each other."

Devon put her hand on his arm and gently turned him toward her. "And I tried tonight, too. You just arrived earlier than I expected. Surely you can understand that with the news about the war, and our worries about Grace and Philip, I would want to spend some time with my parents."

"Or your husband, most people would say." John released himself from Devon's grip by moving away from her and once again sitting in the armchair.

Devon was hurt by the gesture. Why was he avoiding contact with her? His kiss of greeting had been strictly perfunctory, and every time she moved near him or touched him, he moved away. She went and stood in front of his chair. "Well, here I am. But instead of being pleased to see me, you had to start an argument."

"Devon, we had no argument," John pointed out in a voice that he tried to keep reasonable, but which she found patronizing, "until I came out of the bathroom and *you* decided to start one."

His tone caused her to speak more sharply than she had intended. "The alternative would have been to leave you feeling martyred and self-righteous about a perfectly innocent mistake on my part. John, sometimes it seems as though you look for opportunities to become offended by things I do. I can say the most innocent thing, and you always seem to take it as a personal attack."

"There you go! Why do you have to speak in generalities when we're discussing a specific, isolated incident?" John's voice rose a decibel and he threw up his hands in frustration. "Don't tell me about what I 'always' do. Let's just discuss tonight."

"Tonight wouldn't be an issue if it were an isolated incident, but it's not!" Devon replied heatedly. "It's the kind of thing that *always*" — Devon emphasized the word by placing her hands on her hips and leaning toward John — "seems to happen."

John, quieter now, said, "If it always seems to happen, that begs the question of why we're still married."

Devon stared at him, too stunned to reply. She felt a knife turn in her stomach as she reflected on the bitter truth of his statement. He was right, they never seemed to have civil conversations anymore. Agreed on very little. Had almost nothing in common, now that Morgan was dead. Emotionally exhausted, Devon slumped into the love seat.

For the first time, John approached her. He sat down beside her and spoke with more sincerity than he had all evening. His defense mechanisms were gone. What he said came from his soul.

"I love you, Devon. Even now, after all our disagreements. But it's not working between us. I'm worn out. Too tired to keep fighting. To keep asking for things you seem unable to give."

"But John, I love you too," Devon protested.

"I know," John said sadly, shaking his head in resignation, "but it's not enough. I need someone beside me all the time. I need to come first with my wife."

"But you do —" Devon began to protest.

"You know that's not so. You have become a very successful

trainer. And you seldom want to leave Willowbrook. When Morgan was alive, she came before me, too. I'm not saying that's right or wrong. All I'm saying is that it's not what I want in a wife."

"I've tried to —"

John interrupted, "I can't derive pleasure from your unhappiness, Devon. When you try to please me by doing things that you would prefer not to do, I'm uncomfortable. And, of course, I can't force you to want what I want. You can't force yourself, either. I think we're just incompatible."

"John," Devon said, studying him carefully, "is there someone else?"

"Of course not," John said, as though the very notion were ridiculous.

"No . . . I know that," Devon said, looking down at her hands. She was surprised to see the tears that had fallen on them. She had not realized that she was crying.

"Devon, please don't be unhappy . . . you'll see that this is for the best."

"You mean a . . . divorce?" Devon hardly dared utter the word. Her family would be crushed. So would John's. And she would feel cast adrift without an anchor.

"I think it's best," John said, gently wiping a tear from Devon's cheek with his thumb. "I truly believe that Morgan was our main reason for staying together these last few years. Without her, we have very little together."

"Oh, John," Devon said, sobbing into the clean linen handkerchief that her husband placed in her hands.

"I know," he said soothingly. He drew her to him so that her tears wet the front of his robe.

Oddly, now that the rupture was inevitable, they felt closer to each other than they had in some time. The shadow of their love lingered, a poignant reminder of what they had lost.

BOOK TWO

CAIRO, EGYPT

1942

CHAPTER 38

CAIRO'S streets teemed with soldiers from every Allied country and every service branch. But Cairo had always been an international crossroads, and the foreigners were absorbed into the frenetic, tightly packed crowd as foreigners in Cairo had been for thousands of years.

Devon, pushing her way through the throng with Grace, thought they would drown in the tide of humanity. Most disturbing to her were the hands that reached out anonymously to touch her. The natives of the city viewed women in Western dress — many of them cosmopolitan Cairenes — as Jezebels sent to entice them, and they pinched the breasts and buttocks of passersby at will. First-time visitors, like Devon, would whirl about in outrage, only to be confronted by a faceless mass of pushing, sweating bodies. Residents, like Grace, knew better than to fight the inevitable.

"Grace," Devon yelled in order to be heard above the din, "how much farther?"

"Not much." Grace looked over her shoulder and smiled reassuringly at Devon. They were on their way to the famous souk, the outdoor bazaar. As always, the embassy car, a long black Cadillac, had driven them as far as it could, but the streets leading to the souk were too narrow for automobiles, and the women had had to walk the rest of the way.

Devon's anxiety turned to excitement as she and her sister emerged into the area that was reserved for the souk. Entranced by the bounty of glittering clothes, jewels, and brass around her, Devon hurried toward a table laden with fancifully decorated caftans.

"Wait, Devon!" Grace hurried after her, grabbing her by the hand. "Don't let go or you could get lost!"

"You're right!" Devon laughed. "This makes New York look like an uninhabited desert island."

"Ah, the beautifool leddy is eentrrrested in a caftan?" A dark-complected man wearing a red fez with a bouncing black tassel lifted a garment of scarlet cloth shot with gold from the table.

Devon was fascinated by the rolling *r*'s of his speech. Everything said in that musical accent sounded interesting to her.

Devon smiled warmly at the man and took the proffered garment, saying, "This is lovely. How much?"

"I geev you verrry good price." The man smiled to show a row of gold teeth.

Grace discreetly nudged her sister in the side. "Let me!" she whispered.

Devon looked at her questioningly.

"Thees eez the best seelk you weel find anywhere, I assure you!" said the man. "Eet eez a beautifool drayss."

"We may be interested," Grace said.

The rotund little man turned and bowed at Grace, as if sensing her greater experience with the ways of the souk. "Twenty-seven pound eez norrmal price, but for such beautifool leddeez, I geev for twenty pound."

"That's only about thirty dollars!" Devon whispered to Grace. "That's a good price!"

"Excuse us, please," Grace said to the man, drawing her sister away from the table. "Look, listen, and keep your mouth shut, my dear. You may know horse-trading, but I know bazaars."

Returning to the table, Grace resumed her bargaining. "Your offer is very kind, sir, but we only just arrived. There are many other tables."

"Madam weel not find morrr beautifool seelk than thees," the man argued, lifting his three chins in pride. He laid the voluminous garment on top of all the others in a dramatic gesture that sent the shiny silk floating over the entire table.

"I'm sorry, but it's very expensive," Grace argued, running one white-gloved hand over the fabric.

The man looked crestfallen. "Tell me what you weel pay," he countered.

"Four pounds," Grace said firmly.

The man's eyebrows shot up, a look of shock on his face. "Fourrr pound! Eempossible! No, eet eez robbery!" Nonetheless, he fingered the material thoughtfully. With a despairing sigh, he finally said, " I offerrr seexteen and half pound."

Grace pretended to consult her sister, but instead whispered, “Don’t get anxious, you’ll get your dress.” Then turning back to the man with a look of sorrow, she said, “It’s just too much. We can’t go higher than four pounds.”

“But madam, you start weeth fourr pound, I start with twenty pound. I say seexteen and half. You can geev a beet morr than fourr, no?”

“I can’t give sixteen and a half,” Grace said ambivalently.

“You arr verrry deefeecult, madam. I offerrr you for seexteen pound. No less.”

Now it was Grace’s turn to sigh. “I’m sorry,” she said shaking her head, “we’ll just have to look elsewhere.”

“You weel not find betterrr!” the man prophesied.

Grace simply smiled and, taking Devon’s arm, slowly turned to go. Devon did not dare say a word, but she glared at her sister in disgust. A moment later, however, her glare turned into a smile as she heard, “Leddeez, pleez!”

Grace and Devon turned back and waited to hear the man’s offer.

“Look how the cloth falls, so supple, so fine,” he said, holding it against his pudgy stomach and letting it hang to his knees in the approximate shape of a skirt. “And thees beautifool caftan, I geev you for fifteen pound. I mek no money,” he declared, “but thees caftan eez med forr thees beautifool leddy.” He smiled and held the cloth in the air in front of Devon so that Grace could admire the color against her sister’s skin.

“Well . . . it is lovely,” Grace admitted. She put one index finger to her mouth, as though thinking the matter over. “I’ll raise my offer to seven pounds.”

“Rez yourrr offerrr! Thet eez nothing. I cannot tek only seven pound!” The man looked apoplectic.

“I’m sorry, it’s the best I can do,” Grace said.

The man and woman stared at each other in silence, each trying to assess the other’s breaking point. The attractive chestnut-haired woman had a firm, bold stare. She knew how the game was played, the man thought, and he respected her for it.

“Okay,” he conceded, the expression a favorite one picked up from the Americans, “I geev you food frrom my mouth. I geev you cloth frrom my back. You tek forrr seven pound.”

Grace and Devon beamed at the man with such gratitude that he almost forgot that he had let them have the caftan for only one pound more than he would have been willing to sell it for.

"Well done, ladies." The unmistakable accent of a British aristocrat confronted the sisters as they turned to leave the booth. They looked in confusion at the crowd swarming about them until Grace spotted a familiar face.

"Roland!" Grace cried.

Roland Somerset-Smith, handsome in his Royal Air Force uniform, lifted his cap and bowed to the women. The duke of Abersham looked like a cinema ideal of a British officer with his slightly receding dark hair, twinkling brown eyes, and classically modeled features.

"I didn't know you were back in town," Grace chided him. The circle to which Grace and Roland belonged in Cairo was small enough that the comings and goings of its members were known to one and all. Cairene society was in some ways a rather democratic one. Prejudices against other nationalities, religions, and races were largely forgotten as the most sophisticated segment of the population congregated in enclaves separate from the great mass that made up the majority of Egypt. Europeans, Americans, Africans, and Cairenes mingled freely so long as they came from a background of wealth and family connections. The privileged classes gathered at Groppi's for tea and pastries, the Mena House for dinner and dancing, and the Gezira Sporting Club or the Turf Club for cocktails, athletics, and gambling. They summered in Alexandria, ordered custom-made clothes from skilled craftsmen who perfectly copied the latest European fashions, and sent their offspring to the American University in Cairo, the Sorbonne in Paris, or Oxford in England. They spoke French and English with equal fluency. Arabic was hardly needed. Most business transactions were performed in French, and that was the primary language taught in schools, even more commonly than Arabic. Arabic was useful, though certainly not necessary, for bargaining in the souk.

"I'm permanently stationed here now," Roland said, his eyes irresistibly pulled to Devon, despite the fact that he was addressing Grace. "No more shuttling back and forth to London for me. At least not for a while." He was a squadron leader — the equivalent of a U.S. major — in the Desert Air Force, a special section of the Royal Air Force assigned to North Africa.

"Devon, this is Roland Somerset-Smith, a good friend of ours. Roland, this is my sister, Devon Alexander."

"Grace, I didn't think it possible that there could be *another* woman in this world as entrancing as you," he said, bowing over Devon's hand. "I hope you intend to stay in Cairo for some time." The expression in his eyes told Devon that this was more than a platitude.

"I do!" Devon said enthusiastically. "As long as Grace and Philip can endure the imposition."

"We shall have to ensure you have a wonderful time, then. Cairo is an exciting city, as you know." Roland thoughtfully ran one finger over his jaw. "If you ladies haven't any other plans, may I invite you to join me for lunch at the Turf Club?" Roland looked at his wristwatch. "It's almost one o'clock now."

The two women readily agreed to the plan. "We'll go and dismiss our driver then, if you can give us a lift back to the house," Grace said.

Lunch under the blue-and-white-striped awning was so delightful that it stretched into tea, then cocktails.

"Why don't you send my driver with a message for Philip to join us?" Roland asked Grace.

"Wonderful idea!" Grace exclaimed, feeling just a bit giddy from the champagne cocktails.

Roland signaled for their waiter while Grace scribbled a note for the driver, then she settled back quietly in her chair. She studied Roland as he talked to her sister. He was animated as she had never before seen him. It was obvious to her that he was taken with Devon.

And Devon, she noticed, responded to his admiration, happily flirting back. She had not seen her sister so carefree since Morgan's death, almost three years before. There was a healthy flush to her cheeks and, in the flattering pink light of early evening, she looked as though she were in her early twenties.

Indeed, Devon did find Roland attractive. The trait that was most dominant in him — the one that struck both men and women immediately — was his charm. He never seemed to say the wrong thing. He punctuated all his remarks with a dazzling smile. It was the sort of deadly charm that could have been used to ill advantage, but Roland was too kind for that.

At one point, Roland asked Devon, "By the way, are you interested in horseracing? The tracks here in Cairo are quite something."

Devon and Grace exchanged grins before explaining the joke to Roland. And as it turned out, Roland himself had a breeding operation at his family estate in England.

Later, she learned from Grace that Roland was a widower with no children.

In the ensuing weeks, Devon found most of her time taken up by excursions with Roland. He was absent for almost two weeks in late August during the visit of Winston Churchill to British installments near Cairo. Churchill, Roland told Devon, had been very impressed with what he had seen, though on one humorous occasion he had complained privately about a soup made of tinned oysters served to him by the commander of the New Zealand forces.

Then, on August 30, shortly after Churchill's departure, German and Italian forces attacked British positions in Egypt. The Germans were soundly repelled and finally, four days later, retreated.

After the battle, Roland returned to Cairo. He continued to see Devon as often as his duties permitted.

"When exactly do you work?" Devon asked teasingly on a day that had begun with beignets at the Continental Hotel, gone on to lunch at the Mena House's pool terrace, and moved to an afternoon of horseracing at the Heliopolis Club. Now they were enjoying martinis in the shade of the terrace.

"This is my life's mission, don't you know?" Roland took Devon's hand and kissed it, unmindful of the benign stares of those near them. Suddenly his gaze turned serious. "I'd like it to be, you know," he said, searching Devon's eyes for her response.

Devon looked down at her drink, confused.

"Devon," he said, his voice grave, "I'm not permitted to elaborate any further . . . but there will come a time, quite soon now I think, when I will have to leave Cairo."

Devon was surprised by how much she dreaded the thought. "You'll be here for my birthday, won't you? It's only a little over a month away." Devon could hardly believe that it was already early October. The days were still as hot as midsummer in Virginia.

Roland looked sad. "I would love to be more than anything on earth, but I don't think I can." His expression changed to one of concern. "And I wish you'd consider going elsewhere for a bit."

Devon searched his face sharply. "What do you mean?"

"The war is rather close, isn't it?"

"The war is close anywhere you go in the world nowadays," Devon pointed out.

"Not Virginia," Roland countered.

"Granted," Devon said with a smile, "but at this point in my life, I'm more disturbed by my ghosts in the United States than by physical danger here." She shrugged her shoulders and went on breezily, "Besides, didn't Mr. Churchill order that every one of your office workers in

Cairo be issued a rifle? And what about all the reinforcements he's surrounded the city with? I don't think there's anything to worry about."

Roland stared at her for a moment, and it was obvious that he was holding something back.

"What?" Devon asked.

Roland's face reflected his internal conflict. He reached across the table again for her hands and enfolded them in his. "I have no right to tell you what to do, though God knows I wish I did," Roland said. "If I had that privilege, however, I would insist that you leave Cairo just now."

Devon smiled gently. "I know it's what you think best, but I'm just not ready to go home." Although Devon still loved Willowbrook, Morgan's death had created a terrible emptiness in the place. Her divorce from John had exacerbated her feeling of loneliness.

It was not that John had completely disappeared from her life. Shortly after the United States joined the war, in 1941, John had phoned Devon to tell her that he had been selected for a special government mission overseas. He did not supply her with any details about the mission, making it clear that such questions were unwelcome. She assumed that his duties involved espionage, but did not know for sure.

Then in February 1942, John telephoned her with news she found much more disturbing: he had become engaged to Bebe Henley. As soon as she had politely congratulated him and hung up the telephone, she scurried to the bathroom and became sick to her stomach. She was not sure if the nausea was due to jealousy or simple disgust at the idea that John should marry such a contemptible creature. She only knew that she was downcast for days after she heard the news. And after hearing it, she knew she had to escape.

Devon's beloved Willowbrook — the place she had fought so hard for and about with John — simply was not able to fill the void in her heart. She knew it was being well cared for and was not worried about it in her absence.

Roland shook his head with a smile of resignation at her refusal to return to the United States. "You're an obstinate woman, Devon Alexander."

"Yes," she said dryly, "so I've been told."

A few weeks later Devon discovered the reason for Roland's concern when British and U.S. forces launched a surprise attack against the Germans and Italians in North Africa. The date was October 23, 1942.

The German forces were at an extreme disadvantage in terms of personnel and firepower and, perhaps most important, due to the fact that their able commander, General Rommel, had gone to a hospital in Germany at the end of September. General Stumme, who took his place, died in battle of a heart attack on October 24, whereupon Hitler cut short Rommel's convalescence and immediately dispatched him to the battle front.

Just two days after Rommel's arrival, on October 27, there was a decisive turn in the fighting. The Germans launched a full-scale counterattack on Allied troops, and the Royal Air Force responded with two and a half hours of bombing sorties, during which eighty tons of bombs were concentrated in an enemy area measuring three by two miles. The enemy attack was quelled almost before it could begin. By November 8, Allied troops had taken thirty thousand prisoners from the Battle of Alamein.

The battle marked a turning point for the Allies in World War II. Churchill afterward said, "Before Alamein we never had a victory. After Alamein we never had a defeat."

CHAPTER 39

"I'M grateful I was able to be here after all," Roland whispered softly into Devon's ear, mindful of the other guests standing near them. Philip and Grace were hosting the elegant party in honor of Devon's birthday.

Devon raised her flute of champagne to her lips and looked over the rim at Roland as she took a sip. "It makes my birthday much happier, having you here." Devon lowered her glass and looked up at Roland, dimples showing at either side of her smile. She thought he looked resplendent in his Royal Air Force uniform, new medals shining from his already overladen breast pocket.

Devon wore an elegant black gown, strapless and completely plain but cut beautifully to show every curve of her body without quite clinging to them. With the gown, she wore a choker of diamonds and earrings to match. Her hair, tightly pulled into a chignon at the nape of her neck, set off her perfect bone structure. At age thirty-seven, she was more beautiful than she had been ten years earlier. Her skin, always flawless, remained so, but she was slimmer, making her features more strikingly angular, and the headlong exuberance that had characterized her a decade earlier had matured into a quiet confidence that often intimidated those who were less sure of themselves.

"It's lucky that I'm to continue on here," Roland said, giving Devon's hand a furtive squeeze.

She answered truthfully when she said, "I hope we'll be able to see a lot of each other."

"I fully intend that we should," he said, a sparkle in his eye.

The butler came in to announce that dinner was served, and the guests slowly made their way into the huge dining room furnished in French antiques and Oriental carpets. Dinner was a sumptuous affair that began with a saffron-flavored seafood bisque and progressed to roast prime ribs of beef with herbed crust and Madeira sauce accompanied by broccoli timbales and potato caraway croquettes. With this was served a stellar 1924 Mouton Rothschild. The main course was followed by a salad of Boston lettuce, endive, and watercress with mustard vinaigrette; and, finally, Devon's so-called birthday cake. The cake was actually a Grand Marnier meringue torte that with its thirty-seven candles looked like the sun blazing through a puffy white cloud. Devon had insisted that she did not mind her age being represented in candlepower. She thought it was silly to be secretive about such things.

After dinner there was dancing to a ten-piece orchestra playing popular tunes and waltzes. As Devon and Roland danced, he led her to a secluded corner of the ballroom.

"I'd like to have a word with you privately. Is there somewhere we can go?" he asked her.

"Of course." She took his hand and led him down the black and white marble corridor to the double doors of the library. She opened one door tentatively, peeked inside to ensure that it was unoccupied, then went in, closing the door behind them.

Roland settled on a navy velvet sofa and pulled Devon down beside him.

"I was frightened during the Battle of Alamein," he said without preamble.

Devon was surprised at the admission. Roland was a person who always tried to smooth things over. He did not like to reveal unpleasant emotions, though he was open with his happier ones. Devon silently waited for him to continue.

"I wasn't exactly afraid of death, mind you, though I shouldn't like it to occur anytime soon," Roland said with a half smile.

Devon was fascinated by this revelation of his inner self. She dared not speak for fear of interrupting his train of thought.

"I was afraid" — he took a deep breath before continuing — "of dying before I should have the chance of marrying you."

Devon's eyebrows shot up in surprise. The proposal was not completely unexpected, but the beginning of his speech had not led her to believe that this would be its end. "I . . . I'm not certain what to say."

"Say yes," said Roland, in a blunter command than she had ever heard him utter. Even when he spoke to subordinates, it was always with the utmost politeness, always couched with a "please" and a "thank you."

Devon looked directly into his eyes. "I won't insult you by being coy. I've known for some time how you felt, though I wasn't quite sure of the extent of it."

"Well, now you know. But the more important question is, How do you feel?" Roland took her hands in his and stared intently into her eyes, trying to read an answer in her expression.

"I . . . I enjoy the time we spend together. I feel sad when you're not here. I feel happy when you are. . . . I . . . I don't know if that's love." Devon shook her head in befuddlement. Where was the nerve-shattering anticipation, the tingling excitement she had felt for John? Was she no longer capable of such feelings? When Roland touched her, it was pleasant . . . terribly pleasant. When he kissed her, her body stirred. She could easily envision making love with him, enjoying it. But where was the mad, hot desire she had felt for John?

"You're making comparisons, aren't you?" Roland asked sadly.

Devon flushed guiltily. "I'm ashamed, Roland. You don't deserve that."

"No, no, you're perfectly right. Let's discuss it openly, shall we?" he said with that cool civility that was so British. "Alexander, I assume, was your first love, yes?"

Devon nodded confirmation.

"Well, then, that's always something special, isn't it?" Roland didn't want to frighten Devon by confessing that the passion he felt for her was far stronger than any he had ever felt before. He continued, "You needn't feel ashamed of such feelings. They're normal, perhaps universal."

But Devon thought of Sydney, so madly in love with her new husband, Douglas. So in love that she had virtually become a rural hermit. So in love that she had been transformed from a cynical, witty sophisticate into a blushing bride. Hadn't Sydney loved Bart just as passionately at one time? Devon didn't know, and there was no way to find out at the moment.

Roland was so easy to talk to, though, that she found herself asking him the question that troubled her. "So you believe that passion — that first-love passion — only happens once in a lifetime?"

Roland found it impossible to lie to Devon. He looked down at his hands. "I'm sorry to say that I don't quite believe that, no.

"Look, Devon, I hadn't intended to be quite so frank, but I have to confess that I fell in love with you the first moment I saw you." He didn't let the look of surprise on her face stop him. "And now that I've spent more time with you, I love your inner qualities as well," he said with a smile of self-mockery.

She smiled back at him. As always, he made her feel wonderful. Tentatively, as though it were for the first time, she kissed him, a sweet kiss on the lips that, as the seconds ticked by, became a passionate embrace. And when they finally parted, Devon once again felt the flush of desire she always felt at Roland's kisses. It wasn't the uninhibited, unthinking desire she had known with John, but it was desire nonetheless.

"Devon," he groaned, "don't do this to me unless you intend to say yes. I don't know how much longer I can endure your presence without being able to have you."

"Roland," Devon said, tilting her head to one side curiously, "is it only desire that you feel for me? Because if that's the case, you needn't feel that a proposal of marriage is the only way to . . ." She let the sentence hang in midair.

Roland looked at Devon and shook his head, smiling. "Devon, you give me too much credit. If only things were so simple as that. Believe me, I would pounce on that offer. However, the traits I admire in you go far beyond something so . . . commonplace."

Devon returned his smile warmly, more relieved than she would have supposed. She was glad that he loved her, she decided. But did she love him enough for marriage?

As though reading her mind, he said, "Devon, if this were peacetime, I would suggest that we become engaged for a good long time. But that's not the way things are now. I need to know that you're my wife. I want that before I go up again in that plane." Now his expression turned sheepish. "I'm afraid the emotion of the moment is making me resort to maudlin claptrap . . . if I should die and all that rot," he joked.

"It's not maudlin. Things are different during a war," Devon said seriously. "I do understand what you mean."

"Then don't make me wait any longer. Don't take the time to think about my proposal, just say yes. You won't regret it, I promise you. You may not feel the passion for me that you did for Alexander, but, after all, passion isn't always the basis for a good marriage. You know that, don't you?"

"Yes," Devon admitted thoughtfully. She and Roland had everything in common that she and John had lacked. They both raised Thoroughbreds, both loved country life . . . both wanted children. They laughed at the same things, enjoyed the same food, the same pastimes. In short, they were as compatible as two people could be.

With one exception. "Roland, how will your family feel about your marrying so hastily, and an American at that."

"Devon," Roland answered firmly, "I am almost forty years old. Even if my parents were alive, I shouldn't let their views stop me from marrying the woman I love."

"It's not just a matter of family opinion, Roland. You're a member of the aristocracy. Would you want a child who is half American, who doesn't come from one of the great families of Europe, inheriting your title and properties?"

The look of love Roland gave Devon was so strong that it melted her heart. "Yes, as long as he's your child too."

Devon gently released his hands and rose from the couch. She walked to the huge fireplace, almost never lit despite the cool Cairo nights. There was little wood to burn in Egypt. Roland watched her slim, graceful figure as she placed her arms on the mantel and dropped her head down onto them, lost in thought. For what seemed like a very long time, she said nothing.

Finally, the tense silence grew too much for Roland. "You can't think of a reason to refuse me, can you?"

Devon whirled about to face him. "Oh, Roland, I'm not trying to think of a reason. I just want to be sure that I'm being fair to you."

Roland rose and came toward Devon. He took her in his arms and, once again, gave her a long, passionate kiss. She put her arms around him in return, enjoying the warmth of his body near hers. His kiss became more gentle; then, just when it seemed that he would release her, he dropped his lips to the space where her neck met her bare shoulder. The action sent a shiver of enjoyment through Devon.

"We'd be compatible in every way, I promise you," Roland murmured lasciviously in her ear.

Devon closed her eyes and let her head drop back, shifting all her weight to Roland's encircling arms. It felt wonderful to be cherished again, she thought. And if she didn't feel the same kind of love for Roland that she had felt for John, well, who was to say the one kind was better than the other?

"Marry me? Before my leave expires?" he urged, not letting her go.

She lifted her head and straightened her body, but he did not loosen his hold on her. With her arms around his neck, she looked into his eyes and said, "Yes, Roland, I'll marry you."

CHAPTER 40

DEVON, PHILIP, and Grace were in Philip's office preparing to go to lunch together at Shepheard's Hotel when the news came. It was carried in by a flustered-looking secretary who knew of their close relationship to John Alexander. Had it not been for Philip's position at the embassy, Devon would never have known that John was hurt. The explosion in Geneva had made headlines around the world, but the names of those involved had been carefully concealed.

According to the newspapers, the bomb had been planted at the site of a secret meeting of Allied "diplomats." None of the so-called diplomats, however, were known to be part of their countries' respective foreign services, hence the secrecy. A British operative had been killed, along with two members of the Free French. John was fortunate to escape with injuries, but they were severe, according to the cable the secretary handed Philip.

Devon, stunned, slumped into Philip's cordovan leather couch, Grace's comforting arms around her. Philip stood helplessly in front of his desk, not sure what to say.

Devon's heart pounded with fear at the thought of John dying. Even though they were divorced, the memories they shared were an important part of Devon's life. John had been her first love and her first lover. They had had a child together, then shared the tragedy of her death. The bitterness and hostility that had immediately preceded their divorce seemed no more than a distant memory to Devon.

"I have to go to him!" Devon exclaimed, almost to herself.

Grace raised her eyebrows and met Philip's eyes over Devon's head. Grace understood and shared her sister's distress, but she wondered how Roland would feel about Devon rushing off to Geneva to be with her first husband.

"I must get in touch with Roland . . ." Devon mumbled to herself, devising a checklist in her mind of things to do to prepare for her departure. "Philip, can someone on your staff check on flights?"

"Dear, don't you think you're jumping the gun? After all, it's very likely that his wife will be there," Grace said in the gentlest of tones.

"His wife . . ." Devon looked puzzled for a moment, then her face clouded. "Oh . . . yes, of course." There were a few moments of silence as Devon mulled this over. Suddenly, she stood up in a decisive fashion. "Nonetheless, I want to go," she said, punctuating her phrase with a firm nod of her head.

"Devon, do you suppose that it will hurt Roland's feelings if you rush off like this?"

Devon made a small noise of exasperation. "Don't be silly! He'll understand."

"Well . . . all right," Grace said, skepticism apparent in her tone.

And, indeed, Roland was understanding.

"By all means, darling," he said warmly when she phoned him a few minutes later. "I'll be on a mission for a few days in any event, and I'm sure Alexander will appreciate your concern. I understand it was a rather nasty explosion."

Devon heaved a sigh of relief at her husband's supportive reaction. She threw Grace a look of victory as she spoke into the telephone. "I knew you wouldn't mind my going."

That's not quite accurate, Roland thought to himself. It disturbed him that his wife felt compelled to rush to John's side. At the same time, the feelings that made him want to stop her from visiting the wounded man shamed Roland. And since he knew that stopping her was impossible, because of both Devon's will and Roland's sense of fair play, he thought it best to feign complete support for the decision.

"I'd like to see you off," Roland said, "do you know your schedule?"

"Not yet. I'll telephone you."

A few hours later, Roland kissed his wife good-bye and watched her slim figure mount the stairs to the airplane. Just before entering the plane, Devon turned and waved at Roland. His heart swelled with pride and love as he waved back. She looked stunning, her shiny black hair glinting in the brilliant sunlight, her red silk dress billowing slightly from the breeze on the runway. In her arms she carried a mink-lined raincoat, for it would be cold in Geneva. Roland wondered if John would find her as attractive as he did. He did not see how he could fail to do so. It was with a pang of regret that Roland watched the stewardess close the metal door firmly on the hatch. Roland peered down the row of little round windows trying to catch a glimpse of his wife, but he did not see her. He did not stop searching, though, until the propellers started to move.

Devon sank back into her seat and thought about her husband. How she loved him for being so supportive of her trip! Theirs was a harmonious relationship. It seemed that they laughed nonstop when they were together. They seldom had serious discussions; it was almost as though they were still involved in a courtship. Of course, they were newlyweds, having been married only three months.

When she thought of John, she seldom thought of his being lighthearted, though of course they had shared lighthearted moments. But John was more serious than Roland, or at least his serious emotions were closer to the surface. In many ways, Roland was what Devon thought of as a stereotypical member of the British aristocracy—emotions in control, expert at small talk, always pleasant, even in the face of unpleasantness. Devon knew Roland was deeper than that, but he seldom showed it. Being with Roland was a respite from the harsh realities of the world around them: the poverty of Cairo, the tensions of war, and on a more personal level, the ego-bruising, heart-shattering unhappiness of the last three years. To Devon, Roland was like a safe haven in a turbulent sea.

* * *

The cold in Geneva came as a shock to Devon's system, though she had known in advance to expect it. Months of hot Cairo sun were only a memory in the drizzling, bone-chilling Geneva April. It did not seem possible that it was spring when Devon observed the spindly, bare trees silhouetted sharply against the misty gray sky.

Devon checked into the luxurious, family-run Le Richemond Hotel where, in typical Swiss fashion, she found a full tea hospitably awaiting her in her suite. She asked the chambermaid to draw her bath and sunk into a cozy wing chair to enjoy the repast. Once finished, she undressed and made her way to the white marble bathroom where the warm, perfumed water awaited her.

When Devon emerged from the tub she felt like taking a nap, but opted instead to dress for her visit to John. The hotel's concierge had told her that the hospital allowed visitors until eight o'clock. Devon was undecided whether to telephone John in advance of her arrival. She decided against it, choosing instead to surprise him.

She dressed carefully, more carefully than she cared to admit to herself. She discarded two dresses before finally deciding on a pale blue wool suit with chinchilla collar and cuffs. With it she wore a matching blue hat and pearl gray gloves and shoes. She surveyed her reflection in the mirror. The blue suit set off her eyes marvelously, but she wondered if she was overdressed. Would John think she had made a special effort to look good for him? She dismissed the thought as silly. After all, he was flat on his back in a hospital bed — undoubtedly in pain. It was egocentric to suppose that he would even pay attention to what she wore, she told herself.

Still, she wondered if she should change into something more subdued. Then it occurred to her that Bebe Henley might be there. She thought of the stunning younger woman with her blond hair and dramatic fashion choices. Devon decided to leave on the blue suit.

The hotel's Rolls-Royce took her to the hospital, a beautiful private clinic with none of the sickroom smell that characterized most hospitals. A wholesome-looking young nurse directed her to the room of Monsieur Alexander, and Devon proceeded down the hallway, high heels clicking on the gleaming floor.

John's door stood open, but before entering Devon paused outside to listen for voices. She heard nothing, so she peered inside tentatively. The room was painted a cheerful lemon yellow and furnished with rich rosewood furniture. How typically Swiss, Devon thought with a smile.

She tiptoed into the room, wondering if John would be sitting up. Maybe he'd be dozing.

Nothing could have prepared her for what she saw. She stood riveted in place with shock, unable to move, unable to breathe.

John was almost invisible in the crisp white bed, so encased was he in bandages. There were holes for his eyes and mouth, but his head, arms, and neck were like those of a mummy. One leg was raised, held in traction from the ceiling by a pulley. A sheet covered the other half of his body, and Devon could tell from the bulk that there were more bandages underneath. His bed was surrounded by a variety of sinister-looking devices — tubes, bottles, and several metallic boxes with numbers on them. Devon had no idea of their purpose.

It was as though John were an inanimate object, so alien did he look. And there was no sign of life from him! Devon struggled to suppress her panic, but her heart was racing so fast that she was breathless. She could feel herself growing unbearably hot. She braced one hand against the wall, afraid she would faint. Black spots swam in front of her eyes. He looked . . . no, it couldn't be . . . but he looked . . . dead.

No, he has to be alive, she told herself, or he wouldn't be in this room. He would be somewhere else. Somewhere cold and final.

She took one tottering step toward the bed and froze. Her legs simply wouldn't carry her. She wanted to confirm that he was alive, but she couldn't move. Couldn't utter a sound. All she could do was stare in horrified disbelief.

Then John's eyes slowly opened. He blinked at the light. Then blinked again at the sight of Devon.

Devon felt a giddy wave of relief wash over her. He was alive! She gasped for air, trying to steady herself. I can't faint, she told herself. I can't show John how scared I am. If I do he might die. He'll die because he'll *think* he's dying. He musn't know how horrifying he looks. I have to act like I know he's going to live.

She marshaled her forces and, with what seemed like a superhuman effort, made her way to the flowered chintz armchair next to the bed. She tried not to collapse into it. Was she acting normal? Or did her face show her bone-chilling fear?

"John!" she whispered, unable to keep the agony from her voice. There was no answer. The seconds ticked by. She waited for him to respond. Oh God! He couldn't even speak! He just stared at her as though she were a figment of his imagination. The last time she had seen John he had been brimming with male vitality. This broken creature in the bed couldn't be the same man! Couldn't be!

Yet John's eyes were following her every move and she knew more than ever that she had to — for his sake — maintain her poise. But suddenly she was freezing, despite her heavy suit. Absolutely trembling with cold when just seconds before she had been sweating. She forced herself to take some deep, calming breaths. And still those navy eyes gazed at her. She had to pull herself together. She had to be strong. One final deep breath. If she could only touch him, she was sure that some of her own life would flow into him.

"Can you speak?" she asked, her voice a rasp.

It was several seconds before he croaked, "Little."

Tears welled up in Devon's eyes. She blinked several times and looked up at the ceiling, trying to control her distress. Another deep breath. "You must be in terrible pain," she said finally.

John's eyes closed, then reopened in a sign of assent.

"These bandages . . ." Devon reached forward and hesitantly touched the sheet that covered him. "For your burns?"

"No," he croaked, "bones."

It was odd, but even those few uttered monosyllables made him more recognizable. The timbre of his voice — hoarse though it was — was familiar. He wasn't just a mummy in the bed. He was John. Oh, thank God he was alive!

John's eyelids fluttered as he fought the desire to sleep. Then he closed them, giving in to his fatigue.

For a long time, Devon sat silently watching him. She had never before thought of John's death. He had seemed invulnerable. Able to beat any odds. And now he was utterly helpless. An overwhelming feeling of tender protectiveness filled her. She wished she could ease his pain, somehow take it away. But there was absolutely nothing she could do for him. She wanted to weep, to wail like a child at this thought. She felt terrified and so alone. John was the one person who had always seemed immortal to her, irrational though it was. Now she had to muster her courage and see him through this, all the while knowing that she had no control over whether he lived or died. Just like Morgan, she thought in despair.

And thinking of Morgan made the fear close in, grab her. Irrational voices told her that she had failed to save Morgan. That she could fail again.

"No!" she cried aloud. John's eyes flew open, bringing Devon back to the present. She had to calm herself, she realized. She was alarming him. She gave him a half smile, hoping to reassure him. "Rest, John," she whispered, "that's the best thing for you." He obeyed, his eyelids dropping closed almost instantaneously.

Devon watched John carefully and saw that his breath, though unnaturally shallow, was at least regular. She wished his doctor would come to explain his injuries to her, but she didn't want to leave John alone while she went in search of him. She thought about ringing for the nurse, but was afraid that the sound of their voices would disturb John. No, she would just wait. Calmly and rationally. No more panic. No more bad thoughts. She had to be optimistic, for John's sake.

It was a few moments before Devon remembered to remove her gloves and hat. She sat quietly with these objects on her lap, uncertain what to do with her hands, her nerves screaming in distress. She removed a linen handkerchief from her bag and dabbed at her eyes. She put her hands down and stared at John, watching him breathe, watching for any sign of movement. After a few minutes the little piece of cloth she held in her hand was twisted so tightly that it looked wet. Devon saw what she had done to her handkerchief, then smoothed it on her lap.

Trying to distract herself, she looked around the room. It was spacious for a hospital room, and sprinkled with rather good prints of restful landscapes. A stack of telegrams and letters lay on the bedside table. A huge basket of fruit — unopened — rested on a side table between the windows. Several baskets of flowers were also scattered around the room.

Devon stood up and went to one of the bouquets, a vivid arrangement of red roses. She leaned against the table a few moments to regain her equilibrium. Everything is fine, she tried to convince herself. Look, you see how many people are thinking of John? That's good. That will help him get better. Mental attitude is so important. I'm sure he's already much better than he was. The worst is probably over. Aren't these roses beautiful?

She leaned down to smell the flowers, but straightened abruptly at the sound of rustling linen. She turned to see the matronly-looking night nurse enter the room.

"Ah, madam, excuse me, I did not know monsieur had visitors," the woman said in charmingly accented, but perfect, English.

Now Devon found that she was able to smile weakly and actually converse in a normal tone. "I hope it's all right if I stay . . ."

"Of course, madam. It is good you are here finally."

Devon looked at her, puzzled. She had told no one she was coming.

Reading the strange look on Devon's pale face, the nurse said, "You are Madame Alexander, no?"

Devon came closer to the nurse, searching her face. "Haven't you met Mrs. Alexander already?" Devon had not learned of John's accident until almost a week after it had occurred. Surely Bebe had been notified immediately.

The nurse, flustered, did not know how to reply. She turned toward her charge and inserted a thermometer into his mouth. John's eyes opened slowly.

"What exactly are all his injuries?" Devon asked.

"I will send the doctor, madam," the nurse replied, a closed book after her gaffe. "You are family, yes?"

"Well . . ." Devon was not sure how to reply.

The nurse went on. "The doctor will discuss Mr. Alexander with family only. I thought because of the picture that you were family."

"Yes," Devon replied, more puzzled than ever.

Seeing the younger woman's expression, the nurse moved aside a bouquet on the bedside table. Propped against a small alarm clock was a photograph of Devon in her wedding dress. It had been torn and it had blood on one corner. Devon could see that it was held together with tape. Her heart melted at the sight of it. She wanted to put her head on the shoulder of the matronly woman in front of her and sob until there were no tears left. John still carried her picture!

"It was in his personal effects," the nurse explained, "and he asked for it almost as soon as he could speak."

Devon blushed and turned away, avoiding the nurse's curious gaze. Her eyes met those of John. He stared back at her, the thermometer preventing him from speaking.

The blue intensity of his gaze disturbed her and she turned back to the nurse. "When can the doctor come?" she asked brusquely.

"I will send him to you now, madam." The nurse took the thermometer from John's mouth, nodded her head approvingly, then hurried from the room.

"John." Devon turned back to her ex-husband. "Has anyone been in touch with . . . with Bebe?" Devon asked, loath to pronounce the despised name.

"She was here," he said with some effort.

"But the nurse didn't seem to know her."

John turned his eyes away from Devon and stared at the yellow wall. It was at that moment that the doctor entered.

"Madam." He nodded, a stern-looking middle-aged man with a square face and glasses to match. He held out one scrubbed pink hand for Devon to shake. "I am Dr. Durier."

Devon returned the gesture, then asked, "Can you give me the details of Mr. Alexander's injury?"

Like the nurse, the doctor spoke English. His was even accented as though he had studied in England, which, in fact, was the case. "Monsieur Alexander will recover from all his injuries, but he will bear scars. His face, luckily, was attended to by one of the best plastic surgeons in Europe, a colleague of mine here at the clinic. He will look much as before. Perhaps some small scars near his eyes and mouth where he was deeply cut.

"He also sustained two broken arms from the impact of flying objects. And then, there is his leg."

Devon looked at the pulley that supported the bandaged limb. "Yes, I see. It looks as though it will take some time to heal." She turned back to the doctor.

Dr. Durier shifted uncomfortably and looked toward John. John's eyes met the doctor's in an unblinking stare.

Devon looked at John, then turned back to the doctor, her expression worried.

"I'm afraid there is no way to make this easier . . ." The doctor took a deep breath. "It was necessary to amputate his other leg, his left leg."

Devon's head snapped back to the bed. All color drained from her face. Her bloodless lips moved, but no words came out. She felt as though she were choking on her tongue. Her eyes traveled to John's face, but he stared fixedly at the wall.

Devon's vision grew fuzzy as the adrenaline rushed through her. The little black spots returned, parading in front of her eyes. She grabbed the doctor's arm for support.

"Madam!" The doctor grasped her elbow, certain she was going to faint.

Devon did not see John's eyes close in pain. Visions of John — healthy and whole — flashed through her mind. It was their wedding day and they were dancing gracefully together. They were walking through the fields that first time at Evergreen. Riding Sirocco, galloping, galloping. Skiing furiously, racing to the bottom of the mountain. He would never do those things again.

Then she remembered some of the wounded servicemen she had seen. Hobbling. Staring with vacant eyes. Driven crazy with the inability to adjust to their injuries. Stories of suicides — of families torn apart. Her eyes flooded with tears and they spilled down her face.

The doctor awkwardly steadied Devon and led her to the flowered armchair. He eased her gently into it and poured her a glass of water from the pitcher at John's bedside. He watched her take a few jerky gulps. When some of the color returned to her face, he began to explain.

"It is bad, madam, but he will recover. He will be very much as before." He looked at John to see if he was listening. The doctor had earlier reassured him in much the same way, but he did not know if it had done any good. It took weeks, even months, before a doctor could truly gauge how a patient would handle an amputation. John's eyes were open again, but still fixed stubbornly on the wall.

The doctor continued, uncomfortable at referring to John as though he were not present. "He will be able to do many of the things he enjoys. People imagine much worse . . ." The sentence drifted off. The doctor was at a loss for words. Surgery was his strong suit, conversation was not. He plodded on. "We were able to save much of his leg. The amputation begins below the knee." The doctor gave one last attempt at softening the blow. "It will not be the handicap you now believe."

Devon looked over at John. He would not meet her eyes, but she knew he must be terribly distressed by her tears. He had always hated to see her cry. She cried so rarely that when she did, John knew that the hurt was deep indeed.

Devon fought to recover her composure. She would not add to his misery, she resolved. What does it matter so long as he's alive, she chided herself.

She tore her gaze away from John and looked evenly at the doctor. "Well, Doctor," she said, her voice still shaky, "if you say he won't be too hampered, then I believe you." She paused for a moment, trying to collect herself further. She turned toward John again. He was looking at her. She gave him a tearful smile. "The important thing is that you're alive." Her voice grew stronger, full of resolve. "And that you'll be well again soon."

Dr. Durier rarely saw people in such situations regain their composure so quickly. He admired the woman for her strength. She was beautiful and strong. That was good, for it would help to speed his patient's recovery. And the other woman who had come and gone in such haste, the doctor sensed that she mattered very little to the man in the bed — now that the woman in the photograph had finally arrived.

CHAPTER 41

IT was another week before John was able to sit up in his bed and carry on a prolonged conversation. When that day finally arrived, he told Devon what had happened with Bebe, sparing himself not one humiliating detail.

"Oh, she came right away, no problem there. I rather think that she imagined herself as the beautiful wartime heroine," John said wryly. "But I guess seeing me brought her back to reality."

Devon shifted uncomfortably. It was painful to hear such a story.

"Anyhow," John continued, "she apparently had been told that I had sustained serious injuries but not the nature of them. She and her father came into the room when I was awake, so before the doctor even arrived I just blurted out a few words to get the message across. I was still in shock myself over the news, so I wasn't thinking about the impact on her."

"I gather she didn't react in the way you would have hoped," Devon said gently.

"You're right," John said with a roll of his eyes. "She had hysterics, which of course brought the nurse rushing in. Not the one you met; the day nurse."

As he relived the memory, he shook his head like a person trying to get rid of a buzzing fly. He couldn't wipe from his mind the sound of Bebe's voice screaming "No, no, no!" repeatedly. It had taken a sharp slap from Henley to quiet her hysteria.

Devon, in the chintz chair that had become her station beside John, leaned over and placed a comforting hand on his. "I'm so sorry," she murmured.

"After Bebe calmed down, Mr. Henley asked the nurse to leave so they could be alone with me." John's eyes focused on a garden print on the wall opposite his bed as he relived the end of his second marriage. "But do you know that for the rest of their visit she didn't say one word to me? Not one word. And she never looked at me again. Anyhow, Henley returned the next day by himself."

"You're a hero, son," Henley had told him. "You've served your country. I know that's not much consolation at this moment, but I'm very proud to call you my son-in-law."

"He tried to explain about Bebe," John continued. "That she had no mother. How he had been an overly indulgent father. How he had always sheltered her from the realities of life. This amputation was just more than she could cope with. Couldn't stomach it. Henley told me she would be filing for divorce when she got back to America. He was so terribly ashamed. He said he'd tried to talk some sense into her but . . . I almost felt sorry for the poor guy."

"Oh, John!" Devon exclaimed sympathetically.

"Pretty ignoble, isn't it?" John said with a sigh.

"I don't know what to say . . ." Devon shook her head from side to side.

John gave her a wise smile. "That I'm well rid of her." He paused. "You know, I never really loved her, Devon," he said, searching her eyes with his own.

"I wondered when I heard about your marriage . . ." Devon confessed.

John looked at his ex-wife warmly. "And what about you. Are you happy, Your Grace?"

Devon thought of Roland and a smile lit her face. Unlike John, she had been lucky. Roland was kind and generous of spirit. He was a loving husband who had made Devon love him in return. Was she in love with him as she had been with John? Their life together was one of contentment and satisfaction rather than tumultuous passion. But yes, she was happy with him.

"I can read the answer on your face," John said tenderly. He was glad for Devon, but he could not help but feel jealous. It was painful to envision her as the wife of another man.

Devon hadn't been concerned when her period was two days late. That had been back in Cairo. Afterward, the change in temperature, the travel, the stress — all those things could have delayed it even more.

But when the delay stretched into May, she decided to have herself tested. After all, she was at the clinic every day.

"The results are not always conclusive with so early a test, but I believe that you are at least four weeks pregnant," Dr. Huerscht, a Swiss gynecologist originally from Zurich, told her. Huerscht — a world-renowned expert on obstetrics — was a jolly, fun-loving man, and Devon found him easy to talk to.

"I want this child desperately, Doctor. And I want to go home to tell my husband about it in person. Is it dangerous for me to travel at this point?"

"Well . . ." Dr. Huerscht did not look pleased at the prospect. "It would be better if you could wait until the second trimester. Is it possible that he could come here?"

"I'm afraid not. He's in the Royal Air Force, stationed in Cairo."

"Ah, yes." The doctor nodded sympathetically. "Well, I think it is important for you to settle somewhere for your confinement. You are thirty-seven years old. Not too old to have a baby, of course, but old enough for there to be hazards. Return to Cairo now, if that is where you think you will stay for the duration of your pregnancy. I would advise against further travel after that."

A few minutes later, Devon was in John's room. An instinct of propriety stopped her from sharing her news with him. After all, she should tell her husband first, she believed. Also, for a reason she could not identify, she was almost embarrassed to tell John. It was as though he still had a claim to her, and to admit her pregnancy was to admit her lovemaking with another man. It was silly. John knew, of course, that she was married to Roland. But a baby was such tangible proof of that relationship, and she sensed John's vulnerability to that news.

John sat up straighter at the sight of Devon, a grin on his face. "Hello there!" he said jovially.

Devon smiled back and sat in the chair by the side of his bed. His arms were still in a cast, but the bandages had been removed from his face. He would have a scar on his cheekbone and another, smaller one above his lip, but Devon was almost convinced they would enhance his masculine good looks.

"John." Devon hesitated, not sure how he would react to her leaving. "I have to go back to Cairo."

John's face clouded over, but he quickly replaced his expression of disappointment with a hearty grin. "Of course, you must have a million things to attend to. You've been generous with your time to stay as long as you have."

"You have so many visitors all the time," Devon said, "that you probably won't even miss me."

"That's not so," John said wistfully. "You're the only family. At least until Mother arrives." John's father had died of a heart attack the year before. John's mother, who had been visiting friends in Palm Beach at the time of John's accident, had only just been located by the government and was en route to Geneva.

Devon's heart melted at his words. She was tempted to stay just a few days more, but she had already been gone two weeks. Roland had been generous to let her come, but she did not want to take advantage of his good nature. And then there was the baby. She was eager to share the good tidings with her husband. Unlike John, Roland had many times expressed his desire to have children. His first wife had been unable to conceive, a fact they had discovered during the testing that identified her cancer.

The only heir to Roland's title and fortune was a nephew, his sister's son. Roland would have liked a son of his own to inherit his estate, but more than that, he wanted children for their own sake. He would be elated at Devon's news.

Devon looked down at the man in the bed. The magnetism that emanated from him was strong. Vulnerable, incapacitated, needy, heroic, and more handsome than ever — she was undeniably drawn to him, as she had always been. She could almost, almost but not quite, admit to herself that she still loved him in many ways. But he was not the father of her child.

"John, you don't need me here anymore. You're going to be just fine. The doctor says you'll be able to do everything you did before. Even without the —" She cut herself off, not sure whether John wanted to be reminded of the amputation.

"Leg is not a dirty word, Devon," John reassured her. "I can't avoid the fact that it's gone, but neither will I surrender to it. I intend to resume all the activities I enjoyed before. The absence of a leg does not end my life. Thankfully, I can continue my work, I can continue to do everything I did before, except perhaps ski. And maybe I'm deluding myself," he continued, "but I don't think every woman will find me as repugnant as Bebe did, simply because I'm missing part of a limb."

Devon was glad to hear the genuine confidence in his voice. No indeed, women would not find him repugnant — she could see that all too well.

CHAPTER 42

"DEVON, you've given me the greatest gift of my life," Roland said, tenderly taking his wife into his arms. He blinked rapidly to restrain the tears of joy. They were going to have a child! He had never been happier.

Devon hugged her husband with all her might, involuntarily comparing his reaction to John's that long-ago day in Paris. How wonderful for their child to be welcomed into the world with unadulterated joy!

"Do you care very much whether it's a boy or a girl?" Devon asked anxiously.

"Not a bit!" Roland lifted her off her feet and onto the plump flowered sofa that matched the drapes in their bedroom. It was a cheery, thoroughly English room. Devon had created it as a surprise for Roland, basing it on photographs of the conservatory of his country estate. The sun-filled room had been Roland's favorite, with its hunter green walls, white trim, and yellow-pink-and-green-flowered furniture. The bountiful Egyptian sun spilling through the long windows made the room a burst of happy color, which perfectly suited the mood of the moment.

Roland surrounded Devon with his embrace. How he loved her! He had never imagined he could be so happy. He drew back and drank in the radiance of Devon's face for a quiet moment. Then he asked, "When will we have our child?"

What a wonderful way of putting it, Devon thought. Aloud, she said, "Late December, I think." Just like Morgan, she thought with a pang of melancholy.

"Christmastime," said Roland dreamily, not remembering, in his happiness, the sad memories that Devon associated with that time of year, "how wonderful!"

Devon looked into her husband's happy face and all her sadness vanished. Never had she felt so appreciated, so much at one with another person. The baby was a new and beautiful aspect of her love for Roland. It added infinite dimension to her feelings for him.

"I wish you could have the baby at home," Roland said.

Devon knew he meant Abersham. She, too, would have liked to have the child in her husband's ancestral home. Or at Willowbrook, with her mother nearby. But she knew that it was best for the baby if she remained in Cairo until it was born. She told Roland of Dr. Huerscht's warning.

"Then by all means, you must stay here," he said firmly. "I'll see if I can't arrange it so that I remain here until the baby is born."

"What do you mean?" Devon asked, suddenly distressed.

"Darling," Roland chided gently, "it's no secret that our work here is mostly done. They need us in the European theater."

"But they can't send you now!" cried Devon.

"They can indeed. You know many men are separated from their loved ones. I can ask to remain here, but I may have to go nonetheless."

Devon disengaged herself from Roland's arms and stood up. Of course, he was absolutely right. She could not be selfish. At the same time, it broke her heart to think of being separated from her husband when their child was born.

Turning back to Roland, she squared her shoulders and put a brave smile on her face. "I understand that you may have to leave," she said calmly. Then she sank onto the couch and took his hands, adding a plea that was not at all stoic, "But please, please try to stay!"

Roland left the villa a bit earlier than usual the next day. On his way to headquarters, he stopped at the Thomas Cook office to arrange a wire to his solicitor in London. That dispatched, he prepared himself to face his commanding officer with his request to remain in Cairo for the next nine months.

The news, however, was not good.

"You'll be here for a few more months, of course, but every good man is needed in the European theater. I'm afraid you'll be off just about the time that it's most important to your wife that you be here," the older man said, regret in his voice. "What we can do, however, is try to arrange some leave for you close to the due date. Nonetheless, I can't give you any guarantees, old chap." He looked regretfully at Roland, fully understanding the duke's wish to be near his wife for the birth of his first child.

Roland, always correct, revealed none of his distress. "Thank you, sir," he said, "that's all I can ask."

CHAPTER 43

DEVON stood on the balcony and watched the jeep drive out of sight. She had bravely withheld her tears in Roland's presence — it was already too difficult for him to leave her — but now they spilled unchecked down the smooth lines of her cheekbones.

I should be grateful they let him stay this long, she told herself. The baby was due in only two months. Then she, like Roland, would go to England with the child. She knew it was far wiser to remain in Cairo until then. England was cold and wet in October, Cairo sunny and warm. Her obstetrician was a Swiss doctor of impeccable medical credentials to whom she had been referred by Dr. Huerscht, whereas in England the best doctors were serving the war wounded. Here, she had her sister. In England, she had no one. And even the English countryside was subject to bombing raids, while Cairo was now safe from any German threat. Still, Devon wished desperately that she didn't have to be so far from Roland.

She sank into her flowery couch facedown and indulged in a few moments of sobbing. Then, slowly, it subsided. She sat up again and looked at the tear-covered pillow, ashamed at her self-pity. After all, she told herself, her circumstances were no worse than thousands of other women's.

Devon got up and rang for Alice, who arrived moments later with a silver tray bearing several letters and invitations.

Alice bustled around the room as Devon perused her mail. "You didn't eat your breakfast," she chided Devon, clearing the little round table on the balcony. Devon and Roland almost always breakfasted in the warm morning sun.

"No . . ." Devon said absently.

Alice threw her a worried look. She knew Devon was distressed at Roland's departure. But Devon's next words reassured Alice with their normality.

"Grace has invited me to a luncheon for Cecile de la Montaigne. You know, she's marrying Lord Penderbrook. I think I'll wear my lavender silk."

Alice went to Devon's dressing area and located the suit. She checked the hem and cuffs to ensure there were no dangling threads. "I think the skirt needs a bit of pressing," she murmured, throwing the garment over her arm and going toward the bellpull. A few moments later, a young Arab servant arrived. Alice handed her the skirt, explaining what needed to be done, then dismissed her.

Devon looked at her in amusement. "I didn't know you'd learned Arabic," she said, chuckling.

"It's good management practice to make an effort like that," Alice said with a businesslike nod of her head.

"I suppose you're right," Devon said, respecting Alice for her insight. Alice was in her sixties, but her energy had not abated one bit. The household servants respected her and she, in turn, treated them with kindness and respect.

It was much the same way she, Devon, treated the stable workers at Willowbrook. A wave of homesickness suddenly engulfed her. She had never intended to stay away for such a long time. She knew that Willy was a capable manager, but she still wished she could see the farm again. After the baby was born, she'd visit, she promised herself. And after Roland returned from the war, they would all have to spend several months each year at Willowbrook. She knew that Roland would want to live in England, but he had already told her that he would be happy to spend considerable time in the Virginia countryside that so resembled Abersham. She remembered briefly how bored John had become at Willowbrook. Roland would be more suited to life there, Devon thought happily.

She suddenly had a vision of them many years hence. Roland would be gray, her own hair white. They would still be active, would take rides in the woods, work in the garden. They would have grandchildren by then. A lot of them, she hoped. Perhaps she and Roland could have another child next year.

She wondered if Laurel and Chase had received the letter — sent by Grace in the diplomatic pouch — announcing the news of her pregnancy. Devon had waited until after the fifth month to notify them, not wanting them to be disappointed in case of a miscarriage. Devon missed her parents. She wished Laurel could be beside her when the child was born.

Then she shook her head to clear it of such regrets. She forced herself to think of other things. Deliberately, she shifted her thoughts to Roland's sister. Devon wondered what she was like. Hopefully like Roland, kind and witty and good-natured. Roland did not often mention Regina, however, and when he did it was always with restraint.

Well, no matter what, Devon told herself, Roland and I have each other.

CHAPTER 44

DEVON was elated that Roland was able to arrive in Cairo the day after the birth of their daughter. Like Morgan, the child was born close to Christmastime, but in the case of this second child, the birthdate followed Christmas rather than preceded it. Her birthday was January 2, 1944.

"Are you disappointed that she's not a boy?" Devon asked, knowing the answer in advance. She was already sitting in an armchair next to the bed, dressed in the lavishly trimmed red caftan purchased at the bazaar. It was both modest and festive, thus perfectly suited to receiving guests in comfort after the birth of her child.

"Not possible." Roland beamed. "My only regret is that she won't be able to inherit Abersham." The English law of primogeniture often encumbered old properties with prohibitions against female heirs. A male relative, no matter how remote, took precedence over a female direct descendant of the property owner.

"It doesn't matter," Devon said, "she'll have Willowbrook. And," she added, "I fully intend that we should have another child. A boy maybe?"

"That would be grand, but it doesn't matter a bit if it's not." Roland sat on a pouf at the foot of her chair. From his position, he was able to remain as close as possible to his wife and child. "Darling, I have a very exotic name request," he said, looking at Devon with a bit of apprehension.

"Exotic?" Devon gave Roland a sidelong glance, then returned to feeding her child.

"What would you think of the name Francesca?" he asked.

"Well . . ." Devon reflected a moment. "It's certainly not very British."

"That's just the point. I thought of names like Penelope or Rowena, but they seemed . . . not very lively, I suppose."

Devon laughed. "I'd have to agree with you."

"Then there are the shorter names, like Anne or Mary. They're even more boring!"

"I can't argue with that, but how did you arrive at Francesca? It's not the name of an old girlfriend, is it?" she asked with mock suspicion.

"The very idea!" Roland exclaimed with a hearty laugh. "Well, it's ridiculous, I suppose, and not at all as tradition dictates, but I once read a book in which the heroine's name was Francesca. It just stuck in my mind."

"How long ago did you read this book?"

"Years ago. At school."

"And you've been counting on naming your daughter that all these years?"

"Well, I once considered giving the name to a particularly lovely hound, but then I decided not to squander it."

"Thank heavens, because I don't think I would like to name my daughter after your particularly lovely hound."

"Precisely!" Roland said, raising his arm clownishly so that his right index finger was extended in an exclamation point just above his shoulder.

Devon laughed at the pose, then said, "I suppose that since the name hasn't been taken by one of your animals . . ."

Roland sprang to his feet. "Capital! Then you agree!"

"I think it's a lovely name, and I agree," Devon said, amused by her husband's childish glee.

"Francesca Somerset-Smith, I've been waiting for you for a long,

long time," Roland said, tenderly taking his daughter from Devon's arms, "and I intend to make you as happy as you've made me."

It was a moment that Devon would hold close to her heart until the end of her life.

CHAPTER 45

A TERRIBLE sense of foreboding gripped Devon when, on March 31, 1944, she learned that the British Bomber Command had sent 795 aircraft to bomb Nuremberg, Germany — and lost 94 of them. She knew that Roland, acting as fighter escort to the bombardiers, must surely have participated in the mission.

For two days she was almost unable to eat. The circles that appeared under her eyes were so dark that they looked like bruises. Her clear skin erupted with tiny pimples, something that had never happened before.

Then, two days later, euphoria. She received a wire from Roland reassuring her that he was fine. She blessed him for this communication.

Somehow, after those two hellish days, she felt that the worst was over, and indeed, there was some truth to that. The Allies were gaining air superiority over Germany.

Finally, there came a day in April when Roland was convinced that he could bring his wife and daughter to England without fear that they would be killed by a German bomb. He was certain that Hitler's air force would soon be defeated. In any event, the Germans were kept so busy defending their own cities that their attacks against London had abated.

Although Roland did not write these things to Devon for security reasons, he knew she would understand the significance of his news that she could finally go to Abersham. His London town house in Belgravia was out of the question until the war was over.

Devon was elated when she received Roland's letter.

"Grace." She had telephoned her sister immediately. "Francesca and I are going to England!"

The idea of seeing her husband again, of being in his home surrounded by his personal belongings, was almost too exciting for her to bear. It would make her feel closer to him even when he was away, she realized, if she could live in the place in which he grew up.

Roland had arranged for her to fly on a military aircraft to a small airfield near his home, thus avoiding London entirely. It was to be a circuitous and time-consuming trip with several plane changes, but it was the only way to avoid areas that Roland feared might not be entirely safe from the Germans. Not only would the trip be time-consuming, but also Devon had to wait until there were spaces available on an airplane for her, Alice, and Francesca. Precedence was given first to active military, then to soldiers returning home.

And so she waited and hoped each day for a phone call or visit from the RAF telling her it was time to go. Her valises were packed. All she had to do was be ready to go at a moment's notice. Each morning she dressed herself and Francesca for travel. Each morning Alice packed a soft leather bag with diapers and other necessities for the voyage. And at the end of each day, Devon was disappointed to find that there had been no room for them.

Once, only once, she had telephoned British headquarters to inquire about the possibility of a space for her little group. She had been rebuffed with exquisite politeness.

"I know the wait is tedious, Your Grace, and we are sorry for the delay, but so many of our personnel are being transferred to the European theater just now. We will find a place for you soon, I hope."

"Of course," said Devon, ashamed that she should be so impatient about a personal matter when the military desperately needed the space. "I won't trouble you again."

"No trouble at all, Your Grace. Please feel free to check with us again, but rest assured that we have not forgotten you."

Devon awakened to the cry of the street vendor in front of her villa. He came each morning bearing fresh fruits and vegetables. Exotic, luscious ripe fruits that tasted sweeter than the richest dessert. Devon made it a point to savor a mango each morning with her breakfast, for she knew they would be impossible to obtain in England.

There were many things about Cairo she would miss, she thought as she stretched in the fine Egyptian cotton sheets. She enjoyed her premature nostalgia for Cairo because it meant she would soon be reunited with Roland. She found herself reveling in Cairo's attractions more than ever because each occasion might be her last in the bustling city. And, paradoxically, that filled her with happy anticipation of the new chapter in her life.

As had become the norm in the past three weeks, she arose to find a summer-weight wool traveling dress laid out for her to wear. Spring had officially come to England the month before, but Devon knew it was likely to be chilly and damp there.

She rang for her breakfast, then sat on the flowered sofa to await her sister's daily phone call. Grace and Devon, as close as ever, spoke on the telephone each morning at approximately nine o'clock, whether or not they intended to see each other later in the day.

Alice entered the room with a tray of steaming coffee, croissants, blackberry preserves, and, of course, a mango.

"Do you think today will be the day?" Devon asked, her face radiant at the thought.

"If it isn't soon, the war will be over before we even get there," Alice joked.

"Wouldn't that be wonderful!" Devon sighed.

Alice smiled and proceeded into the bathroom to draw Devon's bath. Devon, delighting in the sunny, lazy morning, dreamily ate her breakfast as she read the two-week-old *Washington Post* sent over by Grace.

When she was finished, she bathed and dressed. She had to unpack her makeup case in order to apply her cosmetics, then repack it in case she should be called to the airfield.

She was on her way to check on Francesca when she was intercepted in the cool marble hallway by the butler, a distinguished Arab who inexplicably spoke nearly perfect English although he had never gone to school.

"Your Grace, there is a British officer here to see you."

Devon's face came alive with excitement. "It's time!" she exclaimed aloud. "Where is he now?"

"In the foyer, Your Grace."

"Show him into the conservatory, please," Devon said breathlessly. "Or, never mind, I'll do it myself," she said, sweeping past the servant in her impatience.

As she approached the visitor from the stairway above, she was surprised to see that he wore the insignia of a colonel. She had expected an officer of lesser rank to escort her. As the man turned, she recognized a friend of Roland's.

The smile she offered him was like a resplendent bouquet of roses. "I'm completely ready, Harry!" she cried gaily as she descended the stairs. "I only need to tell Alice to fetch Francesca and we're on our way."

The gray-haired colonel stared at her in seeming astonishment, but said nothing. Then, recovering himself, he stepped toward Devon, hand outstretched. "How good to see you again, Devon," he said in a serious tone. Harry was always serious, Devon thought with an inward laugh. A sweet, kind, and highly intelligent man, but so serious, she reflected as she chattered away about inconsequential things.

"Wonderful to see you! Let me show you into the conservatory. I'll call for some tea and order our things brought down."

Devon sped down the hallway of the villa, the colonel in her wake, until they came to a sunny room filled with tropical plants. The room was glass on three sides, but one of the walls could be entirely opened onto a courtyard, in the tradition of the Middle East.

"Well, what's our schedule? When do we leave?" Devon asked, once she was seated.

The colonel took a deep breath. He did not return Devon's smile. Gravely, he began. "Devon . . . I . . . I'm afraid I have something rather difficult to tell you . . ." he said, then stopped himself. There was a moment of heavy silence. A moment during which comprehension suddenly dawned on Devon. Harry watched her face shift from blissful happiness to horrified understanding, then a mask went down — an unbreachable mask that bore no resemblance to the delightful woman he knew. The roses in her cheeks turned to chalk. Her sparkling aqua eyes turned dull with shock.

Harry watched helplessly as Devon sagged in her seat. She looked as though she were in physical pain. He struggled fruitlessly for words. He had to explain what had happened. How Roland's plane had been downed by enemy fire over Germany. But Devon's expression stopped him cold. She looked on the verge of breaking. And the look on her face was so rife with agony that he dared not utter a word.

"Don't say anything!" she commanded harshly, staring down at her hands. She felt as though her heart was being torn from her breast. At all costs, she had to prevent him from saying the words. If he didn't say the words then it wouldn't be real. Not yet. Not until she could bear it. She knew she would scream if he voiced any platitudes; break down and never stop crying if he offered any sympathy. She would shatter, totally shatter. All there was to say she could read in his eyes. In his stricken expression. Roland wasn't a prisoner, he wasn't injured, he wasn't missing in action. He was dead. There was no doubt, no missing body, no hope at all. He was simply dead. It was that final.

I just don't have the capacity for any more pain, she thought. I can't stand one more thing. Not this. Oh, God! Not this!

Devon started, very methodically, to tear the nail of her index finger. She worked at it a few seconds with a concentration that the colonel found difficult to watch. Finally, it hung on by just a sliver. Devon tore at the sliver until the little shred of nail was severed. But she had severed it too low, and she began to bleed on her white wool traveling dress.

"Oh, look what I've done," she said, watching the blood seep into the fine cloth, "look what I've done . . ."

Harry moved to an ottoman at her feet and took her feverishly working hands in his. "Devon, I . . ."

"Don't." Her voice was rough, completely unlike the graceful contralto he knew. "Don't tell me he died bravely. Don't tell me he's a hero. I know all that already," she insisted fiercely.

Harry obeyed her, only nodding to acknowledge the truth of her words. It was, of course, just as she had guessed.

It seemed as though hours elapsed before either one of them spoke, though it was only a few moments. Finally, Harry had to continue. "We are fortunate in that we were able to recover the . . . that he'll have a decent burial. But you need to go to Abersham. You need to be there now."

Devon looked up at the colonel. "Now?" she cried, deeply bitter at the irony. "After all the waiting, I'll only be able to see my husband now?"

Harry bowed his head. He focused on the spot that the blood from Devon's wound had left on her skirt. "I'm sorry . . . so sorry," he said, shaking his head. He could not bear to lift his head and meet her eyes, so he continued to stare at the spot of blood. And when tears joined the blood, still he continued to stare.

"You . . . you must go," he finally murmured, "this afternoon."

Devon released her hands from his and buried her face in them. Her wound was drying, but a bit of blood smeared onto her face. She looked like a wounded creature, Harry thought. And indeed she was.

"Finally," she said bitterly, "the day has come for me to go to England."

"Devon," Harry asked, looking up at her in bewilderment, "don't you want to know more? About how it —"

"Later, Harry," she said wearily, "when I have the strength. I can't bear it right now."

Harry stood up and awkwardly fumbled with his cap. "Your strength will come back, Devon," he replied. He knew this was so. His military service had schooled him to distinguish the strong from the weak.

His instinct was confirmed by Devon's next gesture. She rose on visibly unsteady legs and forlornly started to leave the room; then, suddenly remembering him and the fact that he was a visitor in her home, she straightened, turned back to him, and said, "Thank you for bringing me this news yourself."

The colonel looked at her, his face mirroring the pain on Devon's. "I'll be back for you at three o'clock, then," he said gently.

"I'll be ready," Devon said stoically. She looked like a soldier facing battle; afraid, but even more afraid to admit it.

CHAPTER 46

DEVON arrived in Abersham with just enough time to prepare for the funeral the following day. She knew she had no claim to the estate, so instead she found a nearby inn where she could lodge in case she was not invited to Abersham by Roland's family. The decision was a wise one, for when she telephoned the estate, she was told by a servant that Roland's sister was unable to come to the telephone. Devon politely left a message, but was relieved when the call was not returned. She could not bear to face introductions with Roland's family on the eve of his burial.

Insulated by grief, she nonetheless noticed the coolness of

Roland's friends and family toward her at the funeral. In fact, aside from a cursory handshake, she was not acknowledged at all by Roland's sister. His brother-in-law — hers too, she supposed — issued a half-hearted invitation for Devon to join them at Abersham following the funeral, but Devon sensed she was unwelcome at the gathering, and lacking the strength to grapple with a houseful of cold strangers, she instead went directly from the graveside to the train station. From there, she traveled to London, where Roland's heirs were scheduled to meet the following afternoon for the reading of his will.

The hostile face of Roland's sister, Regina, was the first sight that greeted Devon upon entering the solicitor's office the next day. Devon's sister-in-law — tall, dark, and slender, like Roland — had the formidable demeanor of one accustomed to having her way.

Seated beside Regina was an apologetic-looking young man with a curiously unformed face. This was Roland's nephew, Percy, and the new duke of Abersham. Devon knew that Percy was twenty-five years old, but his face had the slightly fleshy roundness of adolescence. The whisper of a mustache that struggled along his upper lip was clearly an attempt to look older, but it was not successful. Devon had the impression that Percy was referred to by others in the family as "Poor Percy."

Stepping farther into the room, Roland's solicitor following closely behind, Devon saw that a third person occupied a Regency-style sofa in the corner: Regina's husband, the only person who had bothered to extend civility to her during the funeral. The man, an older version of Percy, wore a resigned, uninvolved expression.

Regina herself was not physically unattractive. Though she was forty-eight years old, her skin had only the barest trace of wrinkles. These she kept at bay with an unceasing parade of costly ministrations. Regina's endowments — her good looks, wealth, and high birth — she did not view as providential gifts. Rather, she considered them her due. The minor irritations of everyday life she considered major trials of her strength. Her strength she manifested through browbeating and haranguing so that, ultimately, most of her relationships ended either in angry confrontation or emotional withdrawal. Her husband and son had chosen the latter route. Roland had chosen neither.

Despite Regina's faults, Roland had genuinely loved her, and she him. After their parents had died, however, Regina had felt it her duty to direct her younger brother in life. He would always gravely agree with her advice, then merrily ignore it. But Roland's charm was so great, his love for Regina so clearly genuine, that it seemed she could forgive him anything.

Roland's new wife was another thing entirely. This interloper, this divorcée, this wealthy American, was a breed well known — and despised — in British society. She couldn't fool Regina with her perfectly tailored, perfectly appropriate slate gray dress. She might look every bit the well-bred lady but she was just another American opportunist, like that Simpson woman who had desecrated the crown of England. Regina was girded for battle.

Roland's solicitor looked from one woman to the other and felt sorry for Roland's widow. Oswald Lyttleton, a rather cynical servant of the rich who had grown wealthy himself, was not given to sentimentality, but he pitied the beautiful American for the ordeal to come. He took the young woman by the elbow and walked her across his antique Persian rug until they stood in front of Regina.

"Your Grace," he began, properly addressing Devon, the woman of higher rank, first, "I believe you have already met —"

"Please." Devon cut him off. Turning her head toward Regina, she extended her hand and said, "I'm afraid we didn't have much of a chance to speak yesterday. How do you do?"

Regina considered the hand for a moment. Everyone in the room held their breath, afraid that she was about to commit an unpardonable rudeness, but her upbringing finally forced her to take the proffered hand. She did this with the air of a person being handed a dirty diaper.

Lord Lewiston rose and, braving a glare from his wife, gave his sister-in-law a polite greeting. Percy blushed and stammered a brief "How do you do," cast a worried glance at his mother, and promptly slouched back into his chair.

Lyttleton scuttled behind his desk as though eager to put the barrier between him and the others, bowed his graying head, and cleared his throat. "Shall we begin?

"Let me first summarize matters for you by pointing out that the entitlement to Abersham must go to a male heir if such a person exists. In this case, to Percy Lewiston." The solicitor studied Devon's reaction, but this was apparently what she had expected, for she only nodded her head.

"Income and rents associated with the estate will also go to Percy Lewiston, as will an additional bequest of fifteen million pounds, to be kept in trust for the upkeep of Abersham." Lyttleton paused and surveyed the room once more. Lord Lewiston was looking at the ceiling, seemingly detached from the proceeding. Percy had his eyes cast down. The two women, however, stared at the solicitor attentively, waiting for him to continue.

"However . . ." Lyttleton shifted uncomfortably in his seat and looked once more at Devon. He was afraid to look at Regina. He could sense her bristling at the word "however." Lyttleton fixed his gaze on the document before him and adjusted the bifocals on his nose. "There are some funds independent of the estate that His Grace had the discretion to distribute at will." Hurrying on, Lyttleton read, " 'I leave the remainder of my personal fortune to my beloved wife, Devon, on the condition that five million pounds of that sum shall be held in trust for my daughter, Francesca, until she attains the age of twenty-one. Trusteeship of said funds shall be held by my wife, Devon. I leave no further instructions as to the guardianship of these monies, for I have every confidence in my wife's financial and personal judgment.' "

"The remainder of his personal fortune!" cried Regina.

"At this time, some nine point two million pounds," announced the solicitor.

"That's outrageous! Why should this . . . this . . . *person* get a sum like that after being married to him for only a year?"

For the first time, Lord Lewiston entered the fray. "Because, Regina, it is Roland's will."

Regina wheeled in her chair to face her husband. "This has nothing to do with you," she hissed.

Lord Lewiston leaned forward on the sofa and opened his mouth to reply, then apparently thinking better of it, closed it.

"Er . . . that's not quite so, Lady Lewiston," Oswald Lyttleton interjected. "There is a small bequest for Lord Lewiston." Lyttleton coughed and went on reading. "To my brother-in-law, Sir Archibald Lewiston, I leave my yacht *Wicked Ways* in the hope that he will enjoy a few interludes of pleasure and solitude so necessary to one's mental well-being."

"I beg your pardon!" said Regina, seeing this as a barb directed at her. Suddenly she thought of Roland — how he used to tease her, to make her laugh — and she burst into bitter tears. The only person she had ever truly loved and admired was gone. How gay he had been, how amusing! He had loved her, too, as no one had ever done before or since. Certainly not her husband or son. No, those two feeble specimens were more afraid than affectionate, she thought, blaming the victims for what she had made them.

"And to my dear sister, Regina, I leave my town house in Belgravia, which we shared during our childhood when it was the home of our parents. In addition, to Regina I leave all the Abersham jewels with the exception of the diamond and sapphire ring, necklace, and bracelet that I offered as a gift to my wife and that I intend she should keep until her death, at which time I would wish to see it bequeathed to our daughter, Francesca."

"But those are priceless family heirlooms!" cried Regina. Snapping her head up from her Brussels lace handkerchief, she saw that Devon was quietly studying her. The young woman's composure seemed insulting. The American had certainly not loved Roland as she had. She did not deserve his fortune. And certainly not those jewels!

"*You,*" she spat at Devon, "you have taken advantage of a hero. You knew he was going off to war, that he would probably be killed. You saw an opportunity to make a fortune. But I intend to contest this!"

"Regina!" Sir Archie sprang to his feet and strode over to his wife. "You've gone too far now! I won't have this." He leaned down and took her elbow, almost forcibly bringing her to her feet. "I think you should take a moment in private to refresh yourself."

"How dare you!" Regina's face was scarlet with fury as she yanked her arm out of her husband's grip. Her son cowered in the adjacent chair, wishing he were far, far away. Devon, pale with anger herself, kept her seat and said nothing, afraid that if she spoke she would sink to the level of Regina.

"Regina!" commanded Archie. "Come."

Astounded by her husband's newfound forcefulness, and the jerk he gave her elbow, which he had recaptured in a grip of iron, Regina followed him from the room.

"I'm . . . I'm s-s-sorry," Percy said, not daring to look directly at Devon.

"Don't apologize," Devon said coolly, "you've done nothing."

The solicitor appeared to be very busy moving the papers on his desk from one pile to another. He, too, did not wish to meet Devon's eyes. So the three sat in silence for several minutes while Regina presumably composed herself.

Indeed, it was a calmer woman who reentered the office, her husband unexpectedly no longer with her. Regina did not sit, but instead walked toward Devon until she was standing directly in front of her chair.

"You" — the word exploded from her mouth like a gunshot — "are an adventuress. I intend to explore every legal means to see that my family is not robbed of what is rightfully ours. If I fail, I intend to ruin you. I will broadcast from every treetop exactly what kind of opportunist you are. You will not be received by anyone here. Furthermore, I will make every effort to ensure that what passes for society in America also rejects you for the low sort of woman that you are."

Devon coolly arose from her chair, pulling on her black kid gloves. She brushed past Regina and walked to the heavy, carved door that guarded Lyttleton's office, her back to the others. Then she turned.

"*You*" — she swiveled her head to face Regina — "have just thrown away a fortune. You see, I believed, somewhat as you do, that I had no right to such a vast sum after only one year of marriage. Furthermore, contrary to what you may believe, I don't need it. As a result, I was going to suggest that the money be added to the fund for the upkeep of Abersham. Of course, that's quite out of the question now. I'll simply give the money to charity.

"Oh and by the way," Devon said, almost as an afterthought, "if I hear that you've said one word to impugn my reputation, either here or in America, I will sue you for slander. And, rest assured, no one in a courtroom will believe that a woman who gives away her inheritance is the adventuress you describe. So be careful, or you may lose a second fortune." Devon stood on the threshold for a moment to watch her message sink in. She was satisfied to see Regina's mouth drop in horror.

"Good day, gentlemen," Devon said with a half smile, "and, of course, good day to you, Lady Lewiston."

BOOK THREE

WILLOWBROOK

1957

CHAPTER 47

"I'M almost as dark as you," Francesca Somerset-Smith said, holding her arm next to that of the coffee-colored boy.

"Not by a long shot! No matter how long you stay out in the sun!" Jesse denied scornfully.

"By the end of summer I will be," Francesca said challengingly. Devon's thirteen-year-old daughter was olive-skinned, much darker than either of her parents. That combined with her springy black tresses gave her an exotic, almost Mediterranean look. She was not as beautiful as her mother had been on the threshold of womanhood. She had none of her mother's innate delicacy. Rather, she was a wiry package of muscles with a slenderness that was the result of endless energy. Still, she was a strikingly attractive child, though she did not believe it. She lamented the fact that, unlike most of the other girls at school, she had yet to develop breasts. She hid her disappointment by clinging to tomboyish pursuits, refusing to be absorbed into the adolescent world of preening and giggling over boys.

Francesca's best friend was Jesse, the fifteen-year-old son of Jeremiah, Willowbrook's former top jockey. Forty-two years old now, Jeremiah was retired from his stellar career in racing and was reentering the world of training. He worked closely with Willy and Devon on the development of racehorses, but his main task was to oversee the younger Willowbrook jockeys.

Jeremiah had earned enough money from prize purses to build a large, comfortable home on a parcel of land sold to him by Devon. She had suggested the transaction once it had become apparent that none of the white landowners nearby would sell to a black man, despite his stature in the horse world.

Because of the proximity of their homes, Jesse and Francesca had grown up together and were as comfortable with each other as brother and sister. They shared a love of horses — both wanted to be jockeys — as well as a love for other outdoor pursuits, such as fishing and swimming.

They sat now on the banks of a fast-running creek that ran through the valley separating Jeremiah's land from Devon's. It was Jesse and Francesca's favorite spot in summer. On a typical day, they would awaken early, meet on the creek's bank to go fishing, and then, without bothering to change into bathing suits, they would jump into the water in their shorts and cotton shirts. Once exhausted from the games they played in the water, they would clean and cook their fish, then laze on the banks for a few hours.

"Well, I may not be as dark as you, but I bet I can outrun you to the stables." Francesca threw out the challenge as part of their daily ritual, though she was never able to outrun Jesse.

No day was without riding, of course, and this they would typically do in the afternoons. They were not allowed to ride any of the Thoroughbreds raced by Willowbrook, but Devon owned several pleasure horses freely available to Jesse. Francesca had her own small mare, Caramel, a thirteen-year-old palomino.

"Hah!" Jesse sprang to his feet. "That'll be the day! Go on, I'll give you a head start since you're just a girl."

"Just a girl!" Frankie expostulated, jumping up with as much energy as her friend.

"You're so easy to rile," Jesse mocked her. "Why do you get so mad about being a girl?"

Frankie turned red with anger and embarrassment. She wished she were a boy so that she wouldn't have to worry about things like being pretty and growing breasts. Other girls made her feel inferior, with their frilly petticoats, training bras, and beribboned hair.

"If you keep pestering me, Jesse Washington, I'll punch you as hard as any boy. Now, let's race, and you *don't* have to give me a head start!"

Jesse leaned over. "On your mark . . . get set . . ." — he paused a moment to heighten the suspense — "go!"

Jesse did not give Francesca a head start, but he did let her carry the lead until almost the end. Then he beat her by a small margin. He wanted to be kind, but he didn't want to lose.

CHAPTER 48

"HOW do you think he's doing?" Jeremiah asked Willy, nodding toward the young jockey circling Willowbrook's track on Royal Flush. The two men leaned on the white fence in identical poses, elbows on the top rail, left foot on the bottom.

"The horse is better'n the boy," Willy grumbled. "Lad's cockey. Horse too. But the horse is entitled."

Jimmy Pritchard was a daring jockey. He took chances many others would not. But he did not alter his strategy to suit the horse; rather, he tried to make the horse suit his style of riding — all-out war in the roller-derby tradition. He had won a number of races for Willowbrook, but Jeremiah was concerned that his boundless daring was too undisciplined.

"He's hard to control," Jeremiah said with a philosophical sigh, pushing himself away from the fence.

"Won't do," said Willy in his usual curt fashion, turning his back to the man on horseback.

"You don't like him, do you?" Jeremiah asked, studying the older man's profile as they walked toward the barn. Willy was approaching eighty, but his posture was as erect and his manner as alert as that of a much younger man. Jeremiah knew that one day he would inherit Willy's title of head trainer for Willowbrook, but he was not eager to see the old man go. Jeremiah had learned that Willy's instincts were rarely wrong, and he relied on those judgments to guide him.

Willy snorted in reply to Jeremiah's question. "Who cares anything about like?" he said derisively. "It's simple. A boy who thinks he's too good to listen to his boss is going to make a serious mistake one day. Can't afford that kind of attitude."

Jeremiah nodded in agreement. But Pritchard was good and he hated to lose him. "I'll try to talk to him . . ." Jeremiah said, thinking aloud.

"Won't get you anywhere with a mule like that one. He's the kind won't take orders from you and you know it." Willy stopped walking and gave Jeremiah a significant look.

"Because I'm a Negro, you mean." Jeremiah confirmed what he knew to be Willy's thoughts. Between him and Willy there were no words minced. They were color-blind to each other, but they were aware of the views of society.

"Yup," said Willy, shoving his hands into the worn pockets of his jeans and looking directly at the younger man.

"Well . . . I'd hate to give up so easily." Jeremiah ran his hand over his face, struggling with indecision. "He's got guts, Pritchard does."

"Yeah, and he needs a good kick in 'em. Or lower," Willy grumbled.

Jeremiah smiled at the older man's words. He had not acquired Willy's ability to command others. As a jockey, he had been guided by Devon and Willy. When he had issued orders, it had been to an animal, not a person. Now, suddenly, he found himself in command of five young men who treated him with varying degrees of deference. He knew it was difficult for the four who were white to look upon him as a superior, despite his celebrity status in the racing world. It was the same old story, he thought with resignation. There were Negro athletic stars, but no Negro coaches. Negro singing stars, but no Negro producers. He had been able to overlook such injustices much of his life, insulated as he had been from prejudice in the safe cocoon of Willowbrook. But he knew that had it not been for the immense influence of Devon and Willy, he would not have been permitted to become a top-flight jockey.

Now, though, Jeremiah knew he would have to command respect as a man, not just as an athlete. And he had to start with Jimmy Pritchard.

"I'll give him one last chance," Jeremiah told Willy.

"He won't thank you for it," Willy warned Jeremiah, "and he won't respect you either."

"All the same . . ." Jeremiah turned his hands palms up and shrugged his shoulders. The two men stopped in front of Willy's office.

"Comin' in? Want a drink?"

Jeremiah chuckled, marveling at the old man's ability to drink whiskey on a hot afternoon yet continue working until nightfall. "No, thanks. See you later."

Devon looked up from the accounts ledger as Willy came through the door. Reading the look of disgust on the old man's face, she asked, "Trouble?"

"Pritchard." Willy didn't need to say more. He and Devon, after more than twenty years' collaboration, communicated in a virtual Morse code of monosyllables.

The old man opened the top right-hand drawer of his big scarred oak desk and took out a bottle of whiskey. "Drink?"

"A drop," said Devon, from her own identical desk. She took a cheap tumbler half filled with water and handed it to Willy.

Willy tipped the bottle to her glass, then took a shot glass from the open drawer of his own desk. He carefully filled it as full as he could without it overflowing, then recapped the bottle and put it back in the drawer. He never had more than a single shot of whiskey in the afternoon, but he never failed to adhere to the ritual.

"What's Jeremiah going to do about him?" Devon asked, leaning back in the old swivel chair and cradling her head in her hands.

Willy sat on his desk, his legs on his chair before him. "Says he's goin' to try to talk to him."

Devon crossed one denim-clad leg over the other. "Probably won't work." She sighed.

"That's what I say." Willy lifted the dusty old Brooklyn Dodgers cap off his head and laid it on the desk top beside him. It was not the same hat he had worn twenty years before, but it was identical.

"I suppose a jockey as good as Jeremiah only comes along once in a while," Devon said with resignation.

"S'pose so," Willy agreed.

Devon turned back to the ledger while Willy took his seat at his desk. They worked for a few moments in silence until the ringing of the old black telephone on Devon's desk interrupted them.

"Is it already so late?" Willy heard Devon exclaim. "I'll be right there, Mother."

Devon replaced the receiver, stood up, and turned to Willy. "You're coming to Alice's birthday party, aren't you? It's an important one."

"Eightieth, right?" Willy asked over his shoulder.

"Right."

Willy said thoughtfully, his back still to Devon, "Fine-lookin' woman for eighty."

Devon stared at him and raised an eyebrow. "Did I hear correctly?" she asked in mock astonishment. "Did you actually just pay someone a compliment?"

"Don't start cacklin'," Willy said gruffly. "And, yeah, I'll be there."

*   *   *

Francesca knocked at her grandmother's door. "Grandmother?" she called softly.

"Come in, dear!" Laurel's voice, still musical, carried through the heavy wood of the closed door.

Francesca opened the door and stood shyly just inside.

"Don't you look lovely!" her grandmother exclaimed.

Francesca smiled. Her grandmother always said she looked lovely.

"Come here and let me have a good look at you," Laurel commanded kindly.

The girl obeyed, crossing the polished plank floor to the delicately carved fruitwood vanity where her grandmother sat applying the finishing touches to her makeup. Francesca adored her grandmother, and was in awe of her femininity. Her grandmother always smelled deliciously of orange blossoms — everything about her was soft and sweet and soothing. Even her room — decorated in watercolor hues of blue, gray, and lavender — had an atmosphere of peace and comfort. Laurel herself was dressed in an impeccably cut gown of silvery gray silk whose luster reflected her snowy white hair.

"Turn around slowly," Laurel told her granddaughter.

Francesca complied, holding out the full skirt of the pink linen dress. "Mother let me wear stockings and high heels!" she breathed, stunned herself by the transformation the new privilege had wrought on her appearance. Suddenly she didn't feel at all tomboyish. She felt almost pretty.

"With your hair pulled into a chignon like that, you look quite grown-up." Laurel smiled, taking her granddaughter's hands in hers.

Francesca impulsively hugged her grandmother, elated at being told she looked grown-up. "I'm so glad you came to live with us!" she said, holding her grandmother close.

"I am, too, dear. I'd have been very lonely at Evergreen without Chase."

Francesca pulled back and studied her grandmother. "Do you miss Grandfather all the time?"

A misty smile crossed Laurel's face and it seemed that she forgot Francesca's presence for a moment. In a wistful voice, she finally replied, "We were together sixty years . . ."

"Sixty years!" Francesca repeated in awe. "That seems like forever."

"It passed so quickly," Laurel said from her reverie.

Francesca was silent. From the expression on her grandmother's face it seemed that the old woman was reliving a happy memory — one that Francesca was hesitant to interrupt.

Suddenly Laurel shook her head brusquely and stood up. "Sometimes I forget that he's gone. Sometimes I feel his presence so strongly . . ."

"Do you believe in ghosts?" Francesca asked in wonder, following her grandmother into the huge walk-in closet.

Laurel turned on the light, then sat on a small bench along the wall opposite the door. Above the bench was a shoulder-high shelf of neatly arranged shoes. Laurel took a moment to contemplate Francesca's question. Finally, she said, "Once I would have told you absolutely not. But now . . . I suppose as one grows older one hopes for a spiritual afterlife. Not ghosts exactly, but . . ."

Francesca sat on the polished wood floor in front of Laurel. "Grandmother, are you afraid to die?"

"Yes, in a way," Laurel answered honestly. "On the other hand, I feel so strongly that I would like to rejoin your grandfather. Maybe in death such a thing is possible."

"I hope it is," Francesca said fervently, "because then I could see my father, too!"

Laurel smiled down at her granddaughter affectionately. "I'm sorry you never knew him. I didn't either. He was a hero, though, and a wonderful man, I know that much. And, one day, I hope you'll marry a man just as wonderful."

"Oh, I'm not going to marry," Francesca said in the most sophisticated voice she could muster. "That's for silly girls! I'm going to become a famous jockey instead!"

Laurel stood up and turned toward the shelf of shoes to hide her smile. She selected a pair of silvery peau de soie pumps and sat back down on the bench, addressing her granddaughter as she placed the shoes on her feet. "You're not fond of boys then?" she asked mildly.

"Boys are okay," Francesca said indifferently, "it's girls who are so silly."

"Well, then, it seems to me that you would be very happy spending your life with a boy . . . er . . . man, I should say."

Francesca's face crinkled into an expression of frustration. "Yes, but boys don't like girls like me. They like girls like Melissa Parrish or Kendra Wilkes. Girls who wear dresses all the time and . . . well . . . you know what I mean!"

Laurel laughed softly and stood up, waiting until Francesca did the same. "You are a very beautiful young lady, Francesca, though you may not know it yet. Just wait a year or two. You'll have so many boys interested in you, you won't know what to do."

With those words, Laurel swished out of the closet, skirts rustling behind her. Francesca followed more slowly, and just before she turned off the light, she paused at the mirrored door and peered into it. She saw a long-legged girl with strong features, thick curly hair, and slanting green eyes. What she wished she saw was a petite, curvaceous blonde with straight, shiny hair, a pert upturned nose, and round blue eyes. Grandmother was so wrong! She just didn't know what boys liked!

CHAPTER 49

"MOM, that's the man you were married to before Father, right?" Francesca asked, peering at the old black-and-white photograph in the display case. Francesca and Devon, in Saratoga Springs for the August racing season, were visiting the National Museum of Racing and Hall of Fame, first opened two years before. The museum's curator — who knew Devon well from her fund-raising activities on behalf of the institution — had recently telephoned her to ask for help in compiling a series of old photographs. She had forwarded several dozen from her early racing years, and was surprised to see that almost all of them were prominently displayed.

Now Francesca was carefully studying a photograph of John Alexander, one arm around Devon, one holding the lead of a racehorse.

Devon remembered that time so vividly. The strife between her and John, the many disputes, the struggles with Willy. None of that was apparent in the photo. They looked loving and carefree.

"Yes," Devon murmured to her daughter, "that was my first husband."

"John Alexander. How come I've never met him?"

"He lives in Geneva, dear. He does something very important for the government."

"Doesn't he ever visit here?" Francesca persisted.

Devon shrugged. "I don't know."

"He was very handsome. Was Daddy as handsome?"

"Different. Your father had tremendous charm. And certainly he was handsome. But you've seen pictures of him," Devon said softly.

Francesca turned and looked directly at her mother's profile. "Which husband did you love best?"

The question took Devon aback. She did not know how to answer. Turning away from the display case, she said, "I loved them both with all my heart, but in different ways."

"If you loved Mr. Alexander with all your heart, why didn't you stay married to him?"

Devon tried to remember back to the time before her divorce. They had fought. About what? What had been so important that it couldn't be resolved? When had their disagreements grown greater than their love? "I . . ." Devon struggled to answer her daughter. "I'm not sure exactly what happened, to be honest. Sometimes, things just make you grow apart."

"Was he mean to you?"

Devon chuckled at the question. "No, of course not," she replied. "He was the kindest of men. He just wanted different things out of life than I did."

"Did he get them?" Francesca asked.

Devon reflected for a moment on the question. John had put his New York business interests in trust to accept a career in what was obliquely called "government." That image did not fit with the one Devon had had of him during their marriage. He had always been a hard worker, but not a man thoroughly absorbed by his work. Play had been equally important. The little she knew of his career since the war led her to believe that he had changed. Yet she still saw his name coupled in society columns with those of beautiful women much younger than he.

Devon answered her daughter. "I don't know if he got what he wanted out of life because I don't really know him anymore."

"Do you hate him?"

"Of course not!" Devon cried, appalled at the idea. Her thoughts of John were always affectionate, her memories happy. She had pushed the unhappy ones to the back of her mind.

"Do you still love him then?"

Francesca asked the question in a normal conversational tone rather than in the hushed voice reserved for museums, and Devon quickly looked around to ensure that they were alone. When she saw that they were, she replied in a vehement whisper, "I don't even know him, Francesca, how could I love him?"

"And he stopped loving you, too?" Francesca asked with the tactlessness of childhood.

"He and I agreed to go our separate ways," Devon replied with dignity.

"But why?"

"Francesca, you're truly exasperating me. This is an unfortunate subject and I'd like to drop it, " Devon declared, turning back to the display case and feigning absorption with the photographs inside. But after a moment, Devon felt ashamed at her own peevishness. After all, the girl was naturally curious to know more about her father and John.

Francesca, however, had already forgotten the snappish words in her excitement at what she saw. "Look, Mother! It says here that you are 'the foremost woman horse trainer in the racing world and among the most highly regarded trainers of either sex. Devon Somerset-Smith was a groundbreaker of the 1930s who transformed Willowbrook Farm from a state of decline to one of the world's most highly respected racing and breeding operations.' And look! There's a picture of Willy, and one of Jeremiah!" Francesca cried. "And one day, I want to be there, too."

Devon laughed. "You will be. You'll own Willowbrook."

"I don't mean that!" Francesca said scornfully. "I mean as a jockey."

Devon wheeled on Francesca and gripped her shoulder. "No!"

Francesca stared into her mother's face, shocked by the sudden paleness of it. "Why?" was all she could utter.

Devon, seeing the expression of bewilderment on her daughter's face, released her. Making an attempt to calm herself, she replied quietly, "Being a jockey is very dangerous. Pleasure riding is one thing, but jockeys engage in cutthroat competition. They don't care who gets hurt."

"I know that!" Francesca said, in the tone typical of an adolescent who is insulted by the condescension of a parent.

"I . . . I don't want you to ride like that. I know you're a good rider, but there's a big difference. And, by the way, just because I'm involved in racing doesn't mean you have to be. You could be anything — an artist, a doctor, a model — anything!" Devon said.

"I want to be a jockey," Francesca said, raising her chin stubbornly and meeting Devon's eyes with a determined gaze of her own.

Devon decided not to argue the point further. After all, Francesca was only thirteen. Thirteen-year-olds were dreamers. She would grow up, fall in love, forget about it, Devon reassured herself. To oppose her would only cause her to cling more firmly to the dream.

CHAPTER 50

DEVON was chairwoman of the ball to benefit the racing museum, so she was up before dawn to go over her checklist of arrangements, Francesca unwillingly at her side.

"I don't see why I have to go!" Francesca complained as they made their way down the quaint street lined with gingerbread-style Victorian houses. Devon had for the last ten years rented the same cozy white house for the month of August. With its wraparound porch and candy-apple-red shutters, it looked like a childhood fantasy of a house, and Francesca loved it. What she didn't like, however, was getting up at the crack of dawn each day to accompany her mother to the vast array of events that filled her schedule. She would have preferred to stay at the little house with her grandmother.

"Mother is too old to look after you all day," Devon insisted firmly, "she gets tired."

"I'm tired," Francesca declared, rubbing her eyes, "and I hate balls!"

Devon sighed. She had been warned that thirteen was the age that would usher in adolescent rebellion. She and Francesca had always been so close that it had seemed impossible, but here she was grumbling about the fact that she was forced to accompany her mother.

"Well, you won't be going to the ball, Francesca," Devon said patiently, "so you needn't worry about that."

With typical adolescent contrariness, Francesca said, "Why can't I go to the ball?"

Devon stopped in the middle of the sidewalk and turned to face her daughter. "What are you thinking? You're thirteen years old. Of course you can't go to a ball!"

"When can I?" Francesca asked.

Devon studied her daughter, astounded that she should even ask such a question. Francesca kept her eyes on the sidewalk. "When you're sixteen."

"Elise Whitney told me that her mother lets her go now, and she's only fifteen."

"Her mother lets her go to the afternoon cotillion. That's not the same thing and you know it. You may certainly go to the afternoon cotillion if you like, but you've always said that you hated that sort of thing."

"I do hate it! I don't want to go to a stupid cotillion!"

Exasperated, Devon shrugged and turned to continue their walk. "Well, then . . ."

"But Elise —"

Devon interrupted Francesca. "My dear, there is one way to ensure that you will never get what you want, and that's by comparing my standards to others. I don't care what anyone else's mother does. I make the rules for our household."

"That's because I don't have a father!" cried Francesca. "If I had a father maybe things would be more fair. You're always telling me what I can't do! Everyone else's mother tells them to ask their father!"

If Devon hadn't been so annoyed, she would have laughed at such a simplistic view of the way families worked. She knew that many of her friends were completely uninvolved in the upbringing of their children. Most of them, at any rate, only rarely consulted their husbands on questions of child-rearing, but Devon knew there was no convincing Francesca of that.

Devon said quietly, "I can't help that you don't have a father. I wish it weren't so."

Francesca was suddenly near tears. She had hurt her mother's feelings. She hadn't intended to, but sometimes her emotions were so jumbled up that she just struck out.

"Mother, I . . . I'm sorry," she said.

"It's all right," Devon said, putting her arm around the girl and drawing her near. Lately, such gestures seemed to mortify Francesca, but now she snuggled closer to her mother, matching her footsteps to Devon's.

"Mother?"

"Yes," Devon said in a soothing voice.

"Do you ever think about getting married again? Everyone else's —" Francesca cut herself off abruptly, remembering her mother's warning.

"Not really. I haven't met anyone I care for in that way."

"What about Mr. Wilder? He's so nice." Francesca looked up at her with teary green eyes.

Devon smiled down at her daughter. "He's just a good friend, dear."

"He acts like more than that," Francesca said with assurance.

Devon thought for a moment. Mason Wilder, publisher of the *Washington Telegraph*, had been her regular escort for the past four years. She was not in love with him, but he had on two occasions proposed to Devon, emphasizing their compatibility, common interests, and mutual friends. He had not mentioned love, but rather respect and friendship. And that suited Devon. She felt affection for Mason, not passion. Sex with him was pleasant. It was good to feel desired and cherished by a man, and she knew that many women her age were not so lucky. But she had neither the wish nor the need to remarry.

"Mr. Wilder is a very nice man, but I don't want to marry him," Devon explained.

"Do you think you'll ever meet someone you want to marry?"

"I don't know. Maybe."

"I hope so," Francesca whispered.

Mason Wilder stood at the bottom of the wide wooden staircase, waiting for Devon to descend. Dressed in white tie and tails, the newspaper publisher was an imposing figure. A huge barrel-chested man, he seemed to cause objects and people around him to shrink by the sheer impact of his stature. And when Mason Wilder laughed, it seemed as though the room shook.

Despite the power of his presence, Wilder was a refined man. A scholar himself, he approached newspaper publishing as though it were an academic exercise requiring all the substantiation and accuracy of a doctoral dissertation. His newspaper was the leading journal in Washington because he insisted on thorough, painstaking research of every story. Wilder, whose newspaper was the realization of a lifelong dream, had invested part of his personal fortune in tripling the personnel of the newspaper he had acquired two decades before. As a result, his reporters each had staff available to check quotes, verify facts, and perform the other journalistic duties usually left to the harried writers. Wilder's newspaper broke the hot stories, and when it did readers did not doubt the facts — no matter how sensational.

Wilder, with his gleaming white hair and robust, tanned body, had about him the look of a man who had arrived. He was shrewd yet not crass, wise yet not pompous, a gentleman, but most certainly not weak. Except where Devon was concerned.

Wilder had been excruciatingly careful to transmit to Devon an air of fond companionship when, in fact, he was deeply in love with her. He knew that if he were to reveal his true feelings he would lose her, for Devon would consider it dishonorable to continue to see a man whose feelings she could not return. She would, in no uncertain terms, inform him that she was not in love with him and that she could not marry him. He could not bear to hear those words, still less to risk the end of their relationship. So he was careful to leave her on her own for weeks at a time lest he grow too comfortable — and thus careless with his feelings — around her.

Still, when he saw Devon appear at the top of the stairs, his heart beat faster. She was so lovely! People told him that he looked fifteen years younger than his true age of sixty-four — but Devon! Gliding down the stairs, her white chiffon dress floating behind her on the light summer breeze, she looked like a young goddess. It seemed impossible that she was fifty-one years old. Her black hair still shone like ebony in the evening light, save for the one streak of pure white that gracefully emphasized her widow's peak. Exercise had kept her slender, while the wide hats she favored had kept her rosy complexion supple. She was as beautiful as any woman he had ever known.

His spell was broken by the boisterous arrival of Francesca. "Mother says I can't go to a ball until I'm sixteen!" she cried without preamble, clattering down the stairs and throwing her arms around the big man.

He lifted her up and swung her around the room affectionately. "My God! You're getting too big for that. I can't lift you anymore!" He pretended to struggle with the girl's weight, then set her gently on her feet in front of him.

"Mother says —" Francesca began breathlessly.

"How could I have failed to hear you the first time?" Mason joked, bending to plant a chaste kiss on Devon's cheek. "And I think that's perfectly correct. My daughters did not attend balls until they were sixteen either." Mason had two daughters, both long since married. "Anyway, I thought you hated to dress up!"

"I do!" Francesca said.

"Then why are you complaining?"

"Well . . ." Francesca stared into space for a moment, trying to formulate words for her feelings. "I'd like to be grown up so I could do anything I wanted!"

Mason threw back his head and his laughter filled the room. Devon laughed along with him, but Francesca looked at them puzzled, not understanding the joke. Finally, Mason explained, "Very few adults are able to do exactly what they wish, and most spend their lives doing things they dislike."

"Don't be in such a hurry to grow up, dear." Devon reached down in a cloud of perfume and gave her daughter a kiss. "It has its drawbacks."

But Francesca, watching the glamorous, self-assured couple sweep out the door, could not believe that adulthood wasn't a big improvement over adolescence.

CHAPTER 51

CHRISTMASTIME in New York always excited Francesca. The city that usually seemed covered in soot was transformed into a fairyland of lights, bells, and evergreen wreaths. Although Francesca loved the vast, quiet beauty of the Virginia countryside in the winter, she preferred Manhattan for the holidays.

On this particular morning, just three days before Christmas, Francesca rolled out of bed and impatiently pulled on the crumpled pair of corduroy slacks that lay on the floor where she had left them the night before. Heavy woolen socks, a sweater, mittens, galoshes, and she was ready for her mission. For the first time, she would go shopping for her mother's Christmas present without an adult along to guide her. She could easily walk from their town house to Tiffany's on Fifth Avenue and Fifty-seventh Street, despite the snow. All year she had saved her allowance. And she had earned extra money after school by helping to muck out the stables at Willowbrook. Her grandmother had loaned her money until her birthday in January, so she had almost one hundred dollars to spend. She would spend it all on her mother, and make gifts for everyone else.

Quietly she descended the elegant marble staircase. She cringed as the closet that held her coat and hat squeaked, and left the door open to avoid further noise. She was almost to the front door when she heard Alice call, "Is that you, Francesca?"

Francesca hesitated, her hand on the knob. She thought about not answering — for she knew she would be forced to eat an unwanted breakfast — but did not have the nerve.

Slowly she walked through the drawing room into the sunny dining room. Bright light poured through the French doors that led onto the terrace with its formal garden and greenhouse. The long Hepplewhite table with its white linen placemats and napkins was invitingly set with cheerful strawberry-patterned breakfast china.

Alice and Laurel looked up from their newspapers as Francesca entered. The two old women shared the silent companionship of those who have known each other a lifetime. Alice, in her retirement, was no longer regarded as a servant, but rather as a family friend. She now dined with the family, and she and Laurel spent most of their days together, contentedly sewing, visiting museums, or reading.

"We may be old, but we're not deaf," Alice remarked with a half smile. "Just because your mother is out this morning, don't think that there's nobody watching you. Sit down and have some breakfast. And don't try to sneak out of the house without it again."

"I'm old enough to decide when and what I'd like to eat," Francesca said impertinently.

Laurel scowled at Francesca's tone and opened her mouth to chide her, but Alice was quicker. "Not by a long shot, kiddo. Now sit," she commanded, easily springing to her feet and taking a plate to the sideboard.

Alice's air of authority brooked no contradiction, and with a sigh, Francesca sat down. After she had gulped down the breakfast of oatmeal, biscuits, and juice placed before her, she asked sarcastically, "May I leave now?"

Alice and Laurel looked at each other and rolled their eyes. "Not until you apologize for your tone and ask politely," Laurel said, leveling a firm gaze at her granddaughter.

Francesca looked at the dainty old woman and suddenly felt like a boor. "I'm sorry. I was just in a hurry. May I please be excused?"

"Yes, you may. Where are you going?"

Francesca's face brightened at the thought. "To buy Mother a Christmas present. Remember I asked you to lend me money? I have almost a hundred dollars. I'm going to Tiffany's," she announced proudly.

The two old women looked at each other in indulgent amusement. "Well, if you need a bit more help, let me know. I think I might be able to arrange another loan," said Laurel.

"Thank you, Grandmother," said Francesca. And with that, she rose from the table, hurriedly kissed both women, and rushed from the house.

Outside, the brisk air invigorated her, and despite the slushy sidewalks, she ran for a few blocks. It felt good to be on her own. She felt extremely adult undertaking such a mission. When she arrived at Tiffany's, she passed through the doors without hesitation, but stopped short when confronted with the vast, high-ceilinged room crammed full with display cases, precious silver, clerks, shoppers, Christmas decorations, and the general noise and confusion of the holidays.

Edging toward the first counter she saw, she stopped and leaned against the display case, trying to get her bearings. Looking inside, she saw men's jewelry. She cast her eyes about the room helplessly, not knowing where to go next.

"Excuse me," she said to a clerk hurrying by, but he did not hear her.

Still holding on to the counter, she walked around the display case toward the back of the store. She saw key chains and silver pendants, earrings, and pearl necklaces, but she had no idea where to start to find a gift for Devon. Her eyes riveted to the display cases, she continued down the aisle.

Suddenly she felt a hard knock on her shin and collided — face first — into the soft wool of someone's coat. "Ouch!" she cried, almost falling backward. The man reached out to steady her, but his companion, a tall, striking redhead, scolded her.

"You silly child! Why don't you look where you're going!"

Francesca turned an angry glare on the woman and opened her mouth to retort, but the man spoke first. "It was an accident," he said soothingly, "she didn't mean any harm."

The redhead shrugged her white fox fur closer about her and remarked, "I don't see how parents can let their children run around alone like that!"

"It's none of your business," Francesca cried, "but I'm here to buy a surprise for my mother, so she couldn't come with me!"

"How dare you speak to me in that tone!" the young woman breathed.

"Calm down," the man commanded both, with a gesture of his hand. In his other hand, Francesca saw what had hurt her shin — an ebony walking stick with a brass eagle head as the handle.

The man turned back to Francesca, and for the first time, she noticed the deep, deep blue of his eyes. There was something vaguely familiar about him, but she could not place him. Yet she was certain she would have remembered meeting him. "You're looking for a Christmas gift for your mother?" he asked gently.

"Yes, thank you, I am," Francesca said in her most adult manner.

The man suppressed a smile at the child's pompous tone. It did not fit with her helter-skelter hair and pointed wool cap.

"Tiffany's is a big place. Do you need any help?"

"Oh, please!" the redhead began sarcastically.

The man turned to her in exasperation, the expression on his face effectively silencing her.

Francesca looked at the beautiful young woman, then back at the man. She dimpled and said, "I really do need some help."

"Well, come along then," said the man. To the redhead, he turned and said, "Why don't you take the car back to your place. I'll catch a cab." And with a peck on her cheek, he left her standing in the middle of the aisle, her coral-painted mouth open in astonishment.

"Won't she be mad?" asked Francesca, giggling.

"Briefly," replied the man, with a dismissive gesture of his walking stick.

"You're nice to help me. I hadn't expected this place to be so big."

"Well, then, let's get on with it. What's your budget?" he asked with a smile.

"My budget?"

"How much do you want to spend?"

"I have a hundred dollars," Francesca said proudly, "but my grandmother said she could lend me more if I see something I really love."

"Why don't we start over here. Pens and stationery. For a hundred dollars, you can probably buy something very beautiful."

"My mother would like a pen. She's a businesswoman," Francesca said proudly.

"Well, then, let's have a look."

Francesca looked behind the counter where busy clerks hurried back and forth. They all seemed to be waiting on customers. Francesca was afraid she would be humiliated in front of the man if another clerk ignored her, but as soon as he placed his gloved hand on the display case, a smiling clerk seemed to materialize out of nowhere.

"Sir, may I be of assistance?" the clerk asked with an obsequious little half bow.

"This young lady would like to buy a Christmas present for her mother," he said, indicating Francesca with a hand on her shoulder.

"Ah," said the clerk, turning to Francesca deferentially, "and what did we have in mind?"

"A pen?" she said uncertainly, looking up at her new friend.

The clerk reached into the display case and pulled out a gray velvet box filled with pens neatly aligned on a satin-covered rack within. "We have some sterling silver pens here. They're very fine."

Francesca immediately saw the one she wanted. It was silver like the others, but had an inlay of mother-of-pearl that added a delicate femininity to it. "This one looks like something Mother would like. How much is it?"

"That is eighty-five dollars, young lady."

Francesca clapped her hands together with delight. "I'll take it!" she cried.

"Very good, miss. I'll have it wrapped for you."

Once payment had been made, the clerk handed Francesca her change, ceremoniously counting out the money. "Thank you, miss. And sir, I'm sure your wife will be very pleased with her gift."

Francesca opened her mouth to protest, but a squeeze on the shoulder silenced her. And for a moment Francesca wished so much that the clerk's words were true. She wished this kind stranger were her father and would always be there to help her.

"Well, can I drop you somewhere?" asked the man.

But Francesca didn't want to lose her new friend so quickly. Seeing her downcast expression, the man looked at his wristwatch. "It's a bit early for lunch. But . . . if we walk very slowly and look in all the shop windows, I suppose we could delay our arrival at the Plaza until eleven-thirty. That is, if you would be so kind as to join me for lunch."

"Oh . . . yes . . . I'd love that!" Francesca cried. Then, suddenly, she stopped short. "But . . . but I'm not supposed to go anywhere with strangers. My mother told me never to —"

"And she's absolutely right," the man interrupted. "Well, then, I shall be getting along."

"Oh, no, please!" said Francesca. After all, she knew she could trust this man.. He wasn't the kind of person her mother had warned her about. He was obviously someone very much like her mother's friends. He was expensively clad in a navy blue cashmere coat, and Francesca could tell he was a man of substance. Besides, she would be fourteen in just a few days. She wasn't a child any longer!

As they left Tiffany's, Francesca noticed that the man limped slightly. She wanted to ask him what had happened, but her mother had told her that such questions were impolite.

After a lingering walk around the block, the two proceeded up the stairs and through the huge brass doors of the Plaza Hotel. The man, knowing what would appeal to the youngster at his side, chose to lunch at the airy Palm Court rather than the more masculine Oak Room at the rear of the hotel.

After they sat down, Francesca removed her hat and woolen coat with its high collar. Now the man studied her carefully.

"Have I done something wrong?" the girl asked, puzzled by his intense scrutiny.

"No . . . no," said the man, shaking his head. "You remind me of someone. Just a bit." His voice was wistful.

"Who?"

"Oh," said the man, staring beyond Francesca into the distance, "someone I knew twenty years ago. Someone who meant a great deal to me."

"When you were young?"

The man threw back his head and laughed, revealing straight white teeth. "Yes," he said good-naturedly, "when I was young."

Francesca blushed, without quite knowing why.

"What would you like?" the man asked, studying the menu.

"Oh, the tea sandwiches and watercress salad!" Francesca said, barely looking at her own menu. "That's what I always have. I love the way they cut the crusts off the little sandwiches," she said in a confidential tone. "And, if you don't mind, I'd like strawberry shortcake for dessert."

Again, the man studied the girl carefully. Suddenly he said, "I don't believe I've asked your name. Would you tell it to me?"

"Frankie," she said crisply.

"Odd name for a girl."

"It's not my real name," she confessed, "but it's what I like to be called."

"Well, Frankie, my name is John. John Alexander."

Frankie's mouth opened in shock. "You're the one!" she breathed, staring at her companion with new fascination.

The man tilted his head and lifted one eyebrow in inquiry, waiting for her to go on.

"You were married to my mother!"

John was stunned. He searched the girl's face, a face that seemed strangely familiar to him, though he could not isolate the traits that reminded him of Devon. Yet she did remind him of — no, wait. It was not so much a resemblance to Devon as to Morgan. Yes, that was it. Morgan. A fist clutched his heart and squeezed it until he could not breathe. His only child. And now, this child. Devon's child. With the same dark hair, the same laughing features. For a moment, Morgan was not dead at all. It had all been a cruel hoax. How often he had awakened in the dark of night thinking that Morgan's death had been a nightmare. Only to be bitterly disappointed. To realize that the nightmare was reality.

And now, this . . . this was like a wonderful dream. He blinked his eyes rapidly to suppress the mistiness that threatened. Morgan, still young enough to be a child — his child — was sitting before him. His eyes drank in her features. Her beloved features. But . . . they were not the same. His stomach plummeted in disappointment. No, it was not Morgan. A child like Morgan. A child like his and Devon's. Only she wasn't his. That was the heartbreak of it.

"You're Francesca, then," he murmured. Of course, he had read the columns announcing her birth. "I should have recognized you immediately."

"I look like Mother?" she asked, delighted.

"Well . . ." He saw the hope in her eyes and did not want to disappoint her. "There is a definite family resemblance." John took a silent inventory of her features. Yes, he was beginning to see it. Morgan, too, had been different from Devon, and yet had resembled her in much the same way this child did. "Your eyes are green, not aqua, your skin is darker, but the shape of your face, your bones, your mouth — all that is the same. Yes, there is definitely a strong resemblance."

"But . . . but Mother's beautiful, and I'm not," Francesca said, hoping for contradiction.

Her words tugged at his emotions. She was so vulnerable. He wanted to protect her, encourage her. Give her all the confidence he would have done a daughter of his own. "Give it a year. You will be," John replied honestly. Then, seeing the disappointment on her face, he added, "It's already there, your beauty, you just need to realize it yourself. Once you have confidence, you will be beautiful." And it was true, he thought.

"Mother's the most beautiful woman I know," said Francesca.

"I haven't seen her in so many years," John said, thinking aloud, "I wonder if she's changed a great deal. Of course, I've seen photographs, but that's not the same."

"Oh, Mother's much more beautiful than her photographs," said Francesca breezily. "Everyone says so."

"Everyone?"

"Well . . ." said Francesca, pausing discreetly while a waiter placed their food in front of them. When he had left, she continued, "Mr. Wilder says so."

"Mr. Wilder?" asked John, taking a bite of his London broil in mushroom sauce.

"Mother's gentleman friend, as she calls him." Francesca picked up a tea sandwich, saw that it contained egg salad, and replaced it, choosing one filled with smoked salmon instead.

Suddenly Francesca saw an opportunity to learn things her mother would not tell her. "Why did you and Mother get a divorce?" she asked abruptly.

John drew in his breath, surprised by the question and the pain it caused. But, of course, this girl couldn't know that. She meant no harm. And he could tell that she needed to know these things. He shook his head. "There's no easy answer to that. It was a lot of things."

"Didn't you love her anymore?"

"Oh, yes . . ." he said, looking down at the table, "we just wanted different things out of life."

Francesca nodded knowingly. "That's what she told me, too."

John raised his eyes to Francesca's and searched her face. "Is she happy?" John asked softly.

Now it was Francesca's turn to look puzzled. Happy? It never occurred to her that adults could suffer from a general state of unhappiness. None of them seemed to go through the roller coaster of emotions she felt every day. "I . . . think Mother's happy. I've never seen her cry, except when Grandfather died."

Focusing on John now, Francesca asked, "Did you get married again?"

"Yes, but I'm not married now."

"Do you have children?"

John paused. He felt his throat constrict with pain. With difficulty, he replied, "I had a child, but she died."

Francesca gave him a sad little nod of sympathy. "Morgan, you mean. We put flowers on her grave every week when we're at Willowbrook. You've sent flowers, too, haven't you?"

"Oh, yes," John said, his voice melancholy, "I've sent flowers."

"I didn't know her, but I wish she hadn't died." Suddenly a thought occurred to Francesca. "If she had lived, you might have been my father. A lot of my friends' parents stay married just because they have children. You hear them talk about it sometimes."

"But then you wouldn't be you." John couldn't help but smile at the eager young face before him. He signaled for the waiter to clear their table. After they had ordered Francesca's strawberry shortcake and John's coffee, he asked, "Do you miss having a father very much?"

"Mother's wonderful," Francesca said loyally. "And there's Mason and Willy and Jeremiah."

"But?" John probed.

"But, yes . . . yes . . . I wish I had a father."

"Well, maybe we can be friends," John said warmly.

"That would be great!" Francesca said enthusiastically. Then her face fell. "But don't you live abroad?"

"Not anymore. I'm in New York to stay," John said.

The waiter brought a six-inch-high confection of white frosting and red strawberries and placed it in front of Francesca with a flourish. Then he poured John's coffee from a silver pot, and placed the pot beside John.

"But . . ." John hesitated. "Do you think your mother would mind our being friends?" he asked.

"Oh no," said Francesca casually. "I asked her if she hated you and she said no."

CHAPTER 52

DEVON'S sound sleep was pierced by the insistent ringing of the telephone on the bedside table. She groggily lowered the thick eider-down comforter and reached for the instrument, not alert enough yet to feel a sense of apprehension.

"Hello?" She yawned.

"Devon, I'm sorry to wake you, but we've had an emergency here." The familiar drawl of Jeremiah's voice on the other end brought Devon instantly to her senses.

"What's wrong?" Devon asked, alarmed. She pushed herself into a sitting position and turned on the bedside light, shivering in the cold night air.

"It's Willy . . ." Jeremiah hesitated.

"Oh, God, no!" Devon cried, fear gripping her.

"Devon, I don't know how to tell you . . ." Jeremiah's desperate sense of loss was evident in his tone. "I . . . I'm afraid he's had a heart attack."

"Please, Jeremiah, don't say he's dead," Devon pleaded.

"I'm sorry, Devon. He's gone," Jeremiah said gently.

"I just can't believe it. He was fine last time I saw him," Devon said incredulously.

"Not according to the doctor, Devon. He told me tonight that he'd warned Willy to cut back on work."

"But Willy never said a word! He worked the same amount as always."

"Yeah," Jeremiah acknowledged softly, "that was the problem. His work was his whole life."

"Willowbrook was, yes." Devon's voice broke as she said the words.

"And you, too, Devon. He loved you very much, you know."

Devon smiled through her tears, the smile turning into a grimace of sorrow. "I never thought that he would get used to me, but one day we were just the best of friends. I don't exactly know when it happened."

"He left a letter for you," Jeremiah said. "I don't know if it's his will or what."

Devon looked up as the door to her bedroom opened. A worried-looking Francesca was standing there, her striped pajamas rumpled from sleep.

Instinctively lowering her voice and wiping away her tears, Devon said to Jeremiah, "I'll be down in a few hours. I'll leave right away." She replaced the telephone receiver, using the few seconds to mull over how to tell her daughter the news. Francesca regarded Willy as family. She would be heartbroken.

"Come here, Francesca," Devon said, gesturing to the empty place on the bed beside her. She pulled back the crisp sheets and waited for her daughter to slide between them. "Snuggle up next to me, Frankie, I have something to tell you."

Devon's use of the nickname startled Francesca, for she knew her mother disliked it. Devon almost never used this form of address, even though Francesca tried to insist on it. But instead of being gratified by its use now, Francesca felt only a sense of disquiet. She drew close to her mother's warmth, curling up against her. Devon put her arm around her daughter so that Francesca's head rested on her shoulder.

"You're getting so big," Devon murmured.

"What's wrong, Mom?" Francesca asked.

"Darling, I don't know how to tell you this. It's about Willy."

Francesca abruptly squirmed out of her mother's arms and sat up so that she was directly facing her. "What's wrong?" she repeated, panic evident in her voice.

Devon deliberately made her voice calm and soothing. "He's been ill."

"No, he hasn't!" Francesca cried.

Devon took her daughter's hands and enfolded them in her own. "None of us knew about it. He didn't tell anyone. And now, I have to go back to Willowbrook. Tonight."

"I want to go too! I want to see him!"

"Frankie, Willy had a heart attack tonight."

"Oh no! Is he going to die?" the girl sobbed.

"Oh, Frankie." Tears streamed from Devon's eyes as she reached forward and wrapped her daughter in her arms. She needed the comfort of a warm body as much as Francesca did.

"Mommy," said Francesca, reverting to the childhood appellation in her distress, "is he dead?"

Devon choked on her words, but she nodded her head against Francesca's, and the girl had her answer.

Francesca was stunned. She remembered the heartbreak of her grandfather's death. Now her heart was breaking all over again. Willy, whom she had seen almost every day of her life — more than her grandfather even — would no longer occupy a place in her world. It seemed cruel that she had not even had a chance to say good-bye. A giant sob escaped Francesca once more. "I want to see him one more time. I want to say good-bye."

Devon studied her daughter's face and saw the determination there. Yes, Devon thought, she's old enough for this. Devon and Laurel had thought her too young to attend her grandfather's funeral. But for Willy, she should be there, Devon decided. She needs to be there.

"Very well," Devon said, "I'll ring for Ettie to help you pack. Don't try to take a lot. We need to go."

Francesca and Devon hugged one more time, then Francesca slid out of the bed and walked out of the room, her back erect. Devon was surprised to feel comforted by the fact that Francesca would accompany her to Willowbrook. Devon had been her own source of strength for so long that she thought she had grown accustomed to it. But now, she found she welcomed the support of her daughter. It was a new, somewhat bittersweet sensation.

*   *   *

Dear Devon,

I guess I don't have much to get rid of. Give my clothes to whoever wants them. If you don't mind, I'd like to be buried at Willowbrook. Somewhere that looks over the stables. I know I'm not family, so if that's not okay, cremate me and throw my ashes on Willowbrook's track. Don't matter too much which you choose, but I think I'd rather be buried. You'll find $25,000 under my mattress. Buy me a tombstone and give the rest to a good cause.

You've been a good boss, and that's something I never thought I'd say. You've also been a good friend. Thanks.

Willy O'Neill

As his letter requested, Willy was buried at Willowbrook. There was a family graveyard there, but none of Devon's family was buried in it, only members of the Hartwick family, Willowbrook's former owners. The Richmond family grave site was at Evergreen. So Devon created a small graveyard just for Willy. It was under a stand of oak trees not far from the big white barn. It was a beautiful site on a hill overlooking all of Willowbrook's acreage. She was gratified that he had wanted to be buried at Willowbrook.

But now, as she stood gazing over the rolling meadows, brown from the winter cold, she felt only a sense of loneliness. She looked at the dozens of people around her, their heads bowed as they listened to the priest recite prayers for the dead. Some of the faces she saw were family — Grace and Philip had driven from Washington, Laurel had accompanied her from New York. Some of the faces belonged to friends. But not one among them had been as constant a companion as Willy. Devon and he had achieved a deep friendship that required no words. More important, there had been tremendous mutual respect between them, hard won on both sides. She felt almost as though a part of her was gone.

Devon looked at Francesca's bowed head. The youngster was trying hard to stifle her sobs, but her body shook with the effort. Devon put a comforting arm on her shoulder, then shivered herself as a cold wind rustled through the bare branches overhead. She felt Mason Wilder's strong arm draw her closer. It was a comfort to have him there, Devon thought, leaning against him gratefully.

As the priest closed his prayer book, Devon walked toward the grave and picked up a small shovel. She dug into the heavy red clay that stood in a pile beside the gaping hole and threw the contents of the shovel on top of the long, shiny box below. The dull thud of the dense clay hitting the coffin sent another shiver through Devon. She laid the shovel down and turned toward the crowd, wanting only to return to the warmth of her home.

Then, in the back of the crowd, like a ghost from the past, she saw a familiar face.

CHAPTER 53

"WORLD-FAMOUS Horse Trainer Dead at 79," said the headline of the obituary in the *New York Times.* The headline drew John Alexander's attention, for he was acquainted with most of the country's top trainers. Putting down his piece of toast, he drew the newspaper toward him with both hands.

"Oh my God!" he exclaimed, throwing his white linen napkin down on the glossy mahogany of the table and rising to his feet.

"What?" asked the redhead, surprised by the sudden movement. She put down the romance novel she was reading and stared at her lover with a look of inquiry.

"Someone who once worked for me just died. A good man," John replied absentmindedly.

"Oh. Just someone who worked for you," said the redhead, picking up her book in one hand and taking a sip of coffee with the other.

John looked with exasperation at the beautiful creature in the white satin peignoir. There was no use explaining to her the impact on him of Willy's death. Ignoring her, John rang for his valet.

"Prepare an overnight bag for me with clothes appropriate for a funeral," he commanded when the man arrived.

"You're going to that man's funeral?" the redhead asked in shock, rising as well.

"Yes," John said brusquely, "I'm going to my room to change."

"I'll come with you!" the redhead announced, already envisioning how fetching she would look in a well-cut black dress and a coquettish black hat.

"No, you won't," John replied firmly. He turned and exited the French doors leading to the foyer of the Park Avenue penthouse. He crossed the black marble floor and proceeded down a long hallway leading to the master suite, the redhead trailing him like a puppy.

"Why can't I come?" Her pretty pout was wasted on the back of John's head.

John did not reply. He entered the bedroom — clearly a man's room, with its hunter green walls and rich leather chairs — and began to dress. He hastily chose a tweed jacket and gray flannel slacks for the drive down. In an instant he was dressed and ready to go.

John gave the redhead a perfunctory kiss on the cheek and headed for the door. "I'll see you when I get back," he tossed over his shoulder.

"When will that be?" she asked, hands on hips in annoyance.

John paused. "I don't know. Day after tomorrow probably."

"I'll wait here," the redhead said, sinking onto the huge four-poster bed behind her.

"No, don't," John said sharply.

"Why not?" she demanded.

For the second time that morning John ignored her. He hurried from the room, leaving her on the bed.

"Williams," John addressed his butler as the man helped him on with his coat, "I should return in three days. Please make certain that the lady is gone by then."

"Yes sir," said the butler impassively.

He had never expected that she would still be so beautiful. Francesca had told him that she was, but Francesca had not known her in her youth. Photographs he had seen of Devon had led him to believe she would still be very attractive. They showed that she had retained her slender figure, that her fine eyes were still full of vitality. But he was unprepared for the magnetic attraction that hit him when he spotted her leaning on the arm of the huge white-haired man. Even in the black coat and veil, even with her features fixed in an expression of grief, John Alexander found Devon extraordinarily alluring.

She came toward him, mouth slightly open in surprise, aqua eyes wide, brushing past many other bystanders.

"John." Her smooth, cultured voice washed over him, deeper now than in her youth. "How kind of you to come."

An electric shock ran through him as he touched her black-gloved hand, enfolding it in his two hands. He was suddenly taken back to the day he had first seen her, in the Magraths' ballroom. It seemed as though the years were fading away, like a dream, and he was meeting her for the first time. He remembered his fascination. She was still fascinating. More fascinating now, with that regal bearing that had grown more pronounced with maturity. He wondered whether she was feeling the same emotions.

Then he noticed the manner in which the white-haired man hurried up beside her and took her elbow. His manner was concerned, solicitous, and very proprietary. John released Devon's hand. He saw that the man was studying him, waiting for him to speak.

"I thought so highly of Willy," said John. "I'm so sorry."

Devon bowed her head for a moment, then raised tear-filled eyes to his. "I feel lost without him. You know, we became the best of friends."

John's eyes stared into the distance, remembering. "You were at each other's throats in the beginning. I never thought you'd work out your differences."

Devon's voice drew John's eyes back to hers. "Our differences seem so insignificant now, after all our years together. I suppose circumstances forced us to stay together in the beginning. Afterward, I'm sure neither one of us could have ever imagined a parting of the ways." Devon looked down as her emotions threatened to overwhelm her.

Seeing her distress, Devon's white-haired companion began gently to urge her forward. The brick path leading from the grave site was only wide enough for two people, so John dropped behind. The party moved toward the gravel-covered drive, where black limousines were waiting to take them the short distance to the main house.

Devon turned to look over her shoulder and saw Francesca walking with John, his arm draped comfortably over her shoulder. Puzzled, Devon frowned at the apparent familiarity. Did they know each other? she wondered.

"Francesca," she called softly, stopping to wait for her daughter, "come along, dear."

Francesca obediently came to her mother's side, but then she turned to John and asked, "Can you stay awhile? Everyone else will be coming back to the house."

John looked questioningly at Devon, who, though confused by the apparent relationship, would never publicly countermand an invitation issued by a member of her family. "You are certainly welcome," Devon said, a little stiffly. She found John's presence disturbing and was annoyed at herself for feeling that way.

"Thank you. I'd like that," he replied with a kind smile at Francesca.

Devon looked from one to the other, then turned and got into the long black car in which Laurel was already seated. Francesca and Mason followed her in.

Devon held her tongue during the ride to the house, not wishing to question her daughter about John in front of Mason. Nor did she have a chance to speak to her alone during the afternoon, since the room was crowded with those who had attended the funeral. But despite the crowd, Devon was always aware of John's presence. Her eyes were drawn unwillingly to him. She found herself furtively studying him. He had aged well. Though he was almost sixty years old, his shoulders were still broad, and he did not have the middle-aged paunch that characterized most men of her acquaintance. His appearance was distinguished — yet still disturbingly animal, as it had been years before.

Later that evening, when finally the house was empty except for the family and Mason, Devon knocked softly on her daughter's door.

She found Francesca reading in bed; a book about horses, of course. The pure white walls of the girl's room were covered in drawings and photographs of horses, and her cherry bookshelf lined with horse figurines. Devon suddenly remembered that her daughter's birthday was only days away. The funeral arrangements had made her lose track of time.

"How are you feeling this evening, sweetheart?" Devon asked, perching on the edge of the blue-and-white-gingham-covered bed. The material had been Francesca's choice. She had wanted something that reminded her of the dungarees she always wore when she went horseback riding.

"Okay, I guess," Francesca said, putting her book facedown on her lap.

Devon took the child's hand in hers. "I think we're both going to miss Willy a lot."

Francesca nodded and squeezed her mother's hand.

"Francesca, I'd like to ask you about something that happened today."

Francesca looked questioningly at her mother.

"Have you met Mr. Alexander before?"

Francesca studied Devon with a slight feeling of trepidation. She wasn't certain what her answer should be. She had intended to tell her mother after Christmas of her meeting with John, since to tell her before that would have revealed that she had purchased Devon's gift at Tiffany's. But Christmas had come and gone almost unnoticed in the days between Willy's death and his funeral. In the family's haste to leave New York, all the gifts had been left there. And it would have been unseemly, they decided, to decorate Willowbrook for Christmas and celebrate the holiday as usual.

"The truth," Devon insisted firmly.

"I was going to tell you . . ." Francesca's voice faltered as she searched for an explanation.

"Where and when did you meet him?"

"At a store when I was shopping for your Christmas gift," Francesca blurted out. "He was nice to me even though the lady with him called me a silly child. He made her go home and then we had lunch at the Palm Court."

Devon raised her eyebrows, clearly signaling an infraction to Francesca.

"Oh, Mother!" Francesca sighed in exasperation. "I knew he wasn't a kidnapper or something else awful. He seemed so . . . so . . . well, *kind*, if you know what I mean. But at the same time, very respectable. No different from anyone else we know."

Devon rose from the soft mattress and began to pace quietly. It was obvious to Francesca that Devon was preparing to lecture her. Francesca burrowed into her pillows and waited for the admonition, philosophically resigned.

As predicted, Devon began, "Under no circumstances — *no circumstances* — are you ever to go anywhere with a stranger," she said sternly. She turned sharply to face her daughter, glaring down at her from her standing position. "You are only thirteen years old —"

"Fourteen," Francesca interjected, "this week."

"Fourteen then. You are too young to make judgments about whether people mean to harm you. Believe me, some people who appear to be very nice can do tremendous harm to young girls like you."

"I was just —"

"Don't interrupt!" Devon commanded. "I have very few rules in this household, but those that I clearly state *will* be observed."

"Are you going to punish me?"

"Yes. You are not to go horseback riding for one week."

"But Mom!" moaned Francesca. "That's the best part of being here."

"I am perfectly aware of that," Devon said, hands on her hips, "that is why I have chosen it as your punishment. And don't assume that air of tragedy. You deserve this for doing something you knew was strictly prohibited."

"All right," Francesca said, eyes downcast. She knew the punishment was fair, albeit unwelcome.

That matter resolved, Devon let go of her anger and resumed her seat on the edge of Francesca's bed. "On to more pleasant subjects," she announced calmly. "For your birthday, I would suggest just a quiet family dinner this year, in view of Willy —"

Francesca interrupted, "Oh, that's all I want. I couldn't have a party so soon —" She cut herself off in midsentence, not wanting to utter the reference to Willy's death. "But, Mother, there is one thing I would like for my birthday."

Devon gave her daughter a half smile, expecting a request pertaining to horses. "What is it, darling?"

"Could . . . could Mr. Alexander be invited to my birthday dinner?"

The question caught Devon unawares and she flushed hotly, without quite knowing why. Confused, she looked around the room, avoiding Francesca's eyes. "Well, I . . . I . . ." Devon hesitated, trying to think of a reason to avoid such a simple request. "He's not really a close friend, and he's certainly not a member of the family," Devon offered.

"I know." Francesca sighed.

Her daughter's tone of wistfulness captured Devon's full attention. "Why? Why should someone you only met twice make such an impression on you."

Francesca looked down at her hands picking at the sheet. "I don't know exactly."

Devon considered a moment. The child had just lost one of the most important male figures in her life. There really was no one else for her, other than Mason, who was as constant or long-standing a presence as Willy. Why should she deny such a simple request of her daughter's? And on her birthday.

"You know, Francesca," Devon said gently, "you musn't invest too much emotion in your friendship with Mr. Alexander."

"Why not?" Francesca asked.

Why not, indeed? Devon asked herself. What could she tell the child? That the man did not wish to be burdened by a family, liked his freedom too much to be encumbered by a relationship with a young girl? His act of friendship toward Francesca would make Devon look as though she were dreaming up feeble excuses. There was no way to impart to a fourteen-year-old the caution she had learned as the thirty-five-year-old wife of John Alexander.

Reluctantly, she decided to grant Francesca's request. "All right, Francesca, you may invite Mr. Alexander. But please make clear to him that the invitation comes from you, not me."

"Oh!" Francesca cried happily, clapping her hands. "I'll do whatever you want. Thank you!"

"And, one more thing . . ."

"Yes, Mom?"

Looking at Francesca's happy face, she decided to temper her words of warning. She did not want to spoil her child's joy, but at the same time, she wanted to protect her from the hurt she herself had once known. "Well, just remember that Mr. Alexander is a very busy man. And if he should ever disappoint you . . . I mean, by not being available, or not paying you the attention you'd like, try to understand . . . it doesn't mean he doesn't like you."

CHAPTER 54

"THAT'S the last straw, Pritchard," Jeremiah said in a quietly menacing tone. "I've given you every chance to shuck that attitude of yours."

"Well ain't you high and mighty," the little man said, his nose almost touching Jeremiah's, his veins standing out above his open collar. "Willy's only been dead six months and you already think you know everythin' so's you can boss me."

Jeremiah, usually slow to lose his temper, was incensed. Still, he did not raise his voice, though he spoke tensely, leaning forward to add emphasis to his words. "I've always been your boss, Pritchard. Got nothing to do with Willy. And it's because of me that you've stayed around this long. Now I'm deciding that it's time for you to be sent packing. I want you gone by noon."

The two had disagreed over a seemingly minor matter: whether it was time to break in one of Willowbrook's prize colts. But it had been only the latest of a long series of disagreements. And Jeremiah had finally decided that Willy had been right. Jimmy Pritchard would not listen to reason. He was as wild and unrestrained as the colt under discussion.

Jimmy's next words proved that Jeremiah's impression was correct. "You got no power over me. Miss Devon'll decide if I'm fired or not!" shouted the young man.

"You're a fool, boy, Miss —"

Jeremiah's words were interrupted by a resounding blow to his jaw. For a moment, he stood on his feet, stunned and seeing stars. Then he fell backward into the mud of the barnyard. From a dreamlike distance he heard Jimmy Pritchard shout down at him, "Ain't no nigger gonna call me boy!" That was when Jeremiah felt a gut-wrenching blow in his stomach. Then he lost consciousness.

The breakfast of the ladies of Willowbrook was interrupted by a loud banging on the kitchen door. The vibrations could be heard through the hallway and into the dining room where Laurel, Alice, Francesca, and Devon sat enjoying the morning sun.

"I gotta see Miss Devon!" she heard a man shout to one of the kitchen servants.

Alarmed, Devon hastily arose, throwing down her napkin on the table. "What in the world?" she said to no one in particular as the ladies all looked at one another questioningly.

She heard muffled responses, then the same voice shouted, "No! Right now! Get outta my way!"

Before she could hurry into the kitchen, she heard footsteps stomping down the short hall that acted as a thoroughfare to the dining room. Then Jimmy Pritchard burst through the door.

"I gotta talk to you," the jockey said, glaring at Devon.

Devon stared icily at the young man. Like Willy, she had recognized him as a troublemaker, and she had often been tempted to fire him. Yet Jeremiah was his direct boss, and Devon was reluctant to interfere. She knew that Jeremiah was having more trouble since Willy's death maintaining his authority as the undisputed boss over some of the white employees. Even some of the blacks seemed to believe he had no place in the number-one position. Devon knew that if she wanted Jeremiah to succeed in his new job, she had to step back and let him take over the operation until he had established himself.

But now Pritchard was intruding on her territory and she intended to put him in his place in no uncertain terms.

On this day, Devon was wearing a crisp navy linen suit in preparation for a visit to her banker in Middleburg. She had decided to borrow money to purchase an adjacent brood farm that had recently been put up for sale. If she was able to swing the deal, she would own the largest Thoroughbred stable in Virginia. The brood farm was highly prestigious, and she was not even certain that the sellers were serious, but her mouth watered at the thought of consolidating the operation with hers. Of course, she could have bought the farm outright with her own money, but she preferred to use the bank's money for her new enterprise — a practice she had adopted for all new ventures soon after taking over Willowbrook.

Pritchard had only rarely seen Devon in such a businesslike outfit. At the stables, she usually wore blue jeans. So the sight of her, authoritative, cool, so obviously above him, made him hesitate for a moment.

Devon allowed a few seconds of tense silence to elapse, then she spoke. "You are intruding, Mr. Pritchard. Why?"

He looked uncomfortably at the two old women and Francesca sitting at the table behind Devon. Then he seemed to gather himself. "I got business with you," he blurted out defiantly.

"I find that hard to believe; however, if you would like to make an appointment —"

"Now!" he interrupted, regaining his natural arrogance.

"I beg your pardon!" Devon said, eyes flashing dangerously. She rang the bell to summon the butler. He appeared almost before her motion was completed. "Greene, would you show Mr. Pritchard out, please."

"I got business with you!" the jockey cried as the huge black man encircled his comparatively small arm with one strong hand.

Devon turned her back on the jockey and addressed the ladies assembled around the dining table. "I apologize to all of you for this scene."

Furious at his summary dismissal, Pritchard cried, "Jeremiah Washington is layin' flat on his back in the barnyard and I'm here to tell you why!"

Devon spun to face the jockey. She studied him for a moment as she absorbed his words. As comprehension dawned, she felt hot anger bubble up in her. "Get out of my way, Mr. Pritchard! If Mr. Washington is in the condition you describe, I'll find out why from him!"

As she started to brush by him, Pritchard caught her arm. "I have a right to be heard, too."

Outraged, Devon jerked her arm from his grasp. "How dare you!" she spat. She turned her eyes to the butler. "Greene, escort this man into my study, please, and see that he stays there." Without another glance at Pritchard, she turned and marched out of the room.

Unmindful of her white-and-navy spectator shoes, Devon tramped through the mud of the barnyard to the office she shared with Jeremiah, as she had once shared it with Willy. There she found most of her staff gathered around the ancient leather couch. Jeremiah was lying there, an ice pack on his jaw.

"What in the world!" Devon exclaimed.

Seeing her, Jeremiah tried to come to his feet, but succeeded only in rising onto one elbow. "I fired Pritchard," the trainer offered, as though that explained everything.

And, indeed, it did explain a great deal. But Devon still had a few questions. "You got into a fistfight with him?" she asked, astounded that this most mild-mannered of men would have done such a thing.

"I wish I had," he replied sheepishly. "No, he hit me without any warning. Next thing I knew, I was flat on my back."

"Kicked 'im when he was down, too," one of the grooms added.

Devon's fury against Pritchard intensified when she heard this. She picked up the telephone on her desk and dialed the main house. When the butler answered she instructed, "Greene, tell that . . . that . . . person" — she expelled the word as though it were a profanity — "in my study to leave at once. Leave not just my study, but this property. I want him out of here within the hour. He'll get two weeks' severance and a half-decent reference provided he meets that deadline and goes quietly. He can phone us with a forwarding address. Tell him those are my orders. I don't ever want to see him again. Is that understood?" Devon nodded as she received confirmation on the other end of the telephone line. Then she replaced the receiver with a sharp click.

"Jeremiah, do you need a doctor?"

"No, thanks, I'm fine," he said, sitting up and waving away the men who surrounded him, "all you boys get away from me and let me breathe."

"Would you gentlemen excuse us, please. I think Jeremiah's fine now," Devon said, gently dismissing the staff. One by one, the men filed out of the office until the screen door closed with a squeaky smack.

Nonetheless, Devon spoke in a hushed tone. "It was more than you firing him, wasn't it?" she asked Jeremiah, pulling out her scratched wooden chair and sitting opposite him.

"Yeah. Same old thing. You know. He always had a chip on his shoulder about taking orders from a colored man. Like today . . ." Jeremiah explained the cause of their argument, concluding, "I was stupid, thinking I could change his attitude. He had an unbeatable way with some of the horses, though. I didn't want to give up on him too easy."

"He can be replaced," Devon said brusquely. "Never keep on a troublemaker, Jeremiah. They're just never worth it. You're a good trainer. The farm is doing fine with you at the helm. Your only weakness is that you're too nice. You're willing to give men like Pritchard too many chances. It's a waste of time."

"Ah, Devon," sighed Jeremiah, shaking his head. "I wish I could be as good as Willy. He commanded respect without even trying."

"It's not every man who can look beyond your color, Jeremiah. Most will, once they get used to the idea. Those that can't, well, they're just no use to us."

"Devon, how come you never even thought about getting a white man for this job after Willy died?"

"Don't be ridiculous! You know our stock inside out. You know my training methods, and Willy's. You grew up here and you've been my friend for almost thirty years. Most of all, you're qualified for this job. What kind of person would I be if I put someone else over you?"

"Maybe a smarter one, Devon. No one has a Negro trainer. Everyone thinks you're crazy to have me. I'm afraid this is just going to cause you a world of trouble." Jeremiah tried to readjust his ice pack, spilling water down the front of his shirt.

Devon laughed. "Here, give that to me. I'll refill it." She bent over him, putting her hand to his cheek to take the pack from him.

"Well, ain't this cozy!" a sarcastic voice came through the screen door. Devon wheeled to find the leering face of Jimmy Pritchard staring at her through the rusty wire. "I guess what they say about black boys is true. Maybe that's why you keep 'im."

Hearing the younger man's voice, Jeremiah stood to his feet and, in two long strides, reached the door. He slammed it abruptly out so that Jimmy, caught unawares, was hit in the face.

Jeremiah was no taller than Jimmy, but he was bulkier because his retirement from racing had allowed him to put on weight. It was all muscle, though. And this he demonstrated by grabbing Jimmy's collar and lifting him off his feet until they reached the wall of the stall opposite the office. Jeremiah slammed Jimmy into it, knocking the wind out of the younger man so that he slumped over. Jeremiah lifted his knee. *Bang!* Right into Jimmy's chin, knocking his head backward. Then he dropped the jockey in the dirt.

Devon stood behind the screen door, aghast at Jeremiah's unprecedented behavior. She kept silent.

"Pritchard, get your ass up if you want to fight. If you don't want to fight, get the hell off this property. Now!"

The jockey shook his head to clear it, wiping blood from his nose with his sleeve. He rose to a sitting position and glared at Jeremiah with hatred. "I'll fight you anytime, nigger." Then he hurled himself at Jeremiah's legs, hoping to bring the larger man down. But Jeremiah was too quick. He stepped aside so that Jimmy fell face first into the dirt. Jeremiah again grabbed his collar, this time at the nape of Jimmy's neck.

"Let me help you up," he said mildly, yanking Pritchard up and throwing him once more against the stall. This time the younger man yelped with pain as his elbow hit the metal padlock. He balled his hands into fists and came toward Jeremiah. "Not again you won't," Jeremiah said with a grunt, hitting his opponent in the stomach with all his might.

Pritchard doubled over with nausea and staggered toward Jeremiah. The black man backed up, ready to strike again if necessary. But before Pritchard could reach him, the younger man fell to his knees and vomited into the dirt.

Jeremiah looked up from the mess to find himself surrounded by his men. Most wore looks of approval, but two of Pritchard's friends went toward the jockey and helped him to his feet.

"You're done for today, Jimmy," one said, leading him out of the barn.

Jimmy signaled for them to stop. With difficulty, he turned to face Jeremiah. "I may be done for today. But I ain't done. Not by a long shot. There's plenty of ways to deal with uppity niggers. Especially ones that put their hands on white women," he spat. "You and that bitch. You'll get yours," he threatened. Then he turned and limped away.

Devon emerged from the office, face immobile. She opened her mouth to speak, but Jeremiah preempted her. Addressing his men he said, "If any one of you thinks like Pritchard, you're free to leave now. We'll give you two weeks' pay and a recommendation. You who stay do so under the condition that you understand I am your direct boss. I hire and I fire. And any man, black or white, who starts the kind of trouble that led to the situation today is going to get fired a lot sooner than Pritchard did. I don't care what color a man is. Work hard, you get rewarded. Make a mistake, you get another chance. But defiance, disrespect, prejudice — those I won't stand for." Jeremiah glared at each man in turn, waiting for one to protest, to turn away.

"Yes sir," said a skinny groom, a sixteen-year-old white boy with dreams of being a jockey.

"That's a deal," said one of the black jockeys.

All around the room, men nodded agreement.

"Okay," Jeremiah said gruffly, "then get back to work."

When the room had emptied, he turned to face Devon. She simply gave a crisp nod of approval, turned on her heel, and headed to her appointment with her banker.

CHAPTER 55

DEVON was in a mood to celebrate. Her banker had eagerly granted her request for a loan to buy the adjoining farm. And why not? she asked herself. She had built Willowbrook into a world-class racing operation. The banker knew he was not at risk.

Then there had been the incident with Jimmy Pritchard. It had been ugly, but Jeremiah had emerged the victor. Devon felt confident that he had finally established his dominion over the other employees. She was satisfied that Jeremiah would deal with any future insubordination swiftly and completely.

Turning to more pleasant thoughts, Devon glanced over at the frothy mist-colored evening gown on the bed and smiled to herself. There was another cause to feel happy. She was fifty-two, yet still beautiful, still desirable, still sought-after. Not everyone could make the same claim at her age, and she was proud of it, though she would never have revealed this to anyone.

Mason Wilder would arrive soon to take her to a dinner at the

Hartwicks'. They still lived in the old Magrath estate, adjacent to Evergreen, Devon's childhood home. Helena Magrath Hartwick's parents had both died, but the entire county still referred to the home as "the Magrath place." Helena, Brent, and their children had remained good friends with Devon, but also with John. Devon knew that John was visiting them, for he had stopped by Willowbrook on several occasions to see Francesca. Devon and Mason both observed this growing friendship with skepticism, but so far John had not disappointed the young woman. Devon resolved to warn John that evening — albeit subtly — about Francesca's eagerness for his visits. She did not want her daughter hurt if John should suddenly decide he was bored with the girl. Devon knew that Francesca had fixated on the idea that John might have been her father, and was fascinated by him as a result. She also recognized that the feeling was mixed with a plain old adolescent crush on a handsome older man. That was perfectly normal and fine, Devon thought, as long as John handled the young girl's fragile emotions with care.

Devon finished her makeup — a subtle application of rose hue on her lips and cheeks, smoky gray around her eyes, and black mascara to match her eyelashes. Then she walked over to the bed and stepped into the gray dress. It was of a pearlescent silk that seemed to shimmer with every move she made. The full-skirted dress bared Devon's shoulders, still youthful and attractive, but it had long sleeves. Devon's arms were muscular, but she had decided that it was inappropriate for a woman over fifty to bare her arms. Francesca and Grace laughed at this notion, but Devon held firm, refusing to give in to the current rage for strapless dresses.

Devon heard the doorbell ring just as she slipped into her silvery sandals. She knew it was Mason coming to fetch her. Francesca's hurried patter down the wooden floor of the hallway confirmed that. The sound of their enthusiastic greetings floated up to Devon and she smiled to herself. Before she left her room, she opened all the windows, drinking in the night fragrances of her garden. It was not quite dark yet — one of those summer evenings when twilight seemed to go on for hours. The sky was streaked with a few faint traces of pink, and Devon breathed deeply, relaxing and enjoying the view. A perfect sense of well-being filled her and she savored it, not knowing that it would soon be rent apart.

Mason tried not to glower as he observed Devon and John talking intimately in front of the Hartwicks' huge marble fireplace. He did not know that the subject of their conversation was Francesca, but even if he had he would not have been comforted. It seemed that they stood a bit closer to each other than was necessary. John touched Devon's arm frequently as he spoke. Devon did not flirt or laugh a great deal, which comforted Mason somewhat, but it was clear that she was completely absorbed in the discussion.

"Francesca's taken a great liking to you," Devon was saying to John.

"And I to her," John said, smiling as he thought of the teenager.

"I'm afraid the friendship may be more important to her than you intend," Devon said with a soft smile.

"You know," John said thoughtfully, "I initially was amused by Frankie. But I'm now finding that her friendship adds a great deal to my life. My parents are both dead. The rest of my family is, well, distant, both geographically and emotionally. Frankie has become very important to me." He took a sip of his after-dinner cognac, then continued in a wistful tone, "I don't know many young people."

Devon did not wish to be cruel, but she couldn't help pointing out that John had never really wanted children. "You could have had more children. I mean, when you were married to Bebe. Or had you remarried."

"Point well taken. I don't think I ever felt ready for that responsibility. I kept on thinking I eventually would, but —"

Devon interrupted, sorry that she had implied some criticism of him. "But you were a good father to Morgan."

"We had a lot of disputes over that at the time, though, didn't we? You wanted to spend more time with her than I did. And that meant living at Willowbrook."

Devon looked down sheepishly. "I seemed to take everything so seriously. I'm sure it wouldn't have damaged her psyche to have been left with Penny a few more times. Or to spend more time in New York. She was a happy child, wasn't she?" Devon looked up at John, not exactly needing reassurance but desiring it nonetheless.

"She was," John said warmly, "and so is Frankie —" He saw Devon wince at the use of the nickname. "Francesca, I mean. Sorry, but she insists on it."

Devon smiled and shook her head. "I know."

John felt her smile resonate through him. She was so lovely. Guiltily, he looked up to find Mason staring intently at them. As though embarrassed at being caught, the white-haired man immediately averted his eyes. He's a good man, John told himself. I wonder why Devon and he haven't married.

"Maybe the amount of responsibility I have toward Francesca is just the perfect amount for me. I haven't had to go through the terrible twos or any of the other monstrous phases of infancy," John said with a wry smile, "but I enjoy a paternal relationship with a girl who, if things had turned out differently, might have been my daughter."

"Yes, that's what she always says."

"She's very fond of Mason, too," John said, with an involuntary nod in the other man's direction.

"Yes." Devon smiled.

John hesitated a moment before going on. He had no right to intrude, but his curiosity about Devon was overwhelming. Finally, he asked, "Have you never considered remarrying?"

Devon blushed. It was obvious John was trying to understand the nature of her relationship with Mason. "I have considered it," Devon said.

An answer that told him nothing, John thought to himself. "Mason seems very much in love with you."

"Oh, and I'm so fond of him, too!" Devon said fervently.

An answer that told him everything.

Suddenly John wondered what it would be like to kiss Devon again — or more. He remembered their first kiss, by a brook in the woods of Evergreen. He remembered the sweetness of the moment, the sheer romance of it. And then there had been the fire in her, that wonderful passion. For years now, he had firmly shunted from his mind the picture of Devon in bed with another man. First Roland, now Mason. He had to admit that it made him jealous.

As if on cue, Mason, with a deliberately casual step, ambled over to John and Devon.

"Grand party, isn't it?" he said heartily. "Nice to see you again, Alexander," he added, clapping John on his back in a friendly gesture.

"Good to see you, too. How's the publishing business?"

"Fine. Fine. Thinking of getting into television."

"It's the wave of the future." John nodded his approval.

Soon the two men were engrossed in conversation, and Devon slipped away from them. Half an hour later, she glanced over to see that they were still talking. It was the first chance they'd really had to get to know each other. Devon was not sure that she liked the idea of them becoming good friends, though she couldn't quite say why.

A few moments later, Devon noticed that some of the guests were beginning to drift away. A glance at the mantel clock told her that it was past midnight. She wanted to be up early in the morning to work with her new colt, so she joined Mason and John, signaling to the former that she wished to leave.

Devon realized that she must have dozed on the way home when the crunch of gravel on her drive awakened her.

"Would you like to stay the night?" she asked Mason. He often spent the night, sleeping with Devon until she awakened at five o'clock, then tiptoeing down the hall to one of the guest rooms. He sometimes wondered if they were fooling anyone with their subterfuge.

Mason wanted to stay, but something about her earlier attitude toward John disturbed him. He sensed electricity between Devon and John. He suspected that the two were still — or once again — attracted to each other. The idea that she had spent a good part of the evening in conversation with John — the first extended conversation Mason had ever witnessed between the two — made him uncomfortably aware of the other man's former claim to Devon. He wondered if he would always feel this way when John and Devon met. I shouldn't give in to such feelings, he reasoned. But he couldn't help himself, and he decided to make the sixty-minute drive back to his Georgetown home.

Devon accepted his decision with a polite murmur of regret but no real disappointment. She was suddenly very sleepy and she looked forward to drifting off in her big soft bed. The house was peaceful and quiet — she had told the servants not to wait up for her. In order to avoid awakening anyone, Devon bent down and removed her sandals.

As she began to climb the stairs to the second floor, she heard a strange noise outside. Puzzled, Devon turned. The horses? The noise was not coming from the direction of the barn, but rather from the vast green lawns in front of the house. Now the noise grew louder. Someone in trouble? Devon's heart raced with apprehension. She ran back down the stairs. Hurriedly, she slipped her shoes back on. The noise was louder. Yes, she definitely heard shouting. Rushing to the front door, she threw it open. There on her lawn was a nightmarish sight. Ghostly figures in peaked caps, some carrying torches, were mobbing her front garden. In a rush of adrenaline, Devon slammed the door and ran into her study. She moved automatically, driven by fear and instinct rather than by plan. With trembling hands, she took her Remington twelve-gauge shotgun from its rack and loaded it.

She ran back into the foyer and stared at the front door, dreading what she would find on the other side but knowing there was no way to avoid it. A noise behind her made her whirl, gun raised. There she saw the shocked faces of Francesca, Laurel, and Alice. Behind them, the housekeeping staff cowered against the wall. They all stared at the gun in Devon's hands. None of them uttered a sound. They were mute with fear. And so was she.

The shouting outside grew louder. Devon gripped the gun hard and approached the door. She put one hand on the doorknob, then looked back over her shoulder at her family. She turned back to the door and stared at her hand on the knob. Her knuckles were dead white. She took a deep, shaky breath, then threw the door open. The sight that confronted her was worse than she had imagined.

There was fire everywhere. Torches that cast hideous shadows on the ghostlike figures crowding her vision. She took a step backward, wanting to flee inside.

"There she is!" cried one of the figures below.

Now there was no escape! She stood rooted to the spot — a dark figure silhouetted against the light from the foyer inside. Her dress flew up behind her, like flames leaping toward the sky.

The men, some on horseback, some afoot, gathered in a group on the lawn directly in front of her.

Then suddenly, absurdly, Devon noticed that some of them were standing in her daylilies. The observation struck her like a slap to the face. Her emotions, already at a high pitch, were transformed from stark fear to blind fury.

She stepped forward rigidly until she was at the edge of her porch. She was panting, bursting with the intensity of her emotion. So much so that she could not even speak.

As if by some invisible signal, the group fell silent. A lone voice, harsh and common, rang out. "The Grand Wizard has a warning for you!"

A different voice now, deeper. "Women who consort with the nigger, women who let themselves be sullied by nigger hands, deserve to die!"

The voice continued, "Today you favored a nigger over a white man. Tonight you will be punished!"

A resounding roar went up from the mob.

"And, after you, we'll just go pay a visit to the nigger!" a voice from the dark gloated. A voice she recognized as Jimmy's. She scanned the group until she spotted its shortest member.

Devon's guts churned with fury — raw, dangerous fury, unencumbered by any civilized emotion. She stood as immobile as a statue, head high, back perfectly erect. Then she raised her gun to her shoulder and pointed it directly at Jimmy.

Her words came out in a harsh growl. "Punishment, you say? Try it. Because if any one of you damages one piece of my property or touches anyone who works for me or any of my family, you will die! I want you to try me if you think I won't use this gun." Abruptly Devon pivoted ninety degrees and aimed at the only lighted area in the front garden — a boxwood alcove with a terra-cotta birdbath at its center. At the edge of the birdbath was a small sculptured sparrow. Before the men's eyes, the clay bird exploded, sending fragments flying a hundred feet. As if in a military drill, Devon cocked the shotgun again and pivoted back so that the weapon was pointed directly at the group of hooded figures.

"All right, Grand Wizard." Her voice was pure venom. "Now it's your turn! And after that" — she moved her gun slightly to the left — "it's yours, Jimmy Pritchard!"

Now several of the men raised shotguns so that they were pointing at Devon. "Don't even think of it!" she spat. "I'm quicker than you and I've probably got better aim. You may kill me, but before you do, I'll get at least two of you. How about that, *Grand Wizard*." She used the title with utter contempt, aiming the gun once again at him.

"We're here to issue a warning!" the voice, less belligerent now, replied.

"Really?" She laughed disdainfully. "I thought you were here to punish me. Well, let me give you a little food for thought. How do you think this county would look upon the likes of you punishing me? Not too kindly, I think. I think you could just forget about jail and courtrooms and formalities like that. I *know* there's several gentlemen who'd come after you bunch with a hanging rope — or worse. And I'd be right there to lead the way, I promise you. Because I know who you men are. I've lived here all my life, so don't think I can't recognize you under those ridiculous dunce caps you're wearing."

"You're not scaring us!" Jimmy Pritchard called defiantly.

Devon noticed that all the men with guns had lowered them. Now she was the only one in a shooting stance. She swiveled so that the shotgun was aiming straight at Pritchard. "I'm not? Then you're even more stupid than I thought," Devon declared. "Come up here,

Jimmy Pritchard. Let's see if you've got the guts to face me without a mob backing you up!"

None of the men said anything, nor did Jimmy move. "Come on over here, you coward!" Devon said in a low voice.

Humiliated and angry, the little man turned to the group. "This here woman shows more respect to that nigger than she shows me!"

"Well, I guess that says something about you, doesn't it?" Devon mocked.

"You're fuckin' 'im, that's why!" Jimmy cried. A few of the men around him gasped. One stepped forward and put an arm on the jockey. "Hey, there, boy. You're goin' too far."

"Jimmy Pritchard!" Devon's voice cut through the night air. "You've got three seconds to get off my property. Then you've got three hours to get out of the county. And, unlike you, I don't make idle threats. At dawn, I'm going to call on some of my friends. If you're not out of here, we'll find you!"

Jimmy started to respond. "You —"

"One!" Devon cried.

"I'll get —"

"Two!"

"Come on, Jimmy," said another man, putting an arm on Pritchard and drawing him away.

"Three!"

Jimmy turned to look over his shoulder at Devon. In a menacing voice Devon said, "Jimmy, you're just too damn slow."

A resounding *boom!* An explosion of dirt, grass, and flowers flew up in the air a few yards behind Jimmy.

Then Devon began to laugh, a full hearty laugh that chilled the blood of the men below. And she was still laughing as the last of them hurried away.

Devon was as good as her word. Soon after dawn she hurried to the local sheriff's office. The man knew the Richmond family well, knew Devon's stature in the community, and was quick to comply with her request.

Devon had been bluffing when she told the mob that she recognized them all, but she had recognized several of them, and these names she gave to the sheriff.

"I'll just go pay a visit to those men. Make sure we don't have anymore trouble, for you or Jeremiah," said the sheriff.

"Thank you, Earl, I appreciate that," said Devon, holding out one white-gloved hand for him to shake.

"I don't take too kindly to men scaring helpless women," said Earl in a grave tone.

Devon simply smiled.

CHAPTER 56

JESSE couldn't take his eyes off Francesca. It was their first swim of the summer, and now that she was sixteen it seemed that her old cutoffs and T-shirt were clinging to a brand-new set of curves. Her long legs, gawky and sticklike a year ago, were now shapely perfection. She was glorious and Jesse, at eighteen, found it very difficult to hide his feelings.

Why had he not noticed the change before now? he wondered to himself. Just yesterday they had gone riding together, laughing and joking as usual. Now, suddenly, he found himself tongue-tied.

"Jesse!" Francesca stood above him, hands on hips in an attitude of exasperation. "Didn't you hear me? Let's eat. I'm starved." The girl playfully wrung her wet hair out over Jesse's shoulders, finally rousing him from his stupor.

"Hey, quit that!" he yelled.

"Okay, but let's eat!" Francesca dove into the picnic basket and pulled out ham and cheese sandwiches, potato salad, pickles, cold barbecued chicken, sugar cookies, and, for good measure, two apples. "Where's the thermos?" Ignoring the paper cups packed by the cook, Francesca poured apple juice into the lid of the thermos bottle, took a sip, then offered the cup to Jesse.

He took the cup from her, careful not to put his lips where hers had been. He was almost afraid the spot would burn him if he touched it.

Francesca unwrapped one of the ham sandwiches lying on the

checkerboard tablecloth and handed it to Jeremiah. Absentmindedly, he bit into it.

"Potato salad?" Francesca asked, chewing her own sandwich. She laid it down as she spoke, reaching for the plastic container. Taking paper plates from the basket, she piled both high with the potato salad without waiting for Jesse's confirmation. After years of picnicking together, she knew what he liked and how much he would eat. "Here, have a pickle," she said, carelessly plopping one down on his plate.

"I'm going to talk to Mom about being an exercise rider," Francesca announced.

"That's nice," Jesse replied dreamily.

"You liked it, didn't you?"

Jesse forced himself to focus on the conversation. "Exercise riding? Yeah, loved it. Till I got too big," he said with a final bite of his ham sandwich. He rummaged through the packages of food on the cloth and picked out a drumstick of the barbecued chicken.

Francesca looked at his broad shoulders as though noticing for the first time that his body was becoming that of a man. "Yeah, too bad for you. You'll be over six feet tall if you grow any more. I guess that means you'll never be a jockey."

"That's okay." Jesse shrugged philosophically. "I can still be a trainer. My dad's teaching me. I'm going to start working for him."

"I thought he wanted you to go to college."

"Yeah, it's crazy. You don't need college for the kind of work I want to do. My dad didn't have any college and look at where he is now!"

"He's the best," Francesca said matter-of-factly, "aside from Mom, of course. Anyway, *I'm* not too big to be a jockey. I'm taller than I thought I'd be, but I still only weigh one hundred and ten."

"Good luck talking your mom into letting you be a jockey," Jesse said with a wry smile.

Francesca took another swallow of apple juice. "One of these days I'm going to be one no matter what anyone says. Uncle John thinks it's okay."

"What's that got to do with it?"

"He can talk Mom into letting me have my way." Francesca grinned. "He always does."

"He does not! Your mom wanted you to go to that fancy girl's school in Washington and there you are! Didn't you get Mr. Alexander to try to talk her out of that?"

"Only because I kicked up such a fuss about it and he felt sorry for me. But I think he secretly thought it was a good idea. That's why he didn't really argue with Mom too much. Anyway, at least she didn't want me to board there. Ugh!" She wrinkled her nose at the thought.

"He spoils you. He knows it's a good idea for you to go to that school, but he just can't say no to you."

"I know." Francesca giggled, pleased with herself. "But I'm like you. I don't understand the reason I need to go to school at all, since I'm going to be a jockey."

"Maybe your mom doesn't see it that way," Jesse pointed out. "After all, she went to college, and so did your grandmother. It's not like in my family. If I went to college, I'd be the first one."

Francesca shrugged, bored with the subject. "Cookie?" she offered, holding out one of the golden confections.

"I don't know. I might be getting full." Jesse lay back and rubbed his stomach, sticking it out for Francesca's amusement. It was an old game of theirs to see whose stomach stuck out the most after their picnics.

Francesca laughed at Jesse, just like always, but she didn't mimic his action. She found to her surprise that she wanted Jesse to think she was pretty. She didn't want him to see her stomach sticking out. The thought made her feel suddenly self-conscious. Without realizing it, she blushed.

CHAPTER 57

"LOOSEN up the reins a little bit, Devon, she can't stay a child forever," John said, looking to Mason for support.

Mason nodded, adding, "She's a good kid. Never been in any kind of trouble. Give her a chance to do what she wants to do."

Devon paced the floor of her study in annoyance. She didn't like it when John and Mason sided together with Francesca against her. She was the girl's parent, after all, her only parent!

Both men sat on the burgundy silk couch, feet up on the mahogany coffee table, watching Devon as she moved back and forth in front of them.

Her movements were as elegant and fluid as a fashion model's, even when she was pacing. Dressed for the cocktail hour, she wore a figure-skimming lavender silk dress by Christian Dior. It had a rounded collar and long sleeves, yet its perfect tailoring showed to advantage just how well Devon had retained her slenderness. Her new short, wavy haircut seemed to emphasize her aqua eyes and fine bone structure. It was hard to believe that she was in her fifties.

"For God's sake, Devon, you're making me tired with your pacing! Sit down, have a martini, and stop worrying!" said John companionably.

The two men looked at each other and nodded almost imperceptibly. Mason stood and went over to Devon, gently taking her arm and guiding her to a fat, flowered armchair. Holding her by her shoulders, he pushed downward slightly, indicating that she should be seated. Meanwhile, John had gone over to the bar cart and poured the contents of the silver shaker into a wide, V-shaped martini glass. He added two olives to the mix, then brought the concoction over to Devon.

"Here," he said. "Don't say another word until you've drunk everything in this glass."

Devon gave the two men a look of mock exasperation, but then she dimpled. They were so silly when it came to Francesca!

John turned away abruptly and went back to his place on the couch. There were moments when John found it almost impossible to conceal his love for Devon and he had to turn away from her immediately for fear he would blurt out something inappropriate. He always treated her in a genial, fraternal manner, even when he felt like taking her in his arms instead. Two years before, when he had first become reacquainted with her, he had thought of trying to rekindle their romance. But his quick friendship with Mason and the older man's obvious love for Devon prevented him from making such an attempt. He sometimes wondered with amusement if Mason had deliberately coopted him with his charm and kindness.

At the time of their reunion, John had not been *in love* with Devon; rather, he had been deeply attracted to her. The love had come later, so many things making it grow. Her confrontation with the Ku

Klux Klan had filled him with respect and pride for her. He admired her bold, authoritative style of managing her business, kicking himself for his former objections to it. He envied her ability to inspire loyalty from her employees — they were happy, it seemed, a rare feat in the business world. She accomplished so much — and appeared to do it effortlessly. But most of all, when he watched her loving relationship with her mother, her daughter, and Alice, he regretted that he was no longer part of her family. It was an impossible situation, yet he enjoyed the company of his two friends — and Francesca — so much that he resigned himself to it.

"Devon," Mason said, his deep voice adding weight to his words, "there will come a time when you will no longer have the right to control what Francesca does. Why let your actions now foster a rift then? If she wants to become a jockey badly enough, she will do it over your objections. But maybe this is just a phase. All young girls love horses."

Devon shook her head. "This . . . this *obsession* of hers has lasted twelve years. It's not just a phase."

"It's not an obsession, Devon," John countered, "it's a dream. Not many people have the talent and opportunity to fulfill their dreams. Why deny your child a chance that is unique?"

Devon looked angrily at her former husband. "That's easy for you to say; she's not your daughter!"

John averted his eyes, hurt apparent on his face.

Mason came to his friend's defense. "Devon! John cares as much about Francesca as if she were his daughter. So do I! We don't want any harm to come to her. How can a woman as God-blasted independent as you deny your own daughter a chance to have what you have — a career doing something she loves!"

"Well, women aren't jockeys!" Devon cried, slapping the arm of her chair for emphasis.

"Hah! That's rich coming from you." John's tone accused her. "When you took over Willowbrook, there were no professional women trainers. You broke every boundary, every tradition that ever existed. Now your picture's hanging in the racing museum! But you won't let Francesca have the same chance. Devon, she's just like you. She's a survivor, a winner! She'll be fine!"

"No!" Devon argued, close to tears. Up from the bottom of her soul came bubbling the source of her opposition. Like a boil bursting, Devon's deepest fears spilled out. "What about Morgan? Things might have been different . . ." She choked on her words. For a moment she was too overcome to speak. Both men stared at her in stunned silence. Haltingly, she continued, "I . . . I could have . . . protected her, but I didn't. I can't let that happen twice!"

Mason got up from the couch and started toward Devon, but then he stopped short. John and Devon were staring at each other, mesmerized. It was as though a camera lens was focusing on only the two of them, blocking out their surroundings — and blocking out Mason. They were reliving a tragedy the depth of which no one around them could comprehend. It was a moment of such deep intimacy, such naked pain, that Mason felt like a voyeur intruding on the privacy of others.

Slowly, John rose from the couch. He went to Devon and took her hands, rubbing them a moment in his. Then he knelt beside the chair and wrapped his arms around her, comforting her. Oblivious to Mason, John crooned to Devon as she sobbed into his shoulder.

"I'm sorry," she said, almost incoherent, "it's just been eating at me. What if the same thing happens to Francesca?"

"It wouldn't be the same thing," John said softly. "The circumstances were completely different. Francesca is strong, used to taking tumbles. And she's a talented rider."

"But jockeys can get killed!"

"So can bus drivers or maids or doctors or housewives. Anybody can get killed, Devon."

"It's not the same," Devon said, pushing John away for a moment and giving him a look of exasperation. "I could stop Francesca from doing something so dangerous!"

"No, you couldn't. Not forever. Just like you couldn't have stopped what happened to Morgan. Not really. And that's what's been eating you all these years. You believe that you did something wrong. But at the time, you thought it was right," John said gently, taking his handkerchief from his pocket and wiping away her tears. "You're not God, and you couldn't have known how it would turn out. You don't have the power to protect your children from death, as much as you would like to." John remembered with shame how he had secretly blamed Devon for contributing to Morgan's death. He had been so foolish, he realized. He was thankful that he had never spoken aloud the words of blame that were in his mind during that period.

Devon took the handkerchief from John's hands and blew her nose, recovering some of her composure.

"I'm so frightened for her, John."

"I am, too. If she truly does become a jockey, my heart will be in my throat every time she rides. But I'll be proud of her, too. And I'll be happy for her. People have to take risks to get what they want, Devon. Sometimes they have to give things up. But I don't have to tell you that, do I?" John's eyes looked deeply into Devon's, and for a brief moment she saw in them the hurt she had inflicted upon him so long ago. Then a veil went down, and all she saw was sympathy.

"I suppose I've been overly protective," Devon said, looking down at her hands as she twisted the handkerchief nervously.

"You've been a wonderful mother," John said warmly, lifting her chin with his index finger and looking into her eyes with a smile.

"Well, I guess I'll tell Francesca the good news at dinner tonight," Devon said, readjusting her skirt and sitting straighter in her chair.

"Good."

"Mason, why don't we —" Devon looked around the room for her friend, then back at John. "Where's Mason?"

"I don't know." John looked around, puzzled, as though he would discover Mason in some corner of the room Devon had overlooked. "I didn't even hear him go."

CHAPTER 58

"CAN you believe it? Mom says I can start as soon as finals are over next week," Francesca called to Jesse. Their horses were traveling single file along the path through the woods, Jesse in front of Francesca. Soon they would arrive at their swimming spot.

"That's great!" Jesse said over his shoulder. "Congratulations! How'd you talk her into it?"

"Like I told you. Uncle John did it."

"Spoiled!" Jesse teased. As they reached the clearing, he dismounted, tethering his horse to a tree. Francesca did the same, taking their food from the saddle pack.

"Swim first?" she asked.

Jesse remembered his discomfiture of the weekend before, and a wash of rose color touched his light-coffee-colored features. "Sure. I wore a bathing suit though. Mom gave me one for my birthday," he added offhandedly. He didn't want to explain that he felt somehow more exposed sitting opposite her in his wet clothes than he would in a bathing suit. He could not explain why exactly, but it seemed somehow less . . . abandoned . . . to wear a swimsuit. He felt safer in it. More in control.

Francesca looked puzzled. "Didn't feel like getting your clothes wet?" she asked.

"Something like that."

"We always dry so quickly, it never seems like a problem. Maybe I should wear one too."

"Maybe." Jesse shrugged, not meeting her eyes as he spread the picnic blanket on the ground.

"Are you going to change into your dry clothes when you get out?" Francesca asked.

"Frankie, I don't know!" Jesse said in irritation. "It's not like I've got some big plan. I'm just wearing a gift my mom gave me."

"Okay, okay! Don't get hot under the collar," Francesca said, returning Jesse's look of irritation. "Maybe I won't even go swimming."

"So don't." Jesse shrugged in feigned nonchalance. He turned and ambled to the water's edge. Soon, Francesca followed him.

"Cold?" she asked. Francesca bent over the water and dipped a hand in. Suddenly, Jesse had the urge to push her in. Stealthily, he backed away from the water's edge and toward her. Francesca spun around, eyes wide. "Jesse, don't you dare!" she cried as he gave her a shove strong enough to send her into the icy brook tail first.

"Oh!" she screamed, laughing and gasping for breath as her head bobbed to the surface, "it's freezing!" She slapped her hand across the surface of the water in an attempt to splash Jesse.

All at once, the tension between them melted away. Jesse jumped into the water, making as huge a splash as he could. Then the water fight began in earnest, both teenagers laughing uproariously as they splashed each other.

After about fifteen minutes, Francesca, gasping for air, said, "I'm getting too cold. I've got to get out."

"Yeah, me too."

Francesca hoisted herself from the brook, sheets of water raining down from her and muddying the bank. Jesse followed. "I've got towels," he said, running toward his horse.

"You do?" Francesca asked. "You really came prepared today."

"Well, you always bring the food."

Jesse grabbed two towels from his saddlebag and came toward Francesca. She was still standing by the bank of the river. Her cutoffs clung to her, but were thick enough to be no more revealing than when dry. On top, Francesca wore a sleeveless cotton top under a plaid cotton blouse. The outfit was modest, more modest than a bathing suit. Jesse was relieved she was not wearing only a T-shirt.

But, as if reading his mind, Francesca said, "As long as you have a towel, I may as well hang this up to dry." She removed the plaid shirt and, for one brief moment, Jesse saw the outline of her sturdy white bra through the sleeveless top. The wet cloth sank into her cleavage, now as full as a woman's, and Jesse could not help but stare.

Francesca's face turned crimson as she followed his gaze. Snatching the towel from Jesse, she hurriedly wrapped it around her.

Together they went to the picnic blanket and sat down. To cover their confusion, they occupied themselves with unloading the contents of the saddlebag.

"Mmmm, chicken salad sandwiches, sweet pickles, olives, potato chips . . . Hey! My favorite! Roast beef!" said Jesse, happily absorbed in the feast.

"Jesse," said Francesca, ignoring the food, "can I ask you something?"

"Go ahead."

"How come you don't have a girlfriend?"

Jesse gave her a bold stare. "What makes you think I don't?"

"Well . . . you never talk about one. And you spend every Saturday and Sunday with me."

"Just days," Jesse said mysteriously.

Francesca's eyes widened. "Who's your girlfriend?"

"Rosie Hammersmith."

Francesca felt a sudden stab of jealousy as she thought of Jesse spending time with another girl. "Reverend Hammersmith's daughter?"

"Yep."

"She's pretty," Francesca admitted. She waited a beat before continuing. "Don't you want to know if I have a boyfriend?"

"Nope," said Jesse with feigned indifference. He reached for a roast beef sandwich and bit into it.

Francesca tossed her glossy black curls and pushed out her lip in a pout. She was annoyed that Jesse didn't seem to want to know whether she was attractive to boys. "Well, are you going out with your girlfriend tonight?"

"She goes to Bible school in the summer." Jesse chewed his sandwich, wishing that Francesca would stop staring at him. "Listen, would you stop asking questions and just eat."

"I'm not hungry."

"Hah, that's a first for you!"

Francesca ignored the remark and continued her line of questioning. "Jesse . . . did you and Rosie ever *do it?*"

Jesse's eyes widened in outrage. "Frankie! That's none of your business." Guiltily he thought of his trysts with Rosie behind her father's church. Jesse had been troubled by the locale, but that had only seemed to excite Rosie more. "We'll move back fifty feet if you're going to be so prissy about this," she had mocked him, "so we won't be on hallowed ground." But she had been so hot and willing that he would have been unable to resist her no matter what the circumstances. He had not known that women could be so *eager*.

Rosie, though, had departed ten days before, and immediately afterward Jesse had become aware of Francesca's blossoming womanhood. The dreams that left him wet and tormented at night were no longer about Rosie. And the guilt he had experienced with Rosie was nothing compared to the taboo attached to his lust for Francesca—which only made it all the more excruciating.

Francesca thought that Jesse looked as though he'd been caught doing something wrong, and once again her jealousy flared. She thought of Jesse kissing another girl, touching her, and she suddenly had the urge to show him that she, Francesca, could arouse him if she wanted to. If she wanted to.

"Well," she said casually. "I don't think I'm ever going to get dry if I keep this towel around me," she said, dropping it around her waist. Jesse immediately averted his eyes, but not before he noticed her two nipples poking out through the wet cloth. Against his will, he felt himself stir. He dropped his sandwich on his paper plate and rolled onto his stomach, cradling his head in his arms.

"I'm not hungry anymore," he announced. "I'm going to take a little nap. And I don't want you to bother me for at least a half hour."

"Fine!" she said pettishly, annoyed that he would literally turn his back on what she considered a most intriguing conversation. She glared daggers at the fuzzy curls on the back of his head, willing him to turn around and face her. But Jesse remained immobile, as though he were already asleep. His pose reminded her of summers past when they had dozed for hours in the hot sun, not saying a word all afternoon. In all that time, there had never been the tension between them that existed now. It must be my fault, Francesca chided herself. Suddenly, she was ashamed of her behavior. What was I trying to do? she asked herself. Jesse's my friend. Do I want him to kiss me, to touch me? Of course not! Jesse's like a brother. But, of course, he was not her brother.

CHAPTER 59

DEVON'S sporty Jaguar pulled up in front of the glossy black double doors of Mason Wilder's Georgetown mansion. The neoclassical structure occupied two acres of a neighborhood in which most of the houses were no more than twenty feet wide. The town on the outer boundaries of the District of Columbia had once been the most sought-after residential area of Washington, had tumbled into a period of decrepitude, then had been resurrected into the high-style real estate that it would remain. Wilder's family had been there from the beginning, his house a sightseer's landmark in a town filled with landmarks.

Devon emerged from her racing green convertible, brushing her full-skirted white linen dress in a vain attempt to smooth out some of the deep wrinkles that had formed during the drive. She fluffed her black waves with her fingers as she climbed the wide brick staircase that stretched across the entire facade of the house. With its massive white pillars and twenty-foot ceilings, the house was a monumental structure.

Before she could reach the front door it was thrown open by Mason, who wrapped Devon into his huge embrace. He kissed her on the lips with fervor, unwilling to release her until he heard the footsteps of his butler behind him.

"Owens, would you please take the bags to the ivory room," he said with a conspiratorial wink at Devon. The ivory room was connected to his by a door. As always, he was certain that they fooled no one. Still, appearances had to be maintained.

"Devon, I'm so glad you could make it," Mason said, ushering her into the house. "It will be good to have you by my side as hostess tonight. Entertaining is always more gracious with a hostess present, don't you agree?"

"Of course," murmured Devon, avoiding yet another of Mason's broad hints.

"Would you care for tea, a cocktail?" Mason asked, leading her to the terrace at the rear of the house. Terrace, perhaps, was too modest a word for the multilevel expanse of herringbone-patterned brick that stretched for two hundred feet in either direction. It was interspersed with fountains and specimen trees, a pergola and an orangerie; all of it constructed in a formal style that perfectly suited the palatial lines of the home. At the outer reaches of the structure stood a pristine Olympic-sized swimming pool surrounded by black wrought-iron tables and chairs sporting red and white umbrellas.

"This looks like a perfect setting for a glass of lemonade," Devon remarked.

"Lemonade it is then," said Mason, picking up a telephone and pressing a button that accessed the kitchen.

A few moments later, a gray-uniformed woman emerged carrying a silver tray. She brought with her not only a pitcher of mint-sprigged lemonade but also a three-tiered tea tray filled with dainty miniature sandwiches, fruit tartlets, and petits fours.

"Are you trying to sabotage me?" Devon joked, unable to resist a quarter-sized lemon cookie covered in confectioner's sugar.

Mason laughed and helped himself to three smoked salmon sandwiches. "We'll be dining at nine, so I thought you might need something to tide you over."

"Thanks." Devon smiled, biting into the cookie.

"How long will you be able to stay?"

"Just the weekend this time. We have to get ready for Saratoga. Less than two weeks away. I can hardly believe it."

"Renting the cottage again?"

"As always."

"How's Francesca?"

"Good. But I'll tell you this. Any hope I might have had of this jockey thing being a whim has been dashed. Jeremiah says she's his most valuable exercise rider. He thinks she has real talent. And, of course, she feeds off his praise. She's up every morning at four-thirty. Can't wait to get to the stables. She used to stay in bed until noon!"

"Well, it's good when young people are motivated."

"I know," Devon admitted, "but I think I may have a problem motivating her to do well in school. She's completely absorbed with horses!"

"I thought girls that age were completely absorbed with boys," Mason teased.

"Not Francesca. Oh, boys *have* started to call, as you saw when you were at Willowbrook."

Mason nodded and smiled, thinking affectionately of how Francesca had bloomed over the past year. She had been so certain that she would turn out ugly!

"But," Devon continued, "I've never heard her mention a special one. And you know how teenagers are. They won't tell you anything about what they're thinking!" She sighed.

"You're luckier than most. At least Francesca admits to having a mother," said Mason with a comical look.

"So my friends tell me."

"Devon," said Mason, shifting in his seat, "I didn't invite you here strictly for this party tonight."

Devon raised her eyebrows inquiringly.

"I feel that I must speak my mind to you, even if I risk losing something very precious."

"By all means," Devon murmured.

"We've been dating — God, I hate that word — perhaps I should say 'keeping company,' for about seven years."

"You could say 'lovers,' " Devon said wickedly.

Mason chuckled. "The term lacks a certain dignity, so you'll pardon me if I stick to more euphemistic phraseology. In any event, I feel that the time has come for us to marry or to put this relationship aside."

"You can't mean that!" Devon protested. "Why would you say such a thing?"

Mason thought a moment before answering, then he said bluntly, "Because you're in love with another man."

Devon's mouth popped open, so shocked was she at his words. For a moment she was confused. Something that had been firmly suppressed in her subconscious began to surface. No! She tried to push the feeling back into dormancy. It can't be true! You know it's true, a mocking voice within her insisted. But I refuse to let it be, she argued back silently. I don't have to act on it. I don't have to do anything at all. It will pass. And until then, I'll carry on as before. *It will pass.*

Devon suddenly became aware of Mason's intense gaze. He was waiting for her to respond. But how? Were her feelings really so obvious that he had recognized them even before she herself had? What if John, too, had guessed her love for him? Oh, the embarrassment! And their friends. Had they guessed? Had they laughed at the three of them, caught in the classic triangle of jealousy, friendship, and love? No, she refused, absolutely refused, to admit the truth aloud. Instead she asked, "If you believe that — and I'm not saying it's true — how can you want to marry me?"

"Because I, my dear, am in love with you," Mason admitted, turning his hands palms up in a gesture of helplessness. At the look of distress on Devon's face, he hurried on. "Oh, I'm no masochist. You are a woman of honor. If you marry me, I know you'll be faithful. And I know that you love me in your own way. I also doubt that you'll ever be willing to marry the man with whom you are *in* love. So, you see, you might as well marry me."

The reference to Devon's honor made her feel ashamed. Resolving to be as honest with Mason as he was with her, Devon asked, "But why should you settle for second-best like that?"

"You could never be termed second-best, Devon. You are the best there is in this world."

Devon blushed. "I don't mean —"

"No, of course you don't," said Mason, leaning forward and taking her left hand in his right one. "But let me ask you this: Do you ever intend to marry John?"

Devon started again at hearing his name spoken aloud. Oh, she hated herself for the involuntary thrill she felt at the sound of that one syllable! The odd sort of relief she felt at being able to confide in her trusted friend Mason. She felt like a volcano that had erupted. But like the lava that flowed from a volcano, her love would have a devastating effect, Devon knew. For Mason was not just her friend, he was her lover — and he wanted to be her husband.

And as alive as Devon's love for John made her feel, she wished it did not exist. She did not want to make the same mistake twice. She did not want these feelings of tremulous yearning, of a battle raging within her. But there it was. She couldn't help it.

That's not true, the strongest part of her argued. You *can* help it. Keep it hidden. Keep it hidden until it goes away.

Mason watched her face intently as Devon mulled over these thoughts. He saw the confusion, the longing, then the firm resolve. Finally, she spoke. "I do *not* intend to marry John," she said emphatically.

Mason believed her. Devon could be inflexible. She could be stubborn. But these traits also meant that she could be strong. He knew there were many unhappy memories associated with her first marriage. But one of the unhappiest was that it represented failure to Devon. And Devon did not like to fail. This encouraged Mason to press on. "Then I'll repeat my question: Why not me?" Mason's voice was an urgent whisper as he leaned closer to Devon. He watched her with an air of expectancy.

Mason's scrutiny, his clarity of insight, disturbed her. Abruptly she pushed the wrought-iron chair backward. The legs made a harsh, scraping sound on the bricks, disturbing the quiet of the afternoon.

Mason sat back in his chair and smiled indulgently. "You always pace when you're confronted with a problem. Did you know that?"

The affection in Mason's voice eased some of Devon's tension. "I know," she admitted ruefully, "I guess I'm not very good at hiding my feelings."

"Depends," Mason said with a shrug.

"Well, I won't try to hide them now." Devon turned and faced Mason squarely. "You deserve better than that."

Mason looked at Devon, patiently waiting for her to organize her thoughts.

"Mason, I'm very happy with things the way they are. Why do you want to change them?" Devon asked bluntly.

"It's very simple, really. I want to have some claim on you. To ensure that you'll always be in my life. I love you and I'm afraid that if we don't marry I'll lose you one day."

"But there's no need for you to worry about that! I'm happy being with you." And she was! Mason was a cozy fire on a winter's night, while John was a pagan bonfire. She was content with Mason. Content to be content. She didn't need more than that now, she told herself.

Mason ran one of his huge hands over his chin in a thoughtful manner. "I'm happy, too. But I won't be if I lose you to someone else."

Devon went to Mason and stood behind him, leaning over to put her cheek next to his. "That won't happen," she whispered in his ear.

The nearness of Devon, the haunting smell of her perfume,

aroused a profound yearning in him. He reached up and covered her arms with his hands. "I'd feel more certain of that if you were willing to join our lives permanently," he remarked.

Devon could see his point. How could he feel certain of her commitment to him if she was unwilling to formalize it?

She straightened, releasing her hold on him. Returning to her chair, she sat down, the white skirt settling gracefully around her legs. She stared pensively at the bright aqua of the swimming pool, trying to decide how to respond to Mason. She did not want to lose him. She enjoyed his company, had come to rely on the security and comfort of their relationship. And Francesca adored him. So why was she hesitant to marry him? Was it simply that she was set in her ways? Should she perhaps give serious consideration to his offer? She knew many women would jump at the chance to marry Mason.

But I'm not in love with him, a small voice inside of her whispered. How can I marry a man I'm not in love with? Love may not be the most important ingredient in a successful marriage, she reminded herself. After all, I loved John. For Roland, on the other hand, I didn't feel the same kind of passion. It was a more gentle kind of love. More mature. Could my feelings for Mason just be one more step along the same road? After all, I *did* love Roland. Maybe if I marry Mason, I'll grow to feel the same way.

But try as she might to convince herself of this, Devon couldn't. There was a difference between her love for Roland and the deep affection she felt for Mason.

"You look undecided." Mason's deep voice broke into her reverie, startling her.

"I am," she admitted.

"That's somewhat encouraging," Mason said, trying for a light tone. "At least you aren't rejecting me out of hand."

"I'd never do that," Devon said warmly. "I think, though, that I need a little more time to consider your proposal."

"I've waited seven years, Devon!" Mason protested. "Can't you at least tell me what you're thinking?"

"I'm thinking that I don't want to do without you. At the same time, I'm not sure I want to change my life at this point. And it could be disruptive to Francesca to —"

"Balderdash!" Mason said with an impatient gesture. "If anything, Francesca could use a permanent father figure in her life. She's always wanted one. That's why she's so fond of —"

Mason cut himself off, realizing how self-defeating his next utterance would be. Francesca had bonded with John in a way she had done with no other man in her life, even Willy. Mason was a little hurt by this, as he was very fond of Francesca. He knew that she returned this affection, but that she felt closer to John. Perhaps she could talk to John more freely knowing that he had returned to their lives as *her* friend, rather than Devon's. Clearly, however, John was Francesca's idol.

"I suppose it's ridiculous to worry about disrupting Francesca," Devon said hastily in an attempt to smooth over Mason's slip of the tongue. "She's almost grown. And she's so fond of you. I'm sure she'd be very pleased if we were to marry."

"Well, if you're not going to marry John and you're not worried about Francesca and you want to continue our relationship, why hesitate?"

Because I'm not in love with you, she repeated silently. And Mason, attuned to Devon's every emotion, saw her answer written clearly on her face.

Feeling defeated, he averted his eyes, staring sightlessly into the grove of evergreens that marked the boundary of his property. His face hardened into a mask of hopeless resignation. That he could feel such youthful longing at his age! Life had built up a core of toughness in him, and Devon had penetrated that toughness.

For years, though, he had had the strength to hide his weakness. Afraid of losing her, he had maintained a distance between them, assumed an air of contentment with the terms of their relationship. She had offered no more, so he had demanded no more.

Until now. Now he had stripped himself bare before her. He had admitted to her that he would take her whether she loved him or not. How ignoble! He had a sudden feeling of impotence.

Seeing the despair on his face, Devon cried, "Mason, don't look that way! I'm only asking for more time to think about it."

Mason turned hollow eyes to her. "Then I have no choice but to wait, do I?" he said with self-mockery. "But I can't wait forever, Devon. Not that I don't love you enough to wait, but it would be too much of a torment." Seeing her stricken expression, he made a halfhearted attempt to lighten the mood. "Oh, I don't mean to use such melodramatic language. It's just that there is a certain amount of suspense involved and I feel as though I've been in suspense for much too long already."

"What do you suggest?" she asked softly.

"Well, I'm a newspaperman, so you'll pardon me if I resort to something as crass as a deadline, but it's the only thing I can think of." Devon's nod of encouragement was a signal for Mason to continue. "What if we say Thanksgiving? You tell me by Thanksgiving what the answer will be."

"All right," Devon agreed.

"And if you say yes, it will give a new meaning to the word 'Thanksgiving,' I promise you," Mason said wholeheartedly.

CHAPTER 60

"I'M worried about that French colt Carte Blanche," Francesca said. She was hot and breathless from her turn around the track with Willowbrook's finest two-year-old, Roll the Dice. She nodded toward a diminutive white horse as Jesse and Jeremiah followed her gaze.

"Why?" Jesse looked up at her. "He's not used to dirt tracks, he's not used to racing counterclockwise, how can you consider him serious competition?" In France, as in the rest of Europe, races were held on grass tracks and were run clockwise.

Francesca studied Willowbrook's star jockey, Kelly Majors, to gauge his reaction to her warning. He smirked at the girl's assessment, sure of himself and Roll the Dice.

Francesca shrugged. "There's something about him. His rider's holding him back in exercise. The horse wants to run, though. Always wants to run."

"So does Roll the Dice," Jesse and Kelly said simultaneously.

Jeremiah, however, was not so complacent. He respected Francesca's instincts even though this was her first summer as an exercise rider. It was also her first official participation in the Saratoga races, so she was on edge, anxious to prove her worth. And she had. She had an instinct for knowing just how much to push her mounts. It was not smart to run a horse too fast in a prerace exercise because it threatened to whittle away at his winning edge. On the other hand, a too-slow exercise session did not provide the horse with the needed warm-up and stimulation. A careful balance had to be achieved, and Francesca was gifted at finding that balance. In addition, she followed Jeremiah's instructions precisely, not taking any liberties as some other ambitious young riders were apt to do. Now Jeremiah watched her handle her prancing mount, soothing him with soft murmurings and a steady hand. She had talent, there was no doubt, Jeremiah thought to himself.

Jeremiah turned to look at the French colt for a few moments, trying to see how the colt ran. He was annoyed at himself for not paying more attention to the French entry. Instead, odds makers had pointed to Gallant Man, to be ridden by Willy Shoemaker, as Roll the Dice's main competition. Shoemaker was a great jockey who knew how to pick winners, and Jeremiah took the threat seriously. But now he was beginning to wonder if he was making a mistake by focusing too closely on the obvious.

Jeremiah turned to Francesca. "Why don't you quit for now. Your mother wants you to meet her for breakfast. But be back in an hour," he instructed.

She nodded and turned her mount back to the stables. She had no need to be told where to meet her mother. Devon breakfasted almost every morning at the track clubhouse, like most of the owners. Laurel and Alice, still energetic participants in many of the racing ceremonies, preferred to spend leisurely mornings in the little Victorian house the family rented.

Francesca used a ramshackle bathroom near the stables to change into a seersucker skirt and blouse — it would have been unseemly to enter the clubhouse in her work clothes — and emerged just as the sun cleared the horizon. As Francesca made her way past the elaborate grandstand trimmed with white ironwork, she admired the window boxes spilling over with geraniums and petunias. The petunias were just opening their paper-thin petals, their scent drifting over the air on the morning mist.

As Francesca arrived, Gloria Vanderbilt rose from Devon's table, daintily kissed the air beside Devon's cheek, then Francesca's, and bid them farewell.

"Did she eat anything?" Francesca whispered, staring after the sylphlike woman.

"Never does," Devon said with a shake of her head. It was an old joke between mother and daughter. Gloria Vanderbilt, a nice woman who enjoyed Devon's company, was rarely seen eating, though she was an avid socializer. She attended the breakfasts, the dinner parties, and the balls, but only rarely put a fork to her mouth. In contrast, Devon continued to enjoy the hearty breakfasts that had been her custom since childhood.

"I wonder how she can stand to sit here and watch you eat waffles while she just drinks black coffee," Francesca remarked.

"She's a stronger woman than I." Devon chuckled.

Francesca picked up a blueberry muffin from the bread basket on the table and began to nibble on it. "You know," she ventured, "Kelly Majors doesn't believe me when I say we should worry about Carte Blanche."

Devon raised her eyebrows inquiringly, waiting for Francesca to continue.

"I think that colt is a threat."

"Kelly's been good for us. He's won a lot of races over the past year."

"He's too sure of himself."

A merry peal of laughter escaped from Devon. "Occupational hazard!"

Francesca smiled and looked down. "I guess so," she admitted. "But Jeremiah doesn't think I'm crazy."

Devon's expression grew serious. "Maybe I'd better take another look at Carte Blanche's stats."

"Isn't it too late? The race is tomorrow."

"It's never too late to change your strategy. Not until the horses are led to the starting gate." Devon threw down her napkin and stood up brusquely. She was wearing a pair of crisp black linen slacks and a black-and-white-striped cotton shirt, suitable enough for the paddock, she decided. She picked up a canvas bag and headed toward the ladies' room, where she would change from black patent leather sandals to ankle-high riding boots.

Francesca followed her mother, a second blueberry muffin clutched in her hand. "Are you going down there now?" she asked.

"Yes. Why?"

"Uncle John was supposed to meet me here this morning. Don't you want to wait?"

Devon hesitated for a moment. Then she remembered Mason's

remarks about her obvious feelings for John. She pushed open the door to the ladies' lounge and went over to a red-and-white-striped sofa. She changed her shoes quickly, then stood up. "I don't have time this morning, dear. Besides, John is here to see you, not me."

Francesca smiled slyly. "Whatever you say, Mom."

CHAPTER 61

FRANCESCA twirled in front of the quaint cheval glass, reveling in the unfamiliar image before her. Was that really she? Were her cheekbones really so pronounced, her green eyes so exotic and slanting, her skin so glossy and tanned? When had her skinny figure developed this hourglass shape? She was still lean, of course, but she had full breasts and a small, provocatively rounded rear end whose shape was subtly hinted at in the white halter-topped gown she wore. Her lively black curls were stylishly swept into a French twist, making her look at least twenty! And she was to attend her very first ball — a real ball, not an afternoon cotillion!

To think she had hated the dress when Laurel had shown it to her! It was deceptively simple on the hanger; its skirt a straight, white sheath of silk moiré with a forest green sash at the waist. It was babyish, she had argued, and unsophisticated. But that wasn't the case at all, she now realized. The square-cut bodice teasingly revealed a hint of cleavage, while the dark sash emphasized her tiny waist and flat stomach. The dress was slit up the back for ease of movement, exposing a flash of her tanned calf with each step she took. A wave of self-confidence surged through her and she raised her chin slightly. She felt beautiful! She couldn't wait for her family to see her. John and Mason would be so surprised. And Jesse! Oh, if he could see her now, he would treat her more seriously. He would realize that she had grown up. That she was just as alluring as the ebony-colored beauty she had seen him with in the park the Sunday before — the daughter of the cook of the Gideon Putnam Hotel. Her name was Lacey.

It had disturbed Francesca, the sight of them together. Lacey had been leaning against a tree. Jesse had been facing her, also leaning against the tree, palms facedown on the trunk. She had stood between his arms, looking up at him with a coy expression, her white teeth a flash in her smooth dark complexion. Francesca had turned away immediately at the sight of them, but not before the summer breeze carried to her the sound of the girl's laughter. In those few lilting notes, Francesca had discerned an adult tone of suggestiveness. Suggestiveness that hinted at embraces in the dark, at bodies fused together in secret acts of intimacy. And the sound of it had stricken Francesca with desire and jealousy.

To make matters worse, Jesse had almost ignored her since she had started working with Jeremiah at the end of June. They had gone riding on a few occasions, but Jesse seemed never to have the time to linger over a picnic and a swim. In addition, Francesca's own work schedule allowed her far less leisure than in summers past.

Jesse had grown even more remote after their arrival in Saratoga three weeks ago. Francesca had at first been puzzled. But after seeing him in the park, she suspected that he had wasted no time in beginning his summer romance with Lacey. As a result, he spent none of his time off with Francesca. And she was lonely for him, both as a friend and . . . she wasn't quite sure what else. She only knew that she missed their time together.

Sometimes when she was in bed late at night, she wondered what it would be like to touch the muscles that rippled across his back. She wondered what it would feel like if his strong arms were to pull her to him and wrap themselves around her. Such thoughts were profoundly arousing to her. So arousing that she had begun to feel a strange flutter in her stomach whenever she saw Jesse.

Now, for the first time in her life, she had the conviction that she, too, could arouse that kind of desire. She suddenly remembered the day in the beginning of the summer when she and Jesse had gone swimming. For a fleeting moment she had thought he had been attracted to her. But she could not be sure. Since then, she had seen no such emotion on his part. And, of course, she could tell no one about her feelings for him. Somehow, though, that knowledge just sharpened the tang of her desire.

With a sigh, she turned away from the mirror. She looked at the white lace shawl on the bed, carefully laid out for her by her mother's maid. She knew that Laurel would insist that she wear it. But it would cover the beautiful dress. Ignoring it, Francesca headed down the stairs.

Francesca did not, of course, see Jesse that evening. But she saw Kelly Majors, and that was almost as gratifying.

The arrogant young jockey's mouth dropped open at the sight of Francesca in the lobby of the Gideon Putnam Hotel. He quickly recovered his composure when he saw that she was closely followed by her mother and Mason Wilder. Hurrying over to them, he greeted his employer and her escort politely while sneaking glances at Francesca. He had not realized that she could look so . . . so . . . *adult*. He found himself stumbling over his words as he tried to make small talk with the trio. Then, much too soon, he was forced to depart to meet his date. But he would remember how Francesca had looked that night.

And Francesca would remember the look on Kelly's face. His face and the faces of all her other acquaintances. Oh, it had been heady to be surrounded by admirers! To dance every dance with a different boy. To have college boys treat her as though she were their age; to have boys her age tongue-tied with self-consciousness and a desire to please. Now she understood the self-assurance of the kittenish blond Marina Witherspoon, a classmate of hers in Washington. She could suddenly understand why her girlfriends talked about nothing but boys. It was intriguing to wield the power of sexuality. What had eluded her throughout her adolescence had suddenly been presented to her like the combination to a secret vault of riches.

The enchantment did not end that evening. The next morning, Kelly's attitude toward her was entirely different. He didn't ignore her or make fun of her comments. He listened to her. He followed her with his eyes. He flirted with her. And Francesca flirted back. Flirted with extra vivacity when Jesse was near. Made sure that her laugh contained that suggestive note that she had found so haunting coming from Lacey.

"What's wrong with you today?" Jesse asked when they were alone in the stable for a few moments. His voice was filled with irritation.

"What do you mean?" she asked coyly.

Jesse rolled his eyes and faced her squarely, hands on his hips. "I mean, you're giggling and carrying on and acting like a . . . a . . ." He shrugged and made a dismissive gesture with his hand. "I don't know."

"Well," Francesca said haughtily, "I certainly don't know either."

"Ah, get off your high horse, Frankie. And stop fooling around. We've got a lot to do today."

"Oh, well, excuse me, *sir.*" Sarcasm dripped from her voice. "I didn't mean to hold up your important work."

Jesse gave her a look of disgust and turned to walk away.

"Wait a minute!" Francesca cried imperiously. "I have something to say to you."

Jesse stopped in his tracks, his back tensed in an attitude of annoyance. He did not turn to face her.

"From now on," Francesca said to the back of his head, "I want you to call me Francesca. I'm not Frankie anymore!"

CHAPTER 62

"LOOKS like you were right about Carte Blanche," Jeremiah told Francesca the following morning. The French colt had beaten Roll the Dice in a surprise victory that had been a windfall for those who had betted on him.

The foursome — Jeremiah, Jesse, Kelly, and Francesca — were lined up along the white rail fence watching the morning exercise. Their focus was on Devon, who was riding Roll the Dice. When an investment as large as that one failed a crucial test, the mistress of Willowbrook wanted to see for herself why.

"I thought that race was mine." Kelly sighed and rubbed his hand across his chin. "We were ahead by a couple of lengths right from the start."

"Yeah, and Carte Blanche really fell behind. I figured right then that he was done for," grumbled Jesse.

Jeremiah looked down at the *Racing Form* he held in his hand. He read aloud once again from the article that described in torturous detail how Carte Blanche had humiliated Roll the Dice. " 'Carte Blanche had fallen behind at least ten lengths, and just when it looked as though the race was going to Roll the Dice, the French colt charged ahead. "That horse went by me so fast, I thought it was a bullet," said jockey Willy Shoemaker, riding Gallant Man.' "

"Shit, why'd he have to say that!" Kelly moaned.

"Because it happened," said Francesca. "At least Gallant Man placed."

Kelly put his hand to his forehead in frustration. "I don't know what happened!"

In response, Jeremiah read aloud, " 'By the final fifty yards, Carte Blanche jockey Benito Rodriguez knew he had won. He looked over his shoulder and saw no competition. So the French unknown galloped to one of the most —' "

The group groaned in unison, interrupting Jeremiah just as Devon pulled up alongside of them. "Reading the *Racing Form*, I see," she said dolefully.

"You got it," said Jeremiah with a shake of his head. "Any ideas now that you've taken him around the track?"

"Yes. I think he may be a sprinter. That race could have just been too long yesterday."

"That's what I was afraid of," said Jeremiah, sighing, "but I didn't want to say anything until you'd had a chance to ride him. On the other hand, it could be that he backs down when he's faced with competition. He's always been out so far ahead of the others that we haven't seen that in the past."

"That hasn't shown up in his workouts, though. And he's run long in practices," Francesca pointed out.

"Horses seem to feel the difference between a workout and a race," said Jeremiah.

"Well, those are two different possibilities and both can be dealt with, but first we'll need to isolate the real problem," said Devon.

Jeremiah turned to his son. "Jesse, maybe you could spend the next couple of days working this out with Francesca's help. I've got to concentrate on preparing Willow the Wisp for Saturday's race." It was common among racehorse owners to include reference to either ownership or parentage in the names of their stock. Thus, for those in racing circles, Devon's pun on the phrase *will-o'-the-wisp* signified that the filly was Willowbrook stock.

"I want to see the condition book for the races next week," Devon said to Jeremiah. "We may want to shuffle some of our stock around, given this development."

Condition books were written by the racing secretaries of each track. They described the eligibility for entering each race to be held in the near future, usually the upcoming week or two. Entries could be restricted to horses of a certain age, sex, or winning record. The length of each race was also specified in condition books. Then there were maiden races, meaning races for horses that had so far never won. A horse "broke its maiden" when it won its first race.

One secret of Willowbrook's success was that Devon and Jeremiah carefully studied condition books from tracks around the country, then shipped their horses to competitions accordingly. Their winning record reflected the discrimination with which they selected races. Thus even Willowbrook's least talented horses had above-average winning records. Those that didn't win but had good bloodlines might either be sold or used for breeding.

While Francesca and Jesse returned to the stables, Devon and Jeremiah retired to the trainer's temporary quarters to study the condition book.

As they arrived at the modest white shedrow, Jeremiah indicated that Devon should wait outside. "I'll bring out a couple of chairs. This may be the prettiest racetrack in America, but the quarters are about the same as any other."

Devon chuckled, thinking of his luxurious custom-built home in Virginia. "You're not used to living this way, are you?"

"Every time I go to a track away from home. But that doesn't mean that I like it. And Irma sure doesn't keep house like this." Jeremiah entered the building, then returned a few seconds later carrying two steel-framed kitchen chairs with cushions covered in plastic.

Devon thanked him and sat down. "Speaking of your family, I want to compliment you on Jesse. He's doing a fine job. He has your way with horses."

Jeremiah shook his head and settled into the other chair. "I wish he would take some time off, though, and go to college."

"He doesn't want to?"

"He thinks it's a waste of time. He always points out that I was a success and I didn't have a college education. How can I argue with that?"

"You told me that he gets good grades, though. He wouldn't have any trouble getting into college," Devon remarked.

"He doesn't care about that." Jeremiah swept his hand downward in a gesture of dismissal. "Ah, what's the use with these kids? They'll do what they want to do."

"You could refuse to employ him at Willowbrook unless he finishes his education," Devon pointed out. "It would be entirely your call, you know."

Jeremiah gave her a smile of appreciation. "I know. And his mother would probably like me to do that. But I'm afraid he'll just go somewhere else then."

A cloud passed over Devon's face and she turned in her seat so that she was squarely facing her friend. "He won't get the same opportunities to advance anywhere else. You know that. So does he."

Jeremiah understood Devon's meaning. "The world hasn't changed much since we started in this business, has it? Rosa Parks, the NAACP, none of it has made much difference in how we're treated every day. After I won the Derby, you remember that, of course every white owner wanted me to come work for him. They shook my hand, patted me on the back. Sent me champagne and the like. One even sent me a woman, did I ever tell you that?" Devon shook her head in the negative. "Anyway, they stopped trying after a while. Knew I was loyal to you. Started calling me Devon's boy. Probably still call me that. Whites don't even know why they look down on us, you know. Because we're inferior? I proved I was superior to all of the other jockeys. Do they really think that the color of a man's skin determines what's inside?" Jeremiah's voice was filled with quiet anger. "You're white, you tell me," he demanded.

"I . . . I don't know." Devon was at a loss. She was embarrassed that many of the people who had treated Jeremiah in such a dehumanizing way were her friends. But if she were to eliminate friends on the basis of their racial prejudice, she would have almost none left. What she could do was to provide opportunities for the people who worked for her, without regard to their color. But what was such a small gesture in a world filled with prejudice? It did nothing to change the status quo. Devon said thoughtfully, "Maybe it would change things in this industry, at least a bit, if we could get Jesse an apprenticeship at another farm. He's so gifted —"

"You mean, then your white friends would know that I'm not some fluke? Some mutant nigger who happens to have turned out intelligent? That there's actually two of us in this world, and maybe more?" Jeremiah asked bitterly.

"Jeremiah! You've never sounded like this before. So . . . so cynical."

"Devon, there's not a Negro in America who's not cynical. Unless he's a total fool. You know what my greatest shame is?" Devon shook her head, indicating he should continue. "You remember that night you — a white woman — had to save me from the Klan?"

"But Jeremiah, they didn't even go to your house after they came to mine."

"Because they were scared of you. They had me next on the agenda, only they wouldn't have been as *civilized*" — he spat out the word sarcastically — "with me as they were with you. Your name carries a lot of weight. You've got power. Power to hurt them. I may have money. And I may have a gun, but I've got no power and the pitiful thing is, I don't see things changing for my son."

"I know a little about what you're talking about. Being a woman means always having to prove yourself. Never being taken seriously. Never being given the same chances as a man."

Jeremiah shook his head. "It's not the same thing. Not for a woman born into a family like yours, at any rate."

"No, not exactly," Devon conceded. "But do you think that anyone else would give Francesca a chance to be a jockey? Oh, they'd let her into their country clubs, I'll admit that. But would they hire her? I don't think so."

"Okay, I see your point," Jeremiah admitted. "There's discrimination, although not that same day-to-day humiliation that my boy will have to face."

"I know," Devon said gently, "but you could get more involved in the civil rights movement. Try to change things."

"I can't tell you how much money I've given to the NAACP."

"But that's not all there is to it, is there?"

"No," Jeremiah said quietly. "I guess I just never got around to doing anything. I hope Jesse will be different. So far, though, I haven't seen any sign of that. Maybe we're too protected at Willowbrook. If I read a book, I can talk to you or Irma about it. Exchange opinions. You're not surprised I know how to read. Or by what I read. You treat me with respect. It's only every once in a while that I have to leave our world. And at the track, everyone's pretty nasty to everyone else, regardless of color."

Devon laughed. "That's true."

"So I've got a real conflict. Let Jesse stay at Willowbrook, where he'll be protected, or make him get out in the real world, where he could get hurt. In the real world, maybe there's a chance he can make more of a difference than I have."

"Jeremiah, you sell yourself short!" Devon exclaimed. "You made history as a jockey and you're doing it again as a trainer."

"Hasn't changed anything," he argued.

"You don't really know that. Change might be slow in coming. That doesn't mean it will never come."

"Naw." He turned his mouth down in an expression of firm disbelief. "I'm always going to be just Devon's boy."

CHAPTER 63

FRANCESCA looked flirtatiously at Kelly Majors. "My mother would kill me if she knew I was here with you."

Kelly looked around the ice-cream shop decorated in bright pink and white candy stripes. They were sitting at a white wrought-iron table with matching chairs. Nothing could have appeared more innocent and wholesome. "What's wrong with going for an ice cream?" asked the jockey with a mischievous grin. "We're together every day at the track anyway."

"I know, but it's not the same. My mother wouldn't approve of my going out in the evening with a man in his twenties. I'm supposed to date boys in high school — no older."

Kelly shifted uncomfortably, wondering if this excursion was worth the risk to his job. He hadn't quite realized the import of what he was doing when he suggested that he take Francesca for an ice-cream soda. It was just that ever since the night he had seen her at the ball he had grown increasingly aware of her allure. He couldn't help himself. He was around her every day. Every time she passed by he noticed the blossoming figure underneath her tight-fitting blue jeans and thin cotton shirts. She looked like a woman, not a child. And she acted older than her years in some regards. She was reliable and responsible about her job. Yet she had an innocence about her that he found adorable. The back side of a racetrack was a rough place, and most of the women available to him were the hangers-on that flocked to professional athletes. They were often sexy, good-looking women, but they were anything but innocent.

Kelly studied Francesca now. Her wide green eyes stared back in a frankly inviting way. The only thing was, Kelly wasn't sure if she knew what she was inviting. Suddenly, the precariousness of his position struck him. He took his elbows off the table and sat back in his seat, folding his arms across his chest. "Listen . . ." he said. "I think you're a great kid, but I don't want trouble with your mother."

"Oh, it's fine," Francesca said breezily. "She went out to dinner with Mason, and anyway, I told her I was going over to a friend's house to spend the night."

"Doesn't she check on you?"

"Of course, but I'll be home before she is. I'll just say I didn't feel well and came home early. It'll be fine." Francesca inserted a spoonful of ice-cream soda into her mouth. A bit of the foam stuck to her lip and she flicked it off with her tongue, Kelly following every action intently.

What made it worse for him was that she wasn't dressed in her work clothes. No, just as on the night of the ball, she wore a dress that highlighted her young beauty. The pink linen frock was deceptively simple, but what it did for Francesca's figure could only have been accomplished by a very expensive garment. It gave her an air of both sophistication and extreme femininity. The full calf-length skirt was supported by fluffy petticoats of a darker pink so that every motion of Francesca's made that peculiarly feminine sound that hinted at frilly things underneath. The bodice of the dress hugged her bosom, pushing her breasts together and upward, where a sweetheart neckline emphasized their soft curves. Wide straps of the same material went around Francesca's neck, halter style, so that her black curls tumbled onto the bare skin of her glossy, tanned shoulders. Francesca, who had just begun to wear makeup — her mother only allowed her natural-colored lipstick and mascara — had snuck into Devon's bedroom and applied eyeliner, rouge, and smoky gray eye shadow as well. Having studied Devon for years, she had achieved the same subtle enhancements as her mother did with such skill. To top it off, she had dabbed on her mother's prized Joy perfume — a heady essence of gardenias that floated on the summer evening. She felt very grown-up, and a bit dangerous.

"You look worried," Francesca teased Kelly, feeling a little superior in spite of his advantage in years.

He gave her a wry grin. "I am," he acknowledged.

Francesca just smiled and took another spoonful of her soda.

It was still light when the young couple emerged from the shop some thirty minutes later.

"I guess we'd better be getting you home," said Kelly, looking around nervously to ensure that no one they knew was in the vicinity. He wondered why in the world he had ever thought inviting Francesca out would be a good idea. And how could he walk her home without someone seeing them?

As though reading his mind, Francesca suggested, "Let's cut through the park instead of taking the road."

"But that's not the way to your house."

"No, it's the way to yours. But mine is only a few blocks farther. If anyone sees me coming from the track, they won't think twice."

Kelly grew more comfortable as dusk fell, and as they entered the park, the canopy of trees made it darker still. The summertime music of crickets was the only sound that broke the quiet of the twilight.

Francesca and Kelly walked side by side in silence. "Look!" whispered Francesca. "The bridle trail. If we go back this way, we'll be certain not to be seen."

"Hey, that's a good idea!" said Kelly. His natural exuberance returning, he reached for Francesca's hand and led her onto the narrow path.

As they walked along the path, Francesca studied Kelly's animated face. It was not exactly handsome; rather, it had a somewhat rakish appearance. Dimples on either side of his mobile mouth flashed when he spoke. His blue eyes, fringed with long black lashes, bespoke arrogance, mischief, and daring. His thick dark hair, fashionably combed back from his forehead, was a silky helmet. He looked every bit the brash young athlete. Francesca wondered if she was truly attracted to him or simply thrilled with the idea that a twenty-four-year-old man was attracted to her.

"This was nice tonight," Kelly said softly, "but I don't think we'd better do it again."

Francesca was hurt. Suddenly she felt like the same gawky child of a year before. She wondered if Kelly thought her ugly.

"Hey!" he said softly. "Don't look so down. If you weren't sixteen, I'd go for you in a minute!"

"I . . . I wonder if anyone will ever like me enough to want to go steady with me," Francesca confessed.

"Sure they will," Kelly reassured her, squeezing her hand. "You're a gorgeous-looking girl."

Francesca stopped and turned toward him, her eyes filled with doubt. "You really think so?" she breathed.

"I wouldn't say it if I didn't."

Francesca blushed and turned back to the path, her eyes cast down at the mossy forest floor. A few moments later, they emerged near the white fence that marked the backside of the racetrack, then progressed to the stables.

When they were in the darkness of the barn, Kelly faced Francesca and took both her hands in his. "Stay out of trouble, kid," he whispered, giving her a light kiss on the mouth.

Francesca felt a spark go through her at the touch of his lips. She had never kissed a boy this old before! She tingled at the adventure of it. She put her smooth bare arms around his neck and returned his kiss the way she had seen people do in movies.

"Hold on a minute!" said Kelly breathlessly, pulling her arms from around his neck. He pushed her against the side of a stall and held her there, his arms stronger than they looked. "You shouldn't do things like that unless you really do want trouble," he chided her gently.

Francesca smiled wickedly. "What do you mean?"

"I mean," he said, not releasing her arms, "you shouldn't kiss a guy like that unless you want more than a kiss."

"What makes you think I don't?" she asked suggestively.

Kelly laughed, white teeth flashing in the dark. "You don't even know what you're talking about, kid. And that's the most dangerous thing of all."

Francesca felt the perverse desire to exercise her new feminine power, and she leaned toward him, struggling against his arms.

"You stay where you are!" Kelly warned in mock anger.

Then, suddenly, there was a flurry in the shadows and an explosion of noise. A yell in the dark, and the little man was wrenched away from her. A confusion of motion, dark and light bodies intermingled, then the sound of flesh hitting flesh.

Moving instinctively, Francesca picked up a nearby bucket. It was empty and she drew back her arm, prepared to slam the metal object into the interloper. Just then, she saw that the intruder was Jesse.

"Jesse!" she yelled.

"Run, Frankie! Run!" he gasped as he wrestled the smaller man to the floor.

"What're you doing, you asshole!" yelled Kelly, wriggling to set himself free from the muscular teenager. He wasn't about to risk hurting his hands — his livelihood — by punching Jesse.

"Jesse, get off of him! Let him go!" Francesca reached into the melee and grabbed the back of the black man's shirt.

Jesse whirled and shook her off. "I'll teach him!"

Francesca lunged for Jesse's arm, pulling him off Kelly. "He didn't do anything, Jesse, leave him alone!"

Kelly used the brief pause to wrench himself from Jesse's grasp. He staggered to his feet and began to brush off his clothes.

"You crazy jackass! What'd you think you were doing?" Kelly angrily demanded.

Jesse looked from Francesca to Kelly, suddenly realizing that his rescue had been anything but welcome. "I . . . I thought you were hurting her," he explained.

"Of course not!" Francesca said, as if the idea were the most ridiculous in the world.

"Well," grumbled Jesse, "it looked like you were forcing her."

"On the contrary!" said Kelly, with a tongue-in-cheek grin. His natural good humor was ebbing back and he began to chuckle at the situation.

Jesse, furiously embarrassed, looked appealingly at Francesca, who also began to smile. "I'm sorry. It looked like he was holding you down."

"She's bigger than me!" cried Kelly, at which the three of them began to laugh.

"And probably stronger, too," said Jesse. As the laughter faded, he looked down at the dirt floor and shuffled his feet. "I'm sorry if I . . . interrupted," he said sheepishly.

"No need to apologize further; you rescued me just in time," Kelly remarked with another grin.

Jesse turned to Francesca. "Does your mother know you're out with him?"

Francesca blushed, but she lifted her chin defiantly. "No. I'm sixteen. I'm old enough to do what I like."

Jesse gave her a look of exasperation. "No, you're not. And your mother would kill you if she knew you were out with a guy eight years older!"

Francesca was annoyed that his words so closely replicated her own words to Kelly earlier in the evening. She put her hands on her hips. "That's none of your business!" she cried.

"I've known you all your life! I know your mother's rules," he countered.

The two glared at each other for a few seconds before Kelly broke in. "Calm down, you two. Francesca, you already said pretty much the same thing earlier and you know it's true." He glanced at his wristwatch. "Jesse, Mrs. Somerset-Smith will probably think nothing of it if she sees you walking Francesca home. Why don't you two get a move on. I'd feel better knowing Francesca wasn't walking around by herself."

Without a glance at Francesca, Jesse began to march brusquely in the direction of the path. When he had gone about twenty feet, he turned to see Francesca still glaring at him. "Coming?" he asked.

"Go on," whispered Kelly, at which Francesca began to move reluctantly forward.

Jesse turned again and continued walking.

Annoyed, Francesca called out to him, "I am not going to run to keep up with you."

Jesse stopped, but did not turn. He stayed where he was until Francesca caught up to him. "You want to cut across the track or go around?" He looked pointedly at her high-heeled white sandals.

Following his glance, Francesca tightened her lips. She bent down and removed her sandals. "We'll cut across," she said stiffly. "No use taking the long way."

They walked along in silence a few moments; then, as if he could contain himself no longer, Jesse burst out, "What the heck were you thinking about, going out with a guy his age!"

"What difference does it make to you who I go out with?" Francesca snapped. She didn't like being chided.

Jesse stuffed his hands into the pockets of his chinos and curled them into tight balls. He remained silent. How could he answer Francesca? He would never admit that it made him sick with jealousy to see another man kiss her.

"Answer me!" cried Francesca, pinching his upper arm to get his attention.

"Ouch!" Jesse yanked his arm away from her. "Don't do that!"

"Well, answer then! Why do you care who I go out with?"

"Because we've been friends a long time. Because I know your mom wouldn't like you going out with a guy so much older. Because

Majors is a playboy. He's got women — grown women, not little girls like you — all over him."

Francesca stopped in her tracks and faced him. "Take a good look at me!" she demanded. "I'm not a little girl anymore. I'm as pretty as anyone!"

Jesse stared at Francesca. The night breeze ruffled her dark curls and caused her long skirt to waft about her legs. Her young, full breasts pushed against the thin cloth of her dress. She was a bewitching sight. And she looked every inch a woman. Jesse's eyes filled with longing, and as Francesca's eyes met his she recognized for the first time the emotion he felt for her.

Francesca took one step closer to him. She was so close she could feel the heat rising from his body. So close that, even though it was dark, she could see the fear in his eyes.

Keeping his eyes locked on hers, Jesse backed away from her. "I . . . can't . . ." He enunciated slowly, shaking his head in the negative to underline his words.

But his body was like a magnet pulling her closer. "Why not?" she said hoarsely.

Jesse could smell her perfume, intoxicating as it mixed with the natural scent of her young body. He could see the dark shadow of her cleavage. Could hear the rustling of her petticoats. His senses were assailed and he felt his strength seeping from him. He looked into Francesca's wide green eyes and saw the desire there. Her lips were moist and waiting. She wanted him. Every fiber of her body was telling Jesse that she wanted him.

Jesse stretched his arm forward as though to touch her, then instantly withdrew it. Francesca could see that he was panting, like a man who had run a long way. A thin sheen of sweat covered his dusky features. She could smell the maleness of him, and it was like an aphrodisiac. She couldn't stop herself from moving toward him again.

Jesse stood hypnotized, unable even to breathe. His emotions were in chaos. Terror, excruciating desire, love, and loyalty collided in him. He wanted to run, but he stood rooted to the spot. He wanted to touch her, but he didn't dare. She was so close now, looking straight into his eyes. Her lips just inches from his. Her breasts almost touching his chest.

The two young people stood like statues, frozen in time and space, oblivious to their surroundings. Then, in slow motion, Francesca tentatively lifted one trembling hand and placed it on Jesse's chest.

Her touched seared him. He lost all will, all ability to measure his actions. And with a moan, he surrendered to his furious desire, enclosing her in his powerful arms.

Francesca slid her arms around his small waist. Through the thin cloth of his polo shirt she could feel the smooth muscles of his broad back, the hardness of his torso. He towered over her, engulfed her. She was fused to him and when he kissed her she felt as though she were becoming part of him.

"Oh, God, Frankie!" he said thickly. He buried his face in her hair. "I've been dreaming of this," he said, holding her tighter still. His lips once again sought hers.

Desire surged through Francesca's body. She was moist and hot, yet she shook with emotion. His kiss was even sweeter than in her fantasies, his body even more enticing, the feel of him even more arousing. She leaned against him for support, dizzy with the feeling that swept her. "I love you, Jesse," she said huskily.

The words were like a gunshot blasting him back to reality. Alarmed, Jesse dropped his arms and backed away from Francesca. "Don't say that, Francesca, not ever!" he said vehemently.

Francesca felt as though the wind had been knocked out of her, so surprised was she at his reaction. "Why not?"

Jesse cradled his forehead in his hand. He was shaking with emotion. "This is such a mess. I'm so sorry!"

"Sorry about what?"

Jesse raised his head and stared at Francesca.

The young woman looked at him blankly. "Why are you looking at me so strangely?" she asked.

"Francesca, you don't seem to understand. We just can't do this!" Jesse's voice was filled with despair.

Francesca took a step toward Jesse and took his hand in hers. "But I love —"

"No!" Jesse hastily snatched his hand back, frustrated that Francesca refused to understand what he was saying. "Our families would kill us if they knew about this!"

"But . . . we could keep it secret." Francesca's green eyes were wide with the faith of the innocent. "And as soon as I'm old enough, we can be married!" She wanted to make him understand that she could face anything — for him.

Jesse gasped in disbelief. "Married! We could never be married!" How could she even talk about something so outrageous! Didn't she understand that people would hate them just for being together? In a sudden panic, he looked over each shoulder, petrified lest they be observed.

"Oh, Jesse!" said Francesca, pleading. "Don't you see that the world is changing? One day, no one will even look twice at a marriage between a Negro and a white woman."

But his face was closed, unapproachable.

"Changing! It's not changing fast enough to do us any good," he insisted fiercely. "Do you remember the night those men came for my father because he fired that white jockey?"

"That's just it, though. They *didn't* do anything to him. They came to Mother first. And she sent them all home," Francesca said, certain that happy endings really happened.

"Francesca, you just don't get it! If anyone knew that I'd touched you — that I'd even had these thoughts about you — nobody would stop them from lynching me! And your mother might be leading the pack!"

Francesca drew back from him, bristling. "That's vile of you to say. You know it's not true!"

"The hell I do!" Jesse argued heatedly.

But the hurt look on Francesca's face melted his heart. "Look," he explained more gently, "this can never work. We wouldn't fit in anywhere in the world, you know."

Tears streamed down Francesca's face as she said, "There must be someplace . . ."

Jesse ached to pull Francesca back into his arms, but didn't dare. He smiled sadly. "Heaven. Only in heaven."

Francesca hung her head, trying to control her tears. Jesse watched her helplessly. He started to lift his hand. No, he couldn't. Because if he touched her again, he might not have the strength to let her go. He shoved his hands into his pockets. "Look at me, Frankie," he said, his voice thick with longing.

Slowly, she raised her head. He stared at her, drinking in every detail of her face and body so that he could savor the memory of it later. Her lashes were wet with tears, her lips moist and swollen from his kisses, and her eyes . . . her eyes brimmed over with love for him.

Seeing her this way, so vulnerable yet so inviting, he knew he could never allow himself to be alone with her again. He took one step backward, then another. Tears stung his eyelids. "I've got to go," he said, almost choking on the words.

"Jesse," Francesca cried, her voice broken, "wait!"

Jesse turned away from her. Then he looked back.

"Don't go!" she pleaded, reaching out for him. But she grasped at air. All that was left of Jesse was the sound of his feet pounding as he fled into the night.

CHAPTER 64

"DAD, I need to talk to you," said Jesse, letting the flimsy screen door slam shut behind him as he entered his father's racetrack shedrow.

Jeremiah looked up from the condition book he was studying at the table of the kitchenette and indicated with a nod of his head that his son should be seated.

Jesse pulled out a worn chair and sat down. "I've been thinking . . ." said the younger man.

Jeremiah, curious, leaned forward and waited for Jesse to continue.

"About college. If you'd still like me to go, then I'm going to apply to Howard University."

Jeremiah raised his eyebrows. This was the last thing he'd expected to hear from Jesse. "That would certainly make your mother proud," Jeremiah said cautiously, "but why this change of heart?"

Jesse dropped his eyes, unable to meet the probing gaze of his father. He was afraid his eyes would betray the story of the night before. He shrugged. "I'd like to get my degree as soon as possible," Jesse said. "Maybe start this fall."

"But that's only a couple of weeks away. You haven't even applied."

"I could go home today. Maybe drive into Washington tomorrow. Try to talk them into taking me. I've got good grades. And . . . well, it wouldn't hurt that I'm your son."

"But I thought you wanted to work at Willowbrook," said Jeremiah, puzzled.

"I'd rather go to college. After I graduate, I'll have my whole life to work at Willowbrook," said Jesse.

Jeremiah sat back in his seat and studied Jesse. Still, the younger man did not lift his gaze to his father's. Finally, Jeremiah spoke. "What's troubling you, son?"

Jesse jumped up from his chair and slapped his hands against his thighs in exasperation. "Why does something have to be wrong? This is what you've been wanting. Well, now you've got it. I thought it would make you happy!"

"Sit down, Jesse," said Jeremiah coolly. When his son had obeyed, Jeremiah continued. "This sudden interest in college must mean that you've taken an interest in a particular field. What will your major be?"

Jesse looked at his father in confusion. "My . . . major?"

"Yes. Your main interest at college. Most people have an idea of what they'd like to study when they decide to apply to college, though I'll admit that most people also probably change their minds."

"I'm not sure," Jesse mumbled.

"Well, then, why Howard University? Why not Tuskegee or some other place?"

"I don't know. Howard's close."

Jeremiah was silent. Jesse shifted on the noisy plastic of the chair as the silence grew uncomfortably long.

"I have a feeling . . ." Jeremiah began, then let the sentence drift away as he became lost in thought.

"What?" Jesse asked apprehensively.

"You're not going to college to try to find something, you're just trying to get away from something. I'd like to know what that something is."

Jesse's head shot up and his lips tightened in an attitude of determination. His brown eyes met his father's unflinchingly. Suddenly, the awkward boy seemed transformed into an adult. "I can't say any more than I have. I'm leaving no trouble. You have a right to know that. If you're willing to help me with college, I'd like for you to do it. I'll do my best to see that your money's not wasted. If you don't want to pay for it then . . ." Jesse shrugged in such a way as to indicate that he was prepared to find his own solutions.

Jeremiah could see that Jesse meant what he said about offering no further explanations. And he realized that this was a crucial moment in their relationship. Would he trust his son's judgment, or would he refuse to give him what he was asking for without more insight into the reasons for the request? No, he decided, he trusted his son to do the right thing. And though he would have liked his son to confide in him, he admired his strength in keeping his troubles — if troubles they were — to himself.

"Well, like I said, your mother will be very happy to hear this. And I guess that I'm pleased, too. If going to college is what you want, then I'm proud to be able to send you."

CHAPTER 65

"JOHN, stop nagging me, I don't know what's wrong with her!" cried Devon in exasperation.

John, lost in thought, jabbed at logs in the fireplace. It was the first fire of the season, it being slightly brisk this October evening. It was also John's first fire in his newly purchased Georgetown home, a charming New Orleans–style town house tucked into a cobblestoned mew. He and Mason were neighbors now. More important, John could keep in closer touch with Francesca, who had chosen for her senior year to board at her girl's school in Washington rather than commute more than an hour in each direction. The decision had puzzled Devon somewhat, as she could not believe that Francesca would voluntarily give up the opportunity to ride each afternoon. Nor had the girl ever before shown a willingness to board at her school. In fact, the contrary was true. But Francesca had used two compelling arguments to persuade her mother. First, that the commute was tiring. Second, that it was easier to study at school, away from the distractions of Willowbrook and with all the resources of the library, teachers, and study partners close at hand. Devon could think of no reason not to give in, though she knew she would miss her daughter.

"Francesca hasn't been the same since Saratoga," commented Mason. Despite his preoccupation with Francesca, he couldn't help but let his eyes wander about the room, admiring the decor of John's cozy library. Everything about the little house was harmonious, yet more stylish than one might have expected of a man living alone. The walls of the room were painted the color of whipped butter — cheerful but soft — and accented with bright white chair rails and ceiling molding. Four cleverly situated alcoves housed bookshelves and window seats built into bay windows. A huge mahogany desk with leather insets dominated one end of the room, while a pleasant sitting area dominated the other.

Mason and Devon were comfortably ensconced in a down-filled sofa covered in rich stripes of rust, navy, and pale yellow, while John paced in front of the white marble fireplace, taking occasional pokes at the smoldering logs.

"She won't tell me what's wrong! She keeps saying it's nothing, but I can't believe that," said John, shaking his head.

"Maybe she has her mind on a boy." Mason chuckled.

"It's not a boy," Devon said dismissively. "She's never been quite like this before. She seems depressed and preoccupied. Even Mother can't get anything out of her, and you know how close they are."

"Well, she'll be visiting this weekend," said John. "I'll try once more to get to the bottom of this."

"If that doesn't work, I don't know what will," murmured Devon. It was surprising to realize that Francesca confided more in John than in any other adult, including herself. When had John developed a paternal nature? How was it that a sixteen-year-old girl felt more comfortable discussing her life with a man not her father than with her own mother? Devon sighed and stared into the fire. After a few seconds, she shifted her gaze back to John. His face wore a pensive, worried expression. Had anyone told her twenty years before that John would be so preoccupied by the depression of a sixteen-year-old, she would not have believed it. His main priority had been to enjoy life. He had shown little concern for the worries of others. What had changed him? Devon wondered. The war? Francesca?

Then suddenly she thought of the photograph she had seen of him the week before in a gossip column. John leaning over a beautiful blonde thirty years his junior at a New York night spot. The caption had read "Statesman John Alexander not so neutral on Swiss beauty." The piece had gone on to disclose rumors of an affair between John and the Swiss actress, who was in the process of divorcing her second husband.

Devon could see how the Swiss beauty, though so much younger than John, would find him attractive. Terribly attractive. He was sixty-two years old, yet he was as handsome and vigorous as ever. As is Mason, Devon hastily added, feeling disloyal.

"Devon! Didn't you hear me? Time to go in to dinner," Mason said, the loudness of his tone indicating that this was not the first time he had addressed her.

Devon looked up with a start to see both men standing above her, hands outstretched, ready to escort her in to dinner. You're a lucky old girl, Devon thought to herself.

She gathered up her black taffeta skirt and walked with the men into the dining room. "You've done a beautiful job with this house, John," she complimented him.

As John held her chair for her, Devon looked about the spectacularly dramatic dining room. Its most prominent feature was a black and white marble floor set in a diagonal checkerboard pattern. The walls were painted a gunmetal gray marbled with subtle hints of burgundy and silver. A massive burled walnut table in the style of Charles X was centered under an exquisitely wrought crystal chandelier. Color was provided by the burgundy moiré upholstery of the chairs, whose backs curved like sleighs. Fluted columns, also painted gunmetal, marked the entry to the room. Providing an accent to each column was a spiral juniper tree in a white planter shaped like a Grecian urn. Like the library, the dining room featured alcoves; in fact, it was almost hexagonal in shape. In each strategically lit alcove was an interesting piece of furniture or an objet d'art. Devon wondered with a stab of jealousy which woman in John's life had contributed to the house's imaginative interior design.

She turned her attention back to Mason, who was saying to John, "You don't think there'll be any serious opposition to the nomination, do you?"

"I'm just not certain I want it, Mason. I've been away from this country enough in the past twenty years. It's time to settle down," John said, with an involuntary glance at Devon.

"But a U.S. ambassadorship is a great honor, and Belgium has always been a pivotal country in European politics!" Mason protested. "As far as the newspaper is concerned, we're prepared to officially back the nomination. You've got the personal and professional background to make something of the post, John."

"All right, all right, I admit that it's hard to turn down such an honor." John laughed, elevating his hands palm outward in front of him as though to ward off any further argument from Mason. Then, growing more serious, he said, "But I don't know if my heart would be in it. I've just bought this place. Started to enjoy having a home again. After traveling so much for so many years, it's nice to do nothing more than go back and forth between New York and Washington."

"You, tired of travel?" Devon exclaimed. "I never thought I would see the day!"

John looked into Devon's eyes. For a moment both relived memories of their tense final years together. Years when John had insisted that travel — to Paris, London, Monte Carlo, Newport, San Simeon, Palm Beach — was essential to his happiness. Now John smiled wearily at Devon. "Even the most delightful pastimes can grow tiring if one does them every day," he said quietly.

Mason broke in. "But you've got a great deal to contribute. You're one of the best negotiators this country has ever had. And, God knows, things have been tense with the Soviets. We need someone in Europe who's negotiated with them before, like you did during the war."

"Are you trying to get rid of me?" John asked in a teasing tone, trying to lighten the conversation. But the remark had the opposite effect. There was a moment of awkward silence in the room as all three realized that the joke might contain some truth.

Devon looked away from the men. Mason, opposite her, let out a great guffaw to hide his embarrassment. John joined in, relieved that the silence had been broken. He had spoken without thinking, and was ashamed for having accused his friend in such a way. After all, even if it was true, Mason had been involved with Devon when John had reentered her life. John knew he had no claim on her.

"Seriously, though, I've of course told the president that I would accept if that is what he wants." John went on to clarify his remark. "What he *truly* wants, not what he feels obliged to offer."

"I think you fulfill the unique requirements of being both politically acceptable as well as diplomatically experienced," Mason avowed.

John smiled wryly. "Well, we'll see what the Senate committee has to say. I think it's out of my hands at this point."

"All right, I can take a hint," Mason said, still laughing. "I'll drop the subject."

In bed later, cradling Devon in his arms, Mason confessed, "In a way, I would like him to be out of our lives."

Devon lifted her head from his shoulder and propped herself on one elbow. It was dark, but the moonlight created stripes of silvery white on their bodies as it filtered through the window. She smiled and kissed him tenderly. She felt relaxed and contented, as she always did when they made love. "We've discussed this. He's no threat to you," Devon said, not bothering to pretend she did not know of whom he spoke.

"Yes, he is," Mason said simply. "But, dammit all, I like the man immensely. Respect him, too. The three of us get on so well that it's always a pleasure to spend an evening together. And yet . . ."

"I know," Devon said softly.

"Have you been considering my proposal?" Mason asked, pulling Devon back down so that her head rested on his shoulder.

"Yes. Do you really intend to end our relationship if I say no?" she asked seriously.

"I have to, Devon. It's a matter of self-preservation. Self-respect, too. I'm not a young man. I want a wife and, frankly, a companion for my old age. I want the woman I love beside me when I die. But if you won't marry me, I'll have to settle for something less." He was silent for a few seconds, then continued thoughtfully, "Or perhaps not. I used to think a great love only happened once. I no longer believe that. Perhaps there is still time for me to find a woman I love who will also fall in love with me."

Again Devon lifted her upper body so she could look directly at Mason. "If you truly believe you can find love elsewhere, Mason, you owe it to yourself to do it."

Devon saw a glint of white as Mason smiled. "I have found love, Devon."

She looked down at his broad chest, twirling one of his wiry gray hairs around her finger. "You know what I mean. I don't think I can offer you the kind of love you deserve."

Mason sighed. "My weakness is that I want you anyhow. Because although I believe I could love somebody else, I don't think I could ever regard anyone, man or woman, as highly as I do you, Devon."

"I feel very honored that you think of me in that way. I'm not sure I deserve it."

"If you didn't, I would know it by now. We've been together many years. I'm hardly a pushover. And I'm not blinded by love. My love for you is an outgrowth of my admiration and respect, not the other way around."

Devon was immeasurably touched by his words. Her eyes filled with tears as she regarded him, so dear to her. "Mason, I can't marry you."

Devon saw his eyelids close. He was silent for so long that Devon thought perhaps he had gone to sleep. She wondered if he was deliberately ignoring her, or if he was simply too hurt to speak. Suddenly she felt awkward and out of place in his bed. She felt compelled to return to the guest room, and as quietly as though he were indeed asleep, she pushed back the covers and began to ease out of the bed. But his strong hand slid across the linen sheet and grasped her wrist.

"No," he whispered huskily, "please stay."

Devon hesitated. "I —"

"Please," he said, but his tone was more one of command than supplication.

Devon lifted her legs back into the bed and covered herself. Mason moved over so that he was on top of her, and she was surprised to find that he was once more ready to make love. Mason made use of Devon's body with a fervor he had never before shown. For Devon, it was an oddly impersonal act, yet exciting for its very novelty. She found herself responding with a passion to match his own. They made love for a much longer time than usual, and when it was over, Mason pulled Devon to his side and wrapped his arms around her, clearly willing her to stay with him until morning. They knew it was the last time they would ever be together.

CHAPTER 66

"I CAN'T believe that's our son graduating from college." Jeremiah squeezed his wife Irma's hand as Jesse's name was called.

Jesse, who had not known his direction upon entering college, had graduated in the top ten percent of his class, attending school even during the summer to cut his four-year program to three. And he would enter law school in the fall.

"*I* can't believe the wedding's just two weeks away," Irma said, dabbing her eyes with a handkerchief. For Jesse had also found love. His fiancée, Céline Thibault, was the daughter of a Haitian immigrant, a baker who had taken his life savings of seven hundred dollars and transformed it into the second-largest chain of bakeries in the Washington area.

"Inconvenient time they picked for a wedding," Jeremiah teased. The Preakness was the following week, and a colt trained by Jeremiah would be the Willowbrook entry.

Irma glared at him in mock anger. "You should be ashamed! Your only son graduates from college and gets married, all at the same time, and you can't think of anything but that race!"

"Well, *you* can't think of anything but that wedding!" Jeremiah laughed and shook his head. He turned his eyes back to the stage and said, "Anyhow, I wish Jesse had been there for the Derby. That was a beautiful win!"

Jesse had avoided Willowbrook for three years, and had avoided the Derby on the grounds that he was studying for final exams. It wasn't that he was afraid to see Frankie again, he insisted to himself. He didn't love her anymore. He loved Céline, wanted to spend his life with her. And he only rarely thought of Francesca. Almost never, in fact.

Still, he felt apprehensive about seeing her the following week at the Preakness. But he had to be there for his father. So he would go. And keep Céline close by his side.

CHAPTER 67

"I'M ready to race and Kelly's been ill. How can you think he'd be better than me?" Francesca stomped her booted foot on the old planks of the stable office.

"We'll have none of that, young lady!" said Devon firmly. "Jeremiah has said that Kelly will ride in the Preakness, so that's the way it's going to be."

"You're the owner! You have something to say about this too!" cried Francesca.

"As an owner I know it would be foolhardy to allow an apprentice to ride in the Preakness. You'll be up against the most experienced jockeys in the country."

"I would have the same experience by now if anyone around here ever let me race!"

"That's not fair, Francesca," Devon said calmly, "we've let you race. And you've done well."

"In races that don't matter!" Francesca moaned.

Devon gave her daughter a sharp look and, with a loud report, closed the cover of the ledger book she had been studying. She carefully replaced her pencil in the top drawer of the oak desk. Only after she had risen from her seat, gone over to the minirefrigerator, and taken out a Coca-Cola did she speak. Still standing, she turned to face her daughter at the opposite end of the little room. "Every race matters. Don't ever let me hear you say otherwise. Every race means money spent and, hopefully, money earned. This is a business. A business *I* built. You do not presently have the judgment to make the business decisions necessary here. This . . . this *caprice* of yours — wanting to race in the Preakness — could cost me a fortune. It is absolutely out of the question."

"But I know the track at Pimlico as well as Kelly does —"

"Francesca," Devon said firmly, "that is my final word."

Francesca struggled to restrain her anger, knowing that a temper tantrum would only demonstrate her immaturity. Voice shaking with rage, yet quiet, Francesca said, "When do you think I will be ready for an important race?"

"Next year, I think."

Another year! Francesca had spent the last two years of her life working her way up to being a jockey. She rode King of Hearts every day during his training exercises. She opened her mouth to protest, but once again remembered to maintain an even tone. "Have you been watching me ride King of Hearts?"

"I have."

"Do you have any criticism of the job I've been doing?"

Devon was pleased to note the gradual shift in Francesca's attitude. She was no longer demanding. She was behaving like a professional: inquiring about needed areas of improvement. The ambitious young woman's dissatisfaction was still apparent, but her approach to it was far more mature than it had been just moments earlier.

Devon sat down on the leather couch and invited Francesca to sit beside her. "You have the same problem as all good young jockeys. Your bravery is greater than your skill."

"You don't think I have talent?" Francesca exclaimed, her stomach clenched at the possibility of such a verdict.

"I didn't say that," Devon said soothingly. "Talent and skill are not the same thing. You have talent, you have bravery, and you have skill. Just not in equal measures. You need to polish your skills." Devon reflected a moment before continuing. "Come to think of it, maybe there's something we can do about that."

"What?" Francesca asked eagerly.

"So far, you've been primarily involved in the training of our two-year-olds. That is, the focus has been on the horses themselves. I think the next step is for us to shift the focus to you as a jockey. Instead of working with Jeremiah, you should probably be working with Kelly. Work on improving yourself rather than the horses."

"When can I start?" Francesca asked excitedly.

"That's up to Kelly. I don't want it to interfere with his training for the Preakness."

"He's still in bed sick," Francesca said, disappointed.

Devon stood up from the couch and went back to the desk. "Well, the two of you work it out," she said absentmindedly, "and I'll let Jeremiah know."

"Do you think he'll mind losing me as an exercise rider?"

"Oh, you'll still be doing that, too, my dear," said Devon, with a grin, "you'll just have to work twice as many hours from now on."

CHAPTER 68

DEVON felt threatened the moment she saw the soot-covered brick building that housed Johns Hopkins University Hospital. It was forbidding, impersonal, and dark. And Dr. George Donatello's office was no better. Painted an institutional green, the tiny room had obviously been designed for function rather than human warmth. Dr. Donatello was seated behind a scarred oak desk that took up most of the space in the room. Devon occupied an uncomfortable wooden armchair squeezed into the narrow aisle between the desk and a set of battered metal file cabinets. But at this moment her surroundings mattered little. Her entire being focused on Dr. Donatello's words.

"The lump is definitely suspicious," he was saying, his manner one of professional detachment, "but I'm afraid that the only way to give you an accurate diagnosis is with a biopsy, Mrs. Somerset-Smith. We can check you into the hospital tomorrow and perform the surgery the day after."

Devon's eyes, full of apprehension, met those of the smooth young surgeon who had just examined the small knot in her left breast. Her family doctor had referred her to him. Had called him "the best man in the region." Why did she need the best man in the region?

Because there was something ghastly and foreign invading her body. Something that didn't belong there. She hated to touch it, hated even to look at her breasts nowadays. She just wanted the hard little lump gone. At first, she had awakened each morning and felt the spot, hoping that it would miraculously *be* gone. But it was still there. The same. Or was it just a little bigger? Was it growing? She had to know. And ultimately, the horrible anxiety had driven her here, to Dr. Donatello.

Now, practically speechless with fear, she was able to utter no more than the word, "Tomorrow?"

"I believe it's advisable," said Dr. Donatello formally.

Devon stared numbly out the grimy window behind the doctor's desk. Despite the dirty panes, the bright spring sunshine poured in through the little opening. Yet Devon was shivering. This is a nightmare, she thought. She had the feeling she was being pushed through a dark tunnel.

Finally, Devon spoke the words that were spinning in her head. "So you must think it's . . ." She couldn't complete the sentence, holding to the ancient, irrational superstition that to avoid the mention of cancer was somehow to avoid the disease itself. Cancer, always spoken of in whispers. Oh God! Was that what was in store for her? She stared at the doctor, unconsciously shaking her head no, urging him to deny her worst fears.

The doctor did not answer her directly. He looked up from the clipboard he was studying, seeming to focus on her as a human being for the first time. This time he spoke more gently. "Do you have any family with you today?"

The words, and what they implied, were like a physical blow to Devon. For a moment she forgot to breathe. The color drained from her face. Struggling to maintain her equilibrium, she replied in a trembling voice, "I came alone."

Devon had been too afraid to discuss her problem with anyone. If she told Francesca and Laurel, they would interrogate her endlessly, push her toward action, urge decisions on her. She needed time to adjust to the possibility that the terrible disease had invaded her body. A disease of withering, wasting death. Slow and filled with excruciating pain. Was there enough time in all eternity to adjust to such a blow?

The voice of Dr. Donatello invaded her thoughts. "Let me explain to you the procedure." Devon nodded dumbly, desperate to find some shred of reassurance in his words. "Our first step is to biopsy the lesion. We can't be sure it's malignant until we've done that. We take a frozen section to the pathology laboratory while you're still under anesthesia. Also a sampling of your lymph nodes. If there is a malignancy, we excise the lesion and perhaps the surrounding musculature and tissue. It depends on the extent of nodal involvement. If there are no lymph nodes involved, we would only remove the breast, not the surrounding muscle."

"You can't mean you'd remove my breast the day after tomorrow?" Devon cried, fighting to control the fuzzy sensation of faintness that was making the room spin around her.

"It's standard procedure when we discover a malignancy, Mrs. Somerset-Smith. That way, you only undergo one operation, one anesthesis, one recovery. Provided, of course, there are no complications."

Now panic swept over Devon. What was this cool young man saying? Complications? Standard procedure? That she could wake up with her breast gone? Devon clamped her eyelids shut. She had to suppress the urge to run screaming from Dr. Donatello's office. Unable to respond to the doctor, Devon slumped forward, one elbow on the edge of the doctor's desk supporting her head.

"Mrs. Somerset-Smith." Dr. Donatello's voice came to her, distant and tinny. "Perhaps you don't realize that many people who have had cancer go on to live normal lives. That's why I recommend quick action in cases like yours."

Devon could not speak. Her body seemed to be made of rubber — weak and wobbly. She did not have the strength to do other than remain as she was, her face hidden in her hand, as though the darkness could provide an escape from reality.

The doctor was accustomed to reactions like Devon's. People did not understand that great strides had been made in cancer care. He leaned forward and spoke slowly and deliberately, offering what he thought to be encouragement. "When the breast is removed early enough, and with proper follow-up care, we have had very positive results."

There was a moment of silence as the doctor's words penetrated the mind-numbing fear that gripped Devon's consciousness. Slowly, she lifted her head and stared at him. "What . . . what do you mean, 'positive results'?" she stammered.

"I mean no recurrence of the disease."

Impossible, thought Devon. Cancer was a death warrant. In a voice filled with bitter disbelief she said, "But everyone I've ever known with cancer has died!"

"That doesn't have to be so any longer," Dr. Donatello said firmly. "If the disease is found in the early stages, then I think you have a good chance to make a full recovery."

Devon straightened in her chair, so that her eyes were level with the doctor's. She searched his face for the truth, wondering if what he said was possible. "You mean," she asked incredulously, "I won't have cancer anymore?"

He gave her a half smile that did not touch his eyes, then said carefully, "Well, sometimes the disease recurs. Sometimes not for five or ten years. But people quite often go on to live a normal lifetime."

"Normal . . ." Devon tried to digest the meaning of Dr. Donatello's words. "Do you mean," she asked, her voice tremulous with hope, "that people are able to do whatever they did before?"

"Yes, for the most part."

Devon stared at the doctor as she tried to organize her thoughts. She was coming to the realization that the lump in her breast would not necessarily kill her — if she entrusted herself to this man. Yet for all this, there was another aspect that she found shattering.

"There's something I don't understand," she began, reflexively folding her arms across her chest as though to defend herself from an assault, "if I only have a lump, why does the whole breast have to be removed?"

Dr. Donatello seemed interested in the question. He tapped the eraser of his pencil on his desk as he explained, "There are, I'll admit, some advocates of removing only the lump in cases where there is no involvement of surrounding lymph nodes. But it's a maverick outlook. In another decade or so, we may have studies indicating that a limited procedure results in a survival rate comparable to mastectomy. But for now, accepted practice is to remove the entire breast as a precaution against further spread of the disease."

Devon's face clouded with frustration. He was talking about her body but she didn't understand what he was saying! "What are these lymph nodes you keep talking about, for God's sake?"

"Under your arm, throughout your body, really, lymph nodes act as the filters for infections and other so-called invasions of your immune system," the doctor said calmly.

"But you'll remove the ones under my arm if you find . . . cancer in them?" Devon's voice rose again in alarm. "Then what will happen if I get a different disease? How will I fight it?"

"It's true that the risk of infection on that side of the torso will be greater," the doctor admitted. "But we must balance that risk against the greater risk of cancer." The doctor looked at his watch and stood up. "So that is my recommendation, Mrs. Somerset-Smith. If you'd like a second opinion, I can give you the name of a good man."

Why did doctors always say "a good man" when referring to one another, Devon wondered bitterly. Dr. Donatello seemed like an automaton, not a "good man." Still, if her family doctor believed that Dr. Donatello was the best, why delay? As it was, she was living almost every minute in fear and suspense. At least if she knew the truth, she could move forward with a remedy. And there *was* a remedy — Dr. Donatello had said so.

"No," Devon said finally, taking a deep breath for courage. "Let's go with the schedule you suggested. I just have one question: If my lymph nodes are all right, then am I going to live?"

For a brief moment, something like sympathy seemed to touch Dr. Donatello's features. And Devon found that expression more frightening than anything that had preceded it. "I don't know," he said softly.

Devon felt a sickening thud at the pit of her stomach. But she wasn't ready to die! She was only fifty-seven years old! There were so many things she wanted to do yet!

"Mrs. Somerset-Smith, will you be all right?" the doctor asked.

Devon looked up and met his eyes. "That's what I just asked you," she replied wearily. Oh, she felt drained. Drained from the tension that made every muscle tight, every nerve raw.

"Mrs. Somerset-Smith, if it's any comfort, I have performed this operation a multitude of times. If we find that the lump is benign, or that the disease is contained within the lesion itself, then there is every likelihood that that will be the end of it. Or we may recommend radiation therapy. We'll know more after the operation."

"But if it is . . . malignant . . . you'll still remove the breast?" Devon asked, hoping irrationally that this time his answer would be different. But it wasn't.

"If there is a malignancy, yes."

"It's crazy, I know, but I never thought about Mother dying," Francesca sobbed into her grandmother's orange blossom–scented pillows. "She always seemed so strong. She seemed immortal."

"Parents usually seem that way to their children," said Laurel. She sat on the bed beside Francesca where the girl lay facedown on the down-filled comforter. Francesca felt her grandmother's hand gently smoothing her curls, and the touch of the old woman quieted her tears somewhat. It was twilight, and Devon had just returned from Johns Hopkins to inform them of her news. With what had been for her an almost superhuman act of self-discipline, Francesca had suppressed her tears of panic until her mother had excused herself, professing a desire to be alone. Then the flood had come, and Francesca had turned for comfort to one who needed it even more. For Laurel would never have believed that she would live to witness the death of her daughter. It was a possibility too heartbreaking to contemplate and she was grateful for the presence of Francesca. In searching for words of reassurance for her granddaughter, Laurel found she was able to find hope in her own heart.

"There's no reason to be speaking of death," said Laurel, "until we know what the situation is. The doctor told your mother that the operation might be the end of the disease."

"But the word just sounds so scary. Cancer."

"It *is* scary," Laurel acknowledged, suppressing her own tears, "but your mother is strong. If anyone can fight it, she can."

Francesca turned over to face her grandmother, propping herself on her elbows. "That's true, isn't it?" she asked hopefully. "Mother is the strongest person I know."

"And she has you and Grace and me to give her even more strength."

Francesca hugged her grandmother, burying her face in the soft blue silk of her dress. The old woman wrapped her arms around her. Francesca clung to the smaller woman.

"Think of it this way," said her grandmother gently, "in forty-eight hours we'll know what the situation is. Whatever the outcome, we'll work it out together."

Francesca lay awake, so worried that she was unable to sleep. She leaned over and turned on the lamp on her bedside table. Peering at the alarm clock, she saw that it was past two o'clock. She was normally up by four-thirty for her morning exercise rides. There was almost no point in sleeping now. Still, she turned off the light and squeezed her eyes closed, willing herself to relax.

Unbidden visions of a future without Devon invaded her mind. What would it be like? She would be an orphan. Her grandmother was old; soon she would die, too. Francesca felt completely alone in the world.

How she missed John! He had taken a post as ambassador to Belgium three years before, when Eisenhower had been president of the United States. It had been expected that John would be replaced when Kennedy took office in 1961, but the wheels of government often moved slowly, and John's replacement had yet to receive Senate confirmation. It was a tribute to John's exceptional qualities that President Kennedy had asked him to stay on in the post until the new man was sent. In contrast, the resignations of most other Eisenhower appointees had been accepted by the Democratic regime.

Francesca calculated the time difference between Virginia and Belgium. She had spent one month with him the previous summer and she could envision him breakfasting before the huge leaded windows that overlooked a courtyard lush with greenery. Then, reaching a decision, she leaned over and picked up the telephone.

* * *

Devon, in the foggy world of half-consciousness, could hear her father's voice, sad, worried. His hand reached out and touched her foot. She tried to speak, but no voice emerged. Then she tried to move her foot. Oh, she hurt! Even breathing seemed to cause her agonizing pain. Why did she hurt so? Then she remembered. She had fallen while riding Sirocco. And more than just her body hurt. She felt as though her heart were broken. John. That was it. John Alexander had left her. Had gone back to New York without even saying good-bye. Tears streamed down her face.

"Is she conscious?" whispered John, leaning over Devon.

"She's crying!" exclaimed Francesca. She rarely saw her mother cry. The sight of it frightened her. Devon looked so slender and vulnerable with the tubes going into her arms and nose! She must be in terrible pain, Francesca thought. She grasped her mother's hand, but there was no responding pressure.

"When will she wake up?" Laurel asked the private nurse who stood quietly looking on.

"It varies from person to person," said the woman. The nurse, highly recommended by Dr. Donatello, seemed both competent and maternal, which was reassuring to Devon's family. "Why don't you all take a few minutes and get something to eat. I'll have them page you in the cafeteria if there's any change."

They hesitated, reluctant to leave Devon.

"Look, if it will make you feel more at ease, why doesn't Mrs. Richmond stay here in case Mrs. Somerset-Smith wakes up," the woman suggested, pragmatically realizing that the others would be able to rush back much more quickly than Laurel if indeed Devon did awaken.

Laurel nodded approvingly at the suggestion while John, Grace, and Francesca filed out of the room.

As they emerged into the hallway, John put his arm around Francesca and gave her a hug. "She'll be fine, darling. The doctor said so."

"But she has cancer!" cried Francesca.

"No, she *had* cancer. The doctor said he got everything. And he got it early. The lump was less than a centimeter and there were no lymph nodes involved. He thinks she'll be fine." The group moved down the hallway toward the elevator.

"How do you think she'll feel when she wakes up and finds out that her . . . that they removed her . . ." Francesca couldn't go on, so distraught was she at the notion of her mother's operation.

"She'll be terribly upset," Grace predicted, "but she's smart enough to realize that it had to be done."

Francesca turned to John. "How did you feel when you woke up in the hospital and discovered they'd cut off your leg?"

"Francesca!" Grace chided, embarrassed by the bluntness of the question.

John chuckled. "It's all right." He pressed the button to summon the elevator. He decided to answer Francesca as bluntly as she had questioned him. "I was shattered, frankly. But I got over it. At first, I didn't see how I could go on. It didn't seem that life as an amputee was worth living. The reaction of my wife at the time didn't help either. But after she left, your mother came to visit me, and she helped a lot." The elevator came and the group stepped on. "And, as it turned out, I've gotten so used to my artificial leg that I hardly notice the difference. I'd rather be alive and missing a leg than dead with all my body parts intact. Your mother will feel the same way, once she gets over the initial shock."

Francesca waited until they had emerged from the elevator before she spoke. Then she uttered the question that had been so desperately troubling her. "But how can she ever feel like a woman again?"

Grace looked helplessly at John, not knowing how to answer. She had asked herself the same question. Yes, she was grateful that Devon was alive, but she wondered how she herself would have felt had her breast been amputated — wondered if she would have been able simply to carry on as before. How would Philip react? She could not imagine ever having the desire for sex again, not if it meant exposing one's scarred body to the scrutiny of another.

But John's reaction was completely different. "As if that matters! Your mother's womanhood has nothing to do with a particular part of her body, and I only hope she realizes that."

"But how can she be as . . . as . . . attractive?" Francesca asked, tears in her eyes.

John turned and faced Francesca, his face darkening with anger. "How dare you suggest that your mother's worth is tied to something so superficial! I don't ever want to hear you suggest such a thing again! And especially not to her!"

Grace put a restraining hand on his arm. "John," she said soothingly, "she's trying to understand."

John sighed. "I'm sorry," he said, pulling Francesca to him and giving her a hug. Releasing her, he continued to walk slowly toward the cafeteria, a hand on each woman's elbow. "Your mother has a beautiful face and figure, yes. But that's not what holds a person's love," he explained, his voice full of emotion.

Grace looked at John wisely. John caught her gaze and held it, a silent confession as clear as the written word.

They moved through the line in silence, passing by displays of food that did little to pique their appetites. All their selections fit on one yellow plastic tray. Francesca chose banana cream pie, Grace a tired-looking chef's salad, and John a ham and cheese sandwich. All three had small cups of coffee. They were not able to endure larger servings of the stale hospital brew, but needed the energy boost the drink would provide.

They chose a spot beside a window in the near-empty dining room. Sunshine lay in stripes of light on the industrial brown carpeting, reminding the group of the warm spring weather outside.

"You know," John said thoughtfully, "I always believed that the expression 'love is blind' meant that lovers did not see each other's faults. Of course, that's how it's always used and I'm certain that it is the intended meaning. But now that I'm older, I've added my own second interpretation of that saying."

"Which is?" Grace put down her fork and gave John her full attention.

"That love blinds you to a person's faults, yes, in the beginning. But as love becomes more familiar, it seems that couples forget the unique qualities that attracted them in the first place. So that couples who love each other, have been married for some years, begin to take for granted the very qualities they found so wondrous in the beginning. They fail to see those qualities as unique or exciting anymore."

"You mean 'familiarity breeds contempt,' to use another proverb," said Grace.

"I hate to be so cynical as to call it contempt; although, unfortunately, that seems to be how the sentiment often manifests itself."

"What are you two talking about?" interjected Francesca.

The two adults looked at her in surprise — they had almost forgotten her presence — then back at each other with smiles of understanding.

"We're talking about how foolishly people often behave toward the very ones they love most in the world," Grace explained.

Francesca's face maintained its puzzled expression. What did this have to do with her mother's operation? She looked from her aunt to

John. They seemed to understand each other perfectly. With a shrug, she took another bite of her pie.

John went on as though there had been no interruption. "Do we ever learn from our mistakes? Does anyone have the ability to keep a fresh view of the one he loves?" he asked Grace. It was not a rhetorical question. He sincerely hoped she would provide an answer. She had been married for almost forty years. Surely if anyone knew the secret of love's longevity, it would be Grace.

"Civility and tolerance play the most important roles on a day-to-day basis, I suppose. That's a rather prosaic answer to your poetic question, I'm afraid," Grace said with a wry smile.

John leaned forward in his seat, looking intently at his former sister-in-law. "There must be more to it than that. Why am I now struck by the unique qualities I dismissed so cavalierly in 1940?"

Francesca's ears perked up at this reference to the period surrounding John and Devon's divorce. She took her last bite of pie and pushed the plate away, sitting back in her chair and following the dialogue as though she were a spectator at a tennis match.

"John, the answer is so simple, I'm surprised you should ask," said Grace with an indulgent smile.

John and Francesca looked expectantly at Grace.

She was blunt. "You were both stubborn, self-centered, and immature. She was no saint. You weren't either. And neither of you was generous enough of spirit to overlook the affronts you slung at each other. To be frank, you each clung to your viewpoints and refused to compromise." Grace folded her arms and sat back in her seat. "Would you like to hear more?"

"No, thank you," John said hastily, "I think I catch your general drift."

"Sounds rocky!" Francesca commented, a sparkle in her eye. She had always been curious about her mother's marriage to John, but neither party would discuss it in any detail. Certainly neither would divulge the reasons for the divorce. Her questions on the subject were either answered in the briefest possible manner or diverted entirely.

"Well, I have one more thing to say on the subject, though you may not want to hear it," said Grace to John.

"Pray continue, by all means," he said with a mockingly courteous sweep of his hand.

"You seem to idealize that period of time. You seem to — pardon the expression — wallow in the romanticism of Foolish Youth letting True Love slip through his fingers. All that rot about yearning and missed opportunities," Grace said, with a dismissive wave of her hand.

"You are a hopeless cynic!" John clucked, with a jokingly woeful shake of his head.

"Not at all. But I am a realist. I see things as they are, not as one would like them to be. Do you truly believe that if you'd given your marriage the old college try, you would still possess the treasure that is Devon?" she asked mockingly.

"Do you deny that patience and persistence in the face of disagreements are more likely roads to marital longevity than avoidance or confrontation?" asked John.

"*Flexibility* is the quality that both of you lacked. And, unless you're a martyr, flexibility cannot be unilateral. So stop flaying yourself for the disintegration of your marriage. It was the fault of both of you. But, there's good news . . ."

"What?" Now it was John's turn to look puzzled.

"I believe that the physical flexibility one loses as one ages may not actually be lost at all," Grace said with a comically professorial attitude, "it just migrates elsewhere. So that one often gains in flexibility of will what one has lost in flexibility of body." She sat back, looking pleased with herself.

"I suppose I've had little opportunity to test that theory," John mused.

Grace sniffed in derision. "Of course not, except in your career. As far as your personal life is concerned, you've been a playboy."

John glanced uncomfortably at Francesca.

"Don't worry about her. She's old enough to hear the truth about her idol. Not that I expect it to dim the luster of your crown in her eyes," Grace said, not unkindly. "Anyhow," she continued, "I know the current situation holds great appeal to your chivalry. But before you get any romantic ideas in your head, I hope you'll reflect very carefully about whether you believe you've both developed the qualities it takes to make a go of it."

"I'm not sure I *need* as much flexibility as before. You see, I think the kind of life that I want now is much closer to that which Devon wants — has always wanted."

"Are you talking about marrying Mom again?" Francesca clapped her hands in excitement.

John smiled at the young woman, gratified by her pleasure. "I haven't discussed it with your mother." Then he shot her a look of warning. "And I would appreciate it if you would keep this conversation to yourself for the time being."

"I think it would be wonderful if the two of you got together again!" Francesca sighed.

Grace addressed John. "You and Devon may want the same things now. But if you remarry, rest assured that there will be occasions that test you."

"That's a given in any marriage, of course," agreed John.

"It has been many years since either of you has had to account to a spouse for your decisions."

"True enough," John admitted. "But, I'll tell you frankly, this episode has been unspeakably frightening. The thought of losing Devon . . ." John could not go on, so overcome was he by emotion.

Grace reached across the table and covered his hand with hers. "I understand," she said gently.

A look of desperation crossed John's face. "I don't want to waste any more time. I've held back all these years. First there was Mason. Then I went off to Europe. Something always seemed to interfere. Now this . . . this has made me realize that to delay further could mean losing Devon forever. I'm not prepared to do that."

"I sympathize," Grace said, nodding, "but remember this: your loss of Devon would be far more irrevocable were you to divorce again than should you fail to remarry. What you have together now is incomplete, but it *is* good."

"But it is incomplete," John said firmly. "I may be over sixty-five, but I'm still too young not to act on my desires. And I'm too old to leave loose ends dangling in my life."

CHAPTER 69

DEVON appeared to take the news of her operation well. She was stoic when she awakened to learn that her breast was gone.

During the weeks of her convalescence, when she spoke of the matter to friends and family, she said, "If it had to be done, it had to be done," in a no-nonsense voice that firmly closed the door to further discussion.

She was out of bed and able to carry on business as usual three weeks after the operation. The apparent swiftness of her recovery hid the fact that she felt like a cripple. She had never before realized how important her physical beauty had been to her, and she was ashamed of such weakness. She despised herself for placing so much importance on something so superficial — she had thought her values were finer. Yet she now understood that her beauty had always been a given, a basic component of her identity. She had grown up beautiful, had always been beautiful, had always been treated with the deference and admiration shown to classic beauties. At age fifty-seven, Devon still possessed a beauty that turned heads. Now, she felt it was a sham.

When a man she did not know looked at her with interest, Devon wondered what his reaction would be if he saw the vivid red scars that slashed her torso. What would he say if she were to undress and he were to see that the full roundness hinted at by the exquisitely cut frocks was in actuality a piece of man-made material hiding an ugly, flat surface. She felt betrayed by the body that had always served her so well. She felt like a freak. She vowed never to let anyone other than her doctors see her nude again. She could not even bear to look at her own body in the mirror.

John's visits were the hardest to endure. There was no point in denying the fact that she loved him. How many times in the hospital had her drug-induced dreams carried her back to that terrible time in her youth when she had discovered that John Alexander had gone home to New York — perhaps never to return — without a word of good-bye to her. She would open her eyes, sweating profusely and near tears, and look around the room to discover John reassuringly posted beside her bed. Then how happy she would be! Until she remembered. She wasn't twenty-five. She wasn't at Evergreen. She was at the Johns Hopkins University Hospital, she had cancer, and her breast was gone!

In the hospital, they had sat silently for hours, holding hands. She had no doubt that his presence had sped her recovery. The knowledge of his love for her — for she could not help but be aware of it — was like a soft cocoon of fluffy down, insulating her from the hurt of reality. Yet as she recuperated physically, she found herself withdrawing emotionally from John.

She discouraged his visits to Willowbrook, pleading fatigue. When he came anyway, she made sure that she was not alone with him. She kept their conversations focused on business or small talk. To John of all people, who so treasured gaiety and beauty, Devon could never reveal her feelings, still less her maimed body.

CHAPTER 70

"I'M sorry you missed the Preakness because of me," Devon said to Francesca, lovingly pushing a wayward strand of hair from her daughter's face. They leaned together against the white rail of the Willowbrook racetrack, watching Kelly ride King of Hearts.

"Don't be crazy, Mom! I couldn't have possibly thought about going to the Preakness while you were in the hospital."

"At least we got to watch it on television. I never thought I would like that stupid contraption, but it came in handy in the hospital, I'll admit."

"Oh, Mom, you're so modern about some things. Why are you so old-fashioned about others?"

"Aesthetics, intellect, honor, manners. I think I cling to the good values. And I'll wager those things are still admired when your grandchildren have grandchildren."

Francesca put an arm around her mother. "I hope so, Mom."

Francesca had become less confrontational toward her mother since Devon's operation. The bout with cancer had made her feel protective. She fussed over her mother constantly, forcing her to take naps, eat well-balanced meals, and ration her strength.

"Well, anyhow, we have Belmont to look forward to," said Devon.

"It would be a dream come true to win the Triple Crown!" Francesca sighed.

"It would be the crowning glory of my career," said Devon dreamily. "A lot of people laughed when I set that record at the yearling sale for King of Hearts. His bloodlines were not all that impressive."

"I'd still rather be a jockey than an owner," Francesca remarked, her eyes enviously following Kelly as he circled the track.

Devon followed her gaze, feeling sympathy for her daughter's strong ambition. "I know that's what you're yearning for now, but it's inevitable that you'll be an owner. And it's important that you know about choosing stock. That's not Jeremiah's strong point, as he'd be the first to tell you. He's invaluable as a trainer, of both jockeys and horses, but he doesn't have Willy's eye for stock."

"Or yours." Francesca grinned at her mother.

"Or mine," Devon admitted with a conspiratorial wink.

She pushed away from the white fence and turned to face her daughter, who did likewise. "You know, we've always operated on the assumption that Jesse would take over from Jeremiah one day. That the two of you would be a team as his father and I are. But I don't think that's going to happen."

Francesca's long black lashes were silhouetted against her golden cheeks as she stared at the ground. She stuffed her hands into the pockets of her riding breeches. "I hear he's going to law school," she mumbled.

"You hear? Didn't you see him when he was visiting?"

"No."

"You used to be such good friends." Devon sighed at the thought of times gone by.

Francesca looked up, but she did not meet her mother's eyes, instead focusing on a fat white cloud that scudded across the sky. "Yes, well, people outgrow each other, I guess. He went away. Anyhow, now he's married."

"I'm sorry we had to miss that, too. But I couldn't let that poor girl, whom I've only met once, postpone her own wedding on my account," said Devon, smiling as she remembered Jeremiah's suggestion that the event be put off. "Céline would never have forgiven me." Devon didn't notice Francesca flinch at the mention of the girl's name.

Francesca's eyes shifted to her mother's face. "You and Jeremiah are best friends, aren't you?" she asked.

Devon chuckled softly. "I'm not sure what that means. I suppose I've always thought of the term in relation to another woman, not a man. But certainly I've shared more travails with Jeremiah as an adult than I have with anyone else I know. I love him dearly as a friend, and I think he feels the same way about me."

"Did you ever feel . . . I don't know . . . attracted to him?" Francesca asked.

"Don't be silly! I've known him since he was sixteen and I was ten years older."

"So?"

"Well, it just never occurred to me."

"Because he's a Negro?"

"I honestly don't know."

"But that night the Klan came —"

"I believe very strongly that racism is wrong," Devon interrupted her. "That doesn't mean that I'm oblivious to racial taboos."

With an intensity that surprised Devon, Francesca said, "I wish racism didn't exist."

"So do I."

"How can you change something like that?"

Devon said thoughtfully, "I don't know that you can. People try. Those who do are brave. Take Jesse, for example. Jeremiah says he's gotten involved with the civil rights movement through his university. And I'm sure that when he graduates from law school, he'll want to get involved in those kinds of issues. I'm sorry he won't be taking over from his father here, but what he's doing is more important. And I know Jeremiah is immensely proud of him. Still, I miss him."

"I do too," Francesca admitted.

CHAPTER

71

"FOR God's sake, Devon, let's get a move on," said John, looking at his watch impatiently as he called up the stairs.

Devon came hurrying into view behind the railing of the second-floor gallery. She leaned against the banister and said, with aplomb, "I haven't kept you more than five minutes. If you simply relax and have a glass of lemonade, you'd find the wait much shorter."

John looked up at her and caught his breath. From this distance, she appeared no more than thirty, with her graceful, limber carriage and her shining black hair. She was wearing a dress of soft rose-colored tropical-weight wool; as always, a perfectly tailored example of the latest fashion. The long, body-skimming skirt and molded bodice displayed her slender figure to advantage. She wore sheer stockings and pale taupe high-heeled sandals, thus creating one long, soft line of color. The dress had blousy sleeves of sheer silk georgette, which would have made the garment look fussy on anyone else; Devon, though, could carry it off. The cowl neck was also trimmed with georgette, which cast a lovely glow on Devon's creamy complexion. As she spoke, she pulled on a pair of taupe kid gloves. "Let me just get my jacket and I'll be right with you."

John sighed. "I suppose I have no choice but to wait."

"Not if you want to sit with the owner of the Triple Crown winner."

"But that race isn't until the day after tomorrow."

"Nevertheless," she said with mock hauteur as she disappeared from view. A few moments later, she coolly made her way down the marble staircase of the Richmond family's New York town house as though there were absolutely no reason to hurry. And in fact, she was dreading the ride to Belmont Park. It would be her first time alone with John since her operation. She had always been careful to surround herself with people when he was present. But it had been impossible to engineer that in this instance. Francesca had invited John to watch her ride in one of the less important races that preceded the Belmont Stakes. He had agreed, remarking that he would be staying at his New York town house during that period. Of course Devon had been obliged to invite him to view the race from her box, and rather than asking Devon to ride with him, he had asked if he might ride with her. How could she refuse? The car was a two-seater, so Devon was obliged to be alone with him for the ride to Belmont. She had, however, taken the precaution of inviting several people to share the box with them.

She paused and readjusted her hat before the huge pier glass that accented the entry from the foyer into the main salon.

"You look marvelous. Now let's go."

Devon gave him a look of exasperation. "We've plenty of time. The others aren't to meet us until two o'clock."

"Precisely why I'm anxious to go. So I can enjoy a few moments alone with you."

"We're alone now, aren't we?"

He gave her a sardonic look. "If you don't count the servants and your mother and Alice upstairs — the ladies are looking extremely well, by the way."

"I hope I look as well at their age."

"You will," John assured her with a grin.

Devon automatically held out her jacket for John to assist her in putting on. His hands rested for a moment on her shoulders as his eyes met hers in the mirror. Devon moved away from him brusquely. She didn't like for him to touch her. It disturbed her, made her feel as though a hummingbird were desperately flapping inside her, trying to escape. When he touched her, it reminded her too acutely of what she would miss for the rest of her life. Devon had always enjoyed the physical side of love and had never anticipated that she would have to do without it. Yet her resolve to end that aspect of her life had not weakened since her operation. When she looked at John and felt her resolve slip, she had only to think of the ugly red gashes on her chest and — more important — the freakishly asymmetrical flatness of the left side of her torso.

"Let's go," she said, picking up a small square Chanel handbag and hurrying to the door. Outside, Devon's green Jaguar awaited them. Devon sometimes wondered if she was too old for the sports car, but then dismissed the thought. Why should she care what anyone thought? She enjoyed it too much to give it up.

After they were settled and Devon had eased the car into traffic, John cleared his throat and said, "Devon, I'd like to ask you a rather blunt question. I hope you'll be as frank in your response."

Devon looked straight ahead, sensing his meaning. "I'll try," she said, promising nothing.

"Do you realize that this is the first time we've been alone together since your operation?"

Devon smoothly picked up the conversational thread and carried it in an entirely different direction. "I'm so grateful, John, that you were there when I awakened. I don't know if I've ever fully expressed how much that meant to me," she said, watching him from the corner of her eye. "And, of course, to Francesca."

The warmth of his voice covered her like a soft blanket. "You are the two most important people in the world to me."

"You're one of the most important people in the world to Francesca, too," Devon said carefully.

"And to you?" John held his breath as he waited for Devon's answer.

Devon fixed her eyes firmly on the road. "I . . . I'm very fond of you, John."

John exploded with frustration. "Christ, Devon! Fond! Am I one of your stable hands or, worse yet, one of your horses that you should be *fond* of me? What a truly repellent word to use!" he concluded in a tone of disgust.

Devon struggled to stay calm. She couldn't bear to hurt his feelings, but neither would she permit herself to reveal her own. "I certainly didn't mean to offend you," she protested weakly.

"But you did!" he insisted, shifting in his seat so that the entire top half of his body faced her. "Why won't you even look at me or touch me? Am I so distasteful to you? Sometimes I think you love me. Other times it's as though you can't endure me!"

She turned her face to him, alarmed at the hurt in his voice. "It's not that at all!" she cried.

"Then what?" he demanded. "We've wasted too much time already. I understood when Mason was in your life that you were off-limits. That's one of the reasons why I accepted the post in Europe. I don't know exactly when the two of you ended it — or why — but I'd like to believe that it left the door open for me. This cancer thing has made me realize that we'd be criminal to waste any more time. I love you, Devon! I want us to be married again!"

"No!" she cried.

John stared at her, struck silent by her vehemence. Then an idea occurred to him. "Devon, are you angry at me for going overseas?"

"Don't be ridiculous!" she snapped impulsively. Then, more quietly, she continued. "It's not that. I just don't want to remarry."

"Devon, we've been through too much together for you to resort to these . . . evasions!" He slapped the dashboard for emphasis. "I want a straight answer. Do you or do you not love me?" He *knew* she loved him. Had felt her love for him growing over the years. Yet he had also sensed wariness on her part. They had hurt each other. Had failed miserably at the most important commitment of their lives when neither one of them was accustomed to failure in other realms. For six years, he had loved Devon anew, and for six years there had always been reasons for his reluctance to declare himself. But all that had been swept away with the cancer. Now, he intended to insist on an answer from Devon.

"Do you or do you not love me?" he repeated.

Devon was staring straight ahead again, her pure profile as closed and stony as a statue. Finally, she spoke. "I . . . I don't know about love anymore, John."

"Don't know? What's that supposed to mean!" he demanded.

"I don't think I'm physically able," Devon said, almost in a whisper.

"Why ever not?" he asked, puzzled. "All they removed is one breast, isn't that right?"

Devon turned shocked eyes to him. She had never heard the words spoken so bluntly or so nonchalantly. It was as though he were relating the latest birthing of one of Willowbrook's brood mares, not a life-altering operation. "How can you be so callous!"

"Callous? In what way?"

"John, a woman's entire identity is tied to her physical appearance!" Devon cried.

"Hogwash!" he expostulated. "To say such a thing is to undermine all the qualities that make you special. Your accomplishments, your courage, your perseverance, your intelligence. Those are the things that make you Devon Alexander!"

"Somerset-Smith," she said quietly.

John looked abashed. "Of course. That's what I meant to say. Look, could you find a place to pull over so we can talk?"

Devon's eyes swept the surrounding area, then spotting an exit that led into a restaurant parking lot, she pulled off the highway. The car rolled to a stop and Devon turned off the ignition.

John leaned across the center glove box and gearshift and took Devon's hands. "Look at me, Devon," he compelled her in a quiet voice.

Devon's aqua eyes searched his deep blue ones, recognizing in them the reassurance she had not had the courage to seek since her operation. His eyes told her that he found her desirable, admirable, a person to be loved.

"Oh, John," she whispered, her voice breaking, "it's so ugly. I couldn't bear for you to see . . . it." She couldn't bear to say the word *scar*.

"It doesn't mean anything to me, Devon. It's you I love. All of you. Not your left breast or your right eye or your perfect nose." He smiled, kissing her hands, each one in turn.

"But the women you're used to. They're all so beautiful!" Devon said, despairing.

"No more beautiful than you are," John reassured her.

"Younger *and* more beautiful," Devon insisted. "And whole."

"So what? I'm not 'whole,' as you put it. Do you find my injury revolting?" John studied Devon carefully as he awaited her response.

"It's not the same," Devon said with a dismissive shrug.

"How can you say that? A man's strength, his mobility, his physical ability are all tied to his masculinity. I used to be an excellent rider and skier. I'm not nearly so good now. Does it make you think less of me as a man?"

"Of course not."

"Then why are you being so mulish about your own amputation?" John saw Devon wince at the word, but he went on, refusing to give in to her squeamishness. "You're not prevented from doing anything you did before. You look the same to me."

"With clothes on."

"Are you saying that when I remove my slacks, you'll find my stump so disgusting that you'll be unable to stomach being close to me?"

Devon smiled, unable to resist a joke. "You just keep your pants on," she said in mock warning.

"I'm finding that more and more difficult to do when I'm around you," he said huskily, leaning toward her and planting a soft kiss on her lips. "Don't you think I've shown amazing strength of character in resisting you for six years?"

"Me too," Devon murmured, kissing him back. As their lips touched, she felt a warm glow fill her. She longed to draw him nearer, to surround herself with him.

"That's better," said John, drawing back to gaze at Devon. He put a hand under her chin and watched her smile at him, basking in the love that shone from her eyes. "Devon, I won't allow you to hide yourself away from me. Not your heart. Not your body. I love every part of you, and I refuse to allow you to be self-conscious about any of it."

"John, it's truly an ugly sight," she said, her voice wavering again. He was convincing, but how would he feel when he actually saw her scars? If he recoiled, she did not think she could bear it. On the other hand, she knew that she would not recoil — would never have recoiled — at the sight of his.

John did not try to soften what he said with euphemisms. He sensed that Devon needed a straightforward response. "Scars are ugly. That's a fact of life. If the only flaws we had were our scars, we'd be assured of a successful marriage this time around. Unfortunately, it isn't that simple. Last time, our physical appearances were perfectly fine, but our personality flaws got in the way of our love. I hope that by now we've learned to be more tolerant of the bad and more appreciative of the good in each other. And I guess I'm feeling lucky — willing to take that chance. After all, not many men are lucky enough to get a second chance to marry the love of their lives."

"*I'm* the love of your life, not Bebe Henley?" Devon teased.

"Please!" John said in mock horror. Then his face melted with tenderness. He leaned forward and, ever so gently, gave her a lingering kiss. "Please, Devon. Let's not waste any more time. Marry me!"

"Well . . ." Devon felt as breathless and flushed as a young girl. She looked into the eyes she had never really stopped loving, and for a moment her misgivings vanished. "I don't think I have the strength to say no," Devon whispered.

John's face filled with joy. "That's wonderful!" He pulled Devon as close as the interior of the car allowed and gave her a long, spine-tingling kiss. "Let's forget about Belmont and elope!"

"We can't," Devon objected, "we don't have a marriage license!"

"We'll drive down to Maryland!"

"But everyone's waiting for us at Belmont!" Devon felt flustered and rushed, but at the same time exultant.

"I refuse to give you time to change your mind. We'll telephone Belmont. Leave word for Francesca. Oh," he said with a sweeping hand gesture that connoted exasperation, "these are all petty details. We've got bigger things at stake here! Our entire futures. Come on, let's go to Maryland," he pulled her to him and whispered persuasively.

"Well . . ."

"Come on," he wheedled.

"As long as we're back for the race the day after tomorrow," said Devon, heady with excitement but trying to maintain a grasp on practicality.

"I'll promise anything for tomorrow if it will persuade you to go to Maryland today!" John said. And with that, he leaned over and turned the key in the ignition. "Drive on!" he commanded, and the little green car pulled out of the parking lot, its passengers giggling like teenagers.

CHAPTER 72

DEVON was amused to learn that almost everyone who knew her had expected that she and John would remarry.

"Like they say, the wife is always the last to know," she remarked to her husband as they dressed for the Belmont Stakes, the third race of the Triple Crown series.

John — chin lifted as he knotted his tie in front of the mirror-faced armoire — said with a smile, "Francesca was as pleased as I hoped she'd be."

John finished his task and turned to face his wife just as she disappeared into the small adjoining room that served as her dressing area. Devon had allowed John to look at her scars and to touch them on their wedding night, but she was still uncomfortable with him watching her dress, particularly when she donned the prosthetic device that regularized her silhouette. John had resolved not to rush her. It had been a major step for her to allow him to see her nude.

Devon emerged from her boudoir a few moments later. They had decided to return to her home until after the Belmont Stakes because he did not want to dislodge her when she was preparing for the most important race of her career. Afterward they would move to John's house, just a few blocks away, while Francesca would return to Willowbrook. This had been a suggestion of Laurel, who had insisted that the newlyweds needed privacy.

"But, Mother, we're not exactly newlyweds. And we're not exactly youngsters either. Besides, we want Francesca to live with us."

Laurel had looked at Devon wisely, with a commanding expression that allowed no room for contradiction. "Don't be foolish, dear. She's nineteen years old and can manage very well without you for a couple of months. You'll be back at Willowbrook by Christmas anyhow, and you can resume family life then. But *everyone* needs a honeymoon. And from the way John looks at you I can see that your sexual interest in each other has not abated one iota!"

"Mother!" cried Devon, truly shocked at her mother's uncharacteristic bluntness. Laurel was usually the most diplomatic of people, employing delicate euphemisms that revealed her upbringing as a Southern gentlewoman.

"What? You thought perhaps I was unaware of sex?"

"It's not that . . ." Devon sputtered.

"Well, then, let's agree that you and John need time to yourselves and that the rest of us will get along fine on our own. We have plenty of help. People to take care of us. And we'll all be reunited when you return to Virginia, although I should mention that Alice and I have decided we would like to travel to London this fall."

London! Why, the two old ladies were approaching ninety years of age! She accused her mother of a ruse to grant her and John a more prolonged period of privacy, but Laurel had flatly denied it.

"Certainly not! How like a child to assume that a parent's plans revolve around them!"

"Mother, I'm far from a child. I'm fifty-seven years old."

"Nevertheless, you are still my child. And, as such, you have very little to say about my travel plans. I'm not senile yet!"

"I'm only concerned that you'll tire yourself."

"Don't you worry, my dear, Alice and I intend to pamper ourselves to an absolutely scandalous extent. A nice, leisurely cruise is what we've decided on. With orchestras and good food and all the other amenities."

With outward reluctance, but secret joy, Devon had endorsed the plan. She *did* want to be alone with John.

CHAPTER

73

PEOPLE turned to stare at the handsome stylish couple as they made their way to the Belmont paddocks. People looked not because of the man's well-molded, determined features, and not because of the woman's petite delicacy and elegant dress, but because they were so clearly monied, so clearly accustomed to privilege, and because, without any doubt, they were Negroes. Negroes, they were called in 1963 by those who wished to show respect to the race. But most of the Negroes that the crowd at Belmont had been exposed to were not as relatively fortunate as Céline and Jesse. The white spectators did not even see the hawkers and stable hands who were black. They were all part of the workings of the racetrack — hired labor with no identity. But these two young people challenged the crowd's stereotypical views.

It was early in the day but already approaching eighty-five degrees. Céline was wearing a white linen dress with a straight skirt. It was of such perfect simplicity, and so well-cut, that the women who understood such things immediately labeled it a Paris original. Jesse was also dressed in white linen, increasing exponentially the drama of their appearance. Under his suit, he wore a shirt of rich sky blue and a striped tie of slightly darker blue and soft beige.

Jeremiah's heart filled with pride when he turned to see the couple approaching. They were holding hands, their white teeth flashing as they smiled at each other. They were destined for great things, Jeremiah was certain. He could see it in their faces. He wondered if they knew it themselves.

"Look, Frankie," said the trainer (he was one of the few people who still called Francesca by her childhood nickname), "here's Jesse and Céline."

Francesca wanted to bolt, but she was rooted to the spot. She felt as though a stone were sinking to the bottom of her stomach as Jesse and his new wife came inexorably toward her. She had avoided an encounter with Jesse for years, and she did not know what she would feel when she saw him. But branded in her memory was the knowledge that she had pursued him — foolishly, dangerously. It made her cringe with embarrassment to think of it.

As Jesse approached, he looked from his father to her, and there his eyes lingered. For Francesca was a beautiful sight wearing the bold crimson and black of Willowbrook Farm. The colors seemed to emphasize her bohemian good looks, even though her mass of wavy hair was confined in a single aerodynamic braid that hung almost to her waist.

Several seconds prematurely, Francesca thrust her hand out in front of her, crying in a voice of false enthusiasm, "You must be Céline, how nice to meet you!"

"Francesca, it's a pleasure," said the young woman with a gracious smile. Céline hurried to take the proffered hand and shook it.

"Hello, Francesca," Jesse's deep voice resounded. Francesca dared not meet his eyes. She did not know whether it was more appropriate to give him a peck on the cheek, take his hand, or avoid contact altogether.

Jesse smoothed over the awkwardness by giving his father a lingering hug. By the time the two men had exchanged a few words of greeting, Céline had already engaged Francesca in conversation.

"Are you racing today?" the black woman asked.

"I'm sort of an understudy. We've got four races today, including the Belmont Stakes, of course. If anyone is ill or injured, then I'll ride. But as of yesterday afternoon, everyone was in good health," Francesca added gloomily.

Céline chuckled at Francesca's downcast air. "From what Jeremiah says, you'll get your chance soon enough. Kelly Majors will be riding in the big race, right?" asked Céline.

"That's right," said Francesca, a little sulkily. She had not expected to be allowed to ride King of Hearts today, of course, but not racing made her feel left out.

"You'll be doing something a lot more important," Jeremiah had assured her during a conversation the week before. "You'll be the pinch hitter if anyone is injured or sick. That means you've got to know all the horses and the conditions for each of the races."

"But the likelihood of my riding is almost nil!" Francesca had protested. "Stakes Day is a great day for jockeys. I could get far more exposure than on a normal day. Why doesn't anyone ever give me that chance?"

"Why? You looking for a job?" Jeremiah had teased.

"I might be if I don't get a chance to show what I can do!" Francesca had stomped off then, knowing that she had to obey Willowbrook's trainer, even if she was the future owner of the farm.

Now, faced with Jesse and his wife, Francesca decided to pull herself together and adopt a more cheerful façade. She did not want Jesse to believe that he was the cause of her mood.

Francesca looked from Céline to Jesse. They were well matched. Handsome, committed, and clearly in love with each other. Then why did Francesca still feel a bond with Jesse? She wondered if he felt the same toward her but didn't dare search his eyes for the answer.

Céline studied her husband's old playmate, puzzled by something in the younger woman's expression. Francesca seemed to studiously avoid meeting Jesse's eyes, as though she disliked him or had wronged him in some way. And yet, the two of them were involved in an animated discussion of the colt that was King of Hearts' main competitor in the Belmont Stakes.

"Do you remember how Frankie sized up that French colt in Saratoga, Jesse?" Jeremiah was saying. "None of the rest of us thought he was much of a threat, but Frankie knew."

Céline saw Jesse fix his gaze on Francesca, as though he were trying to force her to focus on him instead of casting her eyes about nervously. "I remember that. Francesca always had good instincts when it came to things like that."

Francesca smiled briefly in acknowledgment, a glimmer of regular white teeth, a dimple at her cheek, then it was gone.

"Boy oh boy, that Roll the Dice turned out to be a big disappointment as a runner."

"Had good bloodlines, though," Jesse remarked.

"What year was that? 'Fifty-eight? 'Fifty-nine?" Jeremiah wondered aloud.

"It was just before Jesse went to college," Francesca said sharply. All the emotion of that heady summer evening came flooding back to her.

Francesca saw Céline's eyes fix on her. She pretended not to see, focusing her green eyes on a distant horse. Now Céline turned her gaze to her husband. He looked at his watch, a solid-gold Piaget that had been her wedding present to him.

"I guess you need to be getting back to work." Jesse addressed his father.

"I've got time for a Coke. Why don't you let me show Céline around here. You and Frankie probably have lots of catching up to do."

"Oh, not me!" Francesca said, almost before the words were out of Jeremiah's mouth. She blushed as she realized her rudeness. "I mean . . . I've got something I have to do." She looked from Céline to Jesse to Jeremiah with an expression like a trapped animal's. "I . . . I'd love to visit with you and Céline later, Jesse, but I've got to go now," Francesca fairly stammered, taking a few steps backward.

Jeremiah's eyebrows shot up in surprise. Céline looked at her husband and saw an expression of hurt, then relief, cross his face before he carefully composed his features. And suddenly she understood with the sure instinct of a woman in love. There had been something between the two.

"Well, then, Francesca, good-bye." Jesse held out his hand to the young woman.

Francesca slowly stretched her hand out to him. Their fingers met for the briefest of moments and their eyes locked. For a split second, Céline thought that her happy world was about to shatter. But before the thought was even complete, Francesca did a rapid about-face and walked away without a backward glance. Jesse watched her retreating figure for only a second, then turned back to his father.

He had loved Francesca! Céline thought. She felt confused, hurt. Céline wondered if she had been Jesse's second choice. What had happened between her husband and Francesca? Questions deluged her mind. So lost in thought was she that she paid almost no attention when Jesse put his arm around her and drew her to him.

Then, suddenly, she realized, He's mine. I have him. Whatever went before, I have him now. And with a wisdom beyond her years, she decided to leave her questions unasked.

Céline laced her arm around her husband's waist and, despite the heat of the day, snuggled close to him.

"You newlyweds!" Jeremiah teased. "I guess Céline's not interested in a private viewing of the stables."

Jesse grinned. "We'll see you later, Dad. We want to watch the big one with you."

"We've been invited to watch from Devon's box, you know," said Jeremiah.

Jesse raised an eyebrow. "How do you think her friends are going to like that?"

Jeremiah shrugged. "Aw, they're used to me by now. You haven't been around for such a long time, I guess you didn't know that I've got a regular spot beside her." He shook his head. "Change sure is slow coming, but it *is* coming, isn't it?"

Jesse looked skeptically at his father, but the expression of hope on the older man's face gentled him. "I hope so, Dad." For a fleeting moment, his mind traveled back to the night Francesca had tried to convince him of almost the same thing. Then he pushed the memory to the back of his mind. And there, with the crowd milling about them and spirited horses prancing past, Jesse turned toward his wife and bent his head to hers. Oblivious to the stares of passersby, he kissed her, just as he had on their wedding day. This time his pledge to her was silent, but there was no misreading it. Céline knew it was a pledge for life.

CHAPTER 74

DEVON shifted restlessly in her chair. She held a glass of lemonade from which she took nervous little sips, like a bird anxiously aware of a nearby cat as it drank from a pool of water.

Soon their friends would be joining John and her, but it was early yet; only the most committed of spectators (or those without guaranteed seats) had arrived at Belmont Park.

"I think I'd better get down to the paddock," she told John with a glance at her wristwatch.

He leaned over and took her hand in his. "You were just down there a few minutes ago," he teased gently.

She shot him a pleading look, knowing she was being overly anxious. "I know, but it bothers me that Kelly hasn't shown up."

John threw back his head and laughed. "Now you *know* Majors would rather die than miss this race. It's the most important one of his career. He was probably just held up in traffic." Majors had for the past year resisted using the Spartan quarters reserved for workers, preferring, as his income and importance grew, to lodge in nearby hotels. At Belmont Park, that meant one of New York City's many fine establishments. His favorite was the Waldorf Towers, adjacent to the Waldorf-Astoria, where he could strut down the long corridor and assess the charms of the well-heeled female passersby. Majors was still a bachelor and to him New York was a fantasy world of beautiful, willing women.

"I shouldn't expect someone who earns as much as Kelly to be content to stay in one of those awful shedrows out back, but it does annoy me that he cuts it so close before a big race." Devon sighed.

"The day of the one-owner jockey is almost gone, Devon. Most of the new ones want to free-lance, going wherever the prize money and prestige is best. There are perks in being associated with Willowbrook, but there are also a few drawbacks. You're probably not in a position to dictate what he does," John remarked.

"Not unless I can find someone as good who wants to sign an exclusive deal with me," said Devon pragmatically.

"I can think of only one person who fits that description."

"Who?" Devon asked, puzzled.

"Your own daughter, my dear. Or haven't you noticed how good she is?"

"Don't be silly!" Devon exclaimed. "She's much too young to replace Majors. Jeremiah agrees with me, too, or he wouldn't be so careful about when he uses her."

"Majors came to work for you when he was Francesca's age," John pointed out, raising his binoculars.

"Not as my lead man!" argued Devon. "Besides, if she's so ready for this, why doesn't Jeremiah tell me so?"

"Isn't that obvious to you?" John asked, lowering his binoculars to meet Devon's annoyed glare. "She's a woman!"

"Are you accusing Jeremiah, of all people, of prejudice?" asked Devon, outraged by the suggestion.

"I'm not accusing him of anything. But he has spent his entire career in a world dominated by men. How many woman jockeys do you know?"

"But Jeremiah has spent his entire career working for me! A woman!"

John chuckled and kissed Devon's hand. "That I know." Then he continued on a more serious note. "But even though he works for a woman, he probably has a few ideas about the capability of a woman jockey versus a man."

"He's always very complimentary of Francesca," Devon said.

"Oh, I don't doubt that he thinks Francesca is good. Or that one day he'll give her a chance to test her mettle. I just think it seems to be coming slower for her than for a few less capable riders. Take that Luccioni fellow. He's not as good as Francesca, but you've got him riding today."

"He's more experienced," Devon said, defending the choice.

"Nevertheless, he's not as good. He's too cautious." John was silent for a few moments in order to allow Devon to consider his words.

"I can remember so many years ago, Jeremiah and I talked about what it would be like for us in racing. I mean, with him being a Negro and me being a woman. We pledged to each other not to let those prejudices influence what we did." Devon thought back to that moment in front of the Willowbrook stables. Suddenly she remembered John's support of Willy in his dispute with Devon. "How did you become such a champion of women?" she asked in mock suspicion. "I can remember a time when you were very sensitive about my involvement in training."

John gave her a wry smile and shook his head. "I was a fool, I suppose. But we've already acknowledged the mistakes of our youth, I believe. I, for one, don't intend to repeat this one when it comes to Francesca. As for Jeremiah, he probably isn't even aware of what he's doing. But don't forget, he was a jockey before he was a trainer. And one of the world's best. It would probably be hard for him to believe that a girl he watched grow up could ever be ready to take on that world. He knows how rough it is. Knows the prejudices. Part of him may want to protect Francesca from that. Part of him may not believe that a young woman has the strength to go through the battles he went through. And she *will* have battles. There are no women racing, even at the level she's now involved in."

"That's not true, there's —"

John interrupted. "I said at the level she's *now* involved in. There are a few minor-league players. What Francesca is aiming for, however, is the major league."

"And you think we've been unfair to her?"

"Or maybe unaware."

"I'll have to talk to Jeremiah about that," Devon resolved.

"And I suppose you'd like to go down there right now," John said with a comical sigh.

"Come on, you." Devon sprang energetically from her seat and pulled John to a standing position.

John followed his wife through the crowd, his heart filling with pride as men turned to stare appreciatively as the elegant woman passed. As usual for important races, Devon wore the Willowbrook colors of scarlet and black. The figure-hugging red silk skirt was topped by a three-quarter length, round-necked jacket of the same color. She wore the jacket buttoned and without a blouse underneath but had artfully draped a black scarf with red polka dots around the collar. The lively banner, which cascaded to her hips, floated behind her as she moved. On her head she had opted for what by now was her signature, a black straw picture hat with a red band. She had boldly chosen red high-heeled pumps, pleased at the stylish élan they added to her ensemble.

As they approached the paddock, they spotted Jeremiah, a worried expression on his face, conversing with two of the Willowbrook jockeys.

Devon knew immediately that something was wrong. "What's the problem?" she called out as she approached the group.

A look of relief came over Jeremiah's face as he saw Devon. "Am I glad to see you! I was just about to send someone to find you."

"What's the problem?" she repeated.

"There's been an accident. Majors isn't going to make it today."

Devon gasped, uncomprehending. "What do you mean?"

"A car accident on the way here."

"How badly is he hurt?" John and Devon asked, almost simultaneously.

"Broken arm. Nothing that won't heal. But he sure can't race today," said Jeremiah.

The color drained from Devon's face. For a moment, she felt like fainting. Why, on this most important of days, had such a thing happened? *Damn* Majors for staying at the Waldorf! From now on, her jockeys would stay at the racecourse, no matter what. She would write it into their contracts. If times were changing, so would she. She would negotiate each race separately, just as many of her friends now did. But that didn't solve her immediate problem. Devon looked at the jockeys standing near Jeremiah. She couldn't trust any of them with the Belmont Stakes!

"Remember what we talked about before?" John whispered in her ear.

"You can't mean that! Not this race! That's out of the question." She snapped her head around to face Jeremiah. "We need to talk in private," she said, beckoning for him to follow her. She held on to

John's hand, making him part of the group. Even in her anger and confusion, she refused to repeat her earlier mistake of excluding John from involvement in her career. She respected his views, and intended that he should always know that.

"What do you propose?" she asked the trainer.

"Anyone I would have used is taken. We could scratch our entry, I suppose." Jeremiah gave a shrug that indicated he was at a loss.

"Scratch our chance at the Triple Crown! Not on your life!" declared Devon.

"Well, Luccioni's the best of the bunch. But this is the longest race of the Triple Crown. One and a half miles. Long races aren't Luccioni's strong point."

"Do you think Francesca could do it?" John interjected. Devon gave him a look of exasperation. She agreed with John that she and Jeremiah had perhaps overlooked her daughter's skills, but this was the Triple Crown, for God's sake!

But Jeremiah's expression was not dismissive, as Devon would have expected. He scratched his head for a moment as he turned the idea over. "Did you know that she and King of Hearts broke the track record in exercise the other day?" he asked Devon.

"I heard. But you know that a lot of the others probably held back."

"Still, it *was* the track record."

Devon looked skeptical. "You really think she can do it?"

"I know she's hungry for it. Hell, they all are. But she's got even more to prove than most." He nodded knowingly. "I've been there and I can tell you that that kind of motivation can sure light a fire under you."

"Has she got the stamina for a race like that?"

"She's got more stamina than any of these guys. That's why she's best at the long haul," Jeremiah said. "And she's got something else, too. She's got guts."

A look of worry crossed Devon's features. She knew her daughter, given the opportunity, would stop at nothing to win this race. She would take risks, she would put herself in danger. That was the mark of a great jockey, of course, but was Francesca capable of controlling the situation?

"You've got to give her a chance some time," John said softly. "Why not now, when you really have nothing to lose?"

"Nothing to lose?" Devon cried. "Have you forgotten Morgan?"

There was shocked silence from the trio. Devon's words were like a hatchet thrown into the side of a tree. They hit their mark with a dull, deadly thud.

John was the first to speak. "The day you decided to let her begin her career at Willowbrook, you had to come to terms with that possibility. Nothing has changed since then. And you can't now decide, after she's devoted four years to this, not to allow her to advance any further just because you're afraid for her."

Devon looked desperately at Jeremiah, pleading with her eyes for him to find a reason to prevent Francesca from riding in the Belmont Stakes. But her old friend, her staunchest ally, just shook his head. "He's right, you know."

Devon spun on her heel and faced the track. At the moment, it was empty. In her imagination, it became that wintry bridle path where Morgan had fallen to her death. She shuddered.

John, reading her thoughts, placed a hand on each of her shoulders and turned her toward him.

Brought back from her memories, Devon found that her face was covered with a thin sheen of perspiration, as when she awakened from a nightmare.

"Francesca is an excellent rider. She'll make you proud today. I promise," John said. He punctuated his words by leaning down and giving Devon a soft kiss on her cheek.

Devon nodded. Turning to Jeremiah, she said quietly, "Why don't we go and give her the news."

Francesca was taller than the other jockeys, though she had maintained her adolescent weight of one hundred and ten pounds. Still, the extra height gave her confidence. And so did King of Hearts. He was, she believed, one of the greatest Thoroughbreds that had ever lived. It had been her dream to ride in a major stakes race, but beyond her wildest imagination that that race should be the Belmont Stakes, and that it should happen so soon!

She looked left and right at the jockeys beside her. She had drawn a good position, second from the inside. Her only concern was to rein King of Hearts in so that he conserved his energy enough to outlast the others in the final furlong. He was naturally a fast starter, and so was she. But it was a sign of immaturity to handle a long race in such a fashion. No, she would follow the instructions of her mother and Jeremiah. She would prove to them that she could handle this monumental responsibility. She knew they had their doubts about her, though they had tried to hide them. They just didn't realize how good she was, but she would show them! And her grandmother, who Francesca sensed had perhaps more faith in her. When the decision had been made a few hours before to let Francesca ride King of Hearts, they had all decided that Laurel and Alice should be present. The old woman and her companion had dressed hurriedly and trundled to Belmont in the chauffeur-driven 1952 Rolls-Royce that transported them everywhere.

The tension Francesca felt vibrated through her like an electrical impulse and transmitted itself to King of Hearts. He had been like a devil going into the starting gate. Now she was having trouble keeping him from moving about, possibly injuring her or himself. She could feel sweat trickling down her armpits, causing her silks to cling to her. The horse, too, already had a lacy stripe of foam on his neck. It was as though he knew that this was the biggest race of *his* career as well!

Francesca almost didn't hear the starting bell, so nervous was she. Then the gate slammed open and King of Hearts bolted. She could feel him uncoiling joyfully under her, springing in front of his competitors in the fashion she had come to expect from him. But she had to control him! Beside her, the man acknowledged as the world's greatest jockey was similarly holding back his horse, Dragon Slayer. He was on the inside, but drawing nearer to her as though to force her over. From her other side, a second jockey was trying to force her to the rail. Desperately, Francesca searched for a solution. She had mapped her strategy carefully for this race. Run it a hundred times in her mind during King of Hearts' daily exercise. But it had been impossible to predict the actions of the other jockeys. And it was this that she had to grapple with now.

She let her horse fall behind, let the other two jockeys fight it out between themselves. The inside man realized her strategy and tried to edge back over to the rail, but Francesca was too quick. With the inside position hers, she urged King of Hearts forward, and in a burst of speed he surged past his two attackers. Colors blurred, she saw nothing but the track in front of her as she looked straight between her colt's ears. She readied her crop, but didn't use it. A little while yet.

She sensed rather than saw Dragon Slayer gaining on her. She was fourth in the field, but she knew she had no worries from the horses ahead. Dragon Slayer was her main opponent. The black horse was beside her now. Again he drew near, too near, but this time Francesca fought back. She moved to meet her opposition, forcing him to go wide on a crucial turn, losing precious seconds. Again, she was fourth in the field. Now it was time for a burst of speed; she used the crop, and King of Hearts, exultant and finally permitted to release his energy, lunged forward, chasing the horses ahead. It was something King of Hearts could not bear, seeing horses ahead of him. Francesca's job now was to maintain a good inside position while King of Hearts did his job and gained on the horses in front of him. She urged him back to the rail, but not so close that she would risk a too-tight turn.

"She's doing it!" cried Devon, on her feet in the stands. She was gripping the binoculars tightly, oblivious to anyone around her. Leaning hard against the rail in front of her, she trained the field glasses on her daughter, admiring the way she handled the challenge from Dragon Slayer. The odds on King of Hearts had been two to one until the change in jockeys had been announced. Then it had jumped to seven to one. We'll show them, Devon thought to herself, all her earlier misgivings forgotten.

Then, as though she were watching a film of an earlier episode in her life, she saw a flash of color, a tumble of silks. A horse was down! The first horse was down, his rider thrown into the rail. The field was pandemonium for what seemed like an eternity, but it took only seconds for another horse to stumble over the accident, another rider to become a splash of bright color on the track.

Where was Francesca? "Francesca!" screamed Devon, leaning over the rail. Then she saw them! King of Hearts, like the best of hunters, was sailing over the trapped jockey as though he were no obstacle at all. Devon saw the jockey curl into a fetal position, protecting his head with his arms. Now King of Hearts had the lead. Dragon Slayer had avoided the accident altogether and was only a nose behind him. Now Dragon Slayer moved toward King of Hearts. Dragon Slayer's jockey whipped him frantically, but Francesca concentrated instead on pulling inside. As they reached the turn, Francesca, in a bold, challenging move, pulled King of Hearts directly in front of Dragon Slayer. Now she used the crop.

She was ahead! The finish line was there before her. She heard Dragon Slayer's hooves directly behind. Pounding to catch up. Threatening to catch up. She could see his ears, his head as he drew nearer. They were neck and neck. She had to pull ahead. She made her body a flat, aerodynamic sheath, bringing her arms in tightly, and urged King of Hearts forward.

And then they did it! King of Hearts' strong chest snapped the ribbon apart, and like a victory streamer, it flew through the air proclaiming them the winners! Francesca's vision blurred as tears of pride and joy streamed down her dirty face. It took her several seconds before she remembered to stand up and slow the horse. She could hear the crowd, wild with surprise and admiration. They had known King of Hearts could win, but not with Francesca as his rider. They were cheering her!

She looked up at the stands, instinctively searching for her mother's box, but all she saw was moving flashes of color, banners, hands waving at her. At the winner! She circled the track. Headed for the winner's circle. A throng of people holding cameras crowded toward her. A horseshoe of roses was draped over King of Hearts. The first Willowbrook horse to win the Triple Crown! Ridden by a woman! A black man, the head trainer! A woman, its owner! So many firsts! Editors around the world would have a difficult time choosing which was the most important.

And then the people Francesca loved most broke through the crowd and surrounded her. Her mother and grandmother, John and Jeremiah, Alice.

In the background, Francesca saw Jesse, grinning, proud of her. She knew a part of him wished that he could be in her place. He had also once dreamed of being a jockey, but had given up his childhood dream. In its place, Francesca realized that he had found something far more valuable to him. But in that moment she knew that there was nowhere she would rather be than where she was now, celebrating a victory that she had earned.

She beamed with elation as reporters shoved microphones in her face and photographers screamed commands.

"Let's get a shot with her parents!" yelled someone. And Devon and John found themselves yanked into position beside Francesca, one of her arms around each of them.

"You must be very proud of your daughter," said a reporter to John.

"Very!" John replied with a broad grin.

But the reporters were not really interested in John, and he soon found himself pushed into the background, Devon clinging to his arm so as not to lose him in the throng.

"They want to talk to you, not me!" John yelled above the noise of the crowd.

"This is Francesca's day!" she cried back. "Let's escape!" she added with a mischievous gleam in her eye. And they did. Back to their box, now deserted. From that vantage they could look down on the commotion on the field but remain undisturbed.

Feeling like truants, they opened a bottle of champagne. John filled the glasses and handed one to Devon. "Well, here's to Francesca," he said, clinking his glass to Devon's. "I was so proud that everyone thought I was her father," he admitted, taking a sip.

Devon's face filled with love for him. "She thinks of you that way, too."

"I know, and it makes me very happy." John was silent after that. Then he sighed and said, "When I think of the years we missed . . ."

"No regrets," Devon admonished gently. She held her glass aloft so that the sunlight sparkled off the pale liquid. She gazed into her husband's eyes and gave him a radiant smile. "Let's drink to our future instead."